The Secret Bureau:
The Brothers of Death
(Vol. 2)

ALSO TRANSLATED BY NINA COOPER

Emile Gaboriau. *Monsieur Lecoq*
Emile Gaboriau. *The Casebook of Monsieur Lecoq*
Jean Petithuguenin. *The Adventures of Ethel King, The Female Nick Carter*
Charles Rabou. *The Secret Bureau* (Vol. 1)
Antonin Reschal. *The Adventures of Miss Boston, The First Female Detective*
Pierre Yrondy. *The Adventures of Therese Arnaud of the French Secret Service*

Charles Félix Henri Rabou

The Secret Bureau:
The Brothers of Death
(Vol. 2)

translated, annotated and introduced by
Nina Cooper

A Black Coat Press Book

Visit our website at www.blackcoatpress.com

.

ISBN 978-1-61227-592-5. First Printing. February 2017.
Published by Black Coat Press, an imprint of Hollywood
Comics.com, LLC, P.O. Box 17270, Encino, CA 91416. All
rights reserved. Except for review purposes, no part of this
book may be reproduced or transmitted in any form or by any
means, electronic or mechanical, including photocopying,
recording, or by any information storage and retrieval system,
without permission in writing from the publisher. The stories
and characters depicted in this novel are entirely fictional.
Printed in the United States of America.

TABLE OF CONTENTS

Introduction

The story of the Hulet family begins in Volume 1 of *The Secret Bureau* (a.k.a. "Le Cabinet Noir"), with the son of E.T.A. Hoffmann, author of the celebrated *Tales*, Frantz Hoffman, a medical student in Paris, agreeing to help a man seemingly risen from the dead, François-Maximilian Kormer, Marquis de Lupiano,[1] publish his memoirs and the history of the *Secret Bureau*. The Marquis de Lupiano takes part in all the episodes of the story, but changes names frequently, using the various aliases of Monsieur Lelourd, Rempailleux (?), Colqhoum, Marquis Vincente de Samaniego, but always retaining and elaborating on his evil designs, plots, and influence.

The Brothers of Death ("Les Frères de la Mort") begins where Volume I left off, with the Marquis de Lupiano beginning his promised story, anticipating the resumption of Rabou's history of the Hulet family, for centuries the custodians of the French Government's spy system. This secret system, called in English the "Secret Bureau," opens and examines all domestic and foreign correspondence, including those written in code. The secret position is inherited, going from father to eldest son when the latter reaches his majority. If the son is not fit, stupid, or irresponsible, he will be imprisoned, killed, or, if he refuses to assume his inherited position, he will be watched throughout his entire life, never allowed to succeed in whatever he may attempt.

When nearing his majority, Henri Hulet, whose principal characteristic is ambition, has contracted a relationship with the daughter of a rich friend of Hulet the elder. It is advantageous and a love match. Hulet the elder refuses to give his

---

[1] A name later changed to "Vulpiano."

7

permission, but without any reason, except that their fatal inherited burden would, by that match, draw a new family into the Hulet fate.

To try to avoid his mysterious fate, the details of which he has not been told, Hulet junior enters the priesthood, rises in the hierarchy, is punished because of his pride, ambition, and inordinate severity, and sent back to his monastery, hidden as if he didn't exist. But when the Revolution of 1789 begins, he is defrocked, enters political life, marries his former intended fiancée, now a nun who has forsaken her vows. He rises in political life to become part of the Convention Assembly that decided the fate of King Louis XVI. He casts the deciding vote at the Convention for the death of the King. During the Reign of Terror, both he and his father are imprisoned. After the death of his father, who is taken to the guillotine in his place, Henri Hulet is released and leaves public life, retiring to the country,

During his time in the country, he is a model father and useful medical practitioner. Hospitality given during a storm to a passing couple leads to the kidnapping of one of his sons and, finally, to his being summoned to the office of Joseph Fouché, who had recommended the death of Louis XVI, without a vote. Fouché is now head of Napoleon's secret police. He is aware of the function of Hulet's father, and wants to enlist the younger Hulet in the same service for the government he now represents. He has a file in the handwriting of Hulet's father detailing the secret history of the Hulet family, beginning more than a hundred years before. He places Hulet in a private room and gives him a key to the file of the *Secret Bureau*, and leaves him to read his family history.

We return to the Hulet story some ten years later when Henri Hulet is now the head of the Secret Bureau. A chance encounter in Napoleon's office antechamber with another petitioner, whose description matches that of the Marquis de Lupiano, again casts him into the disasters awaiting him.

To continue the Hulet family history in *The Brothers of Death*, and to reintroduce the Marquis de Lupiano, Rabou tells a short tale of a young man who, for a small mistake, is mustered out of Napoleon's army. He tries to commit suicide, but is deterred by a stranger and is inducted into a secret society. Then he fights bravely out of uniform with the military. He is again inducted into the military, rescues a rich young woman, whom he has seen and admires, from a burning building, is offered her hand in marriage, but refuses, even though he loves her. When commanded by the Emperor, he marries her, but on his wedding night he receives a note which causes him to commit suicide.

The stranger he met is the Marquis de Lupiano, who has now organized a group called the "Brothers of Death," whose members commit suicide by lottery.

No read on...

Nina Cooper

ADVERTISEMENT FROM
L. de Potter, Librairie-Editeur,
rue St. Jacques 38, Paris
(1887 edition)

The history of a dubious institution around which the imagination groups the most dramatic combinations, a fable full of originality and interest, which begins with the death of Charles 1st of England, and doesn't reach its denouement until the death of Napoleon, is successively set by the author in England, in Germany, in France, in Scotland, in Italy, in the United States, in Malta and in the African island of Madagascar. In the middle of that truly epic saga, a crowd of secondary characters are dominated by one grandiose character, always surrounded by mystery, the movement and development of which the reader nevertheless follows without tiring, and by curious details about secret societies. In a word, it has all the emotions that history, drama, and the novel can create, united in a framework where grandeur is never to the disadvantage of the unity of the whole. Such are the elements of the book where the somber author of *Contes bruns* and *L'Allée des veuves* has combined all the strength of invention that is characteristic of his talent. Germany, a country where *romans noirs* are always well-received, didn't wait until the author had finished his work, and two simultaneous translations appeared in Leipzig and in Vienna, before a French newspaper had finished publication of the book of M. Charles Rabou, a testimonial to the sensation produced even abroad.

PART I: THE BROTHERS OF DEATH

I. A Marriage under the Empire

It is recalled that in July 1810, on the occasion of the marriage of the Emperor with the Archduchess Marie-Louise, the Prince de Schwarzenburg, the Austrian Ambassador, gave an elaborate reception that a great disaster upset. During the ball, and before the outbreak of the fire which devoured the hall, Mademoiselle Léa de Montgermon, daughter of Baron de Montgermon, one of the richest landowners of the Seine-et-Oise Department, had noticed the presence of a very distinguished and elegant young man, who, with the epaulette of a Captain and Legion of Honor Cross, wore the uniform of the Mounted Guards. For Mademoiselle de Montgermon, that young man was not exactly unknown. Often at Versailles, where she lived and where he was garrisoned with his regiment, she had had multiple occasions to encounter him on the walkways. She also knew that his name was Alfred de Missery, the son of an Imperial Procureur General near one of the Appeals Courts of the Midi, and he was supposed to be someone who had greatest expectations, since the Emperor had particularly distinguished him with this title.

The girl hadn't been mistaken: she had been the object of the young officer's unequivocal attention, and yet, something inexplicable had happened: he had never made any effort to be presented to her father, nor at some other houses where he had easy access, and where he would frequently encounter her. Without a doubt, Léa de Montgermon was one of the most attractive young women at the gathering where chance had just placed Monsieur de Missery in her path. She must then very naturally suppose that, in a quadrille, he had an easy and ready-made opportunity to approach her; and that eternal wooer at a distance would hurry to invite her to dance. However, nothing of the sort happened. With a worried and melancholy air, the incomprehensible lover continued, with remarkable perseverance, to look at her, although discreetly, and to court her, with his looks, so to speak. But he let her fill all the spaces on her dance card, without showing the least ambition to see himself listed there.

However, it wasn't that time for thought was lacking for the late comer, because for an hour, the merciful girl had left a name blank, and secretly reserved a dance. But finally tired of seeing nothing happen, she gave to the first claimant who presented himself the place that she had saved until then. And with a nuance of pique, she had just disposed of her last engagement when the fire broke out. To represent the confusion and frightening disorder that accompanied the invasion of the flames, it must be remember that in the middle of the general "everyone for himself," the Russian Ambassador, Prince Kourakin, was thrown down, trod under foot, covered by those confused groups, and robbed of a magnificent garniture of diamonds, and that, in the number of victims of that disastrous night, there must be counted Princess Pauline de Schwarzenberg, sister-in-law of the master of the house, and who, in the heroism of her maternal love, found a deplorable end.

Separated violently from her parents by the wave of fleeing crowds, Mademoiselle de Montgermon remained exposed to the most imminent peril. She had already fallen, senseless, on a small bench where asphyxiation, if not the devouring invasion of the flames, menaced her beautiful life. But the officer, *who didn't dance,* from the instant there was danger, hadn't stopped watching out for her. Alert and strong, he picked her up in his arms, and managing to make his way across a half-closed partition, at the end of several minutes, made his way outside the townhouse carrying his precious burden.

Great catastrophes don't show human nature under a very beautiful aspect, and in the middle of a frightened and self-interested crowd, it was in vain that the courageous young man sought some sympathetic help that would allow him to give, according to demanding social conventions, a denouement to his generous act. Everyone passed by that beautiful unconscious girl, that he had had to put down on the street pavement, and to whom his inexperience was administering care that was more devoted than effective. It was also impossible for him to know where to take her and what he should do with her after he had brought her out of that swoon.

Finally, however, Mademoiselle de Montgermon regained consciousness and she was immediately able to point out the house of a relative that she knew lived in a nearby neighborhood, where she could very easily go and ask asylum. However, it wasn't without a great deal of resistance that she consented to leave the place of the disaster, where she wanted at any price to ask about her mother and father, about whom fate had left her in a state of terrible anxiety. To get her to leave that place, her savior had to agree to go back to look her dear ones as soon as she herself he been left in a safe place.

The journey was made on foot, the girl leaning in a sisterly way on the arm of her liberator. As she entered her relative's house, Léa found herself immediately confronted with a great consolation: Madame de Montgermon had just arrived at the same place, brought there by her husband. Although he had immediately left to seek news of his daughter, he could equally be thought to be safe and sound, Monsieur de Missery also offered to go look for him, to keep his fatherly despair from leading him into some danger. Shortly thereafter, Monsieur de Montgermon learned through the young officer that his daughter was near her mother and safe. To tell then his ardent gratitude would be so much more superfluous when, the next day, we will have to recount a similar scene at the moment when, back in Versailles, Monsieur de Missery, who hadn't been able to avoid the pressing duty to inquire about the beautiful girl in his debt, found himself this time in the presence of the assembled family. After having submitted to the ovation given him with perhaps a little too much dignity, the young officer was urged to follow up on an acquaintance begun for him under such honorable auspices. As for Mademoiselle de Montgermon, her gratitude was expressed in a way at the same time measured and sincerely felt. Following such a welcome, at the time of some rare visits, difficult for her liberator to avoid, with the eloquence of two of the most beautiful eyes in the world, that, for merit less modest than that of Monsieur de Missery, would have seemed to say things of greater significance.

However, on his part, either through natural lack of social polish, or through some unknown preoccupation, or finally through the fear of ridicule by seeming to aspire to the hand of such a rich heiress, he answered only in a discreet and restrained way the kinds of invitations of which he was the object. Then, after some time, spacing his visits more and more apart, he stopped them completely.

Monsieur de Missery wouldn't have been the most dangerous of seducers if he had conducted himself differently. A young girl, whom a man gifted with all the social advantages and all the exterior graces had made his entrance by saving her life, but, then, instead of seeing herself ardently sought out by this savior to whom she did not in any way haggle about her gratitude, imagine that young girl getting nothing from him but formal and cold attention. Wouldn't that be the way above all others to make himself adored, another Hippolytus?[2]

So it was that Monsieur de Montgermon came to see Monsieur de Missery and, point-blank, like a man who had calculated in advance all the implications of his question, he asked him if he had not ever thought of marriage. The young officer having answered that his age had not yet put him in a position to consider such a serious subject, Monsieur de Montgermon said:

---

[2] Theseus' wife, Phaedra, fell in love with Hippolytus, but was spurned by him; infuriated by his lack of response, she caused his death.

"Nevertheless, it should be considered, because a person to whom it is customary in this country to defer, has begun to take an interest in you."

As Monsieur de Missery asked that Monsieur de Montgermon explain himself more clearly the latter continued:

"Yes, sir, the Emperor, who willingly takes an interest in these kinds of affairs, has been told of your generous devotion for my daughter, and he has wished to do me the honor of setting out some ideas on that subject."

"The Emperor has some special kindness for me."

"Better than that, he has looked into everything concerning you; young women you snatch out of fires, very natural feelings that can be born from such events; he calculates the wealth of the father and mother of young men to whom he destines splendid futures; and then one fine day at Saint-Cloud or at the Tuileries, passing in front of a line of people, he throws out these words which could very well be taken for an order: 'Monsieur de Montgermon, you have, they say, a charming daughter, and they add that you are giving her a dowry of a million; I ask it for Monsieur de Missery, one of the officers of my Guard. The girl must not have anything against my protégé, since he saved her life.'

"What, my dear sir, would you answer to that suggestion, when, what's more, by rare good fortune, the thought of the Sovereign and the father of the family meet so fortunately."

It would have been difficult to throw one's daughter at Monsieur de Missery's head more pleasantly. Everything was said in the short discourse of Monsieur de Montgermon: the good will of the family, that of the fiancée, the brilliant sum of the dowry, and, floating above all that, the will of the Emperor, before which the Officers of the Guard did not usually back off.

Monsieur de Missery—who would believe it?—had, however, objections, if not to this marriage in particular, at least to marriage in general. He then spoke of his own merit with modesty, even carried so far as humility and injustice. Then he told of the perfections of Mademoiselle de

17

Montgermon, with the best felt and the most exalted praise; in faith of which, giving to this panegyric the most unexpected conclusion, he ended by categorically refusing the remarkable honor and happiness that had just been offered him.

"That's all we have to say to each other," Monsieur de Montgermon said, rising, with a quickness and astonishment that can be understood. "You saved my daughter and you refuse her from the hand of the Emperor! One act cancels the other, All I can find as an excuse for you is that you are only lucid in the moments when you are doing generous actions."

And he left without wanting to hear any kind of explanation.

Two days later, Monsieur de Missery presented himself at the Montgermon family and came humbly to request Léa's hand. Not that he had in any way modified his idea about the marriage; not that, considering the habitually serious, and even a little melancholy, turn of his character, he though himself less improper than two days earlier before making the happiness of a woman for whom, besides, he didn't deny he had the most tender feelings; but strange gossip had reached him.

He had learned that, despite the assuredly very justified circumstances in which he had in some sort abducted Mademoiselle de Montgermon, their nocturne tête-à-tête had been the object of malicious comments. Given that, he had not hesitated. Triumphing over his unbelievable repugnance, but being very careful not to let the motives of his new determination be guessed, he had come, as if he had changed his mind, to put himself at Monsieur de Montgermon's disposal. It's clear that if Alfred de Missery was a noble character, he was also a rather eccentric person, unless, however, at this point in his life there wasn't some secret or some extraordinary nuance that would explain his strange behavior.

Whatever the situation, the marriage wasn't long in taking place and it was celebrated at the Saint-Louis church of the Versailles parish with brilliance and magnificence which made it a sort of public event.

That evening, at the home of Monsieur de Montgermon, where the newlyweds were to live, there was an elaborate reception which almost all the officers of the regiment who served with Monsieur de Missery attended.

When the time came for the bride to retire, whose beauty her white wedding gown and her understandable and touching emotion made more dazzling, one can imagine if, among the friends of the very fortunate groom, there wasn't some envy of the happiness that awaited him. Several came successively to shake his hand in a meaningful manner; then, little by little, shortly after Mademoiselle de Montgermon had retired, as the dance was ending, one of the young officers had an idea. Living in the furnished house where Alfred de Missery lodged before his marriage, and, considering that proximity, with closer ties than the others, he had shown a sort of melancholy solemnity, and after telling the groom goodbye:

"Gentlemen," that boy then said, in view of shaking off something like a sentimental fog which he felt despite himself, "I suggest we go to my room to smoke a pipe and cheer ourselves up with a glass of punch. I don't know if you are like me, but I find what they serve here sweet and watered-down. I believe that it was that women's tea which turns me thus to languishing and lamentation."

The suggestion was unanimously accepted and, soon afterwards, our young men were seated at a table around a sparkling bowl where its bluish flame showed the powerful strength of the alcohol. As for the conversation, it goes without saying that Alfred de Missery and guessing the mysteries of the bridal chamber were the major subjects. In the middle of that happy calculation, some hammer blows, struck as if by a hand in great haste to be admitted, shook the door of the house. That first call not being enough to wake up the people in the townhouse, the sound was renewed so loud that one of the punch drinkers had the curiosity to go to the window to see who was knocking like that. After having looked out a moment, he said:

"Oh! Gentlemen, this is unbelievable! De Missery is there at the door instead of being where we thought him!"

The truth of that discovery could be immediately verified, because the house, at the same instant, was opened and the impatient visitor introduced. The bedroom where the happy reunion was being held opened on the corridor necessary to pass through to reach the former apartment of Alfred de Missery. The door was ajar and all the officers were grouped behind it. Their astonishment can be imagined on actually seeing appear the groom, who was immediately surrounded and rather indiscreetly pressed with questions.

Pale and very strongly preoccupied, he gave no satisfaction to the general curiosity, and hurried to regain the lodging where, a few minutes earlier, it seemed unlikely that he would spend the night. He was followed there by the one of his friends, with whom we have already said he had a kind of closeness. But all the questions asked him, he answered evasively:

"It was something unexpected... later I will explain... for the moment I don't know what to say..."

And, finally, cutting short the questions which seemed to weigh heavily on him, he finally asked the questioner to leave him alone, since he had to write several letters which were of a pressing nature. Reported to the reunion, whose curiosity and commentaries can be imagined, that detail capped off their astonishment. Then, after exchanging some more suppositions, they dispersed because happy youthful gaiety had just been struck dead by that inconceivable and sad incident.

Remaining alone, the friend of the groom didn't dare try to trouble the solitude that the groom had wanted. He had to be content with going several times to listen at the door, carrying his worry to the extent of looking through the keyhole. However, he was then reassured in seeing the object of his surveillance seated tranquilly in a back bedroom, the door of which he had left ajar, and still busy writing, without any appearance of noticeable emotion. Doing that several times, the observer, always finding things the same, didn't think he should insist any more, and when the first light of day appeared on the horizon, he went to bed.

He had almost fallen asleep when he awoke at the sound of a door being shut, and, at the same time, he thought he recognized Alfred de Missery's footsteps descending the stairs. He ran to his bedroom door, called out, received no answer, and had no other recourse but to open a window from which he could see what was happening in the street. There he saw the groom walking toward a mail box in the area. After having put several letters in the box, Alfred de Missery came back within sight of the window, saw his friend, and waved good morning to him. Then, without seeming preoccupied, he walked toward the woods that encircled Versailles that could be seen at the far end of the walk.

The hour of that departure, the pathway that Alfred took, gave his friend the idea that there was some affair of honor, and, although he was astonished, in that case, at not being chosen for second, he supposed the inexplicable groom, having just learned some serious attack on his conjugal honor, hadn't wanted to confide in anyone, and had preferred to run the chance of a duel without witnesses. That thought, everything considered, decidedly took root in the mind of the one who had just had it; he quickly got dressed and left precipitously so as to follow the path of his imprudent friend, who in that kind of fight could be exposed to some trap. But nothing happened that would shed light on that supposition. The officious young man vainly beat the woods in every direction. Finally, after several hours had passed in useless searches, he decided to return to the Montgermon residence where he could very reasonably expect that some explanations would be given him.

"Ah! There you are," said Monsieur de Montgermon when he saw his son-in-law's friend arrive. "You probably know about the unbelievable conduct of Monsieur de Missery? Are you coming on his behalf? Are you charged with giving us with some explanation?"

"*Mon Dieu!*" the young officer answered, "here's what I personally know about Alfred's behavior."

And he recounted in detail what he had witnessed.

"I'm lost in all that," Monsieur de Montgermon continued, "and you see us here in the utmost astonishment. Last night, shortly after Madame de Montgermon conducted her daughter to the bridal chamber, and when you and some of your friends had said goodnight to my unusual son-in-law, one of my servants came to tell me that a man had come on horseback and stubbornly refused to dismount what he said was a hard-to-control horse; he was waiting in the courtyard below until Monsieur de Missery came to speak to him. The servant has since explained that the individual Monsieur de Missery came to meet had a sinister face, that he was riding a black horse, seemed to be dressed in mourning, and that, without saying a word, all he did was salute my son-in-law, give him a paper, and immediately ride away at a gallop.

"Without going any further than the vestibule, Monsieur de Missery was in a hurry to open the paper with three black seals that had just been presented to him. At the first words he read, a livid pallor spread across his face; however, he immediately regained self-control, and to compose his expression better, he instantly stopped in front of a mirror before going back into the salon. There, giving proof of great strength of mind, he had, I recall, the courage to answer gaily some jokes addressed to him relative to the wedding night, after which he passed into his wife's apartment, and here's what passed between them:

"He began by thanking my daughter in the most affectionate terms for the honor she had done him in wanting him for a husband; then he reminded her of the incomprehensible hesitations with which he himself had greeted this so little hoped for happiness. 'I wasn't wrong, however,' he continued, 'to doubt my star before that favor; I knew that, from one moment to the next, an unknown power had the chance to separate me from my dearest affections, and, at this moment, Léa, who would believe it? I must leave you without duty permitting me to bargain an instant with that necessity.'

"What's more, he was very tender, swore to his wife that in the morning, without fail, he would have news of him brought to her, and he asked her to keep the secret of his strange behavior only until daybreak. The separation taken place, to the great astonishment of the servants who had to open the door for him, he left the townhouse.

"Brought up to date this morning by my daughter," Monsieur de Montgermon said in finishing, "it was also only at that moment that I learned of the strange ambassador who, taking away her husband from the poor child the first night of her marriage, had all the appearance of concealing some terrible mystery, which I wish and fear at the same time, to be soon cleared up."

Less than a quarter of an hour had passed when that conjecture was sadly justified. In a letter addressed to Monsieur de Montgermon, Alfred de Missery clearly declared the thought of suicide, and, without explaining the motives of that desperate act, he charged his father-in-law with telling his well-beloved Léa the terrible news.

Soon afterward that horrible confirmation, they learned that the unfortunate young man had just been found in a deep thicket of the Forest of Satory with a pistol shot to the heart. A guard had been led by his dog to the out-of-the-way place where the deranged man had taken his own life. A letter to his friend was found in one of his pockets, and—another extraordinary detail—to that letter was attached a will in legal form which named as his only heir an unknown woman who resided in a foreign country.

In the same day another letter, dated from Versailles and addressed to Monsieur de Missery senior, arrived in Paris. It was supposed to be delivered to a village in the Midi where he exercised the functions of Imperial Procurer General. Well before that letter had been classed as outgoing, the Emperor had been told of the suicide of one of his officers of the guard,

23

and a famous order of the day, dated 22 Floréal, year 10,[3] showed the effect the news of that catastrophe had produced upon Napoleon.

"The Grenadier Gobain," wrote the First Consul, "committed suicide because of love. He was a very good man. That was the second event of that nature that has occurred in the corps in the last month."

The First Consul then ordered that the following be the order of the day:

That a soldier must know how to conquer sadness and the melancholy of the passions; that there is as much true courage in suffering with constancy the pains of the soul, as remaining stationary under machine-gun fire. To abandon oneself to sorrow with resisting, to kill oneself to get away from it, is to abandon the field of battle before having been conquered

Now de Missery was not a simple soldier; especially honored by the Emperor, he was an officer with a future and in a happy situation apparently, made to be envied by everyone, surrounded by mysterious circumstances, who had just *deserted* life. Wanting at any cost to penetrate the secret of that inexplicable event, in addition to other measures of the police, the Emperor immediately ordered that all the correspondence that, near or far, could be suspected of having a connection to the object of his search, be stopped at the post and carefully examined.

That measure couldn't fail to reach a letter that carried on its envelope the name of the father of the victim. Stopped by the Secret Bureau, it was immediately placed under the eyes of the Emperor.

The content of the text can be seen in the chapter which follows.

---

[3] 22 Floréal 10 (Republican Calendar) = 12 May 1802 (Gregorian Calendar). The Republican calendar was used from 1793-1895, and again for 18 days in 1871 by the French Commune.

II. The Brothers of Death

My noble and honored father—wrote the young, unfortunate de Missery—when you receive this letter, my heart will have ceased to beat. I myself will have taken my life; but nevertheless I don't die a voluntary death. An oath and an engagement of honor created a cruel and imperative duty for me. All that will be explained to you by an event in my life unknown to you.

Leaving the Fontainebleau School, you will recall that I was attached as aide-de-camp to General S***. At the battle of Essling,[4] the General charged me with delivering an order; that mission was given almost under the eyes of the Emperor, and, to carry it out, I had to pass under fire from a battery that for several hours had been decimating our ranks. When I was in range of the bullets from machine gun fire, taken by a kind of vertigo and having goose flesh, I did a cowardly act; taking a great detour, I let myself neutralize by delay the order I was carrying in my hands. My prudence, however, didn't have any regrettable consequences; I arrived in time and the movement I had been ordered to execute obtained all the result desired. That didn't matter; a delay of a few seconds could have brought incalculable misfortunes. My conscience wasn't alone in knowing my fault. With his eagle eye, the Emperor had seen the way I had dodged my responsibility. On my return he had me called before him, asked me my name, in which he recognized that of an old family of lawyers:

"That's all right," he said to me after I had answered him, "you are the son of a magistrate whose talents and character I esteem. You should follow your father; you will, I am sure, have civilian courage; prudence is one of its principal

---

[4] 21–22 May 1809; Napoleon attempted a forced crossing of the Danube near Vienna, but the French and their allies were driven back by the Austrians.

qualities. I am naming you a substitute to the Court of Appeals in Grenoble, to begin that rank today."

I would have preferred that the Emperor had had me shot, rather than degrade me with that refined contempt. I left the army with despair in my soul and, going back to Paris, where better than anywhere else great shame and great sorrow can be hidden, at the end of some days, I had decided to end my life. One evening, on one of the bridges that cross the Seine, the night dark, the place deserted, the water at my feet rumbling and howling, I was already preparing to jump. At that moment, I felt myself strongly held back Turning around, I saw at my side a short man with a strange voice and with a tone of authority:

"My dear fellow," he said, "you won't be resolving anything by committing suicide. You shouldn't die this way.'"

Unusual in his debut and, like all the rest of his personality, the conversation of that unknown man had a strong and dominating turn to it, which, despite myself, impressed me. Far from claiming to make me renounce my intention, by prodigious irony and witty eloquence, he knew so well how to slander life that he would instead have brought to birth the plan to leave it in someone who didn't even have a reason.

"But suicide," he added, "shouldn't be drunk like this in one breath."

To know how to die, according to him, was an art of which only he possessed the means, and that he himself offered to teach me. In short, from confidence to confidence, I learned that this bizarre person was the head and founder of a secret society, where, to hear him tell it, my somber mental disposition would encounter great relief; in sum, he proposed to let me know the requirements and to let me become a member.

From the first, that man began to hold a sort of fascination for me; on the other hand, every occult association always supposes some great social or political purpose in which the most disinherited and compromised existences can again find a horizon; therefore, I lent an ear to the overtures made to me, and, by accepting the address of my unknown man, whom, as he left me, I saw get into an expensive carriage, I made an appointment with him to visit him the next day.

Located in a distant neighborhood of the city, his dwelling, as well as all his entourage, breathed opulence. As for his person, hardly seen the evening before, it was summed up in a contrast where the greatest expression of moral strength appeared to be combined with the weakest constitution.'

"My dear sir," he said to me without any other preamble, "naturally, and before anything else, I must let you know the economic set-up of our institution. But in case that, everything concluded, you should believe that you should not be one of us, I need some security. Would you please then give me your word as a gentleman that all I'm going to confide to you, you will keep as an inviolable secret, and accept in advance the menace of the greatest vengeance, supposing that you ever happened to break your word."

These conditions seemed only reasonable; I then committed myself to an iron-clad vow of discretion. So then this is what was revealed to me.

Calling himself a passionate philanthropist, the man speaking to me had deeply reflected on the question of voluntary death, and he had arrived at the recognition that, in a great number of cases, it was an indispensable resource. But, at the bottom of that heroic remedy, the instinct of self-preservation always found a certain bitterness. Now, the founder of *The Brothers of Death* had taken care to disguise that bitter taste, and to sweeten in some way the edge of the cup.

"There was not one of the members of this reunion," that dangerous apostle of suicide, continued, "who, before becoming part of this group, hadn't decided to reject the burden of life; but not one also, who, after having known the spirit and the statutes of our sacred association didn't halt on the edge of his supreme resolution, so as not to descend except with calm, dignity and reflection. While waiting for your hour, mutual confidents of our sadness, putting at the service of one another our fortune, our material strength, our faculties of thought, and always carrying on us our will, made out to the community, in the name of a person written in, we soften the passage in a brotherly way, and in this way keeping one's head in dying, one can't say what he encounters of happiness and of consolation.

"The goal itself, it must be said, was finally threatened with being out of date. Once applied to so many friendly arms, several, letting the tree of their life again establish roots, completely forgot to die, so that the association, whose object was to lead to the final act down a gentle slope, had the result of suppressing it among us. Now, that's what shouldn't happen: before men; the institution must live. That's why, when in the course of a year, no associate had broken his hourglass, so as to make a place for those suffering outside, because *thirteen,* the inflexible fatal number of the members of the brotherhood, the name of the associates were put in an urn. Then, the one that fate chose must smile at death, and our oath requires him to execute the command at the same hour, in whatever place in the world he receives his designation."

Forgive your son, my noble and venerable father, for having accepted without horror the secret of that monstrous imagination. But in the state of mind in which it was presented to me, I will admit that it unfortunately spoke greatly to my imagination, and the same man who presented it to me, had everything in himself that can constitute the most dangerous procurer.

Afterward, I knew his life as he knew mine; as famous a traveler as the Wandering Jew, disposing of the immense wealth he had amassed as a pirate, in England he had already given a first form to his funereal creation under the name of *The Sleepers' Club.* Later, a privateer under the French pavilion, he found Paris, the great Babylon, was the place in the world best chosen for the flourishing of his devilish idea. Moreover, everything in that man, courage, intelligence, manner of thinking and of speaking, who at first wouldn't be far from appearing grotesque, was pushed to the grandiose. Powerful most of all through will, of all the passions that move the heart of man, he had allowed only one to live in him, vengeance, and at the moment that I am writing to you, he is, after waiting thirty years, relentless against an enemy from whom he received a mortal offense, and to whom he pours out misfortune drop by drop, patient and terrible in his resentment like a judgment from God.

Once in the circle of such a man, you no longer belong to yourself; you have to follow him, in spite of yourself; and moreover, could I separate my destiny from his, when I had an immense obligation to him, that of my rehabilitation?

As soon as I belonged to him, here is what he advised me to do, and what, if fact, I did. That army in whose ranks I had been declared unworthy to serve, I was going to rejoin. I arrived the eve of the battle of Wagram,[5] avoiding encountering any of those who could recognize me. The next day, as soon as the action began, I mounted my horse and, dressed like a civilian, a riding crop in my hand, as if going for a ride, I had myself seen successively in the most dangerous places. In all the line there was no question of anyone but the adventurous *pekin*[6], as the soldiers called him, who rushed through the battlefield out of curiosity. But the astonishment was greater still when they saw him, in front of a regiment of cavalry beginning a charge and, his riding crop held high, rush into the most dangerous part of the foray. By some sort of miracle, without having received any wound but a large gash to the left arm, I managed to grab a flag; then, my trophy in my hand, I presented myself before the Emperor. I proudly asked him if substitutes of my kind couldn't march on an equal with the oldest grenadiers.

The Emperor decorated me, made me an officer in his Guards, and soon I would go back to Paris, preceded by the renown of my military action, which generally was not under-

---

[5] 5–6 July 1809; a decisive military engagement of the Napoleonic Wars which ended in a decisive victory for Napoleon over the Austrians.

[6] Military slang for a person in civilian dress.

stood; and you yourself, my father, wrote me about it at that time calling it brilliant but foolish audacity. At Versailles, where my regiment was garrisoned, I met the young girl who was to become my wife. Attracted to her by a feeling made more irresistible by the fact that I didn't despair of seeing it shared, I however resisted. The knowledge of all my abdicated future in the hands of the *Brothers of Death,* I told myself that I must not bring anyone into my destiny.

Stronger than my scruples, circumstances made my marriage a duty of honor. Celebrated yesterday morning, that union was contracted under sad auspices. The regrettable state of your health did not permit you to bring your benediction. This evening, right at the time of my wedding night, one of the accursed *Brothers* came. The death lottery had taken place that day. The black number drawn was mine, and however horrible the refinement of fate that in such a moment had thrown me such a sorrowful necessity, my oath does not allow me even to hesitate. In a few minutes, all will be over. But with a somber clarity which escapes from my half-opened tomb, I condemn the man and the terribly depraved ideas which have made me their victim.

My father, it is a dying man who addresses this prayer to you: do not make me break my oath, and may this secret that I confide to your caution and your loyalty remain sacred with you. But nevertheless, by your care, may this horrible society, without being revealed, see itself forced to dissolve, and as a man dangerous for the morality and public safety, may the Marquis de Saint-Faust [7] be rejected from French soil where his abominable fantasies have already spread too much contagion.

Also save the unfortunate man whose death he has sworn; that man is named Vandel [8] and lives in Paris, rue Bar-

---

[7] Clearly the Marquis de Lupiano; why is Rabou coining yet another name for the character is unclear.

[8] A fake identity concocted by Hulet the elder, as readers of Volume 1 will recall.

bette in the Marais. Thus at least my death would not have been useless and that this little good that it is given me to do at this supreme instant, does not leave me without consolation.

Now, goodbye, my noble and venerable father, great has been my sin, but great also will have been the expiation. I do not despair of your benediction at my tomb, and at the moment of descending into death, I dare still to call myself your respectful and affectionate son,

Alfred de Missery

III. The Great Interview

The same day that the letter that has just been read was intercepted, the clock at the Tuileries striking a quarter to midnight, the clerk of the Emperor's office saw appear, in the waiting room, that man with so little patience by which, some months earlier, in a way as unusual as unexpected, he had been dispossessed of his snuff box. This time, that petulant person didn't come alone; it was with Desmarest, Director of the State Police,[9] and two officers of the peace that he made his entrance. That disagreeable escort at least gave him the advantage of not being condemned to a long wait in the ante-chamber, as at his previous visit. Hardly had he arrived when he was turned over to the Chamberlain on duty, who immediately showed him into the Imperial sanctuary.

Given in the middle of the day, the order for his arrest couldn't be carried out except at a late hour in the evening. Because of that, a feverish impatience at this moment was manifest by the Emperor who, as everyone knows, knew less than any man in the world how to wait for his wishes to become reality. On the other hand, given the extreme curiosity that his prisoner had created in him, Napoleon, as soon as he was left alone with him, quickly brought forward the light from a lamp placed on a desk encumbered with maps and papers. With a brusque movement, he removed the lamp shade

---

[9] Pierre-Marie Desmarest (1764-1832)

31

which, in concentrating on a single spot, left the rest of the room in relative obscurity, and inundated with light the face put before him.

"Monsieur," the Emperor, for whom that strange behavior served as an introduction, then said, "I wanted to see the face of a man capable of the most monstrous conception that has ever been brought about by human depravity."

"Before coming in here,'" the prisoner answered, "I suspected that the treatment of which I am the object, must be explained by some displeasure that I have caused Your Majesty, but these first words, continue to leave very vague the crime of which I am guilty, and I would dare to ask him for more precise information."

"All right! Monsieur, read this," the Emperor interrupted, and he put in the hands of the accused the original letter of Alfred de Missery.

Without appearing disconcerted the least in the world, and, on the contrary, taking his time, as if he were dealing with a host in every way his equal, the prisoner approached the lamp, trying to recognize the address of the letter, and began to read with the slow calmness of a man that nothing is pressing and who wants to inform himself in depth.

Either because of natural impatience, or in the affectation of that great freedom of mind, the Emperor thought he saw a lack of respect, and didn't let the letter that he himself had presented be read to the end. Quickly taking back the accusing letter, he said:

"Besides, all that detail is not necessary. Your intention to found in France a religion of suicide is demonstrated by this letter, and this very morning, a young man with a future fell victim to the infamous statutes of an association that recognizes you as its chief. That is what is established here."

"Obviously, I am unlucky with letter-openers!" was all the Marquis de Saint-Faust answered in a conversational tone and in addition not seeming to take much thought about the accusation brought against him.

"What do you mean about the letter openers," the Emperor asked quickly, perceiving with anger that he was going to have to defend a practice of his government when, by the overwhelming accuracy of the fact stated, he had believed he was terrifying the guilty man. "Do you claim that this letter has been taken from you?"

"From me, no, but from a person who evidently didn't have time to receive it and to pass it on to your Majesty."

"From this you conclude?"

"From this, I conclude that all governments are alike, and that I really am unlucky. Before this, in England, an intercepted letter caused me trouble, which I fortunately got out of. Then, the only two times that the fundamental article of our statutes has been applied, instead of two men of heart, I encounter two traitors and two perjurers by whom our secret has been given away."

"You are mistaken," the Emperor answered, deigning to support the memory of the unfortunate young man that he had honored. "The one you are calling a traitor and a perjurer, by carrying out with a prodigious innocence the order of this bloody pact, at his last moments understood the horror, and only wanted to see to the salvation of other victims. With this letter that you have not read to the end, he implores his father to see to the dispersion of your horrible society. But at the same time, he begs him to keep its secrecy and not to compromise your safety."

"My safety! It's a question of saving a man when an idea is put in peril!"

"You are playing a role!" the Emperor shouted impetuously. "It's not possible that naive ignorance of himself could be a crime. That terrible callousness that you would have believed here is not on your conscience."

"What! Sire, to come to the aid of a desperate men who are going to die alone, abandoned; shed on their last moments the consolations of friendship, to delay, so as to make it an authoritative act of their own will, a resolution that may have

33

been only a nervous reaction or a mental derangement, you call that a crime!"

"And that unfortunate man, obliged to rush ahead to death, even at the hour he had, more than ever, passion to live, will you say that you have not carried the most odious of refinements to assassination?"

'But, Sire, that's to make me guilty of cruelty, or, rather of a simple combination of the sort. What has to be seen, is that, without me, that young man would have finished up a year sooner, and having on his life that he was going to desert, that stain of infamy that your Majesty yourself had printed there."

"So, you are a benefactor of humanity, and by Imperial decree, I should authorize and regularize your sinister association!"

"Sire, no more than the duel, suicide is not the resort of the powerful of the Earth. For everything having to do with the destruction of his being, barricaded by human liberty, the individual is sovereign."

"Another reason to crack down with the greatest rigor on those who, like you, dare to push detestable excitement to the distraction and the abuse of that liberty."

"I am in your Majesty's hands and you understand without my telling you so, that even yesterday, having my name in the urn, from which it could as well have been drawn as that of that young man, I am in advance prepared, even for death, if you denounce me."

"And I," the Emperor said quickly, "I believe that your name could not be drawn out of the urn; in the moral as well as in the physical domain, I have always seen anarchists push victims ahead of them, and keep all the chances of safety for themselves."

"Sire, I dare say that your Majesty has less right than anyone to address that insulting suspicion to me. Some time ago, I had the honor of delivering at your door some telegrams from the Governor of the Ile de France. Your Majesty read them, and you could see if, engaged as a privateer under the tricolor pavilion flag, I spared my life."

"So, is this what is put before me, to see united in the same man the greatest courage and this cold perversity? Marquis de Saint-Faust, by making me myself your judge, I prove to you that I don't see in you an ordinary criminal; strange misfortunes, perhaps explain your inconceivable ambition to pose in some way as the genius of evil. I still find in that letter the trace of a terrible injury you have received and which you are desperately pursuing with vengeance.

"Let's see, let me read in your life, where, I admit, cruel provocations of destiny perverted the moral sense in you. Open your heart to me. Situated as I am, seeing things from above, it is impossible for me to understand, even to excuse, certain aberrations of human thought outside the reach of the ordinary."

"Sire," the Marquis respectfully answered, "I don't want to make stupid comparisons, but you and I are two extremes. Me, at the bottom of the abyss and the most humble of the disinherited, you, touching the last limits of prosperity and glory, you couldn't hear my sad cry, there is too much distance between us."

"Well," the Emperor, more and more conciliatory, said, "keep your secret, but give me your word of honor to dissolve your terrible association. Glory! I can give you as much assets in your life as you would like. Generals are found by the handfuls in France, where the soil produces them. But seamen are rare. I offer you a promotion in the naval fleet. With your talents and your courage, I don't know to what ranks and honor you might reach."

At that proposition, the serious face of the Marquis seemed to be lit up with a smile that the Emperor took for acceptance; nevertheless, he wanted to know the exact meaning of that change of expression. To the demand of an explanation, Saint-Faust answered:

"A thought came to me."

"What is it?" his illustrious questioner asked.

"Well! Sire, you are offering me a rank in the Imperial Navy, and I, I dare to offer Your Majesty a place in our humble congregation."

"My patience, Monsieur, is not inexcusable," the Emperor exclaimed in a menacing tone.

"Sire, another word. Your eagle flies very high, and it still tries to fly higher. There exists the law of gravity, which brings objects back to Earth from this constant movement of ascension. Now, it's my opinion that your Majesty is wrong to disregard suicide... Some day in his life may come when suicide may be his last resource."

"Enough!" the Emperor said, getting up impulsively. "With certain desperate mad men, there is no place either for punishment or for clemency. I will treat you like the Marquis de Sade."[10]

That said, the Emperor rang quickly, and addressing the Chamberlain on duty who immediately appeared:

"Take the gentleman away,'" he continued, "and tell Desmarest to come speak to me."

In three minutes, the Head of the State Police had received his orders, and when, with the Marquis, he again got into the vehicle that brought them, he said in a low voice to the coachman:

'To the Imperial lunatics' asylum at Charenton!"[11]

---

[10] Donatien Alphonse François, Marquis de Sade (1740-1814), philosopher, writer, politician, mainly known today for his works of pornography and violent sexual fantasies; he was incarcerated in mental institutions 32 years during his 74 years. He was elected to the Convention during the French Revolution of 1789, but was arrested by Napoleon in 1801.

[11] Founded by the Brothers of Charity in 1645; the aforementioned Marquis de Sade was also interned there.

IV. It is in leaving this way that I tell you goodbye

Deprived of his liberty, the Marquis de Saint-Faust must no longer have appeared to be a danger to Hulet. But, as if that implacable man had foreknowledge of his approaching imprisonment, the same day that his sequestration started, like those meteors that, before disappearing, leave a devouring trail behind them, he had just shaken out into his enemy's life what we could call *the last venom* of his revenge.

Recovered from the repercussions of his wound, Alexis Hulet again began that pursuit of pleasure which both the instinct of his age and an impressionable nature, compelled him to seek with a dangerous and passionate ardor. There had already been some disagreement between father and son, the first not accepting that anything in the austere routine of his household could be modified, and the young man not easily adjusting to the necessity of coming back monastically every evening before ten o'clock, which made him say jokingly that Cinderella herself, then in fashion in the opera of Nicolo,[12] had at least until midnight.

The day we have said that the Marquis de Saint-Faust was busy delivering a final blow to Hulet, young Alexis, waking, had found a letter on his night table. He didn't recognize the writing, and it contained only these words:

Every morning, your father goes out before daylight, which explains why there is that early bedtime that you are familiar with. The worthy man goes, he says, to hear the early daybreak mass at his parish. Follow him one of these days; you will learn how he goes to church and the lovely *profession that he follows.*

That letter that he had just read with great perplexity, seemed to charge his father with immorality and gave him much to think about. It was of a vagueness that was frighten-

---

[12] Nicolas Isouard (also known as Nicolò) (1773-1818), a French (Maltese-born) composer; his *Cinderella* was first staged in 1810.

ing, and, however, it was a precise accusation offering proof—but just how to consider that proof? A son spying on his father! Doesn't that very idea turn one's stomach? And what conscience could even think about it? After several days of anxiety, Alexis Hulet finally made a decision. He went to see his father in his study where he spoke to him thus:

"Father, it isn't for an explanation that I dare come to ask you for. I don't expect it from you. And I add that it would be useless. My respect as a son is not at the mercy of the first slander. But you, yourself, have told me that you have a mortal enemy. The suspicion that he wants to throw between us, he could address it somewhere else where it would have more chance to be accepted. Here is a letter that I received. There is no place for a response from you to me. Think it over."

Hulet took the letter from Alexis' hands and the latter, with an admirable refinement of discretion and delicacy, went to stand in front of one of the windows of the house and looked outside, turning his shoulders to his father. He would even have reproached himself if he had watched his father's expression during a reading which might have caused him some emotion.

Almost immediately Hulet recalled his son, and without showing the least mental upset said:

"The man who wrote you that," he told him, "is henceforth fortunately powerless to take any action in our life. As for the present revelation, it only hastens very little the approaching time of a confidence that I will soon have the duty to make to you," and going to pick up a sealed package in a locked file cabinet, he continued: "here are some family papers that I ask you to read carefully. When you have read them, I will have to talk to you, and make some arrangements with you."

Saying that, he handed him the manuscript that eleven years earlier had been given to him by the Minister of Police. Profoundly intrigued, as can be imagined, the young Hulet ran to shut himself up in his bedroom and read what follows.

PART II: THE APOSTLES OF NUREMBERG

V. The Manuscript

Hulet 1st, 1649. The dogma of the original sin and its re-alization is the destiny of some families, where the sin of the original stock descends from branch to branch, right down to the last generation.

My son asked me one day: "*Are you the Executioner?*" He couldn't know how right that was; to retain in our de-scendants a hatchet blow given in the past by our great-grandfather, that's a history I want to write for the instruction of our grandchildren.

In the morning of January 29, in the year 1649, a boat-man named Smith was waiting on the banks of the Thames for some passenger to take a place in the boat that his job was to constantly row from one bank to the other. There was then great quiet on the borders of the river; almost all the boatmen, as well as the people in other jobs , having gone to Whitehall to attend the execution of Charles 1st^r of England, who, at the good pleasure of Oliver Cromwell, was going to be put to death by his subjects.

Not approving of the violence being prepared, Smith, hadn't wanted to go like the others, to see the royal blood flow, and when he considered the way that the powerful of the Earth often end, he was expecting to take patiently the hard work and the humility of his profession. Soon, because of the increased traffic activity around the place where he was sta-tioned, the boatman suspected that everything was finished and some of his colleagues that he questioned told him that in fact the King had just died with surprising courage and calm.

Just as he received these sad details, he saw, coming to-ward his boat, a person with an unusual appearance. That man was dressed like the butchers of the period, in a kind of straight white linen smock. Above a gray beard he wore a mask that entirely hid his face, and, as a hat, had his head covered with a wig of white hair, very long and very tangled, which by itself would have been enough to make him unrecognizable.

He was nevertheless recognized by the people talking to Smith, if not in his person, at least by his costume, because immediately, when they saw him, they said to the boatman: 'That is the man who cut off the King's head.'

"In order to avoid taking him in his boat, the boatman hurried to detach the mooring rope that held it to the bank, and got ready to move into the river, but some marching Musketeers, accompanying the man in the bloody mask, shouted to Smith to keep his boat moored, but the man named Smith, pretended not to have heard them. So, they threatened to put a bullet through his head, if he didn't obey. Knowing that group of soldiers was very capable of carrying out what they threatened, the boatman submitted to the intimidation, and the man with the grey beard got into the boat, that immediately pulled out into the river.

As they were in the middle of the river, Smith noticed that the sinister passenger's whole body was trembling, and so he asked him:

"Are you the executioner who cut off the King's head?"

"No, it wasn't me," the masked man replied. "That's true; I swear as a sinner before God."

But he said that in a changed voice and began to tremble even more than before. Then, with an even more threatening voice, the boatman continued:

"I can certainly see by your fear that you really are the executioner that cut off the King's head."

"No, no, it wasn't me. It was someone else dressed as I am."

"All right, you claim it wasn't you. If I was sure that it was, I would sink my boat."

"Eh no!" the passenger answered with much emotion. "Believe me, I was not the one who did *the thing*. The men in the Parliament wanted to use me, but I refused. Then they held me prisoner in Whitehall, and forced me to put on this dress. Then someone else, dressed just like me, took charge of the job, and afterward they took us outside in different directions."

"Some work!" exclaimed the boatman, "when they hide the worker just like that!'"

Saying that, he began to row as fast as his arms could, as if to be sooner free of the companionship of this executioner by duplicity. Just as they were going to dock, the masked man was back in control of himself, and taking a piece of gold out of a very full purse, he tried to pay Smith.

"I don't have change for that piece of gold," the boatman answered.

"That means, you scoundrel, that you want to keep all of it. All right. So be it. Drink to my health."

That fellow's familiarity wasn't to the boatman's liking and so he replied:

"You're very business-like now that you're on solid ground. Just a minute ago, in my boat, you were more humble. It certainly was you who cut off the King's head. They must have paid you handsomely."

"And if that is so?"

"See, here's what I do with your Judas generosity," said Smith, and he threw the gold piece into the river.

"Well! Do you know what your impertinence means to me!" said the passenger and he approached with a threatening gesture.

"Leave, murderer!" the boatman shouted, keeping him at a distance with his oar. "Leave, and may the curse of God and of all righteous people be forever on you and your posterity."

"So be it!" the executioner said, trying to laugh.

Then, as he saw that some people had stopped to watch the argument between Smith and himself, he decided to leave the place and soon disappeared into one of the hideous little streets near the place on the river where he had disembarked.

The boatman was not wrong. It's very true to say that two executioners had been seen appear on the scaffold where King Charles was decapitated, and all historians have reported that detail. But the one who had dealt the mortal blow was, in fact, the man who had just crossed the river. He was a captain in the cavalry regiment of Colonel Hewson [13]—and his name was Hulet!

That Hulet was married and had two sons. With his salary, a small patrimonial fortune, and the dowry his wife had brought him, he could have lived comfortably, but he was a gambler, a drunkard, dissipated, and was always near bankruptcy.

Hulet's ax stroke, that he used with remarkable dexterity, with one blow separated the head from the trunk. But his cold-bloodedness as an executioner didn't last beyond his bloody butchery. Afterward, he was seized with that trembling we have seen him with in Smith's boat. In his right arm and hand there remained a kind of nervous tension for the remainder of his life.

The shady streets through which Hulet had made his way after having crossed the Thames, was similar in London to what was in the past the Rue de Glatigny in Paris, called the *Val-d'amour* because of the degenerate population that lived there. Hulet had more than one acquaintance in those licentious streets, so much so that, feeling himself with money and in addition to not wanting to return to his wife in the dress which he was still wearing, he decided to enter somewhere there so as to distract his thoughts with a little debauchery, while someone went to get him clothes at a second-hand store.

As soon as he had taken off his mask and was recognized by the Pollys, the Sallies, and the Sinclairs[14] of the place, he

---

[13] Colonel John Hewson (Hughson) (died 1662) was a soldier in the New Model Army and signed the death warrant of King Charles I, making him a regicide.

[14] Note from the Author: A character in a certain house in *Clarissa Harlow*. Note from the Translator: *Clarissa Harlow*

was greeted by great bursts of laughter. People wanted to know what his masquerade was for. The joy redoubled when he threw several pieces of gold on a table and said that he had received an inheritance from an old uncle and wanted to celebrate. Wine was brought out and a happy time began. But while someone had gone to get clothes from a near-by tailor that the Amphitryon[15] needed, one of the prostitutes who lived in the house who had just been present at the death of King Charles, returned. Finding Hulet, minus the mask, the uncovered face of the executioner, which had caused a great commotion among the people, she shouted:

"Divine Goodness! Monsieur Hulet, are you really the executioner who cut off the King's head?"

Hulet tried to turn the thing into a joke. However, at that comment made by the unexpected arrival, all the faces dropped; all the glasses were halted midway and replaced on the table with a little noise. To put a good face on the thing, Hulet wanted to empty his glass, but as he lifted his arm, they saw, on the top of his right wrist, some small red stains. Then there was a general every-man-for-himself exit, and Hulet shouted in vain:

"What's causing these fools to fly away like a flock?"

But he remained alone in a tête-à-tête with the madame of the house. An experienced woman and understanding her world better, that woman, while at the same time sharing the feeling of repulsion felt, even in that place, by the presence of the regicide, thought she should, first of all, put some formality into getting rid of him.

"Everyone, my dear and honorable Monsieur Hulet," she said to him, "does whatever he wants, and to be charged with his execution, you probably needed to avenge some terrible

is an extremely long novel written by Samuel Richardson in 1748. The "certain house" is a brothel.

[15] The husband of the virtuous Alcmene, whom Zeus seduced by assuming the form of Amphitryon, resulting in the birth of Hercules. The name has become synonym with "host."

injury that King Charles must have done you when he was in power. But, here, you know, we are not republicans. The Saints, the Presbyterians, and the Fifth Monarchists [16] are not good company and they can't enjoy the society of poor sinners like us very much."

"That is to say," Hulet replied, "that you are politely throwing me out."

"Not really, but you came here to change clothes and they must be in the bedroom upstairs, and when would you like to go up there now?"

"Have you ever seen such insolence!" shouted the regicide, becoming angry.

"My dear Monsieur Hulet, please calm down. There are so many other places in London where you would be very welcome for your money."

"To be thrown out the door by you, you Devil's puppet, I really don't know what's happening to me."

And Captain Hulet stood up with a murderous look on his face.

"Do you want to decapitate me too?" the provocative madame asked him with terrible calmness.

At that tense moment, Hulet seemed to be about to attack her; but the dragon-woman held him off with a bottle that she had picked up, and that she seemed ready to use violently. At the same time, she shouted to her servant:

---

[16] The Fifth Monarchists were active from 1649 to 1660 during the Interregnum, following the English Civil Wars of the 17th century. They took their name from a prophecy in the Book of Daniel that four ancient monarchies (Babylonian, Persian, Macedonian, and Roman) would precede the kingdom of Christ. They also referred to the year 1666 and its relationship to the biblical Number of the Beast indicating the end of earthly rule by carnal human beings. They were one of a number of nonconformist dissenting groups that emerged around this time.

"John, go to the door and tell passers-by that we have the executioner of the King here and we will put him on display for free."

Threatened thus with another assemblage of the people of the neighborhood, among whom he knew that his action wasn't popular, the Captain decided to beat a retreat, announcing that someday he would come back to set fire to that house where, rejected even by prostitutes, he had just experienced the worst contempt. He hurried to be rid of his scaffold clothes, and threw them in the first trash can he found on the street. When he entered his home, he found his wife dressed in black. She had again put on the mourning clothes that she had worn several months before on the occasion of the death of a parent.

"So who is dead?" Hulet asked, suspecting right off that the dress was because of him.

"A man is dead," answered Madame Hulet, without letting herself be intimidated, "but it isn't for him that I'm wearing mourning. I am, as you know, a good republican, and his death was perhaps a necessary sacrifice for liberty."

"Then what do these gloomy clothes mean?"

"I am in mourning for your honor," answered the courageous woman. "You have struck a blow that can never be recovered from."

"Miserable woman!" Hulet shouted, threatening to strike her.

"Here," Madame Hulet said calmly, "first read this letter. You can beat me afterward."

The letter was from Tomlinson,[17] who was charged with conducting Charles 1st to the scaffold, and who fulfilled that

---

[17] Matthew Thomlinson (1617-1681): English soldier who fought for Parliament in the English Civil War. He was a regicide of Charles 1st. He was a colonel of cavalry in the New Model Army, and one of the officers presenting the remonstrance to parliament in 1647. He took charge of Charles 1st in

mission with humanity and respect. He walked beside his prisoner with his head constantly uncovered. He was also Madame Hulet's uncle. The letter read:

Your husband, my dear niece, is a villain! A man to de-capitate the King couldn't be found. For two hundred pounds that scoundrel took charge of that horrible work. Cromwell had promised him that he would keep that bargain secret, but something happened. Several others knew it as well as I, and sooner or later, you would have learned it. As no one wishes to live under the same roof as that vile executioner, you may, if you so wish, come to my house with your children. Henriet-ta, my excellent wife, will make a room available to you. In case your husband would want to trouble you in that asylum, know that I have the necessary powers to shelter you from his persecution.

"Well! Why haven't you left?" Hulet coldly asked after having read that letter.

"No, my duty is here. Don't I have the misfortune to be your wife?"

"Then you will conduct yourself in my house as befits a submissive and obedient wife. And, first of all, go take off that sentimental disguise, which offends my eyes."

Madame Hulet obeyed, but at the same time declared that the mourning she no longer wore, she would carry eternal-ly in her heart. Her word was severely kept; a smile was never again seen to spread over her lips; narrowly shut up in her house, where she silently accomplished her duties as mother and wife, she was living remorse for the regicide, and the tor-ture was even more terrible in that never by a word, nor by a gesture, did she ever allude to the past. She accomplished that so well that her husband never found, by a fit of anger, any opening to avoid that sad torture.

In other ways, the unhappy man didn't have any better luck. When he spoke to Cromwell, who had become Lord Pro-

---

1648, until the execution, but refused to be his judge. He fol-lowed Cromwell to Scotland in 1650.

tector, about the advancement he had been promised, the usurper brutally answered him:

"Were you not paid?'" and he turned his back on him.

In his two sons, Hulet equally had no consolation. The elder was very like him, and, something worth noting, from birth, he had on his right hand two large wine-colored stains that could pass for blood stains and were perhaps a warning. In addition, that child had a character which was at the same time violent and hidden. Through all his instincts, in which there was no sign of generosity, he was strongly drawn to evil, and as soon as his character became established, he began to give his father great worry. The younger, on the contrary, had a likeable disposition and face. But noticing, without knowing the cause, the coldness between his parents, he had taken his mother's side and Hulet couldn't expect from him either caresses or an expression of strong affection.

To sum up, the great day of expiation arrived. The Restoration took place. Charles II wanted to avenge the death of his father and searches were made for all those who had played a role in the regicide. Cromwell and some others who had been buried before the Restoration were dug up and thrown into the garbage. Those who were still living saw themselves brought before a court of justice. Hulet had always thought that, for lack of judicial proof, he could never be convicted. He neglected therefore to provide for his flight, and, besides, his debauchery had made him so poor that he would never have been able to live in exile. One of the first arrested and brought to justice, he denied the fact of which he was accused. But, with a terrible play on words:

"I will prove that you are the one who struck the blow," the Advocate General Turner said, "and I will snatch off your mask."[18] And in fact the Magistrate produced a secret register

---

[18] Francis Turner (1637-1700). Here, Rabou departs a little from history. Charles I's executioner was masked and there is still debate over his identity. The commissioners had approached Richard Brandon, the hangman of London, but he

47

of Cromwell, who was an exact and regular man in all his expenses, where he had mentioned two hundred pounds given to Captain Hulet and the *service* for which he had received them.

His sentence was pronounced to him in these terms:

You will be dragged on a stretcher to the place of execution. There, hanged, and still alive, you will be mutilated: your entrails will be snatched out and you, still alive, they will be burned before your eyes. Your head will be cut off, your members divided into four quarters. Your head and your members will be given to the King. And God have mercy on your soul.

The sentence was carried out, and that is how our great grandfather, the first of the Hulets ended.

VI. The Manuscript (Cont'd)
The elder and younger branch

1649-1660. The same judgment that condemned the regicide to death pronounced the banishment of his family. And in any case, Mistress Hulet, her husband's crime having become public, had received legal notice; she wouldn't have wanted to live in England. At the end of November in the year 1660, she sold what remained of her former comfortable life and sailed with the two children to Hamburg, one of the free

---

refused, at least at first, despite being offered 200 pounds. It is possible he relented and undertook the commission after being threatened with death, but there are others who have been named as potential candidates, including George Joyce, William Hulet (or Hewlett or Howlet) and Hugh Peters. On 30 January 1649, Captain Hulet was the officer in charge of the soldiers at the execution of Charles I. After the Restoration, Hulet was indeed convicted on 15 October 1660 for his part in the regicide, but he was not executed along with the other men who were tried with him: Daniel Axtell and Francis Hacker. Turner played no part in these proceedings. A transcript of the trial can be found online at: *http://www.axtellfamily.org /axfamous/regicide/DanielAxtellTrial1660.htm*

Hanseatic cities, where one of her relatives was established and was doing business on Groningerstrasse.

Her elder son was then eighteen years-old, but she wasn't a happy mother for him. Younger by a few years, her second son, in whom each day excellent qualities developed, was her consolation. That young man, being then at the Johanneum, [19] a secondary school then with a great reputation, where he finished his studies in the most brilliant manner, became intimate friends with the only son of Baron de Kormer, a rich Hanoverian gentleman. Taken to Hanover, in the middle of his friend's family, the young Hulet, through his mental endowments and the sweetness of his character, was so well able to gain the affection of the Baron and Baroness, that they soon developed the habit of calling him nothing but their second child. The death of Mistress Hulet, occurring suddenly during his absence, resulted in his being established in that other family. And soon an event, equally sorrowful to him, changed in the most unexpected way the whole economic destiny of his life.

The young de Kormer died as a result of a fall from a horse during a hunt. Left without someone to inherit the name, and despairing, as can well be imagined, the Kormers transferred all their affection that their sorrowing hearts remained capable of to the one that they already cherished and who had been their son's friend. Devoted to consoling their old age and their loneliness, the young Hulet saw his affectionate cares crowned by splendid gratitude.

We have, among our family papers, a legal document dated January 8, 1675, from the Baron and Baroness confirming the adoption that gave Charles-Edouard Hulet as their heir all the titles, prerogatives, household furnishings and property, and generally all inheritance, present and to come. Following that good fortune, the adopted son was not long in making a

---

[19] The *Gelehrtenschule des Johanneums* is a Gymnasium in Hamburg, Germany. It is Hamburg's oldest school and was founded in 1529 by Johannes Bugenhagen.

rich marriage, from which he had several children. Thus, on that strain of the detached Hulets, the name of Kormer is grafted and brought alive again. We have every reason to believe that the descendants still exist in today's Hanover.

As for the elder Hulet son, when he arrived in Hanover, he had haphazardly finished his education. With the help of the relative with whom his mother had taken asylum, he was placed in a commercial establishment, where, unfortunately, neither through his diligence, his taste for the work, nor by the regularity of his habits, did he give a very high opinion of himself. Often warned by Mistress Hulet that he was not pleasing his patrons, he had little respect for these maternal exhortations, and he always ended by reproaching her for her revolting partiality for her Benjamin son.[20]

With that reply, the irreverent young man believed he had victoriously answered the just reproaches that the disorder of his conduct had merited him. And, in sum, everything proved by the sempiternal reproduction of that argument that, basely jealous of a brother who had always been kindly disposed and affectionate toward him, he had toward that brother the most regrettable feelings. For those with such envious natures, success is offensive to them. Thus, when the older Hulet learned about the advantageous situation of fortune his brother had come into, he took advantage of it to break off all relationships with him. With the base feelings of his heart, clothing himself with a sophism of virtue, he wrote to Hulet the younger, that "*renouncing the name of his father, when that name was branded and cursed by human justice, seemed to him the worst cowardice.*"

"Would anyone like to know how, for his part, he went about honoring that name he claimed to retain and wear with pride? No longer restrained by fear of his mother, who, during her lifetime, had stopped him at the incline of the worst behav-

---

[20] Biblical reference: Jacob and his second, favorite, wife, Rachel, had two sons, Joseph and Benjamin, his youngest and the favorite of his twelve sons.

ior, soon after the death of that virtuous woman, he left the modest employment which was his livelihood; then, when no one any longer knew his method of existence, he began a life of luxury and debauchery for himself which couldn't keep from bringing about the most harmful suspicions and comments. In fact, in order to explain the miracle of a destitute laziness which could, nevertheless, support scandalous expenditures, people began to think that he was affiliated with a band of smugglers; some others even went so far as to say with a band of counterfeiters, two versions that certain mysterious habits, especially nightly sorties, equally authorized.

VII. The Manuscript (Cont'd)
The Blue Child

At the time the last descendant of the Hulet name gave such a deplorable direction to his existence, a new type of phenomenon took place in the city of Hamburg. Into the bosom of that republic of merchants, in a place where the general ledger, the bill of exchange, the discount rate, the promissory note and the due date, talk about and the arrival of ships, and the state of the Stock Exchange, were the only preoccupations which seemed to merit the attention of an honest man, a poet was born; that unusual event perhaps needs some explanation.

To pick up things a little further on, one fact must be stated first. A prodigious number of bastards and abandoned children had always been found in Hamburg. That fact is explained by the mass of foreigners and the immense population of sailors, true migrating birds, that business daily drew into its walls.

In 1597 an orphanage had been founded where the products of that infinitely too numerous anonymous fabrication could be deposited. By means of a *tour*[21] set up near the door

---

[21] A kind of round cabinet set on a turn table and placed in the middle interior of a wall. It could be turned, allowing the newborn infant to be sent from the outside into the inside; former-

of the establishment, the infant was introduced and admitted without any other formality. But setting up this *tour* later became the occasion for a horrible event. Its capacity was taken advantage of, to slip infants already several years old into the orphanage, which was against the purpose of the foundation. The administrators of the pious institution thought they could curb that abuse by reducing the dimensions of the *tour* to that expressly calculated to fit a newborn infant.

That new regime soon gave a terrible criticism in action. One day, an unnatural mother placed her fruit cut up into pieces in the *tour*. To that horrible deposit was joined a paper on which was written: *To fit the charity measured in inches.* That crime, by striking in the strongest manner the imaginations of the people of Hamburg, was finally turned to the profit of the interesting class of small unfortunates, to which the victim belonged. Instead of bargaining about their charity, given the decidedly amorous nature of eastern women, the Magistrates, to apply a great remedy to a great evil, provided the necessary funds for the establishment of huge house for abandoned infants where the administrators did not have to submit to any kind of restriction, and soon that orphanage didn't have another like it in all Christianity.

The poor infants costing a great deal to care for and to bring up, the naturally calculating mentality of the people of Hamburg, without using a lot of words, which had become very expensive and very precious, it was with a kind of passion that each one in the city helped with the prosperity of the establishment where the infants were placed. Not satisfied with knowing that the objects of public pity were well nourished, very well taken care of, and when they left the orphanage provided with a good job, they wanted these dear little ones to enjoy their life, and it became the custom every year, on Saint John the Baptist's day, to parade them through the

---

ly installed by monasteries and hospitals which allowed infants to be deposited there without the person making the deposit being seen.

streets, attractively dressed in pretty sky-blue costumes, the orphanage uniforms. That truly civic festival, politely called the *Festival of the Orphans,* was of all those celebrated in Hamburg the most popular and the best attended.

Marching two by two, led by those among them who had distinguished themselves by their good conduct, recognized by a crown of laurel, the children adopted by the city were greeted with the benedictions of the city as they passed by. There was no citizen so poor who didn't want to give them some gracious present of sweets or toys as they passed by. To the passionate interest shown on every face, it looked like a big family celebration. It seemed as if a great fatherly love animated with the same sentiment all the inhabitants of the same city at the same time.

A banquet was prepared outside the city in a big tent decorated with garlands of flowers and leaves, where, the parade over, the innocent troop was seated. In that spot, more than anywhere else, the crowd was helpful and compact. All the parents brought their children over and over again to be witnesses of that touching spectacle, and making it the occasion for some fatherly speech to arouse in those young hearts the ardor of charity.

About ten years before the Hulet family came to Hamburg, a poor musician named Adam Kraft, whose natural genius for mechanics had made him an organ-maker, was at the Orphans' Festival, to which he had brought a charming little girl named Christiana. Born to a woman whom he had passionately loved, that child had had, on coming into the world, the misfortune to cost the life of her mother.

As a musician and a maker of musical instruments, Adam Kraft was hardly less misplaced where he practiced his industry and his art than was the poet who will be talked about after this. Because if the people of Hamburg didn't need odes and elegies, they didn't care a great deal for music, and aside from some repairs which the poor artist was employed from time to time to make on the organs of Saint Nicolas, Saint Peter, and Saint Michael, the only three churches that remained standing in the city after it had embraced the protestant religion, he found almost no work.

However, as he was full of invention and prodigiously clever with his hands, aside from some singing and harpsichord lessons that he found to give throughout the city, by means of loads of small turned, sculpted, and chiseled works, by the application he made in the mechanics of some children's toys, and in addition by some secrets of chemistry which he possessed, and which he used for making imitations of lacquer and for the fabrication of expensive varnish, he always managed, one way or another, to find some work. Nevertheless, with so many resources, or to put it more accurately, because of the multiplicity of those resources, Adam Kraft just managed to make a living. Alongside the sad memory of his wife, whom he thought about constantly, despite the time that had passed since their separation, there was constantly placed another more poignant thought: to know the fear of never being able to set aside a dowry for his daughter in a way that would be able to establish her somewhat comfortably.

The day that Christiana's father took her to see the parade of the *Blue Children,* as it was also called, in that procession there was the seed of a poet who would one day flower in Hamburg. And it was likely due to the circumstance of not being anyone's son that little Karl should be the cherished child of a muse, because, born into some family in his country, at his fifteenth year, he would have been willingly or forcefully installed in an office or behind a counter. In a routine of interest rates, commercial letters, goodbye inspiration!

While waiting until he was a man of genius, little Karl was a handsome infant with a fresh, rosy complexion, long, golden-blonde hair, on which his precocious intelligence, and the sweetness of his character had merited that they place a laurel crown. That laurel as a recompense for the wisdom of poor orphans destined for the most part to be obscure artisans, was, speaking as an absolute, a rather bad idea. But in this particular case, it became an emblem, since it was placed in advance on a head where it would one day flourish, the seed for it already put there by the hand of God.

Was it the *language of fire*[22] that became visible to Christiana? Was she only touched by the beauty and the sad expression on the face of the orphan, or was she even more carried away by the charming smile and the sweet voice with which he thanked her in return when, turning red, she put a little present in his hands? What is sure is that, at first sight, that little girl was taken with a kind of passion for the beautiful *blue child.* Three or four times, in order to see him again, her father, who usually did what she wanted, was willing to run to the head of the procession where the object of that sudden adoration was in the first row. During the meal under the tent, Christiana had to find a way to be placed among the spectators in a way so as to have her favorite in sight. That evening, the next day, and all the other days, after that first encounter, she didn't stop repeating with a little capable tone beyond her years:

"*Mon Dieu*! Papa, *Mon Dieu*! How happy I would be if I had a little brother like that one!"

By dint of hearing that wish repeated, Adam Kraft, who was the best of fathers, one day had an idea. Two days before Christmas, he was at the orphanage and after having received information about the character of young Karl, which was found to be excellent, he declared his intention to take him home with him and to rear him as his son.

It was known that he was not rich. The orphanage administrators with whom he was dealing, thought it their duty therefore to point out to him that he was taking on a great responsibility. If the musician had had any hesitation remaining, that would have been enough to confirm him in his intention. He answered proudly that, despite the small amount of en-

---

[22] Possible allusion to the word of God which was made audible to Moses through the burning bush in the desert and again in a burning bush by the Messiah to Saul of Tarsus (Saint Paul).

couragement given to the fine arts by the citizens of Hamburg, he had the means to bring up two children by his work. In addition, as his reputation for morality was irreproachable, and that, what's more, a good administration would put in the hands of those who asked for them the greatest number possible, since that would be so many fewer for the city's upkeep. Little Karl was turned over to him, and needless to say, Karl happily lent himself to the fortune he had been given.

It wasn't without deep resolve that Adam Kraft had chosen the approach of Christmas to accomplish his good intentions. In Germany, it's Christmas Eve when children receive their presents. Another charming ceremony added to the happiness prepared for them that beautiful evening. When the time came, care was taken to keep them in a dimly-lit room, and to intensify by a little wait their impatience for the surprises prepared for them. Suddenly the door is opened and they go into the sanctuary blazing with light. The family has put together there all the presents in advance. A green tree, the sun of that festival, shining with little candles, candy, and golden walnuts, occupies the center of a wide table covered with a shining white cloth. The presents are arranged all around it, even those to be given to the servants. Each object carries in advance the name of the person it's going to make happy. It would seem that the tree had shaken all that happiness from its branches.

Christiana had been told in advance that she would receive a surprise which the greatest efforts of her imagination could give her no idea. She had therefore dreamed of gigantic dolls, household utensils as complete as the sterling silver service that was used at the meals in City Hall on party days, jewelry for her, and finally entire boxes of bonbons and toys. At first, her disappointment was extreme; her father had seemed to place around the tree only the most ordinary presents and that were known to be less to her taste. But after having amused himself for a minute with her disappointment, she was told to go look under a large blue drapery which hid an object without showing the shape. When she found herself face to face with little Karl, who was hidden there, she blushed, turned pale, went through all the emotions of the most delightful joy. Then, finally, having no words to express her happiness in front of the one she adored, she had at first remained mute:

"Ah! well!" she exclaimed, "Papa didn't lie to me when he told me I would be nicely astonished and nicely happy." But she hastened to add: "But is he with us forever, and not just for a visit?"

"*Für immer (*forever)," replied Karl, hugging her. Was that, like the laurel crown, a view of the future?

VIII. The Manuscript (Cont'd)
The Blue Child (Part Two)

Reared then together, these two children grew up and loved each other like brother and sister and there was never a cloud between them, except that sometimes Christiana reproached Karl for being too much a *serious gentleman.* She didn't know, poor child, that those who have been destined by Providence to the hard labor of thought, carry in themselves a depth of natural melancholy, and obligated to put part of their heart into their work, they instinctively concentrate their feelings inside and do not show them at every moment and with every word in the daily commerce of life.

Adam Kraft had intended to train young Karl as an instrument maker, and Karl did his best to profit by the lessons of that able teacher. But his vocation was elsewhere, and as soon as that was revealed to him, he was a poet as God had intended him to be.

Poets like to feel sorry for themselves and lament. When they have no real sufferings, they invent imaginary ones. They find that to look unhappy is interesting. Karl didn't miss exploiting his birth's bad case, and often in his verses he wrote in very touching terms about the misfortune of not having a family.

"Are you not happy to be with us?" Christina asked him. "Am I not your sister? You think that other people would have loved you better?"

Thereupon, Karl had to make some great changes in the enumeration of his woes, but he held firm to his regret in not having known his mother. It seemed that sort of regret couldn't do anyone any harm, because if there was rivalry on the part of the musician and that of Christiana to be a sister and a father, they couldn't claim to give him back his mother because that role remained vacant in the family.

But Christiana didn't understand anything about these subtleties and the refinement of sadness.

"You are happy," she said to Karl, "or you are not happy. Since you have been in our home," she added naively, "I'm happy. I would have loved my mother very much if she had lived, but since she has never existed for me, I'm not going to search to see if I had known or not known her, in order to find an opportunity to be gloomy, and to cause pain to those that I *know* and who are there alive."

That was to talk good sense, and what was even better, with good sense from the heart. But actually, the more these two young people advanced in age, the more a great dissonance was apparent in them. With a loving soul and capable of all the depth of attachments, Christiana had straightforward reasoning and a healthy and orderly mind. Not putting any finesse to her role as a woman, she thought that it was possible to be beautiful and to be useful. To love for some time a good man; to become his promised one, and soon afterward his companion; then to raise the children and take care of the household in trying to maintain order, economy and good humor, that was all the law and the prophets, and she never dreamed of anything beyond that.

On the contrary, Karl was one of those who never knew, always asking himself, where the narrow path of life led. To understand their path seemed to them sickening, unbearable; not to understand it at all seemed to them terrible torture. Concluding that man was never made for terrestrial paths, they climb on the wings of their fantasy, and look for aerial roads where the sounds and the faint smells of the positive life can no longer reach them. It's also in these high regions that they must finally meet some heavenly girl who has never degraded her nature by keeping a book of household expenses or making conserves or pastry. Other women may have all the tender sentiments, affection, pity, even devotion in a profound degree. But they never give their love to solid qualities; to get into their heart, it's first necessary to pass through their imagination.

Started together, but come to a place where their path in some way diverged, the young girl and her friend, the poet, would not walk together for very long. Each day they grew further apart from the denouement where, without having yet said so, the thought of both Christiana and Adam Kraft was moving, but which Karl had never had in view.

In that circumstance, an important person arrived in Hamburg from Vienna. He was the Commissioner that Emperor Leopold I was sending to the free Imperial city, over which he had suzerainty. The diplomat's mission was to reconcile the very ancient debates between the Senate and the bourgeoisie, which would have, if left to ferment and to become embittered, ended in a revolution.

This conciliation being difficult and long, the Imperial Commissioner, who was named Count of Nesselburg, had brought his whole household with him. The Countess of Nesselburg was remarkably beautiful, and her husband was jealous of her as much as possible, but with this nuance: that he wanted nothing of that furious conjugal worry that tormented him to show. To admit that a woman could deceive you was, in his opinion, to admit to himself the inferiority of his own merit. These kinds of things could be said to himself, but vis-à-vis the public, his vanity advised him to show on the outside absolute and entire confidence.

Karl saw Madame de Nesselburg. She was the embodiment of all the ideal he had never encountered, neither in Christiana or elsewhere. He therefore fell in love like a poet, and it must be added, like a man feeling all the absurdity of his passion, he gave in nevertheless to his seduction. From that moment, he became less and less attentive to Adam Kraft's shop, went to spend entire days on the shores of the Alster,[23] spoke sharp and impatient words to Christiana, and ceased even to be for her an attentive and kindly brother. Poetry, however, took its place and it was only stanzas, sonnets, and elegies to the lady of his thoughts. In fewer than two months he had made a volume from all of those pieces, got a bookstore to publish it for him, and, if he was no further along in his love, Karl at least saw his reputation grow by that publication.

With Christiana, things went even worse. In the past, when the poet gave voice to his flights of poetic suffering, she scolded him gently, finding nevertheless his verses beautiful and loving to hear him recite them. But when the secret poetry written to Madame Nesselburg appeared, without realizing completely what she was experiencing, the young girl instinctively felt that the unhappy lover's complaint was not without an object. And wasn't she going to imagine that the wife of a burgomaster who came to visit them from time to time must be the Iris in flesh and blood for whom Karl was sighing! From there, some nice, perfectly premeditated, rudeness to the poor woman and some biting criticism of the verse that the young girl thought addressed to her. The poet wouldn't have worried about thirty humiliated and turned away burgomaster wives, but to dare not to find his verses beautiful! So what was Christiana thinking of, and was that a definite rupture between them that she wanted to bring about?

Adam Kraft, however, was aware that something extraordinary was taking place in his house. Christiana no longer sang as she usually did. She was pale, obviously depressed, and more than once he had surprised her with tears in her eyes. In addition, Karl had ceased being any help in his work. He fled from any amusements, stubbornly searched for solitude.

---

[23] River that flows through Hamburg. (Note from the Author)

The young man was in love; that was clear. The instrument-maker took him aside one day and spoke to him like this:

"Karl, I have a lot to complain about you. For a long time, poetry has caused you to neglect the work that is our livelihood, and that is regrettable. However, I'll ignore that, knowing that you're aren't absolute master of these seductions. What's more, you have love on your mind."

At that Karl felt a shade of red spread over his face. He saw his secret was out.

"Yes, you are in love," Adam Kraft repeated, "and I'll let that pass also, but what's more, you are proud and can't be trusted, and in one or the other case, I find you equally guilty. Have you, or have you not, given me the right to call you son?"

"Ah! Master," Karl exclaimed. "You at least don't doubt my gratitude. The poor *blue child* will always remember his origin and the poor house from which your kindness came to get him."

"In the first place," Adam Kraft answered, "that's a first misunderstanding. When I speak to you, dear boy, of the ties of affection that must be between us, it isn't to take credit for what you call my kindness. If you were in a poor house, you didn't exchange it for another richer one. Your situation would have been taken care of by the Administrators of the Hospice as well as, and perhaps a great deal better than, it has been with my help. All the benefit has been on our side, since I gave Christiana a brother she passionately desired."

"You are arranging that with the delicacy I know you capable of. But you have nonetheless given me a situation that I could not have hoped for."

"I don't know about that," the musician continued. "I wanted to do more for you, but that has turned out to be very unfortunate for all of us."

"How is that?" Karl asked. "I don't understand very well…"

"It's clear, however. A long time ago, I arranged that you would be my daughter's husband. Christiana has easily become used to that idea, and you, loving her madly as you do, nothing seems simpler than this marriage. But here's the point: on one side there's the gentleman who is suffering; and on the other, a little girl suffers very softly, and is fading away. Nothing takes place because a satanic pride has come between the two of them."

"But I swear to you," Karl replied, "that as concerns Christiana, any more than you, I have never considered the project that you are talking to me about."

"Well! Unfortunate boy, that's a new grief against you, because that's to think at the time and to act in a vile manner. You think that because you are a bastard and without a family, I disdain your alliance, and by the fear of a refusal, you would prefer to let Christina die of sadness and put yourself on the way to follow her than to bring up the question with me."

"But, after all," answered the poet, trying to take advantage of the door that had been opened for him to escape the trap that he felt he had fallen into, "you can't say that I am a very desirable son-in-law."

"For a senator, without a doubt, or for a bourgeois, but me, I'm an artist. I don't have any stupid prejudices. My daughter loves you; you love my daughter. You're not asking me for her, but I'm giving her to you. Is that now understood and will you still make an elegy about it?"

The poet's embarrassment was mortal. He well understood that not to accept the offer made to him, was to blow down the beautiful house of cards that his adoptive father had for years constructed with love. As for Christiana, if he had had illusions as to her sentiments, attributing all her attachment to a brotherly feeling, the veil from his eyes had just been dropped in a way so as to be in no doubt. And he, never had he loved her in any other way, and now he must, after the gratitude that he must have for the father and the daughter, be in the position of outraging one and driving the other to despair by a refusal!

At the moment, he saw a way to gain time, and answered that, before anything else, Christiana needed to be consulted.

After all, she hadn't spoken. Young girls were often strange and the causes of their hidden sadness could easily be misunderstood. As for himself, he had never been struck by anything that could assure him that he was the cause of his adopted sister's concern.

At that, Adam Kraft responded that he was a big simpleton not to have yet seen clearly into his fiancée's heart. Nevertheless, he didn't resist the idea that she be asked for an official explanation and, to delay everything, the examination of conscience was adjourned until after supper.

IX. The Manuscript (Cont'd)
The Loves of the Poet

That interval, short as it might be, was largely taken advantage of by the traitor Karl. Two hours after his conversation with Adam Kraft, he had left his hospitable roof, leaving by way of adieu a hypocritical and rambling letter, where he rather cowardly exploited the pretext the musician had furnished him, the idea that you couldn't prudently, and without great chances of regret, marry a bastard. The unfortunate man, when he was all duplicity and ingratitude, still attributed to his behavior the appearance of delicacy and refined generosity!

Often nothing seems to bring good luck like bad behavior. When leaving Adam Kraft's home, Karl went to the bookseller who had published his poetic works to learn if he couldn't employ him in some way, because he still had to think about earning a living. Monsieur de Nesselburg bought books at this bookstore. He had read Karl's verses and had spoken of them in flattering terms. At the same time, Monsieur de Nesselburg had asked the bookstore owner to find some intelligent boy with a little education to become a secretary, which was hard to find in Hamburg, where bookkeepers were more common than intellectuals.

Karl having become available, the affair was arranged on the spot, and two days afterward, he saw himself installed at the townhouse of the Commissioner. Living under the same roof as the lady of his thoughts, breathing day and night the same air as she, he had the opportunity to see her, to speak to her. He even sometimes ate at the same table when Monsieur de Nesselburg, who had immediately treated him with kindness and consideration, did him the honor of inviting him to the table, rather than letting him eat in his room, as had, in principle, been the arrangement.

If Monsieur de Nesselburg was gracious toward his secretary, the actions of the Countess were not different than those of her husband. She also had read the verses that were a secret homage to her. Although she didn't go so far as understanding that they were addressed to her divine beauty, they had made their literary fortune with her, and she spoke of them to their author, deigning to praise them. She did more; she asked him to write some for her, and often had long conversations with him where she scolded him for his sadness and discouragement. At the end of a few weeks living in his terrestrial paradise, the poet began to feel another torture, that of having constantly at hand a beautiful tree filled with magnificent fruit which he wasn't allowed to touch. It was not, however, because the Countess decreased her kindness, far from that. From one day to the next, she became more affable and friendlier, and it was not impossible to find, in certain regards, signs of a gentle interest that she, when not observed, let fall on the poor *enfant bleu.*

Finally, there was this of happiness for the young secretary, that, despite his jealous instinct, Monsieur de Nesselburg seemed to be a thousand leagues away from taking umbrage, and thus the whole path taken by these humble beings that are not distrusted can't be known. That's the story of those underground animals that dig with little sound and in the shadows of vast domains, profoundly eroding the soil underneath. But certain irritable and worried personalities need constant occasions for concern, and even the good side of Karl's situation was one of his most cruel bitterness.

"*She* probably treats me with distinction and kindness," he told himself, "because in her eyes, I'm one those men of no consequence with whom any whim can be safely ignored, including that of kindness. If I could doubt it, you have only to look at the attitude of that Count. If he found me, I think, in his wife's bed, he would ask himself what that proved and if I had ever been daring enough to raise my desires to such a high place."

When one has happiness, as little as it may be, it should never be spoken ill of; that makes it fly away.

Karl was not at all content with the enormous conquests that he had made in the field of his desires, and instead of calculating the distance crossed between the child of public charity and the man he had become, he complained and analyzed the Countess' kindness. However, into that love affair there came a complication that made him very much regret his past.

Jealous of his wife in general, Count de Nesselburg was also jealous of someone in particular, and we can't say that there didn't seem to be some appearance of reason to his extreme worry that a certain person in particular caused him.

Seventeen years younger than her husband, Madame de Nesselburg had been brought up with one of her cousins, the young Conrad de Grundheim. First page to Emperor Leopold, then officer in his Guard, that young man, as soon as he could fall in love, had developed an ardent passion for his pretty relative, and he wanted to be her husband. But the two families, whose consent was needed, prevented that above mentioned wish. And considering at least the very resigned manner in which Madame de Nesselburg had shortly thereafter married the Count, it was apparent that Conrad de Grundheim hadn't made the ravages in her young girl's heart that in many circumstances makes *cousinage* of cousins.

Therefore, beaten on the field of legitimate love, Conrad loudly announced the intention of falling back on poaching. He even told his foolish claim to the husband who, on the outside, at least, only laughed about it. In that way, become a sort of wager, the young officer got from Monsieur de Nesselburg a kind of tolerance and some marvelous familiarities; thus, at any hour, when the officer was in Vienna, the amorous young man could come and be received by the Countess. In the summer, when the two spouses had gone to try to find some coolness and shade under the forest of some manor, one fine day, Conrad arrived, declaring that he came to spend a two-week furlough with them, and there, in the presence of the husband, who gave in with good grace to all those follies, there were no flirtatious moves which he did not make.

While Monsieur de Nesselburg's mission was in Hamburg, Conrad had gone to fight the Turks and harvest laurels. From that campaign he brought back a beautiful slash to his face and as soon as the wound had healed, he went straight to where the Countess was, to finish, he said, his convalescence. In addition, he didn't make any fuss about it; it was at the townhouse of the Imperial Commissioner that he moved in and made his home We're going to see how Monsieur the poet / secretary was going currently to spend his time.

At first, he was stupefied by the tone and the manners that the new arrival used with the Countess. Then he was taken aback on seeing the husband, as if he was pleased to encourage the most audacious enterprises directed against his rights, not worry about the declarations made point blank, nor the length of the tête-à-têtes, nor the most symbolic bouquets, nor finally all the signs of the most declared and the most audacious sentiments.

As for the defector from the house of Adam Kraft, what he suffered from that rivalry is understandable. But soon, as a result of Conrad's presence, bitterness that he had not yet suspected was revealed at the bottom of his cup. Before everything else, he noticed that the young officer, as if he guessed him to be competition, treated him with disdain and an intolerable haughtiness. Not only did he not at all obtain from him that politeness and that regard to which he was accustomed on the part of those who frequented the Count's house, but twenty times a day, his proud rival found a way to remind him of the enormous distance that birth and rank put between them. More than once he had even had to submit to certain not very courteous outbursts against poetry and poets which he had trouble not reacting to strongly. Those were undoubtedly great sorrows, and nevertheless he was still at the foot of his cross, and his crucifixion had not yet begun.

Either Madame de Nesselburg, watched by her noble cousin, was ashamed of the kindness that she had, up until then, shown the poor secretary; or she feared causing anger to a love that, like her husband, she took lightly, but which could have deepened under that insignificant surface; or finally, the lesson given her, suddenly changing allure and manners, she began to treat the unfortunate Karl with a distressing coldness and to be toward him as rough and as much the great lady as she had until then been indulgent and forgetful of her rank.

The sad rages which the application of that new and terrible regime caused the unhappy young man were such that, if continued, would have pushed him into some unfortunate extremity. He went so far as, to himself, plot to publicly insult the man he considered the author of his suffering. But there is this in the rivalry of the gentlemen of the men of war, that one fine morning, a *rejoin* letter saves you. The war against the Turks had been reignited, stronger than ever. Conrad had largely recovered from his wound. A letter came to him in Hamburg, and instructed him to return to his regiment with the shortest delay possible. What then happened in the goodbyes between Madame de Nesselburg and her cousin, it goes without saying, Karl didn't know, since he had nothing at all to do there and was not called on. But it can be believed that the separation was somewhat tender. The beautiful cousin, for several days, remained sad, dreamy or preoccupied. Sometimes, without being in love with Conrad, just seeing leave a relative and a childhood friend who was going to confront the possibility of combat, the Countess could decently show some worry. Indulgent, because he believed he was on the point of being reintegrated into his happiness, Karl was the first to take advantage of that explanation. But, the poor boy, how far he was from the truth!

He had in vain hoped and waited, nothing of his past was given back to him. As under the reign that had just finished,

Madame de Nesselburg was dry, haughty, then soon malevolent, aggressive. She seemed to take pleasure in annoying her former protégé with words, and finally, with an unequivocal premedication, inflict on him the continuation of the most bitter treatment that an unhappy lover had ever had to endure.

Enduring it with despair for some time this harshness finally made the martyr beside himself, and finding, even in his torture, stimulus for an audacious step, he took it on himself one day to ask the Countess what fault he could be guilty of to have merited to that point the loss of the honor of her kindness.

"But," the Countess said, "I don't recall, my dear sir, having been toward you either good or bad. Your functions are ordinarily with Monsieur le Comte. You have, I believe, taken his kindness for mine, and there is some confusion in what you're saying."

It was difficult to put a man more rudely in his place. Insisting nevertheless, he replied:

"*Mon Dieu*! I may have used a very ambitious word, but I would have sworn that in the past your good heart had covered me with a little pity."

"And why pity? I don't know that you should be pitied. My husband has consideration and kindness toward you, as he has, in general, toward all his servants."

"Ah! Madame, with a single word you have said everything," the unhappy Karl said in a stifled voice.

At the same time a nervous spasm contracted his face and he had to go lean against a piece of furniture, feeling himself faint under the sad emotion.

The Countess apparently regretted the harshness of her last words, since she stood up quickly, went to get a bottle of smelling salts and insisted that the too impressionable young man use it. Then, as he declined in a respectful and expressive gesture, while at the same time taking advantage of this expression of interest,

"But also," she continued in a softer tone, "what strange words did you just say to me?"

The young man's loss of strength was only passing. Standing up again with pride, under the blow he had just received, he said:

"You are right, Madame, a valet should never show in any way that he has been shown kindness or severity. Kindness to him is pure caprice, which he shouldn't get used to. And if I remain a short time still in this house, I will consider that as understood."

"Are you then threatening us with your departure?" the Countess asked ironically, recovering very quickly from her kindness.

"I am one of those, Madame, who doesn't threaten anyone and everyone humiliates."

"That means that you are saying: *If I remain in this house;* that implies an idea of leaving. But, in any case, you understand that is a decision that Monsieur de Nesselburg must be told, and not me."

"I will have the honor to inform him immediately," Karl answered.

He had just been obliquely told in a manner, as polite as it was ingenious, that his departure would be seen without any displeasure. That said, he bowed respectfully and started to leave. The Countess responded only with a cold and indifferent gesture, which implied: *Perfect, dear sir, as you please.*

Almost at the same moment, she picked up a piece of tapestry and had already started that work even before the one dismissed had left the apartment.

X. The Manuscript (Cont'd)
The Origin of the Secret Bureau

A few rapid preparations and a note left by the valet to the Count gave Karl back his liberty. But at least, that time, he didn't have any worry about material existence, which so much complicates a great sorrow. Some savings made during his employment had made him above need until things changed.

The next day, he was in his bedroom at the Black Angel Inn where he had gone to take refuge, still greatly moved by the very brutal *dénouement* of his novel, when, much to his astonishment, the Count de Nesselburg appeared and said something like this to him:

"So what happened, my dear Karl, between you and Madame de Nesselburg, that made you believe you should so briskly leave my house?"

"For some time I have believed that the Countess didn't find my presence pleasant; having had an occasion to make sure of that, I had to act as that misfortune advised me."

"And you couldn't understand the cause of that coldness she showed you?"

"Not really," the secretary answered aloud; however, aside to himself, he thought: *Couldn't he suspect?*

"Well, me, I'm going to tell you why: for Madame de Nesselburg, you are a boy who is a great deal too observant and clairvoyant."

"But if that observation is true, how could that possibly harm Madame la Comtesse?"

"Don't women always have a thousand and one secrets that they don't like to revealed?" said the Count.

"'But I don't know any secrets that I might be able to reveal.'"

"You are lying, my friend," Monsieur de Nesselburg said quickly.

"Sir," Karl said with vehemence, "I am no longer in your service, and I have the honor to receive you in my dwelling."

"I mean," the Count continued, "that you have noticed as well as I have what's apparent to everyone, and it's because of fear that you don't see it very well and that you decided to leave."

"Then," Karl demanded impatiently, "what have I seen?"

"*Parbleu!* That between my wife and her cousin there is an affectionate understanding; do you understand me now?"

"If it's a question of that, sir, let me point out to you that Monsieur de Grundheim's courtship is so openly indiscreet that you seem to attach very little importance to it; your casual confidence even seems to encourage it so that it even takes place under your eyes."

"Young man," the Count replied, "either my wife considers Monsieur de Grundheim's sighs of no consequence, and I would then be extremely ridiculous to worry about them, or the passion of that impertinent young man was contagious and then all my conjugal anger would only have hidden the inconvenience I have noticed."

"However, Monsieur le Comte, a woman is halted on the verge of falling, and extreme liberty can create the danger."

"In the case of good women, I know only those whose wise behavior can stand alone and without limitations," the Imperial Commissioner continued sententiously. "With the others, I would know immediately what I was dealing with, and my principle is to give them free rein."

"That, however, doesn't provide for exceptions; all women can't be a Lucretia.[24] It seems to me that helping their virtue a little wouldn't be considered wasted."

"Me, I don't give any help. I observe; I make sure and I take revenge if I'm deceived."

All that was said like a Blue-Beard[25] in a tone that would produce an effect even on a man less naive than the poet. Dominated by good intentions, instead of trying to add to the venom that the jealous man seemed to have, Karl declared that, with all the freedom of observation which he seemed to

---

[24] Lucretia the Chaste, wife of Collatium, raped by Sextus Tarquinius, King of Rome, when he returned to Rome, leaving the rest of the warriors in the field. Lucretia donned mourning, sent news of the rape to her father and husband. Sextus Tarquinius was killed and Lucretia stabbed herself. Rome banished all members of the Tarquins and Rome became a Republic. Possibly also refers to Shakspeare's version in a poem published in 1594 dedicated to the Earl of Southampton.
[25] Charles Perrault's 1697 fairy tale about a nobleman who has murdered his first six wives.

have been allowed, he had never discovered anything in the conduct of the Countess of which she could be accused.

"That's what we would know better," the Imperial Commissioner answered, "if we could read certain letters that she addresses to Madame the Chanoiness[26] of Valdorf in Vienna, one of her best friends, the plague of husbands."

"But have these letters become more frequent lately?"

"You see, young man, that the Countess was right, and you are a far more dangerous observer than you wish to appear. Well, yes, those letters have become more frequent for some time, and women are not suddenly taken with that furious activity of correspondence without there being a secret in progress."

"I'm going perhaps to say something stupid, but, in certain cases, can't the husband's authority extend to demanding to see those letters?"

"To have jealousy talked about," the Count exclaimed with disdain, "to compromise myself with the feline dexterity of a woman! What are you talking about!"

"Then you're thinking less about something violent than about intercepting something from that correspondence. That can hardly be done except in diplomacy."

"No, I wouldn't want to intercept anything, but I would like to read everything and, in doing that, you can come to my aid. Yes, you, my dear fellow, although that seems strange to you. Every day the world gets more perfect and I want to tell you a secret that you will keep for me."

"Certainly, if I agree to."

"And let's even say that you don't keep it. Here's what I can always tell you: with their thick and totally commercial air, they are clever people, these Hamburgians!"

This beginning was so strange and so far from the former direction of the conversation, that Karl began to give the

---

[26] Member of a religious order in the *ancien regime* which enrolled almost exclusively women from the nobility.

Count an astonished look; was he delirious or was he making fun of him?'"

Without seeming to notice the effect of his opening remarks, the Count continued:

"Yes, really, for the needs of their stock exchange and negotiations, these merchants ended up putting their hand on a very curious procedure: to know, before your neighbor, the exchange rate of a loan, the price of merchandise, that, in summary, is all the genius of high commerce. But instead of undergoing torture to read horoscopes that are always a little problematic, if a way could be found to know for certain, wouldn't that be a fortune earned?"

"Exactly. But if I remember, we were talking about the letters of Madame de Nesselburg to Madame the Chanoiness of Valdorf?"

"Now," the Count continued, without paying attention to the way in which he had been brought back to the subject, "what did the good people of Hamburg do? They remembered that more than once, some letters with valuable commercial contents had reached them widowed of their contents. There must therefore have been some employee at the post clever at opening a sealed letter without anything being noticed. The law intervened without discovering anything. Cleverer, when it was a matter of great interest for them, a few rich business men, contributing to a common fund, finally put their hand on that clever artist, and having brought him in, spoke to him like this:

" 'Dear Sir, you have taken a profession that will get you hanged, and that for having appropriated for yourself some valuable things that you don't, more often than not, know how to negotiate. Instead of this adventurous profession, here's what we want to offer you: you will continue to unseal letters as in the past, but instead of collecting our bills of exchange under the seals, you will only collect news and information which you will share with us. By means of that help, you will have, each year, a revenue of a thousand thalers[27]and, what's more, that very precious blessing, a clear conscience.' "

"But that proposition was odious!" Karl exclaimed, interrupting.

"But let me then say,'" the Count coldly continued, "the beginnings of everything are always puny and not very pleasant. Do you know anything uglier than a new-born?"

"That abominable traffic was continued?" the naive secretary asked.

"As in the city of Rome, the idea grew, became institutionized, so that several men were employed, whereas in the past only one hand had been needed. Then, finally, the gentlemen in the Senate found out about that hidden practice and transported it from the commercial domain to the political regime, where it had a wider application. They turned it to the profit of the general interest by using it to find out about the intrigues of dangerous minds and diplomatic secrets."

"So," the poet said, thinking aloud, "that commerce that lives only by honesty and good faith, and later the government, that is to say the guardian of public morality, gave a body to that infernal idea!"

"Yes, my friend, and you can count on its making its way around the world. Already in Hamburg it has established roots so vigorous that now it can oppose the power that would try to suppress it. Now, you understand, what can serve the general order can take care of private business as well."

"Ah!' Karl said with disgust, "that's how you hope to discover the secret of that correspondence…"

"Yes, I don't hide that. And I will add that, as I wouldn't like to see my personal secret open to just anybody, although in general the gentlemen of this *Secret Bureau* are reputed to be of proven discretion, I would like the assistance of a friend."

---

[27] A silver coin accepted throughout Europe for upwards of four hundred years.

"You probably haven't come, Count, to suggest that I be that accommodating person?"

"But of course! That's a small part of your functions as a secretary. To write letters for me, or to unseal them, that's part of the same family of functions that are logically linked together."

"I am no longer your secretary, and if I still were, I would leave your service rather than lend my hands to that infamy."

"That's too bad for you, my dear boy. After all, that's a career that I'm offering you. Those functions receive a very honorable salary, and with your poetry, that you will in the future be able to write without any risk, I doubt that you will ever be out of work. Besides, my wife, I am the first to admit it, has been rather hostile toward you and I thought that, finding an opportunity to give her back the same..."

"If I could think about revenge, I would wish her to merit it," Karl quickly interrupted, "and that she not begin by taking away my self-esteem."

"Well, you are refusing. That's your business. I will ask someone else, and we won't be any the less good friends because of that."

Saying this, the Count got up, and his former secretary went with him to the door with that ceremonial courtesy due to their respective situations. When he was about to leave:

"A propos," said Monsieur de Nesselburg, as if an afterthought, "I have told you my secret in confidence..."

"Very well, sir, you can count on my discretion."

"No, you can do whatever you like with this subject, and it isn't to me that you will have to give an accounting for what I have just revealed to you."

"How's that? What do you mean?"

"I am sorry for my lack of prudence; it never occurred to me that you would refuse. I have retained a place for you that had become vacant in that fearful association that is always careful to kept its membership to twelve, not counting the President. As it now knows that you have its secret, not seeing you among its members, very probably it will be concerned about what you can say, and you must expect, I think, some bad reaction in its fashion."

"But, sir, what you have done is terrible: to place me perhaps between the sword and infamy!"

"Probably. I have been very careless. I was believing in your devotion for my person, and I was wrong not to inform you before enrolling you. I really would offer you help in leaving Hamburg, but frankly, I think that precaution would be dangerous. From this moment, you will be watched and the least unusual change in your habits would only hasten the catastrophe."

"All right, sir," Karl said, pretending more resolution than seemed needed faced by the peril revealed to him, "I will take care of my safety as well as I can."

"And I, if I can, will find a less virtuous man, but bad luck for the Countess. Blood calls for blood, and if I obtain proof of her infidelity, the adulterous woman and her accomplice, will, because of your prejudice, cruelly atone for their lack of prudence."

That nice consolation given, the Count de Nesselburg finished his departure, and left the poor poet with an understandable emotion.

XI. The Manuscript (Cont'd)
The Apostles of Nuremberg

Many things were true in the strange confidence that had just been given to Karl. From 1660, an institution equivalent to our *Secret Bureau* had existed in Hamburg. Founded on the commercial instinct, developed and consolidated by political interest, it had also borrowed something from those mysterious ideas and that taste for mysterious association which, since the famous secret tribunal, had not ceased to be current in Germany.[28]

In his position as Imperial Commissioner, he had been initiated into all the secrets of that little state over which he had come to be regent. Monsieur de Nesselburg had found out about the existence of the *Secret Bureau (Die Schwartze Kammer)*[29] and he had immediately thought of using it for his jealous curiosity. But the manner in which the young man was enrolled without his permission, everything hadn't happened as he was told it would. Although he hadn't for a long time had any suspicion of a man he called one of his servants, the Count had finally briefly glimpsed Karl's passion for his wife.

Following his jealous ways, back at his home, without showing anything about his discovery, he immediately conceived a plan to distance the poet from his house by affiliating him with the shady agency. He saw more than one advantage to that scheme. If the secretary refused, he would run the risk of being stabbed by the associates of the group, who, in fact, would not hesitate, for their own safety, to take, if need be, the life of an indiscreet person. In that way, an insolent love would have its punishment. If, on the contrary, which seemed more probable, that worthless man hurried to take advantage of an independent and comfortable existence, his jealousy would be informed about what was nearest to his heart, the

---

[28] The Vehmic courts, or *Vehmgericht*, a vigilante tribunal system of Westphalia active during the later Middle Ages, based on a fraternal organisation of lay judges called "free judges." Proceedings were often secret, leading to the alternative titles of "secret courts" or "silent courts." The peak of activity of these courts was during the 14th to 16th centuries, with scattered evidence establishing their continued existence during the 17th and 18th centuries. They were finally abolished by order of Jérôme Bonaparte, king of Westphalia, in 1811.

[29] Rabou here uses the German translation for "Black Cabinet."

Countess' feelings for her cousin, and in addition, the stigma of the stain from the profession to which Karl had descended would be good revenge for his presumptuous love. Finally, to triumph from the hesitation that could be foreseen, between an absolute refusal and an immediate determination, the Count had counted on the influence of fear and more still on the young man's passion for the Countess. Seeing himself disdained and learning that someone else was more fortunate, if nothing but a desire for revenge it seemed he must enter into the plans made for him. Everything was then weighed and calculated in the Imperial Commissioner's mind. Only his vile and wicked nature had kept him from foreseeing a chance by which the principal result of his black cleverness was neutralized in his hands.

That chance was that, instead of being like him, not caring about the life of others and basely jealous, Karl was frightened of the danger that menaced the life of the Countess and, an unhappy lover, he nevertheless had the generosity to devote himself to the one who had so cruelly rejected him. When then, shortly thereafter, the young man, changing his mind, wrote to Monsieur de Nesselburg that he had thought about it and was at his orders, he already had his plan made out. If the Countess was guilty, he would give the jealous husband only false extracts of the correspondence, and by his hand, the woman for whom he sacrificed his honor would be warned of the perils surrounding her. We won't say either that he didn't enter the virtuous determination of that devotion with a little of that furious curiosity that a mistreated lover always has, to know, in fact, if another was better received than he. And then, isn't there something unusually attractive about the idea of being permitted to see into the most secret thoughts of a beloved woman, and to read her heart like an open book as if her heart had become transparent?

However that may be, the evening of the same day the interview took place between the Count and Karl, at first without a result, everything was arranged between them, and the generous young man had obtained the happy certainty that he would have to furnish the jealous man with just the copies of the letters and not the letters themselves, in which case he would decidedly have refused the mandate.

"Three quarters of an hour before midnight," Monsieur de Nesselburg had said to him on leaving him. "You have only to go to the borders of the Alster at the place called *Teufelsort* (the place of the Devil). You will soon be joined by a man who will ask you: '*How many are they?*' You will answer: '*They are thirteen.*' Then you will follow that man who will lead you to a place where the ceremony of your reception will take place. Beginning tomorrow, you will be working. An order will be given for all letters of Madame de Valdorf and of my wife to pass through your hands. I am counting on your fidelity and your intelligence to transmit to me everything that concern the subject in question and others if there are any."

"And these copies, how do I get them to you?"

"You will put them, like all the other work with which you may be employed, into the hands of the President of the Bureau. I have people in the Senate Chancellery by whom everything will come to me."

Eleven forty-five was been struck by the Saint Nicolas clock when Karl arrived at the *Teufelsort*. The solitude there was profound as was the night and the silence. He waited for some time, looking around him as much as the thick darkness would allow him. Suddenly he shivered. Without having heard any sound of footsteps, he felt a hand placed on his shoulder from behind, and at the same time someone said very low in his ear:

"*How many are they?*"

The poet answered with some emotion:

"*They are thirteen.*"

"Then follow me," the unknown man said, "but first put on this mask, so that I don't see your face, just as you won't see mine."

Karl adjusted the mask he had just been given on his face, and almost immediately, he heard the sound of a little spring which closed. Then the carton covered with velvet adhered so tightly to his face that it would have been impossible for him to take it off later if he hadn't been told the secret.

"Oh! oh!" he said gaily to show his composure, "there are a lot of precautions."

Saying this, he found that there was a little apparatus at the opening of his mouth which changed the sound of his voice completely.

"Yes," replied the unknown man, "the Apostles don't know each other. The *Master of the Works* is the only one who knows their faces and their names."

Karl wanted to continue the conversation, but his conductor said sententiously:

"Speak only when necessary." And at the same time he told him to follow him.

When they had arrived at a long alley behind the Senate building, toward the place called *office of the writers,* he entered the building through a hidden door which was opened with a combination lock. After having gone through a maze of corridors and uninhabited rooms filled with deposits of archives, by descending a spiral staircase, they came to an arched antechamber closed by an iron door. Karl was left in that place by his conductor. Soon after, dressed in a strange costume and holding a bunch of big keys, the conductor came to get him and told him to pass with him into a neighboring room. An unusual spectacle was waiting for them there.

Around a long table and in the seating arrangement and the costume that Leonardo de Vinci gave the characters of his famous *The Last Supper,* sat Jesus Christ and ten of his apostles; two seats were vacant. That of the one who was introducing Karl and that of the recipient were waiting to complete the number twelve, sacramental in that reunion. There is reason to believe that the painter, if he could have been present at that kind of initiation, wouldn't have greatly approved of the masks and the black gloves with the ends cut off, plus a Louis XIV wig, the fashion of which then was beginning to penetrate into the north countries, and with which Jesus Christ and the apostles had complicated their antique dress. But those were precautions taken to keep from recognizing each other. Karl himself, before entering the room, had to don a longue robe with a hood, and he had been told to hide his hands in the fashion of a monk.

To understand the dialogue which was going to be established between the President, or *Master of the Works,* and the introducer of Karl, it's necessary to know that the tomb of this saint is in Nuremberg, in Saint Sebald's Church. Around the reliquary, made of gold-covered bronze, the sculptor placed the figures of the apostles, which are considered masterpieces and enjoy an immense popularity in all of Germany.

"Is that you, Saint Peter?" the Master of the Works then asked on seeing the introducer of Karl enter. "Who is the man with you?"

"A blind man who wants to see the light."

"And who will show him the light?"

"Those to whom it has been said: 'You will be like the gods, knowing good and evil. *Et iritis sicut dii, scientes bonum et malum.*'"

"Those words, Saint Peter, are those of the Serpent to the Woman—and the Serpent lied."

"One can lie to the Woman; but the Apostles of Nuremburg cannot be deceived."

"And these Apostles, who are they?"

"Those that the sculptor put to guard the tomb of Saint Sebald, and who were twelve like us."

"But those are figures made of bronze and how is there clairvoyance in a figure of bronze? It has eyes but it cannot see, ears but cannot hear, and a mouth but cannot speak, hands that cannot touch."

"So we have taken only their names. People of flesh and blood, we have eyes to see with, ears to hear with, strong and clever hands to break through all obstacles, and a mouth not to speak."

"And there is nothing in us made of bronze?"

"Oh, yes, there is. Our heart is made of it."

"And this blind man who is looking for light, is his heart of bronze too?"

"He is present here, Master, ready to undergo trial .Tap on his chest and see what sound it gives out."

"Our procedure, as you know very well, Saint Peter, is not to require proofs; those are the play of children and free-masons. For whoever wants to come to us, we have but one requirement: Do you know how to hold your tongue and give your life?"

"You heard him," said Saint Peter, turning to Karl. "Do you know how to hold your tongue and give your life?"

"I can keep a secret," Karl said, "but what do you mean by 'give your life?'"

"There is always a traitor among twelve who are brought together," the Master of the Works replied. "Jesus chose a dozen men and Judas was among them. Our Judas, where is he? Let him give his name so he can be known."

"I," the Introducer then said, "am Peter."

"And I, Andrew, Peter's brother."

"And I, James the elder."

"And I, John, James' brother."

"And I, Philip."

"And I, Bartholomew."

"And I, Matthew the Publican."

"And I, Thomas."

"And I, James, Alphaeus' son."

"And I, Simon."

"And I, Jude, brother of James the younger."

The eleven members of the reunion reported successive-ly.

"That one must be Judas!" the Master of the Works ex-claimed, pointing to Karl. "He is the only one who hasn't giv-en his name."

"You are mistaken," Karl answered. "I am not Judas."

"You are the last arrived among us and the least experi-enced; if you are not the one I said, you will at least play that role. Until someone new replaces you, at our reunions you will do all the servile work, since we do not allow among us either serfs or valets. Now, do you want to swear? Here is the oath:

"*I swear to be a loyal and faithful apostle; never to reveal the secret of the apostolate, nor any of the secrets that will come to me in the exercise of my sacred ministry, nor to turn them to my advantage, pleasure, or happiness. I swear to love, to defend and to aid the members of our holy college, when I am required to, even those who might be my enemies. If I fail to keep such promises, at any hour and in any place the two-edged sword here, the point everywhere, has the right to my heart's blood, of which neither emperor, magistrate, of other protector has the right to save a drop, and in that case I don't expect even from God the salvation of my soul.*"

That said, they applied the point of a long sword to Karl's heart, and he repeated word for word the formula of the oath. After which, under the name of Judas Iscariot, he was declared one of the twelve. Then he was told the secret of the spring to detach his mask, a false hairpiece and gloves, like the others wore, were given to him. And, last of all, dressed in a yellow robe, he took one of the vacant sets, while the one who introduced him went to take his place among the twelve.

"To announce the end of the séance, the Master of the Works used this bizarre formula: "*Now that the zodiac has its twelve signs, the works are closed.*"

Then one of the associates gravely rose and left. A minute later, at the sound of a bell, a second one left, and the others did the same at minute intervals right down to the eleventh. Each of the Apostles found himself alone in the vestiary, while he took off the costume covering his city clothes in which he could have been recognized. The same great precautions were taken at the entry of each of those very discreet associates. The alley that led to the outside door of the palace where they went to do their nocturnal work was narrow and dark, and if, by chance, two Apostles chanced to meet there, warned by the sound of their steps, they had an agreed-on signal among themselves to keep themselves at a distance. But, actually, that encounter was almost impossible. Twelve minutes before the hour set for the reunion, every associate was bound by the rules to station himself outside the palace at a spot marked out in advance for him. When the clock struck, no one started walking until he had counted on his wrist a certain number of pulsations, calculated to let a sufficient interval elapse between the arrival of each of them at the secret door.

When the eleven Apostles had left, and when the Master of the Works was alone with the newly elected member:

"Your name and your face," said the high dignitary, placing his finger on his forehead, "so that I can engrave it here."

The one spoken to took off his mask, but before he had time to say his name:

"Karl!" the Master of the Works exclaimed, making a gesture of great surprise. "Well," he added coldly, "I see I know it by heart. Now, reflect upon your oath!"

XII. The Manuscript (Cont'd)
A Girl's Revenge

Just the next day after his initiation, Karl learned some strange news. Someone informed him right out and without any preparation, by asking him if it was true that Christiana, his adopted sister, was going to marry that Englishman, the son of the regicide, who had on his hands the bloodshed by his father, that dealer in contraband, that counterfeiter, in a word, that living enigma called Hulet.

In the first place, the choice of a husband hardly pleased Karl, who had heard bad things spoken of Hulet. But in addition to that, if Christiana had married God the Father, the former preferred fiancé, for his part, would certainly have found something to criticize. Monsieur the poet didn't want the daughter of the musician, but to learn that she was committed elsewhere was a disagreeable surprise. The human heart has a number of hidden movements like this that it is not very aware of.

Having to reproach Christiana for the bad taste and the lack of prudence of her inclination, the dethroned and forgotten lover would be careful about attacking on the matter of fidelity and constancy in affections. He felt how ridiculous that quarrel would be on his part. But that was one more reason for him to be scandalized, sadly moved, as he said, on learning of the fall the unhappy girl was going to take. In any case, what he had just learned was, for the forgetful and ungrateful young man, an occasion to be worried about what had taken place in Adam Kraft's household since he had left it, and here's what he was told:

A little good luck seemed finally to have entered the artist's life. It was a matter of a distant relative who had made him his heir, and that inheritance must have given him a little ease and a somewhat comfortable situation because he was seen to be spending money, for Christiana most of all, that he always wanted to dress well in the latest fashion, but then also for his table where he rather frequently invited some friends and even the burgomasters. Overall, however, it didn't seem that either he or his daughter had a great deal of taste for this change in fortune. Christiana was almost always serious and sad, and, as for Adam Kraft, who had given up any kind of work, in that situation, he was rarely in a mood that made it appear his soul was content. Periods of turbulent and foolish gaiety were followed by periods of dark melancholy that he couldn't shake off, they said, giving way to drinking an immoderate amount of wine and liqueurs. From all of that, Karl was led to conclude that worry about his departure still weighed on the two hearts in which he formerly occupied so much place. But then a stronger reason was how to explain that unusual, that incomprehensible marriage.

This was known about the marriage:

Adam Kraft didn't appear very enthusiastic about it, but his daughter insisted on it. Besides, making the acquaintance of Hulet was in a circumstance to be remembered. Wandering around in the city at night, as in the past, Hulet one evening had heard a voice in a side street calling for help. He had found the musician stopped and in the hands of two criminals. Those put to flight, the artist's savior had then taken him back to his lodgings and had courteously, the next day, come to ask about him. The liking for Hulet that Christiana had immediately shown, introduced into her home in that way, was then explained as gratitude. And as the girl could now be taken for a rich heiress, the suspicious personage didn't make any resistance to the benevolent attentions offered to him. However, since this marriage was agreed on and set, Christiana wasn't noticed to appear happier, and, on the contrary, she seemed to show a doubling of melancholy.

All that was very extraordinary and seemed to indicate that, following an unhappy love affair, the musician's daughter threw herself at the first man she saw without knowing very well the man to whom she was giving her hand. As a consequence, Karl, in his soul and conscience, thought himself obligated to approach his adopted sister. And, while going back to a house where he had made such a bad exit didn't seem a perfectly agreeable duty to him, he decided to present himself at Adam Kraft's house and did so almost immediately.

Arriving there, he was met by a servant, a great novelty in the poor household he had known. That girl told him that *Mademoiselle* was alone in the house and that she didn't know if *Mademoiselle* would want to receive a man she had never seen.

"Your *mademoiselle* knows me," Karl answered, and he gave his name.

He was expecting Christiana to run to meet him, but he was taken into a room very formally furnished where, on the contrary, he had to wait as in an antechamber. Christiana finally appeared. She was very pale and very haggard notwithstanding her rich attire. Her approach was constrained and she asked with a little irony, which, however, had nothing of bitterness in it, what had made Karl remember them.

The visitor gave as an excuse his many occupations and the extreme dependence on him in the position he occupied with Monsieur de Nesselburg.

"I left it only two days ago," he added, "and my first visit has been to you."

"My father," the girl answered, "will be grateful for that attention."

"But you, Christiana, you aren't speaking for yourself?"

"I, too, am charmed to see you."

The words were said in a tone that somewhat belied it.

"All right,' Karl said, "you're angry with me. You didn't understand how much delicacy and devotion there was in my conduct. It's a very cruel to tell oneself, but my birth was and always will be an obstacle."

"Not a word about the past, please," the artist's daughter said. And, to change the conversation, she added: "What are you doing since you no longer have that position that took so much of your time?"

Karl had a thousand reasons not to answer that question. He hurried to pass on to another subject, more interesting, he said he knew about her impending marriage:

"Yes, as a matter of fact, I'm getting married," Christiana answered without any embarrassment.

"And you know that man to whom you're giving your hand very well?"

"Obviously, since I'm marrying him."

"But everyday a young girl can ignore the background of a man, or even, being told about it, she can, following a heart more sensitive than farsighted, badly engage her affections."

"What you say is very true, Monsieur Karl."

"Well, if that is true," the visitor continued, pretending not to understand what there was in that remark directed to him personally, "allow me, Christiana, to call your attention to the choice you have made."

"*Mon Dieu*!" Christiana exclaimed, "you can't tell me more bad things about Monsieur Hulet than I have already been told, and that I don't already know."

"That means that you think he has been slandered and he has the most regrettable fascination over you. But a reputation is not made without some foundation and when it's a question of the happiness of a lifetime..."

"Did I tell you that I pretend to be happy?"

"However, you must love him, since you're marrying him?"

Christiana just smiled scornfully.

"But if you don't love him," Karl continued more heatedly, "is it then true that you are sacrificing yourself for spite, for wounded ego?"

"You are mistaken," Christiana interrupted. "I'm not sacrificing myself; I'm avenging myself."

"You call that vengeance when all the effects of you resolution will fall on you?"

"I believe it will weigh on others too, Monsieur Karl."

"Then, I don't understand you anymore, Christiana. If I should give in to the most violent jealousy, you wish, at the price of all your future, to buy this pleasure of torturing me. Is that possible?"

"You're not at all jealous; why should you be? Also, it isn't your jealousy I'm hoping for."

"But, after all, to marry a man compromised to this point, a profligate, a scoundrel who is even suspected of crime!"

"And you can add that these crimes, if he hasn't committed them, it's certain that he will commit them. In case you have ever been near him, didn't you notice that he has something like blood on his hands?"

Those words were said with such frightening cold-bloodedness, that it made the one who heard them think they were due to some mental derangement. Noticing that Karl was looking at her with a kind of fear:

"I seem very unusual to you," Christiana continued. "Listen to me. You're going to understand me. Although you have been very hard on me and you have never loved me..."

Here Karl interrupted her and was profuse in protests.

"If you loved me or not, I don't believe you have a heart completely without pity," the girl continued, "and if you had been the cause of the unhappiness of someone, you would have remorse that would trouble the tranquility of your life."

"So that's why, learning the folly you were going to commit, I came here to stop you."

"That's why I will persist in my idea right to the end. I know very well the sort of man I'm marrying, and to what point I will be unhappy with him. But I want my unhappiness to be on your conscience, and no matter how your life turns out, you too will not be happy because I will never cease being a living remorse for you."

With his life of the imagination, Karl, better than anyone, was made to understand everything there was at the same time of delicacy and of depth in that vengeance. The plan had been laid out to him with a simplicity and a coldness of resolution which made the idea more frightening. He was so afraid of it that, without calculating exactly how far in the future he would be faced with it, he asked:

"So then, if I told you that your father's former plans could be taken up again, you would break off with Hulet?"

"At the same instant, and, although you don't love me, I still won't be worried about the happiness of both of us. I am not repulsively ugly, after all. I am neither stupid, nor wicked. Well! with that, when you love someone as I do you from my earliest childhood, (and here the poor girl's voice broke and big tears rolled from her eyes), you can be very sure to make her happy, even when that person doesn't try."

"Well, then, send that man away," Karl started to say, because the emotion of the charming girl had become contagious. But a thought and an incident at the same time kept him from completing the sentence begun. The thought was that of his affiliation with the *Secret Bureau* that had very much changed the economy and limited the freedom of his future; the incident was that of the servant opening the door and announcing Monsieur Hulet.

When he entered, the intended fiancé seemed more than a little astonished to find a young man he didn't know in a tête-a-tête with his future bride. At the same moment, his notice of their mutual emotion added still more to the bitterness of his surprise. He cast a dark look at Karl and Christiana. Then, approaching his promised fiancé, he kissed her hand, asking: "So, who is this gentleman?" in a low and commanding tone.

"The gentleman is my adopted brother," Christiana replied. "We haven't seen each other for some time, and when you entered, we were talking about the former marriage prospects that existed between us."

"The subject was well chosen and seemed to move you a great deal."

"But, Monsieur," the girl said, as if she took pleasure in defying the rather natural annoyance of her future husband, "no one can keep the past from being the past."

"That's without a doubt, but I prefer that the past remain in its place and that it's remembered that the present is the present."

"That's remembered, sir, and the proof is that I'm going to ask Karl to leave us so that you are completely free to make a scene when he has left."

At those words, Karl stood up, and he understood all the harshness of the character to which Christiana planned to link her life. Despite the clever words that almost committed the supposed fiancé to show at least a semblance of better humor, that shameful jealous man remained silent and seemed, by the coldness of his attitude, to want to hasten still more the retreat of the man with whom he was angry.

As for Christiana, she was very little concerned about increasing for herself the chances of a disagreeable explanation the moment the poet left.

"Karl," she said, putting herself again on their former footing, "think about what we were talking about a while ago, and tomorrow morning, if I have not received a letter from you, that's the end of it, and things will remain as they are."

Showing much more politeness than Hulet had shown, Karl, before going out the door, bowed to the somber fiancé. Just at that moment, he surprised a look that followed him with an unspeakable expression of animosity.

I don't know, he thought, *but it seems to me that there will be blood between that man and me.*

XIII. The Manuscript (Cont'd)
A Seance in the Dark Room

No longer having any hope so far as Madame de Nesselburg was concerned, Karl was ready to appreciate the moral value that he had suddenly found in Christiana. In his eyes, she was no longer that little girl totally devoted to household occupations, and capable, of course, of a kind of middle-class sentimentality. Naiveté mingled with strength, strong and real passion, combined with resolution and cold logic, that's what now impressed him in the character that he had, until then, believed completely self-effacing.

But he, on his side, the step he had taken the evening before was very serious, the job to which his foolish love for the Countess had led him, seemed to him to have something so stigmatizing, that he had to ask himself if, as an honest man, he could, at that hour, pick up the jewel that he had just found in his path. On the other hand, however, if he didn't throw himself across the cruel sacrifice that his adopted sister was contemplating, what fate the unhappy girl was preparing for herself! It's understandable that, in this conflict of ideas and feelings, Karl's perplexity was extreme, and a resolution, itself very delicate to take, was found to be the only and last resource that he believed he could take.

"Yes," he told himself, "Christiana is a trustworthy girl. I will confide the terrible secret of my initiation to her and make her the judge. If she wants me despite that stain, I will be her husband; if, on the contrary, her contempt for my mistake is stronger than her love, at least I will persuade her to take back an unworthy choice. And as, after all, in the feeling I now have for her there is more esteem that overriding passion, well, I will comfort myself with seeing her belong to another if he can make her happy. And as for me, I will have learned what the love of great ladies costs imprudent men who wish to look at the sun and are blinded by it."

In any case, a letter couldn't here take the place of an explanation, and, while waiting until he could see Christiana and consult with her, if need be, on a way to escape the constraints of the suspicious association of which he had become a member, the new Apostle was still going to take possession of his occult functions. That was a compelling need of his position. Still too clumsy as to how to remove safely the contents from a letter, Karl didn't need to be guilty of breaking a seal, and under the tutelage of the Master of the Works, he only made some extracts, of which he didn't even understand the interest. The séance then was for him rather empty and monotonous, and he wondered if, before the remorse that always accompanied a dishonest act, boredom must not be the first punishment for the miserable man he had become.

The custom was to open first the letters that they supposed were the least rich in information; as for those that appeared of more serious interest, they were reserved. In that way the attention and vigilance of the workers were kept in suspense right up to the last moment.

Then, when the new initiate was the least expecting it, he suddenly saw arrive in his hands a letter that the Master of the Works had had passed to him already unsealed, addressed to Madame the Chanoiness de Valdorf. That letter, if he had not at first recognized the handwriting, its address would have told him everything. Obviously, faced with the revelation so close, the poor man in love must have felt a certain excitement, but he prided himself on imitating a certain impassive look shown to him by his colleagues. And with a coolness that he tried to make as obvious as possible, he opened the envelope. At that supreme moment, he didn't doubt that Monsieur de Grundheim's triumph was clearly manifest.

However, this semblance of strength of soul scarcely lasted, and anyone who had looked under the mask of this very unconcerned reader would have noticed that, at reading the first lines, his face had changed color three or four times and, at that moment, the agitation in his soul began to be revealed on the outside by a trembling of his hands which communicated itself to the paper.

Dear good friend, wrote Madame de Nesselburg,

I have followed your wise advice. I have been unkind, without pity, to that unhappy young man. I have gone so far as to insult him, and I have forced him to leave our house. During the three days since he left, have I been happier and calmer? Have I stopped for one instant thinking about him? When he was here, doing his work for my husband, I could better remember the distance there was between him and me. Now I forget the social situation to remember only the man. Ah! How wrong you are, my friend, in making absence a heroic remedy! Yes, when you have lost your heart to someone without merit, not to see them might help you to cleanse it; but when your love is well placed, absence, rather, is like a halo around the virtues that charmed you. Me, I would reject the old saying, "Absence makes the heart grow fonder," and I would say: "Those who are present are wrong; because, present, they are happy, don't suffer and don't appeal to memory by pity, that perfidious intermediary."

What is he doing now, the poor child? How his heart must be torn apart and full of bitterness! How he must tell himself that I am a hard-hearted and disdainful woman! Those are the thoughts that come back to me constantly, and you wish, dear friend, for this regime to be cured! At the time I was behaving naturally and truthfully toward him, when I was treating him with the regard and the kindness to which his devotion and the precious qualities of his heart and his mind had a right, I wasn't even aware of loving him. But from the moment that, to avoid Conrad's watchfulness, I tried to reverse my behavior and since the period, most of all, where, to follow your advice, I exaggerated my pretended bad will, it seemed that thus restrained and harshly reined in, my poor heart rebelled, and I no longer know what to do to hold back its impetuous momentum.

Well, he is no longer here. Now I have no chance or opportunity to see him. Leaving, I am at least sure while suffering cruel torture, not to let myself go to any compromising admission, and that is, you will tell me, a great blessing! Yes! Just as letting a member be amputated which would have caused the loss of the whole body. But, for all that, is the operation less painful, and isn't there still in the nerves an eternal memory of that part of the "me" which has been separated, and which sometimes is still felt?

God be thanked! Monsieur de Nesselburg's mission is coming to its end, and I think we will soon leave for Vienna. That change of place, I hope, will do me good. Oh! Is it in the middle of these merchants and stockbrokers that I must fear losing my poor reason!

Carried in such a little expected way into the heaven that had suddenly opened to him, happy Karl didn't lose sight of another less celestial interest, and which, on the contrary, from what he had just read, only required his concern more urgently. In fact, it wasn't any more about Monsieur de Grundheim's good luck but of his own that he now had to reroute the jealous Count. As a result, he picked up a pen and with the energy of happy love, the most beautiful inspiration in the world, he began to rewrite for Monsieur de Nesselburg the counter-letter below:

Dear good friend,
You don't need to defend yourself, just by the frequency of your letters I suspected you of a tender sentiment. And then, no one always returns in this way to talk about one man, even to speak ill of him unless he has made a little impression. Besides, why are you hiding from me? Can't you be released from your vows and marry the man you love! I see you come very nicely to marriage with joy. You were so opposed to it in the past! I repeated in vain to you, "It's a happy situation, whatever is said about it," and give you as an example the happiness of my union with Monsieur de Nesselburg. You

94

were still thinking that I wanted to pretend to you, and there was a little gossip about misunderstanding between my husband and me.

If I have to confess everything to you, I'm afraid for some time, for his peace of mind and for mine, the visit my cousin Conrad has made here recently was truly beginning to worry me somewhat. Not that I pay the slightest attention to his sighs, but he is so indiscreet about it that Monsieur de Nesselburg, while having decided not to take his foolish passion seriously, could get angry , and I have already noticed some signs that this game he overlooked, didn't please him very much. God be thanked! the scatterbrain has gone to rejoin his regiment. My husband having again become calm, I gave up the idea of taking up the matter with him, as I at first thought I would. Beside, between us, this was only a cloud, because Monsieur de Nesselburg has a great heart, as well as a great mind. Men like that recover easily from their mistrust. Only fools and wicked men hang onto appearances and make mountains out of a piece of straw.

God be thanked! Monsieur de Nesselburg mission is coming to an end, and we will soon, I think, leave for Vienna. You ask me what I have done with "my poet." He is no longer in my husband's service, and frankly I'm very glad. These makers of rimes are always ready to find a muse in a woman, and I'm a little afraid that this young man who has, or pretends to have, melancholy airs, might make me the lady of his thoughts. That probably wouldn't be a great shame, you understand, but I am naturally kind, and don't like to be forced to humiliate people and put them in their place. So, goodbye, dear friend, and be more trusting.

That letter written as being the copy of the one given to him from which to make extractions, Karl carried to the Master of the Works. Giving it to him, his heart fluttered a little for fear that he might have the idea of comparing it with the original. But he saw with unimaginable gladness that Madame de Nesselburg's letter was again sealed and that his so-called excerpt, marked with a number at the top went to take its place with the general analysis made by the Master of the Works.

As a debut, the audacious young man had just faithfully fulfilled his role as Judas, and it seemed to him that Monsieur the Imperial Commissioner, by the communication he was going to receive, would find himself quite reasonably side-tracked. As for his good fortune, Karl couldn't at first be completely aware of it. The eruption, if it can be called that, had occurred so suddenly, and the proof so fugitive in his hands, that it had the effect of a dream. He needed to collect himself to assure himself of its reality and its extent.

XIV. The Manuscript (Cont'd)
A Badly Kept Secret

To feel oneself loved, that was a great deal, without doubt, and Karl acknowledged to himself that Madame de Nesselburg, without knowing it, had recompensed his devotion magnificently. However, enjoying all the delights of the feelings of his new situation, the poet didn't avoid finding more than one problem there. How could he get to his divine Countess? How to get her to drop that furious discretion into which she had until then withdrawn? Above all, how to warn her of the danger of her correspondence that still wasn't sure of being so fortunately evaded.

It goes without saying that it was no longer a question of Christiana. From the moment the splendid Madame de Nesselburg appeared on Karl's horizon, as pale Phoebe [30] vanishes at the bright rays of morning light, the musician's daughter saw herself immediately relegated to a lower plane. And as to the kind of engagement that had been made with her the evening before, now only the way to think of what would happen next. However, partly because of childhood attachment between them, partly by the fear of seeing himself infected with the remorse with which he had been threatened, Karl was

---

[30] The Moon.

brought back to think about the unhappy object of his disdain, and would rather have wished to find an opening to prevent this marriage of despair that Christiana was contemplating.

The day passed without his having put his hand on the expediency he was searching for, a way to avoid, because of his silence, that raw and bleeding heart becoming exasperated and hastening the solution. He was careful to write a letter full of good words, and without committing himself more positively than he had done the evening before, he made an effort not to retract too expressly either. A great deal later, he went to the *Black Room,* where his functions called him almost every day. Busy as the evening before with some rather insignificant extractions, he had his mind elsewhere while writing and it wasn't hard to figure out what faraway region towards which his thoughts were straying. His distraction wasn't such, however, that he didn't notice a rather bizarre incident that had just happened.

Placed not far from him, the Apostle wearing the name Saint Peter, by means of a goblet of boiling water, was preparing to melt some seals. A clumsy movement shook the vase, and the boiling water, spreading, reached the left hand of the letter opener. The pain made him cry out, and his first instinct was to take off the glove soaked with the devouring liquid, continuing the torture of the first sensation. At the same time, all regards were toward that naked hand where there were two large stains the color of blood. Recognizing that sign, Karl thought: *That's Hulet!* and he immediately understood that was Christiana's salvation.

The next day, very early in the morning, he was at Adam Kraft's house, and after having justified as well as he could, his resolution never to be his son-in-law, he asked him how a man sensitive and honest, such as he was, could consent to give his daughter to a man as positively discredited as Hulet was.

"My daughter wishes it," the musician answered, "and besides, no precise fact has been uttered against this young man. His life is said to be mysterious, but in total he doesn't wrong anyone; and if he accumulates expenses, he pays them. And seeing that the magistrates who were informed against him take no actions, it must be assumed that he has been slandered."

"I myself know a precise fact," Karl said quickly.

"Be careful!" Adam Kraft said to him. "You have to be very sure of what you say."

"Listen," the poet continued seriously. "I know that I am accused here of ingratitude, because, after all, I am not master of my heart that hasn't permitted me to respond, as I would have wished, to the kind overtures of which I was the object. Well? If I received goodness, today I will pay it back, because there is a secret in my life that I am going to confide to you."

'No one asks you for a secret," the musician quickly answered. "No one here, vis-à-vis you, claims to be a creditor."

"Then it's to my brotherly attachment to Christiana that I owe this sacrifice. At no price should she marry that Hulet, who has an infamous occupation."

"And where did you learn that?"

"In my position with Monsieur de Nesselburg, I can learn a number of secret things."

"If they are secrets," Adam Kraft said severely, "you are wrong to reveal them."

"There are situations in life," Karl replied, "where between two equally regrettable necessities, it's necessary to choose the one that weighs the least on the conscience. Christiana, an angel of honesty and virtue, can't become the wife of a police informant."

"Don't tell me that!" the artist said with an incredulous look. "That's the accusation that's brought against every man who surrounds his life with a little mystery."

"But do these nightly sorties of Hulet have to be explained in detail…"

As if impatient with coming up against popular gossip, like some kind of ghost stories, Adam Kraft said:

"That's what's going around."

"These nightly sorties," Karl said, "lead him into a kind of cavern where, against the honor and security of families, he violates the secrets of letters."

"That accusation is very serious, both for Hulet and for the Government," the musician remarked.

"So, I confide this to your discretion; but could I see your daughter, my sister, sacrificed when I know about that infamy?"

"Very well, Karl," the musician then said, "I will try to profit by your revelation. But your stay at the house of Monsieur de Nesselburg has made you the holder of some very dangerous secrets!"

Then, as he was about to leave, Karl held out his hand to his adopted father, asking him if he was still angry with him.

"I'm not angry with you," he said, "but I won't shake hands with you. You have done too much harm to Christiana and to me."

And with that he took leave of him.

XV. The Manuscript (Cont'd)
The Confession

The orphanage where Karl had been placed possessed magnificent gardens; with a small tip given to the concierge of the establishment, the public was admitted to visit them. In his infancy, the poet particularly liked an alley of linden trees where he often separated himself from the other infants, his comrades. He went there to hear the sound of the wind and the rain in the leaves and to lend an ear to the song of the birds. More than once, when Madame de Nesselburg was kind to him, he spoke to her about that dear walkway where he had composed delightful verses.

Everything that has just been recounted took place precisely at the time of the flowering of the Linden trees. Happiness is a pathway by which the imagination goes back to the beginning of life. In the very happy ecstasy into which the discovery that his heart and that of his beautiful mistress felt

alike plunged him, Karl remembered the trees of his childhood, and when leaving Adam Kraft's house, he thought about
visiting them. Seated under their shade, breathing their sweet
smell, despite some worries that he must have about the future, it seemed to him that his present life was blessed. However, he had not exhausted his good luck, because, at the same
place, almost at the same time, a thought, easily explained by
sympathy, brought Madame de Nesselburg there. It was not in
the knowledge of the secret that he had surprised, that the
happy lover had the audacity to speak to her. He thought first
of the present more pressing situation, that of providing for her
safety.

"Please excuse me, Madame, if I dare interrupt your
walk," he said, "but Monsieur de Nesselburg believes that you
have a declared liking for Monsieur de Grundheim, and he has
your correspondence watched to acquire a justification of his
suspicions."

"Monsieur de Nesselburg, is stupidly jealous," the Countess replied disdainfully, "and I find you strange, Monsieur, to
make yourself his echo here."

"Your letters, Madame, are more than watched, they are
intercepted and opened. The things the last one contained,
addressed to Madame de Waldorf, was not the only one."

"And who then is the agent of these infamous extractions?" demanded Madame de Nesselburg with understandable emotion.

"Me, Madame," Karl coldly replied. "To shield you from
your husband's threatening suspicions, I made myself totally
infamous, I, who now am in danger of my life for warning you
not to write anymore."

"But that letter," exclaimed the Countess, having only
one thought about all he had just told her, "you don't dare tell
me you have read it?"

"I have read it, Madame, and at your good pleasure I will
remember the contents or forget them."

"And you thought you understood them, and you didn't
understand that, from one end to the other, they said the oppo-

site of what they seemed to say, being nothing else by a joke and pure irony?"

"If it troubles you, Madame, to avoid once in your life being found good and kind, just say that you don't want that confidence to have reached me, and I never knew anything about it."

"And in any case, Monsieur, if it pleases you to attach some meaning to those words, you have seen how I treat presumptuous men. You have had a taste of my harshness and indifference. You will now feel my hate if you dare conceive some foolish thought."

"I am not thinking, Madame; happiness is felt and not thought about. I give you permission to heap on me your coldness, your contempt. I can now wait; I have patience and courage for years."

"And also, impudence; to dare confess to me that you have lent your hands to such a monstrous procedure!"

"Eh! Madame, if it wasn't me, it would be someone else, and that one would be working for Monsieur de Nesselburg. I had to read that letter, understand that, to tell your husband what it did not contain."

"Well, Monsieur, since you know so much, you must have read that a short time from now, I will leave Hamburg. You will, I think, give me entirely the benefit of your absence. I won't see you in Vienna, where I will have, I warn you, powerful help against the insolence and the duplicity of my husband."

"You have more than that, Madame, to carry out your orders: the fear of displeasing you, devotion until death, courage, and, in a word, every sacrifice. However, I dare insist on one point: Monsieur de Nesselburg is odiously jealous; your writing, your actions, even your thoughts, are watched and it extends even to your life, if the Count's suspicions increase. That, Madame, is what I wanted to tell you, only that, and otherwise I wouldn't have dared to try to stop you for one moment."

"With that understanding, Monsieur Karl, I thank you."

"And I too, although the future for me is very sad."

"*Mon Dieu*! Who knows the future?" said the Countess, throwing a kind word as they separated.

"I, Madame, I know mine, but I'm not complaining. An angel appeared to me one day, then it went back to Heaven."

These last words were said with such true feeling, that they touched the Countess' soul. Giving way *in extremis* to a kind feeling, she bent down, cut from the grass one of those humble daisies used by the superstitious curiosity of lovers, then, giving it to Karl:

"Take this," she said, "from the angels to children who promise them to be good."

Madame de Nesselburg couldn't see the very happy man press the white flower to his lips; he still hadn't recovered from his happiness when she was already very far away.

XVI. The Manuscript (Cont'd)
The Awakening

Following the order for entry arranged between the associates, Karl arrived last to the place of the reunions. The evening of the day he wouldn't have hesitated to call the happiest of his life, entering the room where his colleagues were assembled, he was astonished not to see work in progress, nor any appearance that they were going to open letters that day. The silence, rarely interrupted, that usually reigned between the somber workers, seemed to have taken on unusual solemnity. It was evident that something extraordinary and unaccustomed was going to happen. As soon as Karl was seated, the Master of the Works spoke:

"Brothers," he said, "the association is in peril. This evening, the three alarms were struck at my door. A profane person knows the secret of the order; the name of one of its members has been revealed."

"Let him die!" shouted with one voice all the Apostles, Karl, however, excepted.

"I then denounce the death of Adam Kraft, the musician," said the Master of the Works. Then, addressing Karl: "Judas, you do servile work here. The order charges you to nail shut the mouth of this profane person. You have three days. May your arm have ability and strength!"

"Why kill Adam Kraft," Karl asked, "if he did not search for this secret that came to him?"

"And how do you know that?" all the Apostles said at one time.

"And how do you know that it didn't? Isn't that what you should know first of all?"

"All right, Judas," the Master of the Works said. "I like that spirit of justice in you. But then a traitor spoke to the musician. That traitor, do you know him?"

"It's up to you and not to me to identify him. The three blows of alarm were not knocked on my door. I am not the Master of the Works."

"Judas! Judas! Be careful," the high dignitary said, "your name is Judas!"

"A name chosen by chance," Karl replied.

"But also a name of misfortune. I myself accuse you of being the traitor. Do you deny or admit it?"

"Whoever makes the accusation should have the proofs. Produce them."

"You know Christiana, the daughter of Adam Kraft?"

"I know her."

"One of our members is supposed to become the husband of that girl. That marriage, who wanted to break it off?"

"I," the poet courageously answered. "I wanted to."

"And what did you say to the father so that he also wished it?"

"You must know that. You seem to know everything"

"And what did the father say to his daughter?"

"Can my eyes and ears see and hear inside families to know what a father and daughter say to one another?"

"And what did the daughter say to our vigilant associate who this evening knocked three times at my door?"

"Christiana is not a woman to denounce anyone. I told you that; I know her."

"However, she's the one accusing you. Are you confessing or denying?"

"And if I deny, what will happen?"

"There's a crucifix near here. You're going to swear beneath it."

Up against an oath he couldn't take, Karl wanted at least to end with courage. Looking around at the assembly with disdain:

"It's my life that you want," he said, "then take it. After all, to die by you is worth more perhaps than living with you."

In another meeting, that insult would have raised an outcry. Here, everybody remained calm, and only a deadly silence responded.

"Here is the oath you took before entering the order," said the Master of the Works, coldly, picking up a black parchment on which the formula was engraved in white letters. "See," he said, after having read the oath, "at the bottom there are interlaced a dagger, a pistol, a cup and a rope. Choose how to pay for your sin."

"I will choose the hemlock," Karl answered. "But Adam Kraft is not guilty. He didn't himself want to know the secret."

"We know that," the high dignitary replied. "Justice will be done to everyone. You can go in peace."

Having thus spoken, the Master of the Works rose and the Apostles after him. They formed a circle and all together shouted three times "*Misfortune*" passing a black candle, on which they spat, from hand to hand, and the last one who received it blew on it, extinguishing it.

Having then opened a door, Saint Peter said to Karl, pointing to a long, poorly lit corridor:

"I brought you in; now I take you out. Come with me."

"Where are you taking me?" Karl asked.

"To the room of poisons," the Apostle answered. "There are four punishments: that of fire, that of iron, that of the rope, and the one where death is drunk. You chose that one."

One against twelve, resistance would have been useless, and it didn't have the dignity of resolution.

They came to a sort of crossroad formed by four cells with open doors, through which Karl saw a seat, a table and, beside a lamp, an instrument of death. In the one he entered, the shaking of the ground underneath his feet and that of the Apostle, caused a greenish liquid placed in the cup on the table to move about. Soon afterward, the condemned man saw in a corner an object shining under the light from the lamp. It was the iron of a shovel that had been used in advance to dig an open and gaping grave beside him.

"Before two hours elapse, this poison will have taken effect," the Apostle said. "Then a man will come to deposit you in your bed. If you have not done the work, he will do it."

At the same time, he closed the door, and soon the sound of his feet was lost in the distance.

Alone then, the condemned man looked around his prison. Around him he could measure the thickness of the walls by the door opening. That door itself was strong and tightly closed, consequently there was no hope of escape.

"Well!" he said, speaking aloud to himself, as is commonly done in emotional situations, "my happiness was really a dream. Awakening from it is bitter. This morning under the linden trees, who would have guessed that? Adam Kraft would have spoken to his daughter, she to Hulet, Hulet to the Master of the Works. Yes, a woman taking vengeance; that's what must have happened. It's true that I acted badly toward Christiana, but I would never have thought she would do this. To die, that's nothing, but to repose like this in a corner, far from all regard and all human memory, I, who dreamed of an immortal name! And I would have conquered that name," he said, striking his forehead and his breast, "because I had something there, and also something there. Well, it was my destiny. Born badly, die badly. Mother," he exclaimed after a moment of silence, picking up the cup and raising it to his lips, "you abandoned me, but in my last moments, I bless you and pardon you."

And he drank the poison in one swallow. Just as he replaced the cup on the table, there was the sound of a key in the lock of the door and the door opened slowly. To Karl's astonish gaze the form of a woman appeared. He looked at her a moment, and, in the uncertain light of the lamp, he recognized Christiana.

"Here to witness my agony!" said the dying man, rising quickly from his seat. "Leave. This is too much."

"Listen to me," the young girl commanded. "Afterward you can judge me. Yesterday morning, you came to the house where your infancy found asylum. It was to me that you should have spoken. You had nothing good to tell me. You preferred to speak to my father. Me, I was at the door and I heard."

"That explains everything," Karl then said, interrupting.

"You're mistaken; you don't know anything, but a number of things were explained to me then: the sudden opulence of my father, a suspicious place where he went every night and where one evening I had the idea to follow him right to the door. Other men went in mysteriously after him. Magistrates surrounded him with care and respect and came to eat at his table. Then I understood everything."

"So," Karl exclaimed, "Adam Kraft was one of those men?"

"Better than that, he was their chief, and it was more to you, his adopted son, that he owed that obligation."

"How could I have done what you're saying?"

"When you left our house, my father, who loved you like a son, suffered mortal sorrow. He became greatly discouraged and he then became open to secret suggestions, which had been made to him for a long time, that he use, in the service of a suspicious work, the manual cleverness and some of the chemical secrets he possessed. Fortunately, he turned down those offers. Suffering from your abandon, suffering from my sadness, he thought that surrounding me with ease and luxury he would elude our sadness. And he put his hand to this infamy."

"You are right, Christiana, I have been very guilty," said Karl, better than anyone in a position to understand where the bad fortune and the dangerous empire of the opportunity led.

"Enlightened by the revelation about Hulet on the horrible work my father was doing, I pressed him with questions," Christiana continued, "and he confessed everything to me, and, also through him, I learned something else that struck me to the heart. You didn't love me, but you loved elsewhere. Tell me, Karl, if this is not true?"

"But your father himself," Karl asked, "where did he find that out?"

"He didn't know it. I guessed it. Didn't you live under the same roof as Madame de Nesselburg? Weren't you the only one charged with opening her letters? Would you have consented to take part in that infamy if it was not to be revenged on her or to remove her from some danger?"

"Then you, too, in a spirit of vengeance, you told Hulet everything?"

"Hulet! He doesn't know anything! Kept at home by the accident he had, he wasn't present a while ago at the meeting and he can't hope to heal for a longtime."

"Then it was Adam Kraft who, without provocation, without any necessity, delivered me over to his pack?"

"Without provocation! Unnecessarily! And his oath which was a duty to him, and me who asked him for it?"

"You Christiana, that's impossible!"

"Impossible to the point that I was one of those hooded members of that pack. I came in Hulet's place, I took the role of Saint Peter. Those masks disguise the voice so well that you didn't even suspect when a while ago I spoke to you."

"So I told the truth. You are here to enjoy my agony."

"No, I've come to save you."

"It's too late; the cup is empty."

At that point, Christiana began to smile, then, continued:

"You aren't going to die," she said, "because, prepared by my father, that poison is only an innocent drink. Let's get to work now. Cover up the grave, and while your devilish associates believe you are enclosed in the cold ground, you will be, far from Hamburg, *a living dead man,* and barely remembered by these men of blood."

"But if it isn't by Hulet, that deception will be discovered soon. Then it's your life and that of Adam Kraft. I don't want mine at that price."

"In an hour, my father and I will set sail for a country overseas where he will go to hide his sin and I, too, to console him."

"You won't go alone. I want to follow you."

"Cover up the grave first of all. Then we will see."

Then Karl had the strange privilege of burying himself. They then left the funeral enclosure, and in several minutes Adam Kraft was reunited with his two children. He said only one thing to Karl:

"Do you now believe you would have been a worthy husband for Christiana?"

"I wouldn't be here now," Karl answered, "if I hadn't come to make everything right."

"Listen, Karl," Christiana said, "yesterday I told you that, without being loved by you, I could still be your wife. But I didn't know then what I know now. Free, you would have appreciated me later. Now your heart is taken elsewhere. You may no longer be able to love me."

"But that love for someone else is senseless, without a future, without children."

"Even with that, her rivalry frightens me. More beautiful than I am, more attractive, your preferred one would still have the merit of being inaccessible and distant. That would be too much."

"Then what do you want," Karl exclaimed, "that you stay without love, a heart of gold like yours?"

"Don't deceive yourself. Today, you're talking out of gratitude, but I have learned to judge men of your temperament. With them, imagination is more powerful than the heart. From your childhood, I reproached you for not loving me as I wanted you to. Ordinary and calm attachments, long-term commitments in which there is the eternal and the irreparable, that's not what you need. Let's break it off here. Follow your path, and I mine. In whatever part of the world we are thrown, I will have you in my memory, and may you also," she added with a slightly altered voice and holding out her hand, "remember me. Father, embrace him," she said to Adam Kraft, and the two threw their arms around each other, sobbing.

At that moment, someone knocked loudly on the shutters of the door.

"Let's go! Let's go! Passengers on board," shouted the harsh voice of a sailor, "the wind is picking up."

"Christiana, I beg of you..." Karl cried out, throwing himself on his knees, his hands held out toward his adopted sister.

The girl bent over to raise him, held him a moment tight to her heart; then disengaging herself from his hold, she quickly took Adam Kraft's arm, that she clutched as if she wanted to flee from temptation.

XVII. The Manuscript (Cont'd)
The End of the Apostles of Nuremberg

Madame de Nesselburg was right when she had said to Karl: "Who knows the future?" Two years after the events that have just been recounted, the Lieutenant of Police, La Reynie, sent to Monsieur de Louvois, Secretary of State of War, General Superintendent of the Post, and Principal Minister of King Louis XIV, this report:

Paris, May 29, 1679
Excellency,

A most extraordinary event took place this morning at the church of Notre-Dame-des-Victoires. A particular circumstance requires that I must give Your Excellency an immediate and detailed account of it.

A great number of carriages were stationed outside the aforementioned church, where took place the marriage of that wealthy foreigner who has been so much talked about lately because of her folly in marrying the tutor of the children of Monsieur the Duke of Vantador. Being herself a member of the aristocracy, and the widow of a chamberlain of His Imperial Majesty, one would have thought she would have done it secretly and would have wished to make her misalliance in the night, very quietly, between two candles. But according to her friends, she wouldn't hear of this at all and said she would get married at noon, in sunlight, inviting everyone she knew at the Court and many important people from the city.

This great number of carriages, lackeys, and, most of all beggars, who are always around at these kinds of occasions, had already been the cause, before the spouses came, of a disorderly scene. A poor man, who wasn't known in that area, and who wasn't licensed to beg there, started a quarrel with some other mendicants who, not knowing either his name or his face, wanted to make him leave. But as he didn't feel he was the strongest, he found a way to get on better with the crowd by drawing from his pockets three or four handfuls of small change from across the Rhine that he threw to all the rabble. They then had great respect for him, after having wanted to rend him from top to bottom, because he was, according to them, either some great lord in disguise, or at least some very opulent poor man doing that work for his pleasure.

During the mass that followed the nuptial benediction, the husband, whom they say was born in Hamburg, where they are all of the Reformed Religion, which, let it be said in passing, makes even more strange his stubborn decision to marry a woman who was born, and is, a good Catholic. During the mass, as I was saying, that heretic took no part in the ceremony and remained seated, looking very distracted. But that way of behaving didn't turn out so well for him, because during that time, he was glancing irreverently from one side to the other; it wasn't clear exactly what he saw, but he was seen to suddenly turn with a frightened look toward a small chapel. Everyone looked the same way after him, but without discovering anything extraordinary.

However, shortly thereafter, his fright seems well justified, because, when the ceremony was over, on the way out of
the church, having already taken possession of his wife, as he
was holding her by her arm and going forward with her to get
into the carriage, that same poor man who had previously
made a scandal, quickly approached the husband and pronounced distinctly these words which several people heard:
"From the Apostles!"

Then he struck him toward the region of the heart with a
dagger with a long handle, which he then threw at the victim's
feet. At the same moment, with great presence of mind, he
threw around him like rain that same small change that he had
already used, so that, in the excitement caused by the audacity
of the murder, and in the tumult of the beggars, pages, and
lackeys rushing to pick up that bloody windfall, he had the
luck to escape.

The husband didn't survive but a few hours; the blow
had penetrated one of his lungs. On the blade of the dagger,
easily recognized as a product of Germany, which is stored in
the Châtelet for evidence, was engraved a figure of the Apostle
Saint-Peter, with this inscription: "The Apostles of Nuremberg."

I had some research done, and I found that, two weeks
ago, a man, that by his accent could be taken for an Englishman or a German, had registered at an inn located near the
Place Maubert. That man spent rather large amounts of money and often went out at night disguised. What's more, he was
frequently busy writing in his bedroom. A servant was able to
see that he was working on a memoir. Its title was: A Monsieur le Marquis de Louvois, Superintendent General of the
Post.

The above-mentioned man, whose name was Schwartz,
went out the morning of the murder and has not returned. He
left only some clothes of little value at the inn. As for the
memoir that seemed destined for Your Excellency, it hasn't
been found.

Our searches are continuing, and I don't despair—

111

I interrupt this report to announce to Your Excellency that the man has just been arrested. I will immediately send you the result of his interrogation.

Monsieur de La Reynie's report was answered by the following note:

As soon as the present order is received, Monsieur the Lieutenant of Police will send to Versailles, under a good escort, the foreigner using the name Schwartz. The Lieutenant of Police will take care that this foreigner cannot communicate with anyone.

Louvois

The man called Schwartz was none other than Hulet, the Apostle of Nuremberg, and here is how he became the executioner of the Association's revenge:

The son of the regicide was of the school of Cromwell. He belonged to that heinous race that likes to contemplate the features of a dead enemy. Following the execution of Charles Ist, his ambitious and fierce successor visited him in his coffin. Cured of burns from the accident that had led to the indiscretions of Karl, Hulet the Apostle hadn't recoiled from the idea of satisfying a sacrilegious curiosity. He had dared to violate the sepulcher of the man he detested with the double title of denunciator and rival. The tomb of the condemned man, widowed of his cadaver and the disappearance of the Master of the Works, whom the Apostles learned shortly thereafter was none other than Adam Kraft himself, told them the truth. Their execrable code condemned the musician, his daughter, and the victim who had escaped his death. The sentence couldn't be carried out against Christiana and her father. Departed for a faraway country, they were never heard from again. But it was known that Karl had passed over into France, and Hulet was dispatched there—a mission that he ardently solicited—in order to be the executioner of the indiscreet revealer of secrets, wherever he might be.

As for Karl, arrived in Paris, and finding himself without a means of livelihood, the refugee poet had become a tutor of children. But he had committed the mistake of entering a house where his great notoriety made him stand out. Because of that, shortly after Hulet arrived in the French capital, not only did he find Karl's trail, but, at the same time, he learned of Karl's good fortune as far as Madame de Nesselburg was concerned. She had become a widow and was disposed to crown the devotion and constancy of the man who loved her with the gift of her hand.

With a refinement of cruelty, the murderer waited for the very day of the wedding so that death would seize the unfortunate man at the height of his glorious felicity. At the same time, to avoid punishment for the crime he was going to commit, having heard about the hard character of Minister Louvois, who believed that despotism could never be too firmly established, he thought about bringing to France the institution of the *Secret Bureau*. He told the Minister in advance about the murder of Karl, giving it the character of an official punishment ordered by a foreign government. As such, that murder, like that of Christine of Sweden had carried out against her servant, Monaldeschi,[31] didn't fall under the control of ordinary justice, where at least the intervention of the justice system would have raised the serious question of civil rights. As for the political problem, here is how the Marquis de Louvois solved it:

"Monsieur," he said to Hulet, as soon as he had been brought before him, "if it pleased the King, my master, to consider you an ordinary assassin, without even asking you to justify the powers with which you are accredited as a diplo-

---

[31] When Queen Christine of Sweden abdicated, she went first to France, where she insisted on maintaining her royal title and rights, as well as her property in Sweden, and a large income. Marquis Monaldeschi betrayed her and she then, at Fontainebleau, sentenced him to death and had the sentence carried out, without notification to French authorities.

113

matic murderer, I would have you immediately hanged and we would see how the gentlemen magistrates of Hamburg would get you taken down. But," he added, coming to the proposition of installing in France an organization dedicated to the violation of the secrets of letters, "it may be convenient for the good police of a country that its government have private means of being informed. See, therefore, that two days from now, you present me with a plan for a *Secret Bureau*. But be careful not to introduce into that institution any of those mysterious and romanesque forms that the politics of a little city-state like Hamburg judged necessary.

"The King, who is pardoning you on condition that you serve him with devotion and zeal, has sufficient power to put under the single safeguard of his good pleasure and his will every type of innovation that he may judge useful to introduce into his kingdom, and the discretion to continue to allow other affairs that His Majesty doesn't intend to make known to the public, that he doesn't need to complicate it with extraordinary precautions to keep that secret from the public."

Without taking too much thought about the haughty form that Louis XIV's Minister used to greet his offer, Hulet hurried to draw up the organization of the project that had just been created for him. He wrote to them again to propose a union between the affiliates in the two countries. But to his great astonishment, both of his letters remained without an answer. Finally, believing that his indiscretion vis-à-vis Louis XIV hadn't been to the taste of the Apostles, that he knew were very ticklish about their incognito, he began to fear from them a treatment like that he had himself had come to mete out to the unfortunate Karl. For his security, he believed he should refer that worry to his new master and protector, the Marquis de Louvois.

Several days later, the Minister sent him and extract of a dispatch addressed by the Ambassador of the King of France to Vienna, which should have removed his worry. Somewhat incompletely informed, but in any case, not pleasing Monsieur

de Louvois and Louis XIV very much, the imprudent diplomat
had written:

*Through the intermediary of a lady of first rank, there
has been discovered in the city of Hamburg an association of
a very dangerous type which threatens to spread throughout
Germany, and from there throughout the rest of Europe. These
people don't draw back from any kind of crime, uniting themselves by oaths and terrible trials. To better attain the ends
that they set for themselves, and which have, they say, much
rapport with the famous "Secret Tribunals," they intercept
correspondence, and, as a result of their discoveries, commit
all kinds of violence.*

*Once drawn into that infernal association, and later hav-
ing married the widow of the Imperial Commissioner, Count
de Nesselburg, a young man, interesting in every way, wanted
to recover his freedom. Fearing then for their secret, his former accomplices had him followed right to Paris, where the
marriage had just been concluded, and there the former member was audaciously murdered. The dying man told his wife at
the time of the murder that the executioner as a man named
Hulet.*

*I hurry to transmit this information so that the King's
justice can be helped in the searches that must be underway.*

But Karl's widow wasn't content with pursuing the assassin with punishment. She had wanted to go higher and punish the Association for which he had acted. The Emperor, at
whose feet she threw herself as soon as she arrived in Vienna,
had no sooner found out about the monstrosity revealed to
him, than he dispatched to Hamburg a Commissioner with
orders to pursue the destruction of that evil den.

His Majesty's envoy didn't at first have all the ease in
fulfilling his mission that he would have supposed. The city
magistrates themselves, as well as the principal men in the
Senate, appeared to be terrorized by the Apostles and seemed
to ignore the existence of that secret power. The Imperial

Commissioner then went to the bourgeois City Council. There he found a more loyal group. The organization, its members, and its statutes were not long in becoming known. There remained the question of doing away with them slowly and without public scandal, because it's the essence of secret societies to leave long remnants behind them when they are not vigorously exterminated. But His Majesty's Imperial Commissioner had provided for that danger by sending as Commissioner the famous Italian Caraffa,[32] who, after the repression of the troubles in Hungary, had gained a terrible reputation because of the thirty executioners that he always had with him, always keeping them busy. As a compensation, that harsh justice, in that circumstance, terminated everything without almost any sign of the repression appearing in public. He needed only a few stones, a mason, and some mortar. Waiting until one evening when the Apostles were assembled at the usual place, while they were following their dangerous practices, Caraffa had the exits from the caves, with very little noise but very solidly, walled up so that in a century or two, perhaps, the pick of some worker will uncover the tomb where these miserable men were buried alive. Then there will be trouble explaining the crime and the punishment.

At that place in the manuscript, Alexis Hulet was interrupted in his reading of the manuscript by his father, who had come to see him in his bedroom. Then the conversation that can be read in the following chapter took place between them.

XVIII. From Father to Son

"Father," said young Alexis, "what a gloomy story! And did all these facts take place in our family?"

---

[32] Antonio Caraffa (1646-1693): General Commissioner in the Imperial Hapsburg Army. After the conquest of Turkey, he was appointed Military Governor of Upper Hungary and Royal Commissioner of Transylvania.

"Yes," the former Convention member answered, "the name Hulet was originally ours. But where are you in the manuscript?"

Alexis showed him where he had stopped.

"In a few words," his father stated, "I'm going to bring this story up to our days. The hour for dinner is approaching, and I don't want it, when we are all assembled at the table, to be a matter of what you have just read. The secret that you will shortly know is at its end, and you will know why, vis-à-vis your mother and your sister, I use discretion."

That said, he still took the precaution to ask his son to listen to him without interrupting. He then began thus:

"Having thus escaped the fatal destiny which did away with all the Apostles of Nuremberg, Hulet, their former affiliate, became, as you have just learned, he first director of the newly-created *Secret Bureau*. Established in France, he married, and, until the revocation of the Edict of Nantes,[33] he lived a tranquil and honored existence in his adopted country. But when religious persecution broke out, he was among the first to be affected. Born in England, brought up and having always lived in the Reformed Religion, he refused to sacrifice his religious convictions to the demands of Monsieur de Louvois. And, finally, to get away from the persecutions of which he was the object, he resolved to take refuge abroad. But the most severe measures to halt the emigration of Protestants had been put in place. Besides, in carrying out his functions as the Director of the *Bureau du Roi,* he possessed too many important secrets for his project of flight to succeed. Had special instructions concerning him been given, or was he just the victim of general orders? However it was, while trying to cross the border, he was shot and died in one of those *dragonnades* [34] that Minister Louvois had created."

---

[33] Signed in 1598 by Henry IV, it gave Calvinist Protestants freedom of religion. It was revoked by Louis XIV in 1685.

[34] The *Dragonnades* were a French government policy instituted by Louis XIV in 1681 to intimidate Huguenot families

"An end almost as unfortunate as that of his father's!" Alexis couldn't keep from remarking.

"And violent, too," Hulet the elder continued, "as had to be that of his son, who, brought up by his parents to be instructed in the Catholic Religion, was in his turn placed at the head of the *Secret Bureau*. After having fulfilled those functions under three reigns, the end of that of Louis XIV, the Regency of the Duke of Orleans, and a part of the reign of Louis XV, one day, taking apart a voluminous dispatch that a criminal industry had filled with a strong dose of explosive powder, he intercepted, so to speak, the death that had been intended for the owner of the letter, and died from the result of the explosion, which, in any case, would have left him blind and horribly disfigured."

"But, father," Alexis exclaimed, as if struck with sudden enlightenment, "I hope that that terrible heritage, very obviously from the finger of God's justice, hasn't come down to us?"

"Let me finish," Hulet the elder continued, "and don't prejudge anything. The elder son of that Hulet whom we have seen meet such a deplorable end, who is also the author of the manuscript you have just read, was your grandfather. Me, I was his only child. As it does to you, it seemed to him that to become Director of the *Secret Bureau* was a fearsome heritage, and he went about trying to avoid it, for my sake. That result obtained, he believed he had done much for my life's happiness. Only one thing in his foresight he couldn't know: the dark denouement of all his predecessors that awaited him, on the scaffold in '93. As for me, following the false direction that he had pointed out to me, thrown into wanderings and travesties without number, I had to, whatever I did, follow the

---

into either leaving France or re-converting to Catholicism. This involved the billeting of ill-disciplined dragoons in Protestant households with implied permission to abuse the inhabitants and destroy or steal their possessions.

hereditary tradition, and, in my turn, today, I am the Director of the *Secret Bureau*."

"You, father!" Alexis exclaimed, astounded.

"Don't get excited, son," the ex-member of the Convention continued, "and in a question where the highest interests of society are at stake, let's not put either the deceptive illusions of youthful ideas, nor the silly prudery of the commonplace. To penetrate the secrets of families, that's a great evil, without a doubt, but a great benefit also when the discovery of those secrets turn to the profit of the State, which is the great family of us all, and which it is necessary to protect before everything. Evil is not so evil when, turned from its true end and direction, epistolary surveillance becomes an instrument of intrigues and wouldn't be used for just one purpose. But that danger has been carefully provided for. In a period when, on the invitation of Bonaparte, First Consul, I accepted this grave mandate, I made two conditions: the first was that, placed in complete independence from the police, I would remain exclusive master of the employees working under me; the second that I would be authorized to establish in that administration of which I was going to be the chief, order and morality that had never been observed until then."

Hulet the elder, having been able to deliver that long exposé of the interior regime of the *Secret Bureau,* his son, under the first emotion of the revelation that had just been made to him, found no other words but an exclamation of terror.

"But death," he finally exclaimed, "is for you at the end of these functions, that obviously God has condemned."

"Everything makes me believe that, in fact," Hulet the elder replied, like a man who had for a long time foreseen that future, "for me, as for those who went before me, the end of my mandate must not be happy, and probably the same destiny awaits you after you have succeeded me."

"Who, me? That I do that work? Don't count on it!"

"Are you afraid, son?"

"Afraid, yes, of dying in infamy!"

119

"Infamy! Look at my life, however! Do you know any better organized and as pure? And, if in my habits there was something to correct, wouldn't it rather be an excess of austerity?"

"Expiation from a cry of conscience," answered Alexis, who, along with his casual and impressionable nature, was often gifted with a sense of observation beyond his age.

"No, Monsieur," Hulet the elder answered with dignity, "I do not expiate, I practice. Given the principle, having considered my functions as a calling, I created for myself an existence following the logic of that idea."

"You are hiding from yourself, however, father, because those morning sorties, with a pious pretext..."

"...Are necessary for one who holds a secret not his own. As for the rest, let's not argue anymore. If you were not governed by prejudice, I would be able to see how to convince you by making you comprehend what there is, on the contrary, consoling and honorable in the high confidence and in the immense and truly discretionary power invested in us. I would even try to speak to your imagination by making you see both the valuable study of the human heart and the almost romantic interest in certain revelations coming to us. But I have something better to tell you: you will follow me, because, by a decree from on high, it's the law of our family, I followed my father and he, his."

"Never!" Alexis replied with strong emotion. "A respectful son, but before everything a free man."

"Free!" repeated Hulet the elder, shrugging, "when on the corpses of three of our grandfathers, your grandfather was able to write: *The dogma of original sin is realized in certain families where the contamination of the root stock reaches from branch to branch right up to the last generation.* And he, did he avoid his destiny? And me, fifth in that sad dynasty, and after having come back to it after a long detour, am I not, more than all the others, a striking example of the fatality which is over us?"

"But what a memory!" Alexis said. "On the list of the judges who sent Louis XVI to death, there is the name Hulet. But, father, your name is Vandel!"

" 'I told you that in the past I was named Hulet, and if it is true that with one blow of a hatchet, the executioner of Charles Ist soldered the curse that weighs on our race, do you believe that it was reserved to the judge of Louis XVI to stop it and make it miraculously disappear?"

"Then your arrest was unjust?"

"I don't know. I voted according to my conscience, but it might have been led astray under the inspiration of democratic thought that didn't want justice to place a great distance between just any criminal and the one Providence had placed at the head of a great nation. Perhaps, also, we made a mistake in wanting to make the scaffold an instrument of political power. Who can say if, one day, with the march of civilized ideas, the instrument of death won't grow weak and fall? But only we, from father to son, executioners of kings, will gain nothing by that clemency and in the rays of the new light rising on the horizon of humanity, the bloody stain of regicide will only point out our name the more."

"No, father, with that light also, that shadowy practice of which you want to make me the instrument, must disappear."

"Don't believe it, my child! That may be said, perhaps, but governments have their necessities which have nothing to do with absolute morality."

"Well! Let others do the work. Me, I won't do it!"

"But what are you pretending? Your education has been conducted in view of that future. With your knowledge of the languages of the Orient, you will be special, the most useful and the most distinguished of all our employees. No other career is open to you. Accustomed to be strong-willed and obeyed, the Emperor called me to these functions in the name of heredity, and he has always understood that we would recruit from among ourselves. He would pity me if he heard about resistance that my paternal power couldn't in two words lower."

"Father, filial obedience ends where human dignity begins."

"Be careful, Alexis. Up until now, you've lived off me. Without support in the world, having a taste for luxury and pleasure, what would you do if, following your obstinate revolt, I withdrew my support from you?"

"So be it," Alexis answered. "I will leave this house. I will, if need be, call on public charity. That is better than eating the bread of infamy."

"Once more, think about it," Hulet the elder answered. "Your ill-considered threat could well be put into effect, because very certainly I will not support this caprice of puritanism, lasting beyond a certain time."

"Immediately, Monsieur," Alex said, rising. "I'm going to embrace my mother and my sister…"

"I command you to wait and to reflect until tomorrow. Now, not a word to anyone about this, and to obtain your discretion, I'm not going to tell you about the dangers you might run. I count only on your loyalty. Above all, in our family, silence. Women are never sure depositories for secrets."

Alexis answered that, so far as his discretion was concerned, the *Secret Bureau* could rest easy. Then Hulet the elder left the bedroom, leaving Alexis with conflicting thoughts, as can well be imagined

The next day, Alexis presented himself to his father with airs of bravado. His face looked calm and beaming. Asked about his decision, he answered:

"Father, Providence seems to support my ideas of independence. Yesterday evening, I was walking along through the streets, when I happened to meet a young Englishman that I met two years ago during my stay in Constantinople. He also has had an unusual destiny. After a great number of adventures, he is today an officer in the service of Fath Ali Shah,[35]

---

[35] Fath-Ali Shah Qajar (1772-1834) was the second shah of Iran. He reigned from June 1797 until his death. His reign saw the forced and irrevocable ceding of Iran's integral northern

and in that position he followed Mirza Babba, the Persian Ambassador,[36] who has resided for some time in Paris."

"What does that have to do with our conversation of yesterday?'" Hulet the elder asked in a somewhat disdainful tone.

"For use in his relations with Parisian life, of which he is an ardent admirer, Mirza-Babba wants to hire an interpreter knowing both French and Persian. People like that are rare. So, in proposing myself to occupy that position, I was almost sure to be employed."

"And you are going to work for that foreigner?"

"I start immediately. Eagerly welcomed by him, I didn't hesitate to accept his offer, given the kind of banishment that you pointed out to me yesterday. What he offered me included nothing that was not honorable. Even later, when he leaves for Persia, I will be eligible to accompany him."

"Monsieur," said Hulet the elder, realizing that the prompt placement Alexis had found for himself had just upset all his calculations, "you take charge of your life in a very casual manner. You aren't yet of age, and you should at least seek advice."

"But, Father, the position that chance has sent me is not one of those that one should have doubts about accepting. It has a great future before it, and if you don't have other prospects in mind for me, except those it is impossible for me to enter, you yourself would be first to rejoice about my luck. What would be more natural than to go search for fortune in Persia, when all careers in your own country are closed to you, and when you have the rare skill of knowing Persian?"

"And you are also probably going to embrace Islam?" Hulet the elder, who felt he was out of logic, asked ironically.

---

territories to the Russian Empire following the Russo-Persian Wars of 1804-13 and 1826-28.

[36] Mirzxa Babba appears to be fictional; the Persian ambassador sent to Paris was Askar Khan Afshar who arrived in July 1808 and met Napoleon on 4 September 1808.

"No more than the young Englishman who was the intermediary for me in this good fortune; not any more than a great many other Europeans who are drawn to the court of his father, Abbas Mirza,[37] heir to the Persian Crown, who, they say, is very enlightened."

"All right, Monsieur, when are you leaving us?"

"To be more accurate, this isn't leaving you. If you agree to it, from today I will begin my functions. But Mirza Babba will still be in Paris for a long time. I will therefore come often to see my mother whom I will, in this way, have a long time to prepare for my separation, if, later, I must leave for Tehran. In that way, also, nothing will be apparent to her of the little disagreement between you and I. And I would be very happy, father, if not only its appearance but its memory too could be wiped out"

"I don't hold it against you," Hulet the elder said, "so much more so that this is fragile, like all human work. Providence, when it's time, will blow away your prudence and throw you back into its path."

"You are saying that, father, with a faith that astounds me."

"Yes, my child, you can be sure of it; you will come back to us. Now embrace me; go say goodbye to your mother and your sister, and may my blessing go with you. We need union and strength for the sad unknown that the future reserves for us. And you will always find me indulgent."

Touched even to tears by those words full of forgiveness, Alexis rushed into his father's arms. But how could he believe in his prediction? At that moment he was happy; misfortune for him was predicted, and he wasn't twenty years-old.

---

[37] Abbas Mirza (1789-1833) was the crown prince of Persia. He developed a reputation as a military commander during the Russo-Persian Wars, as well as through the Ottoman-Persian War of 1821-23. He is noted as an early modernizer of Persia's armed forces and institutions, and for his death before his father, Fath Ali Shah.

XIX. Mirza Babba

Since Reza Beg,[38] who in 1715 was presented to Louis XIV, there never had been a Persian Ambassador in Paris. With the purpose of creating for England an enemy in the very heart of its Asiatic possessions, Napoleon had tried to renew the former relations of France with the court in Tehran. His advances, greeted with eagerness and gratitude, were not long in bringing to Paris, General Mirza Babba as the Ambassador of Fath Ali Shah. It was for this diplomat that Alexis was to be employed as a secretary. This master that he consented to serve was one of the greatest lords at the Persian court. Important by his birth, he was equally so by a certain degree of intellectual culture, which made him a relatively advanced Muslim.

Loaded down by the Emperor with magnificent presents, among which should be noted the armory, more or less authentic, of the two conquerors of Asia, Tamerlane and Nadir Shah,[39] his Majesty's Persian envoy made his entry with extraordinary pomp. And in the middle of the brilliant cortege there was a following of at least eighty persons, all dressed in sumptuous and picturesque costumes. Two details in particular had excited Parisian curiosity to the highest degree. One of those unusual things was a person dressed completely in red, walking in front of the Ambassador's vehicle with a gigantic cutlass in the dimensions of the one history attributes to the

---

[38] Mohammad Reza Beg was the Safavid Iranian mayor of Erivan and the ambassador to France during the reign of Sultan Husayn, and indeed led the embassy to Louis XIV of 1715.
[39] a.k.a. Timur (1336-1405), a Turco-Mongol conqueror and the founder of the Timurid Empire in Persia and Central Asia. Nadir Shah (1698-1747) was one of the most powerful Iranian rulers in history, ruling from 1736 to 1747, when he was assassinated during a rebellion.

125

ogre in the adventures of *Le Petit Poucet*.[40] The other one were two huge chariots, similar in form to the rolling houses that circus entertainers take from fair to fair. Carefully closed and padlocked, the two vehicles were so placed as to give no hint as to their contents. However, seeing several Blacks, with immense pendants hanging from their ears, a scimitar in their hand, and with a look both grotesque and forbidding, escorting the two heavy vehicles, it seemed the contents could be easily guessed.

Leaving his country probably for a very considerable time, Mirza Babba hadn't committed the mistake of his compatriot Uzbek in *Les Lettres Persanes*.[41] Instead of abandoning the "delights of his heart" to all the hazards of absence, bringing as part of his suite the most loved women of his harem, it was for the transport and the security of these essentially delicate and fragile objects that the heavy material he had watched so closely was destined.

As for the man with the cutlass, at first sight, he seemed something rather fearsome, because he was, it must be said, the executioner of the Ambassador, to whom were attached, like him, a poet or storyteller, a cook, and a doctor. But, everything considered, this fearful executioner was only a matter of form, which every great Persian lord took with him on his travels as a personification of his right over life and death. Very rarely did this bogeyman have occasion to exercise his bloody ministry. At the most, he was employed to chastise faults against discipline and then he had only to use his big

---

[40] *Tom Thumb*. Charles Perrault's fairy tale about a poor family with seven sons; unable to feed them, they abandon them in the forest. The children are saved by the youngest, the eponymous hero.

[41] *The Persian Letters*, written by Charles de Secondat, Baron de Montesquieu in 1721, purports to be letters by two Persian travelers, Usbek and Rica, sent back to their friends. Their reactions to life in France allows Montesquieu to criticize French society.

saber as a paddle. However that may be, this executioner, the ambulant harem, that numerous and magnificent following, was such as to strongly affect the imagination, All that spectacle resulted in making the Envoy for Fath Ali Shah an impressive object of curiosity which can scarcely be understood today.

Women most of all, either because they gave this faithful lover credit for the courteous way he treated his beautiful slaves, or because they were not beyond giving these pearls from the Orient a little competition, were in a frenzy to gain access to the Ambassador's townhouse and to be received by him. Claiming that essentially he was a barbarian of no importance, the fashion was, even among the greatest ladies, to go in a celebrating party without a previous introduction, to the residence of the illustrious foreigner. Gossip was spread later that in the conversation of the Sublime Envoy, bottles of rose perfume flowed like the words. He saw himself assailed by such a large number of people that reduction was necessary.

To save a little of his life and of his time, from duchesses, middle-class women, actresses, local dancers, and other charming birds of prey who came to pillage, he was forced to announce by way of newspapers that in the future he would no longer receive anyone except those with a letter of introduction. And it was to respond to those demands that, when he first entered into his functions, Alexis was primarily employed. However, while guarding against the turbulence of that feminine eagerness, the Ambassador was far from appearing the enemy of the beautiful sex. His harem, as much as could be known, was composed of an exquisite choice of young slaves stolen from classical lands of the Caucasus. However, he was not less appreciative of the attractions of Parisian beauties, but in whom he found something lacking in the matter of plumpness. Let's even say that sometimes he showed his feelings for them in a somewhat dubious way.

So, one evening, when he had been particularly attentive to the beautiful Princess F***, to show her his exalted admira-

127

tion, he slipped behind her during a quadrille. Suddenly cutting off a piece of her sash with his sword, to the great amusement of those assembled, he pressed it to his heart as at a tournament in the past a loyal chevalier would have done with his lady's colors.

Another time, with the purpose of studying European culture, unfortunately passing it through the ear of a Muslim, when he was visiting the Ecouen House,[42] struck by the beauty of some of the students of Madame Campan,[43] their reunion seemed to him to be a slave market. He had the bizarre idea of asking the official accompanying them, if, at a reasonable price, some of those charming girls could become his property and part of his harem.

Fortunately, those lapses if civilization by the Illustrious Diplomat were not frequent and, to make up for having reverted to naïve sensuality which could have compromised his reputation as a courteous and polite man, he shortly thereafter showed the beautiful Princess F***, whose sash he had suddenly cut off, all the indications of a most respectful and a most platonic passion.

"In the course of that gallant behavior, conducted in the fashion of the novels of Mademoiselle de Scudéry,[44] Alexis Hulet's work as secretary wasn't mediocre help to the Sublime Envoy. To keep that love, which was always in danger of exploding *à la turque,* at a respectful distance, the Princess, who was, besides, amused by it, had cleverly led it to an epistolary

---

[42] A private Catholic school for girls in Paris.

[43] Jeanne-Louise-Henriette-Campan (1752-1822), educator and lady-in-waiting to Marie Antoinette, appointed by Napoleon as Headmistress of the first Maison d'éducation de la Légion d'honneur in 1807.

[44] Madeleine de Scudéry (1607-1701), French writer. Her lengthy novels, such as *Artamène, ou le Grand Cyrus* (10 vols., 1648-53), *Clélie* (10 vols., 1654-61), *Ibrahim, ou l'illustre Bassa* (4 vols., 1641), *Almahide, ou l'esclave reine* (8 vols., 1661-63), were the delight of Europe.

standing. It was then a question, for the amorous Persian, of a letter every two days. The regime was hard. His inspiration, little by little, dried up, and his embarrassment would have been mortal if, coming to take its direction in hand, Alexis hadn't been charged with taking up the challenge.

An intelligent boy and very knowledgeable about the customs and literature he was to parody, he had soon created for himself a florid and colorful style like that spoken by Covielle of *The Would-Be Gentleman*[45]. In that nonsense language, in several months, he had laid out before the Princess all the commonplaces of love, under his pen illuminated with all the sparkling splendors of the Orient.

Happy to no longer have to write his letters, Mirza Babba had great esteem for his clever interpreter. Reigning over the heart's secrets and rising to the rank of someone indispensable, Alex saw himself showered with presents. He was no longer an interpreter; he was a confident, an intimate counselor. In that capacity, be it said in passing, he was the object of the jealousy of all the Diplomat's retinue. He found he had in each functionary of the Embassy an enemy ready to render him all the bad services of which envy is capable. The young Englishman through whom, as an intermediary, he had gained access to the house, had to be exempted from that category. Considering him as his creation, the young Englishman was the only one to rejoice at his good fortune and continue to show himself kindly disposed and devoted.

---

[45] *Le Bourgeois Gentihomme* of Molière creates a nonsense language for the valet, Covielle, who helps his master, Cléonte, trick Monsieur Jourdain, the Would-be-Gentleman, in order to obtain the hand of his daughter, Lucile.

PART III. THE GEORGIENNE

XX. Georgiana

It goes without saying that, in the townhouse on Rue de Monsieur occupied by Mirza Babba, the women he had so carefully guarded the day of his arrival, lived in a completely isolated part of the lodging. Whatever the distractions given to the Sublime Envoy and his ethereal correspondence, as well as some other encounters more worldly, the regime of his harem transplanted to Paris had lost nothing of its rigor and severity. Living under the same roof as the beautiful recluses, Alexis had yet to see the corner of an eye or the fold of a dress or a veil. Despite some furtive attempts of curiosity, the only revelation he had obtained from that charming neighborhood, which he had often dreamed about, was, from time to time, some faraway sounds of voices married to the melancholy accents of the lute. Then, one day, as he passed by, some movements he thought he had detected behind a louvered door, the rather sharp voice of a eunuch had reprimanded.

How many times, since that glimmer of intelligence came from the enemy location, Alexis, without appearing to think of evil, had gone close to the window where he had heard that vague and almost inaudible brush. That's what none of our readers will find unbelievable. Everyone knows the prodigious attraction of mystery and forbidden fruit. The curious young man, without letting anything be known that could compromise his credit with his employer, walked up and down in front of the door to the harem. But continuing this maneuver for several days in vain, he began to despair of seeing anything follow the beginning of the adventure, when, one evening, by the light of a full moon, he saw a daisy fall at his feet from one of the slats of the door. A melancholy symbol, that flower which blooms under the autumn sun, seemed to signify for him a plaintive beauty in chains, sighing for him and offering him her heart if he could set her free.

Leaving, with new interest in his walks, for which a new envoy recompensed, this time he was spoken to with a bouquet made up of fresh rose buds, a bunch of forget-me-nots, and two pansies with large velvety leaves. That bouquet could be translated like this:

"I am beautiful and fresh like the rose; the more I see you, the more I love you. Think about me; I think about you."

To tell the truth, that advice was completely useless. Not only did Alexis think about his mysterious correspondent, but dominated by that single idea, he little by little lost his caution. From day to day, less reserved in his actions, he had already tried to open the entry to the harem. And it was taking a great chance that if noted by one of the eunuchs that, just as he began it didn't lead to a great outburst. Love, however, seemed to protect him, because while he was planting perils, it was new favors that he reaped. To the language of flowers there was substituted the written word. In a note from the same lucky louvered door, he was told in one of the strongest of the Persian dialects:

"If you love me, that's good; you are also loved. But love is a flower that grows at the top of a sheer rock, and, to cut it, it takes a strong heart and agile feet."

She went on to describe herself: Sixteen years-old, white as a lily, eyes black as a starless night, that was the woman who had written the note. Her name was Georgiana, after the name of her birthplace, Tbilisi in Georgia, and while in chains, she was nonetheless a girl from the nobility. Tsar Erekle II,[46]

---

[46] Erekle II (c.1720-1798), was a Georgian monarch of the Bagrationi dynasty, reigning as the king of Kakheti from 1744 to 1762, and of Kartli and Kakheti from 1762 until 1798. His reign is regarded as the swan song of the Georgian monarchy. Aided by his personal abilities and the unrest in the Persian Empire, Erekle established himself as a de facto independent

the last Prince of the Georgians, belonged to her family. The wicked Circassians[47] put all her relations to death, then sold her for the harem of Mirza Babba, a man who adored her but that she couldn't endure.

"Does such a slave please you?" the note concluded. "Then come set her free. Only two eunuchs guard the door at night. One key to open it, one good dagger for the two others. If the day when you will come could be known in advance, hashish or opium would have confused the minds of the two guards. But iron, you know, produces better sleep. After a week, you will no longer be expected; that's all the time it takes to climb the sheer rock, if the heart is strong and the feet agile."

The beautiful slave, as can be seen, both in her jerky and elliptical style and in her plans for escape, was concise, resolute, and gaily directing events. But for Alexis, a little more familiar with civilization, two men to put to death, a false key to make, put him in mind of the Penal Code, very fitting to make him grow cold. And then, as much in love as he was, when the moment came to take action, Mirza Babba's friend hesitated. Violated hospitality, a nice, easy, peaceful existence, when it was a matter of embarking blindly into the great ocean of adventures, gave him something to think about, especially when he loved an unknown woman on her word, and whose face he had yet to see.

---

ruler, unified eastern Georgia politically for the first time in three centuries, and attempted to modernize the government. Overwhelmed by internal and external menaces, he placed his kingdom under the formal Russian protection in 1783, but the move did not prevent Georgia from being devastated by the Persian invasion in 1795. He died in 1798, leaving the throne to his moribund heir, George XII.

[47] The Circassians are a Northwest Caucasian ethnic group native to Circassia, many of whom were displaced in the course of the Russian conquest of the Caucasus in the 19th century, especially after the Russian–Circassian War in 1864.

On the other hand, the word of Georgiana, that girl of noble blood, brought down to the condition of a slave, those flowers, that ingenious language, that proud, decided note, keeping her dignity so well in her advances, all that spoke very much to the imagination, and balanced the counsels of cold logic. Summing up, Alexis felt that woman in his heart; but to approach her and possess her, he really saw very few ways, when at the moment he had the least hope, an unexpected event solved it.

One day, the beautiful Princess F***, the one to whom Mirza Babba had declared himself to be her *cavalier servant,* had the idea to laughingly say to him that it wasn't at all nice of him not even having the idea of showing his gallantry by arranging for the lady of his thoughts, some party or diversion in the Persian taste. Just that comment was enough, and a few days afterward, some friends, men and women from her usual group, were one evening united with the one who had been thus provoked.

In every country, from the largest to the smallest, festivals seem to take place in families: dancing, music, lights, fireworks, however they are put together always form the basis. And here, too, the host was limited in what he could do, the Princess, who didn't want to stir up gossip, having required that everything be done in a small group, and only among her intimate friends. It's not necessary then to expand on for a long time the colored and transparent glasses incised with the Princess' monogram, or about the ballet where dancers from the Opera replaced the real Tehran dancers, or finally the fireworks and torches from Bengal which crowned the ballet.

What's important to our story, is a splendid dinner, half French cuisine and half Persian, around which at the end of the evening, the Ambassador's guests sat down to table. Toward the end of the meal, finding employment for the poet, or storyteller, that he had in his suite, Mirza Babba had him come in, carrying an instrument from his country. That man dedicated, in honor of the Princess, an entire, very long, chanted poem that he improvised, both words and music. Allowed to sit at the table with the guests, Alexis took charge of translating that poetic homage, abridging it a great deal. Here, as a consequence of that jealousy felt by all of the Ambassador's personnel, as is already known, something comic happened to the young secretary, by whom it is proven that the *genus irritabile* [48] is really true in every country.

While Alexis was making the verses created in her honor intelligible, doing them the inestimable service of shortening the interminable lengths that are the genius of the Orient, the improvised poet suddenly rose in a fury and threw himself at his master's feet.

"Excellency," he said to him in the little French he had learned during his stay in France, "take my head, if that pleases you, but I can't let that traitorous and wicked man reduce my verses to nothing, and that a nightingale singing with a full throat becomes, as he translates it, a broken-winded, crippled, and hairless camel."

Challenged in that way, Alexis hastened to explain the well-meant intention with which he had made some cuts. Mirza Babba approved of what he had done and told the poet to calm down; the poet, seeing his adversary put in the right, continued to complain with more bitterness, and he lost respect so much that they were obliged to evict him from the room, still complaining. That expulsion was without punishment. Ambassadorial discipline, which he had just broken with such irreverence and noise, probably reserved some other correction for him.

Rather malicious by nature, and, as has been said, not taking her suitor too seriously, the Princess chose just that moment to compliment him for the order of his party.

"Only, my dear host," she added, "I would tell you to perfect satisfaction of these ladies and mine, you have selfishly left something out."

---

[48] Poets, irritable people. (Note from the Author.)

The Diplomat immediately spoke up, asking that some-one point out to him the lack for which he was guilty, saying that he would take it to heart and repair it, if there was still time.

"You pay court to me admirably," the Princess contin-ued, "by seeming to think about something a thousand leagues from what I want to talk to you about. But the question here does not concern my jealousy. Here, curiosity is the strongest. The beautiful slaves that you keep under lock and key, frank-ly, we had hoped that you would at least let us see them."

At that sudden attack, the Excellency's face turned a great deal darker.

"Madame," he said with embarrassment, "that would be showing very little generosity."

"Oh, no," the Princess said. "Those ladies and I are thought about in two different ways, me the soul, they the senses. There is no possible conflict. Besides, we know very well that a harem, that's an object of luxury, as are in France collections of gems or a gallery of paintings."

"Princess, I drink to you," then said Mirza-Babba, in or-der to cut short that displeasing subject of conversation. And in one swallow he empted the glass of champagne that was in front of him.

"That's always good," Madame de F*** continued, "and to avoid the question, on a point that you have until now shown yourself very stubborn; you are letting yourself finally become civilized."

That comment must be understood as dealing the ex-treme sobriety of the Muslim. According to the rigorous doc-trine of the Quran, at the most sumptuous tables, in the middle of the most animated reunions, Mirza Babba always had water as a drink. And if, from time to time, he let himself be de-bauched with a glass of champagne, to get around his con-science, he was persuaded that he had been poured sparkling lemonade, an orthodox and inoffensive drink that Muhammad had neither foreseen no forbidden.

Calculating that a host is always a little at the discretion of his guests, and seeing an opportunity to shake that eternal level of seriousness in the mind and face of the hydrophilic diplomat, one of the Princess' friends stood up and traitorously lifting her glass, said:

"Excellency, you don't want to make women jealous."

"It is I, Madame, who am honored," the Ambassador replied with perfect courtesy, and he hurried to return the toast.

Everyone then claimed the same favor, and although keeping his head in that cross fire, the man besieged was careful not to toast with a full glass. All the guests satisfied, in that dangerous encounter he found he had absorbed more of the strong liquid than he had during his whole life. The effect on one who seldom drank was quickly noticed, it goes without saying. His eyes bright and shining, his complexion flushed, his speech high and frequent, the Sublime Envoy soon showed in all his person the work of that strong stimulant. And this time, his majestic impassiveness was threatened with serious failure.

"Do you know, ladies," said the Princess, without abandoning the delicate subject she had introduced, "a while ago I said the Ambassador was selfish. It was perhaps cautious that I should have said."

"If I had been," the Ambassador gallantly replied, "would my heart be placed where it is?"

"You don't want to show us those beautiful recluses," continued Madame F***, "but I believe you have your reasons."

"Eh! Madame, stars beside the sun, has that ever been seen?" the Diplomat asked, turning his languorous eyes toward the Princess.

"Forget that comparison," Madame F*** replied. "It's my opinion that, in fact, we could be shining stars beside some mediocre creatures, and because of that there is no attempt to compare them to us."

"I am too gallant to contradict you," Mirza Babba replied, but in a tone that he himself somewhat contradicted.

"I can't talk about His Excellency's slaves," Alexis, who had his own reason to interrupt at that moment. "Although living with them in this house, I am very far from knowing about their existence. But I can affirm, having lived in the Orient, that often in fact the harem is a deceptive sign. So, even the beautiful women of Georgia, who are so much talked about by travelers, I have seen them in Constantinople,[49] and, well! they are not up to their great reputation."

"Ah! You have seen them in Constantinople," the Ambassador said ironically, "in the Sultan's harem, without a doubt."

"No, but in the streets, where, when the French pass by, they voluntarily find some way to put aside their veil, so that they can be seen."

"And these women from Georgia that you glimpsed appeared to you as only slightly beautiful," the Sublime Envoy continued, still with the same tone of pity.

"Well!" Alexis said, cleverly piquing the Diplomat's vanity, "I have encountered some working girls in Paris who certainly were more so."

"Well, my dear fellow," Mirza Babba answered sharply, "the ones pointed out to you as from Georgia, were some street-walkers from Cairo, or perhaps some women from Africa."

And, as if to congratulate himself on that joke, which supposed that Alexis was very little competent to judge the matter, to tell the difference between black and white, he drank some swallows of his "sparkling lemonade," no longer counting how much.

"*You're a goldsmith, Monsieur Josse!*" [50] the Princess said gaily.

---

[49] Istanbul.

[50] Quote from a character from *L'Amour Médecin* (1665), a comedy of Molière: "You are a goldsmith, Monsieur Josse, and your advice smacks of a man who wants to get rid of his merchandise."

"Who is this Monsieur Josse?" asked the Sublime Envoy, whose study of French civilization hadn't gone so far as to be introduced to Molière.

"A man who points out the value of his merchandise like you, who, seeing enthusiastically you laud their beauty, it's very evident that you have some Georgiennes in your collection."

"I have one, Madame., he said in such a dry way and so sure of himself, that it was clear that he meant, one par excellence, a treasure, a perfection, a miracle.

"After Monsieur Alex's little revelation, I admit," the Princess said, "that I would be prodigiously curious to see her."

"If you saw her, Madame, I honor your character enough to think that, woman as you are, you would do her full justice."

"Yes, but while waiting, you keep her hermetically hidden."

"Through politeness, Madame," said the Sublime Envoy, that the prolonged contradiction and fumes of the wine were beginning, on the contrary, to make extremely impolite.

"And also as a measure of security, and in order not to have anything to back down from."

"Well! Madame, you shall see her," exclaimed Mirza Babba, who had cleverly been made to lose control of himself.

He spoke some words in Persian to one of the people of his entourage. Several moments afterward, with a frightened look and out of breath, the chief of the eunuchs entered. Mirza Babba had made his decision and, without hesitation, gave him the order to bring in Georgiana. That command was so counter to all the ideas of Islam, that the eunuch to whom it had been transmitted, and who now heard it directly repeated, couldn't believe that his master was serious.

Obligated however by an imperial gesture to admit the reality, he threw himself tragically at his master's feet. He begged him not to make him commit such a flagrant violation of the laws of the harem.

As we have already said, Mirza Babba had begun not to know himself. Resenting that resistance, he became furious, spoke of cutting off the head of the one who had insolently contradicted him. And if his guests had shown any curiosity, that decapitation, would have been served to them as dessert in the sense given to that word by the gastronomy of the Middle Ages. Finally, at the powerful intercession of the ladies, the all too zealous servant was excused for his behavior and soon afterwards, he brought in, covered with several veils, according to Persian custom, the beautiful slave.

Whatever the opinions before the examination which must have surrounded the appearance of a beauty praised so highly, the effect of the first view was immense. As for Alexis, he experienced neither happiness nor admiration, but it seemed to him that a powerful electric current had just struck his heart. He remained as if struck by lightning under the splendor of the attractions revealed to him.

Recovered from that lightheadedness, one thing seemed strange to him. Seated beside Mirza Babba, the young girl, having for the first time a view of the world, glanced around her with astonishment, and looking most of all at the dress of the ladies, she seemed not to recognize the man with whom she had communicated. She gave him no look of preference or intelligence. However the term of a week that she had fixed had not yet expired.

From the first moment of her appearance, the Sublime Envoy had assumed the triumphant pride of ownership. His eyes shining and moist, his nose swollen, and one of his arms reposing nonchalantly on the beautiful slave's waist, with the other hand, he was busy filling with treats the plate he had put in front of her, taking no more care for his other guests than if they had not been present at that scene. But the Tarpeian Rock[51] is near the Capitol; a combination of the influence of

---

[51] Tarpeian Rock: steep hill near the Capitol in Rome from which criminals were thrown to their death as punishment. The Latin phrase *Arx tarpeia Capitoli proxima* (the Tarpeian

wine, which he wasn't accustomed to drink, the diverse emotions of being disobeyed, of anger, of satisfied ego, which he had just experienced! Suddenly, the Ambassador's expression changed; he collapsed, slid out of his seat, and if his faithful servants hadn't come forward on a sign from Alexis to run to him and carry him out of the room, that would have completely destroyed the Muslim's dignity. The Sublime Envoy would have disappeared under the table, like two or three nationalities accustomed to these sorts of eclipses, and that we are too polite to name here.

As favorable as the opportunity to say some words to the young slave in Persian, which the others would not have understood, appeared to the young secretary, a generous instinct led him to hurry after the sick man; and when, an instant later, he came back, announcing that sleep and some cups of tea, would take care of that ridiculous indisposition, the fierce chief of the eunuchs, either on an order given or simply as a result of his zeal, had come to again seize his prey and already the sad Georgiana was back in the harem.

A little scandalized by that denouement, the Princess hurried to call for her carriage and thus gave the signal for a general retreat. As some of her friends tried to preach indulgence to her, remarking that it was a kind of instantaneous plot organized against his temperance to which the Diplomat had succumbed., she replied:

"*Mon Dieu*! Turks are Turks. It's useless to give them a veneer of civilization. Muhammad always reappears."

XXI. The Next Day

The following day, Alexis, still in bed, tried to explain to himself why Georgiana, at their unhoped for meeting, didn't seem to recognize him. He had just decided that, under the eyes of her master, apparently fearing being drawn into some

---

Rock is close to the Capitol) means that one' s fall from grace can come swiftly.

indiscreet revelation of her sentiments, she chose to be cautious, maintaining a strong reserve that was perhaps easier. Just at that moment the young Englishman to whom he owed his position with Mirza Babba entered, saying:

"What did you do yesterday to the Sublime Envoy? This morning he's a fierce wild boar, hitting right and left with his snout. The whole embassy is terrified. He has already mutilated two of his people."

"Mutilated! How's that?" Alexis asked, terrified.

"Oh!" the Englishman continued, "the thing is less serious than you might believe. In Persia, there is a kind of punishment more burlesque than terrible. When the case isn't found to be serious enough for impaling, decapitating, or strangling a man, they cut off one side of his mustache or beard. Besides, the Muslims, who are very careful of their hair, hold it a great dishonor to be thus dispossessed. You can easily imagine the look that operation can give a man."

"But who are the poor devils that that despot treated that way?"

"His doctor first, whose crime was to have let him be poisoned at last night's meal."

"Poisoned! He's certainly dishonest! The dear man was dead drunk from Champagne, and what could his doctor, who first of all is an ass, do—besides he was not present?"

"Then," the Englishman said, "that explains everything. His Highness is furious over having compromised his *gravitas*, and to justify the profound attack to his Muslim dignity, he's transferred his anger to the poor doctor, who pays in that way for the crack to the head of his august client."

"And the other person tormented?" Alexis asked.

"The other one disciplined was the maker of the *Thousand and One Nights,* the poet who, in the exercise of his functions, committed, it seems, a serious irreverence."

"It's true that, yesterday, he let himself go with a rather grotesque outburst of ego; now that he's been so severely punished, I reproach myself for having, although very involuntarily, caused it."

141

"Be less concerned for that one. He's a little shady fellow who's setting up an ambush for you which I've actually come to warn you about."

"An ambush for me!"

"Yes, for you, and on this subject, I have to tell you about morality. You've lived in the Orient and should know how touchy the Muslims are about their women."

"Of course, but how did I seem to have forgotten it?"

"Oh! Come now!" the Englishman continued, seeming to be a perfectly well-informed man, "don't act innocent. Your looking into, your wandering around, the harem have been noticed and are known by the whole house to the point that it is on that lack of caution that the sinister mechanism has been built that may perhaps cost you your life."

"That's saying a lot, I think," replied Alexis, who nevertheless couldn't do anything else but appear a little intrigued.

"Not at all; you were in a very bad position, because, if you escaped the serious side of the danger, you were at least exposed to great ridicule."

"*Diable*! That is even more serious," replied Alexis.

"Here is the fact. That damned poet, having noticed that you walked up and down around the harem, got together with the chief of the eunuchs. From behind a persian blind door, they threw some bouquets to you, then a letter that, as a novelist, the creator of all that intrigue fabricated in the name of one of the women most loved by His Excellency, and you, a naive fish, swallowed that hook fabulously."

"Then these Persians are a plague!"

"They are just valets, jealous of a favorite, and seeing you on a bad slope, did what was necessary to roll it to the bottom. But if you will believe me, there is a way to turn that scheme against them; take the letter you received to Mirza Babba. The handwriting will leave no doubt as to its author, and that way, not only will you prevent suspicions of jealousy if they intend to raise them against you, but more so, you will give a good correction to your enemies."

"If it's only a matter cutting off one side of their beard, I certainly wouldn't hesitate, but to have written in the name of his cherished slave, to have compromised her in a love intrigue, don't you think that Mirza Babba's anger, upon learning that audacity, is capable of having the head of the perpetrators cut off?"

Alexis had scarcely finished that sentence full of clemency than someone came to tell him on the part of the Ambassador, that he should come to him.

"Let's hope that that rascal of a poet hasn't preceded you with some revelation in his fashion, and that it's not about Georgiana that Mirza Babba wants to talk to you," the Englishman said. "I am terribly afraid, above all with the attitude that he seems to have this morning, wanting to quarrel with the whole house."

"We'll certainly see," Alexis said, "and in any case, he can't act toward a French subject as he does toward a Persian subject."

The moment Alexis entered the quarters of the Ambassador, that he found seated on his divan, smoking majestically, he had no doubt relative to accuracy of the information of his friend, the Englishman. Georgiana, that he saw, or rather that he glimpsed, under her double veil, seemed to have been brought there for a confrontation, and he got ready for a rough encounter. Nevertheless, putting on a good face, he began by asking the Ambassador, with interest, news about his health.

"My health," Mirza-Babba replied, "then you think I was sick yesterday?"

"Sick, no, but slightly indisposed."

"What! You didn't see that it was a pretended indisposition to get rid of those women whose cackling had pushed my patience to the limit? I thought you were more perceptive, my friend."

"I admit," responded Alexis, who immediately recognized a man intent on saving his dignity, "that I didn't recognize this ploy of high diplomacy."

"Decidedly," continued the Ambassador, still trying to put himself in control of the situation, "that relationship with the Princess can't continue. The role of a platonic suitor, that I have constantly to play with her, finally exhausted me. Yesterday, she acted in a way that brought about an opportunity for a rupture. I picked up the glove and just now I have written to her so that neither she, nor any of her friends, will any longer want to play with me."

"So, that tender tie will be broken permanently?"

"Yes," Mirza-Babba said casually, "henceforth I will only deal with women of my harem, with those terrible Georgiennes who aren't worthy to be compared with the Paris streetwalkers."

"My Lord," Alexis answered. "I must admit to Your Excellency that, since the demonstration that you were kind enough to afford us, my opinions have been considerably modified."

Responding in this way, was the young secretary right, or was he wrong? That's what he himself didn't know, because the allusion to which he had responded could be a little revenge for what he had said the evening before, but it could also be a trap to introduce the touchy subject of his actions around the harem, assuming that Mirza Babba knew about them.

"I am happy to see you drop your prejudices," the Ambassador said. "However, that encourages me in an idea. But first, there's something that I must tell you: we are separating."

"You are no longer pleased with my services?'" Alexis asked, a little astonished by that sudden conclusion.

"But, you understand, that correspondence with which you have been so involved, having henceforth ceased, your services, while still pleasing me, have become absolutely useless to me."

So, the young secretary thought, *the Englishman was right. The dear man no longer wants any witnesses of his dis-*

orderly conduct near him and he is taking revenge also on me
for the tear he made in his Muslim dignity.

"However," Mirza Babba continued, "in leaving each other, I have it in my heart to leave you a souvenir. Speak frankly, and tell me what you thought about the beauty of Georgiana, that girl I showed you?"

Sidestepping the question which still seemed dangerous to him like a Jesuit, Alexis answered:

"Yesterday, you saw the impression she made on all your guests."

"Well, look at her again and see whether the candles were not enough."

And at the same time, he drew toward him Georgiana, who, until then, had remained standing at his side with the immobility of a statue. With a gesture of his hand, he made the double veil, under which this miracle of beauty was hidden, disappear. And thus, with another infraction of Muslim law, he put the excitable young man face to face with the young slave, who was like a ray of sun coming from behind a cloud.

At that moment, forgetting all caution, Alexis couldn't keep from saying:

"Certainly the *houris*[52] of your paradise could not be more beautiful."

"Well," said the Ambassador, "since she is to your liking, take her away; she is yours."

Astounded more than what can be told, Alexis looked at the Ambassador in astonishment, and finally asked if he was speaking seriously.

"Absolutely; that woman belongs to me; she pleases you; I'm giving her to you."

"In France," Alexis said, still struck by surprise, "we don't have such a procedure; a woman gives herself; she can't be given."

"As you like," Mirza Babba answered, explaining his marvelous generosity by a single statement. "If you don't take

---

[52] Beautiful young virgins promised to the faithful in paradise.

her, I know what to do with her. But what's certain is that she will no longer remain in my harem; eyes have seen her!"

This *I know what to do with her* had been pronounced with such a strong voice, that Alexis became frightened, and, while holding to his scruples about accepting a woman like a piece of furniture, and probably without her having given her consent to the transaction, he was very curious to know what fate, supposing that she didn't become his, was reserved for Georgiana.

"In the Orient," the Ambassador calmly answered, "when a woman ceases to please us, we call in a slave merchant and give her to him. I am told that there is the same business in France for women."

"But, Excellency, that idea is awful!" Alexis exclaimed.

"Do you think so?" Mirza Babba asked, while continuing calmly to smoke his hooka. "Well, there is a man attached to the Embassy; I can call him and tell him to break that cup that I no longer want to drink from, so that others can't drink there after me."

That one sentenced summed up all the jealousy and all the Muslim egotism, and Alexis understood that, the evening before, he and the Princess' friends had played with a tiger which, after having seemed tame for some time, under their imprudent provocation, had just reverted to his nature. Nevertheless, he tried to restrain him by threats, speaking to him of French law that protected all those who lived in its territory, even going so far as to cite the example of Christine, Queen of Sweden, who, for having put into effect the fantasy of doing away with a servant by whom she thought she had been betrayed, had incurred the anger of Louis XIV. And he added that, under a sovereign who was both Emperor and King, the murder of an unfortunate and innocent slave could have more serious consequences for its author.

'In the enclosure of this townhouse," Mirza Babba proudly answered, "I am not in France; I am in Tehran, where I have over all my people the right to life and death and I will make it seen."

At the same time he ordered the person with the huge sa-ber to be called. The Parisians finally saw they were not abso-lutely wrong in being worried about the man. Alexis couldn't doubt that the danger to the repudiated slave was very real. And perhaps he was not angry about the kind of violence done to him, since, supposing the young slave didn't have the sen-timents for him she was said to have, she had been in his thoughts for a long time, and she was one of those triumphant and incisive beauties that tear the heart apart at first sight.

Making up his mind, her new master said in Persian:

"Georgiana, His Excellency Mirza Babba has given you to me. Do you want to go with me?"

From the moment her veil had fallen off, placed before a mirror where she had seen her graceful figure reproduced from her head to her feet, Georgiana had given no attention to any-thing else. Without stopping that contemplation, to which she gave all her attention and all her soul, she replied:

"Mirza-Babba is my master. I am his slave. What he does is well done."

"But," Alexis said, "in this country, women are not slaves. They freely follow those their heart has chosen."

"Will I see Paris?" she demanded as her eyes lit up when pronouncing that name, which evidently must be for her syn-onymous with supreme happiness.

"Without a doubt you will."

"Well! Let's go!" said Georgiana in a passionate voice, from which it could certainly be seen that one of the dreams of her existence had been realized.

However, Alexis believed he shouldn't leave Mirza Babba without telling him some words of goodbye. As for the beautiful slave, already at the apartment door, her shoulder turned to the master she was leaving, she didn't even glance at him. Only, during the short conference between what might be called her present and her past, two or three times she could be seen glancing around with a look of impatience and anxiety.

His leave-taking done, Alexis went to join Georgiana. On a gesture that he made for her to go ahead of him, the young girl rushed forward, happy and light; one would have said a white dove that, finding its cage partly open, flew into the heavenly countryside, to join air and freedom.

XXII. What Happened to Georgiana

For Alexis, in the adventure that had presented itself, there were two paths to follow: either see in Georgiana a fallen creature, the remains of a barbarian's lechery, and, in this way, take her first in a liaison as one of those pieces of good luck which, without heartbreak or combat, unfolds, with some sacrifices of money, until all the pleasure has been extracted, or treat her seriously as his protégée, as sort of a sacred trust, that Providence had put into his hands with the mission of initiating her into our customs and our civilization.

At twenty, all love affairs are serious. So, Alexis took the second path, and, instead of treating the encounter lightly, once Georgiana was temporarily installed in a furnished apartment, a kind of resource always at hand in Paris, he began to look into how he could provide her a future, for which he admitted he had all the responsibility.

Having only small resources, a result of savings from his salary at the place he had just left, could he, with that small savings, provide for his own existence and establish that of Georgiana at a certain level? The life of a student in an attic where singers tell you that love and contentment are riches, always has a down side which seldom smiles on him and besides, where would love be when Georgiana was only with him, at the most, out of gratitude? And happiness, how to reach it with a woman accustomed to all the comforts and all the carefree life of the harem, and from that suddenly transported into an atmosphere of difficulty and privations?

Alexis believed he had found a solution to his embarrassed situation: going to find Princess F***, interesting her in his charitable action, persuading her to help him with her great influence and her credit. In taking this step, there was truly honor and courage, because the poor young man had a great deal of love in his heart. However, he couldn't at all hope that, being his helper by giving Georgiana her powerful patronage, she could at the same time, leave her at the mercy of his hopes and his desires smoldering in him. Without being stopped by that egotistical consideration, he generously made his sacrifice, and going to see Madam de F***, asked the honor of seeing her. But all kinds of memories about the Persian Ambassador recommended him badly to the Princess with whom Mirza Babba hadn't made a very courteous parting. Notwithstanding repeated attempts, our philanthropist didn't manage to be received. Suspicious of the motive which made him excluded, he decided to write, and in a very pathetic letter he recounted the way in which he had saved the life of the beautiful slave, and the difficulty he found to give an honorable continuation to that act.

Letter for letter, he received the following response:

I read, Monsieur, with great interest, the repudiation of Mademoiselle Georgiana by our former friend the Ambassador and the somewhat romanesque devotion that decided you to take her off his hands. But what do you think I can do with a girl without education, not even speaking any of the European languages? And in any of the conditions where she could be placed, she has the misfortune to carry her beauty with her, to become the subject of worry or embarrassment for the mistress of the house. All, it seems to me, that can be done is to offer you a letter for the Mother Superior of the The Daughters of the Madeleine, where they accept girls who want to be reformed. If your protegée does not object to that view of herself, and, most of all, if you yourself agree, Monsieur, let me know by sending me a note, and my letter of recommendation will come to you without delay.

*Princess de F****

If Alexis had looked at his situation by the bright side, he would found that he had often met comedy in the march of human destinies, and that idea of making a nun of a concubine would have seemed to him a rather diverting bit of the bizarre.

But as is already known, the good young man was acting as a serious protector, and without speaking about the general tone of the letter, which appeared to him to be from a dry and heartless woman, one word, that of *conditions*, that implied that Georgiana would be made into a chambermaid, or a children's' governess, filled him with indignation. *They want to drag her down*, he said to himself, *because she crushes them all by her beauty*. And Alexis' generous anger was on the point of creating in his mind the thought of a desperate and extreme remedy by suddenly giving him affluence, a way permitting him to make Georgiana queen of the world, before whom the charms of the most elegant and sought after women would be eclipsed.

However, when he wasn't thinking of a more tranquil and modest possession, the terrible step that he himself would have to take wasn't at all one of those done with a simple access of annoyance, without considering what followed and without much reflection. To go ask the *Secret Bureau* to pay the expense of his good deed, that was a flash of weak will which, rapidly crossing his free will, hardly left a trace. Also by that phenomenon of thought that the idea you reject often makes you put your hand on the idea you were looking for, Alexis came to extract from the malicious opening Madame de F*** had suggested, a scheme, in his opinion very workable, that he immediately began putting into effect.

That idea was to place Georgiana in a boarding school of young ladies. Here is the sequence of circumstances and memories by which Alexis was led to think of this solution. The day the duel with the Marquis de Saint-Faust took place, in which he almost lost his life, when he was brought from the Bois de Boulogne, following the great quantity of blood he had lost, he was overcome by a lapse of consciousness which worried his witnesses. They were then near the village Thernes and an isolated house occupied by an institution of young ladies was the only place that could lend assistance.

Received by the Mistress of the establishment with perfect kindness, for several hours Alexis was the object of intelligent and rapid care to which he probably owed his salvation. Since then, several visits had acknowledged his debt of gratitude. And, although in the great distractions of Parisian life that relationship was almost lost, as soon as Alexis thought about the former obligation to the charitable head of the institution, he didn't despair of interesting her in his protegée's fate.

Alexis had reproached himself for using simplicity with a person not even known to himself, and it was with a complete and naïve admission of Georgiana's true situation that he asked pity for her. The success was beyond what he had asked. A woman of imagination, and, it must be said, having some ideas of about the way education should be conducted, that outside rumors said bordered somewhat on charlatanism, the mistress of the boarding school approved of any way that would call attention to her establishment.

"Certainly," she said to Alexis with a vivacity of speech and impressions that were peculiar to her, "we wouldn't make the mistake of telling the public that poor child is an escapee from the little pleasures of Monsieur the Persian Ambassador. But she will be seen here in her picturesque dress, her Caucasian beauty, surrounded with an air of mystery which will make the greatest effect. To add to the naked truth, some little ornamentation will be necessary. We will be very close to reality and play a good joke on your Mirza Babba, in saying, as the greatest secret in the world, that she is his daughter, the one the old monkey no longer wants in his harem. What's inconvenient is the acquaintance of an already mature woman with my innocent troop. That's something I will take care of. She will have little or no communication with my younger or older girls. She will eat at my table and live in a private room. There is only the music teacher who worries me a little. These singers of romantic songs have an aptitude for turning women's heads."

"But," Alexis said, throwing himself into that deluge of projects and plans, "there is a very simple solution; that would be not to have your new student take music lessons, or to have a teacher a little more mature or a little less seductive."

"Old teachers!" shouted the Headmistress. "Yes! Really! That's the most offensive thing that can be imagined to destroy a boarding school! People who, horrifying the students with their tobacco, bring to their instruction the bad disposition of their kidney problems or of their rheumatism, and who, their reputation already made, charge an exorbitant price."

"But, after all, for Georgiana, the arts are not the most pressing thing. The first thing is that she should learn French. She doesn't know the first word at the moment. And in the beginning, it will be very necessary that I be part of her instruction, because I have an advantage over you, my dear teacher, of being able to give her the elements of grammar in the language that she speaks and that I also know."

"That means that the gentleman professor won't be unhappy to have an opportunity to come see his protegée almost every day?"

"On the subject of my visits, Madame, I will leave that to you, whatever you find convenient. However, I would point out to you that I am the only person who, for that poor girl without a country, represents friends, family. In addition she seemed to me to have great aspirations for that freedom that we are still going to delay for her, and, really, having taken away from her the routine of the boarding school, to suppress all intervention on my part would be misplaced and dangerous."

"You plead your case marvelously," the Headmistress responded. "And you are a man of honor and wouldn't want to repay with a scandal the courageous hospitality that I am giving your young girl in my house."

"Now," Alexis said, "there remains the matter of settling between us the conditions of the room and board."

At this point, a real battle of generosity took place between the two parties. The Headmistress said that Georgiana, being an advertisement for her by her presence, would already do a great deal to lower the costs of expenses. Alexis, while admitting that he was not a Russian Prince, insisted on knowing the current price of room and board and on paying something extra, seeing the exceptional position made for the new student.

From this debate and from some explanations that the ex-secretary for Mirza Babba was led to give about his position, there resulted a solution as agreeable as it was unexpected. The Headmistress of the boarding school suddenly realized that, given his travels, Alexis would be an excellent geography teacher. What's more, she thought that a course in Oriental literature, while not claiming to teach the students the difficult Oriental languages, would give them, in translation, a smattering of its masterpieces. It was, in fact, to institute a very exceptional instruction, that in our days would be called a *specialty*. At that point, every battle was terminated. The price of the instruction given by Alexis to the students of the boarding school would take the place of the cost he himself would be asked to pay for the hospitality given to the beautiful slave. However, that's the way of the world. From being someone asking for help, and prevented from doing so by the Headmistress, he ended up by being one of her collaborators and men in her confidence. He had come humbly to ask for a service, and it was only up to him to persuade himself that he was the one who rendered it.

XXIII. Still Water

Things thus agreed on, there remained to make the principally interested person agree on the arrangements. Alexis went at it with skill. He explained to the future boarding school student that, taken by surprise, he couldn't immediately arrange a suitable habitation and proper living accommodations. He had decided to place her temporarily in a house where, surrounded by care and consideration, and being certain that he would visit her every day, she would, better than anywhere else, become accustomed to the habits and ideas of the country in which she was destined henceforth to live.

Either because she had little will power, or from the habit of passive resignation to which she had been broken by the discipline of the harem, Georgiana showed no opposition to the arrangement proposed, but it must also be said that she revealed no great warmth of gratitude for the devotion of which she had been the object. Because of this, there was no way for Alexis to hold on to an idea with which he had been for a moment pleased to delude himself. It was clear, even when Georgiana hadn't confirmed it to him by her mouth, that everything in the advances where he had so naively allowed himself to be taken in, were part of the imagination of the poet. In no way had that charming girl been part of that comedy, and, after their meeting, nothing in her showed the germ of some tender feelings. In a word, already very much in love, and having given himself at first sight, Mirza Babba's successor had to do everything to get paid in return, and to go from being useful, as he had been, to becoming likable.

What's more, in the question of bringing about that nice transformation, he seemed to encounter many great conveniences. In addition to the time he spent one-on-one with his beautiful pupil, in the evening, in the drawing room of the boarding school, at the table of the Headmistress, where he was frequently invited, in some outings that the Headmistress arranged, accompanied by Georgiana, who took the arm of the man in love, he had incessant opportunities to see and be near his pupil. What's more, by a thousand attentions and a thousand acts of kindness, in showering her with a mass of those charming nothings that women use, and that fashion constantly puts in circulation in Parisian businesses, he seemed to have the luck to be able communicate some ardor to that heart until then lukewarm toward him.

However, after several months had rolled by, Alexis still hadn't made any remarkable progress, and the thermometer of his love showed only a slight elevation. Georgiana was, if you wish, more casual with her suitor, but she was not more tender. Apart from the fact that a certain natural laziness in her seemed to protect her even against the fatigue of being in love, it must be believed that the constriction and stain in the bosom of which she had lived had first obliterated, then dried up, all her ability to feel. Passive, even in her desires and her best laid out aspirations, she let herself somehow fade away by evaporation at the breath of the least resistance, lacking the smallest amount of energy to follow them and bring them about. It was the same way that, after showing an unusual ardor for liberty and the sojourn in Paris, having, to tell the truth, only changed prisons and submitted to that regime that Madelon of *Les Précieuses ridicules*[53] called a terrible diet without amusements, she did not complain and didn't even think of enlivening, by a little of that love she had at hand, the desolate monotony of her new existence. She preferred, if it can be put like this, to love herself, to constantly be busy with concern for her charms, which she constantly looked at in the mirror. After she had dressed ten times and changed dress ten times, after using a number of marvelous cosmetics, perfume, treasure of beauty, which cost Alexis considerable expense, she nonchalantly stretched out on a couch. She let the days of her life go by, one by one, without seeming to think about anything else or wanting to go beyond that.

It was easy to see that the opinionated Headmistress of the boarding school couldn't see the education she had taken on herself to direct turn into that sort of moral stagnation. And in her ardent desire to give life to a nature of marble, it was not long before she herself had to encourage her young teacher to be the Pygmalion of his disappointing statue.

But nothing came to disturb the surface of that beautiful still water. It was very true that if, with infinite trouble, Alexis had obtained a passable result from his French lessons, from the point of view of intelligence as well as of soul, that admi-

---

[53] Molière's 1659 one-act satire in prose. It takes aim at the *précieuses*, ultra-witty ladies who indulged in lively conversations, word games and *préciosité* (preciousness).

rable form seemed closed and walled up. Let's say, however, that finally an influence appeared with the ability to conjure away that dullness of heart and mind, and who finally gained access into Georgiana's indifference. She was one of those sad creatures, at one hundred franc a year, exactly the wages of the cook for the house, when meagerly paid, she accepted at the boarding house the harsh functions of spy and Assistant to the Headmistress.

Twenty-five-years old, with a character at the same time both ingratiating and haughty, a quick and audacious mind, and even with the cruel devastations made by smallpox to her face, even to the way she carried herself, there were certain traces of faded beauty. Such was that girl who, in her conversation, otherwise lively and engaging, returned a little too often, perhaps, to talk about a happy, and even splendid existence from which she had been dispossessed.

That liaison, without Alexis approving of it a great deal, continued for several months, more and more fervent, when one day, arriving at the boarding school, Alexis was greeted with strange news. That morning, Georgiana and the Assistant Headmistress, her inseparable friend, had disappeared together from the house.[54] Seeing himself repaid by that ingratitude for the honorable devotion that he had shown, the poor young man at first persuaded himself that he was extremely resentful. But looking into his soul better, he noticed that he experienced still more displeasure than anger, and that actually the lover much more than the misunderstood benefactor was fading in him.

Then, but a little late, he reproached himself for the virtuous abstinence which turned out so badly for him. He thought that, with a creature picked up from where he had found her, he had treated her with ridiculous delicacy which

---

[54] The notion of lesbian lovers eloping isn't new; readers of *Le Comte de Monte-Cristo* (1845) will recall that the same thing happens with Eugenie Danglars and Louise d'Armilly at the end of that novel.

she could neither understand nor appreciate. From there, to his wounded ego, to his exalted desires constantly delayed, to his indignation against the advisor who had evidently inspired Georgiana's determination, he formed a furious passion to find her traces, and there was no way to know to what folly or to what desperate act he might have been carried if a servant in the house hadn't come to his aid with information.

That girl remembered having heard a part of the plan of escape which was whispered near her. The event then made her remember several things that at the time hadn't struck her attention. She could tell the man in love an address where the two fugitives could probably be found very easily. Alex didn't lose a moment to go to the place pointed out. It was a pied-à-terre that the Assistant Headmistress had furnished with debris from her days of splendor to which she had so frequently alluded. It was convenient for her to find that as an asylum on her free days or when she was dismissed from some position. The haughty way she habitually treated Headmistresses of the institutions that employed her rarely allowed her to make a prolonged stay in any place.

Luckily for Alexis, when he reached the apartment of the Assistant Headmistress, he found she was absent, otherwise, it is not probable that he would easily have put his hand on his conquest.

He was very decided to take back the mistakes of his first encounter with Mirza Babba's slave and to speak as the heir to the rights of Mirza Babba.

"I was deceived," the former slave answered with humility.

Recognizing the tone of authority with which in the discipline of the harem she was accustomed to being treated, authority immediately regained its empire.

"Deceived by whom?" Alexis asked.

"By *that woman* who promised me that my existence would be very happy if I would do as she told me."

"So, then, your existence was not at all happy where I placed you?"

"Not too happy. I was still in prison."

"And why didn't you say so?" Alexis asked, softening. "You were there to at least learn the language of the country where you must live. But that wouldn't have lasted a long time."

"*She* said that it would, because you're not rich."

"To please you, it's absolutely necessary to be rich?"

"Mirza Babba was rich and he didn't please me."

"And nevertheless, you didn't think about leaving his harem?"

"If I could have, maybe; besides, he was within his rights."

"What are you calling his rights, that of force?"

"First of all, he bought me, and then the *Qadi* [55]would have found me for him."

"What! The *Qadi*? What does the *Qadi* have anything to do here?"

"Oh, yes, sir, my companions in the harem always told me that a Muslim could have four legitimate wives, and as many others as he wished when he could keep them in his house, feed them, and give them everything necessary. But if he doesn't give them everything that's necessary, and if the *Qadi* finds out about it, he will order him to resell them, and he will be forced to."

Alexis couldn't help smiling on seeing how little progress the poor girl had yet made in European ideas. But at the same time, that remark led him to become aware of their respective situations. The truth was that he had taken charge of Georgiana's fate, and that he didn't have the means to provide for her existence, and, above all, for that existence of comfort and interior luxury women of the Orient are accustomed to. Some naïve admissions of the young girl and the situation she had been drawn into could foretell strange projects. Wanting

---

[55] Magistrate or judge of the Shari'a court, who also exercised extrajudicial functions, such as mediation, guardianship over orphans and minors.

to go into depth of what he thought he had uncovered, he continued:

"But," Alexis said, glancing around him in a room rather badly organized, where, next to some remnants of opulence there were traces of extreme poverty. "I don't see that your new *protectrice* and friend has provided you with an existence very superior to the one you have left."

"But I told you right off, the woman deceived me."

"But then, just what did that deception consist of?"

"Well then, that she was supposed to introduce me to a person a great deal richer than Mirza Babba."

"Unfortunate woman!" Alexis exclaimed. "You were being led to your ruin, and you didn't even hesitate to leave me, despite all the affection I showed you!"

"Oh, truly I did hesitate, and I felt that it wasn't good to leave you, but she told me that I would be doing you a service, that a woman is more expensive in France than in the Orient, and that you would never suffer from it."

Very little is necessary to bring back a man very much in love. That simple regret for their separation, rather coldly expressed by Georgiana, was like a balm to the wound of Alexis' heart. It wouldn't even have taken much for him to see on the part of the discreet girl, a respectable devotion to leave the situation there, to release him from a future that could be foreseen as too heavy for him to bear. However, that forgetfulness didn't extend to the perfidious woman who had exploited that generous sentiment in the interest of her own odious projects. Wanting to get to the bottom of everything, with some solicitude Alexis asked:

"But then, that person richer than Mirza Babba, that you were supposed to meet, have you seen him?'"

"Mirza Babba wasn't young," Georgiana answered, "but he was always richly dressed and his beard was perfumed with rose water, but that man who came to see us here, that I was told was rich, just think, sir, he was ugly, with dirty clothes, his nose smeared with tobacco, and he smelled with a terrible odor when he wanted to kiss my hands."

"And, nevertheless, you let him?" Alexis asked, not without worrying about the answer.

"Him!" the girl exclaimed, in a tone of disdain that couldn't leave the truthfulness in doubt. "On the contrary, he went away very angry."

"And now?"

"Now, Herminie (for hat was the name of the Assistant Headmistress) told me that I had missed out on my happiness. She maintained that he was very rich, and because I laughed in her face every time she told me about his hotels, his furniture store, as rich as that of the Emperor, she began to treat me so terribly that I even thought about leaving her house. But where would I go, a poor girl, in a country she doesn't know!"

"Come, Georgiana," Alexis told her, "I'm taking you away."

"Again to that ugly boarding school?" the beautiful slave asked in a tone that seemed to make her decision depend on the answer to that question.

"No, you won't go back there anymore. But promise me never again to see that girl who wanted to ruin you."

"Then let's go, immediately, so she doesn't find me here anymore," Georgiana answered, hurrying to pack her belongings.

This counter-kidnapping was brought about without any obstacle; only Alexis would have liked not to have heard a question addressed to him by Georgiana just as they left the apartment of the Assistant Headmistress.

"Couldn't that ugly old man dressed the way I told you, be a rich man?"

XXIV. One should never say, "Fountain I will never drink your water"[56]

Two weeks had hardly gone by since Georgiana was back in Alexis' hands when we find the splendid young woman installed in the boudoir of a cute apartment situated in the rue du Helder in the heart of the Chaussée d'Antin. If our taste were for those inventories of fixtures or for those memoirs of tapestry-makers that a certain school of story-tellers would like to make us accept as descriptive poetry, and if, most of all, letting us go into that mania for inventory, we were not condemned in this particular case, to paint one of the most disgraceful things that has ever existed: to see furnishings from the Imperial epoch, from the floor right up to the corniche, all the rooms making up that habitation would be material here for a whole chapter on furniture, and we have enough ego to believe that an official auctioneer for a public auction, himself, wouldn't succeed better.

But so far as we can know, our readers are at this moment, pressed by a curiosity different from that of seeing placed before them Sèvres *porcelaine*, some *chiffons*, some little *bureaux*, some couches and some displays of figurines. What they are most in a hurry to know is the part that ugly old man, whose opulence Georgiana so little credited, could have had in the make-up of that comfortable little establishment of which we have just said she was in possession. The answer will be short and simple. In the good fortune that had visited Mirza Babba's former slave, the ugly old man had absolutely no part. The proof was in the boudoir where Georgiana was lazily couched on an ottoman, sending around her the smoke of a long jasmine pipe. Here came Alexis, carrying a magnificent bouquet that he himself had bought from the *belle*

---

[56] French saying derived from the story of a man, never sober, who said he would never drink water. Once, when he was totally drunk, he fell into a fountain and was drowned. Moral: Never swear to never do something.

floriste, that beautiful Madame Prevost, gone today, as are her flowers, but at that time in all the bloom of youth and glory. Nothing remains now but a boutique and a name.

To see the careful dress and the somewhat triumphal air of our young friend, everything must equally suppose that his fortune, like that of Orestes,[57] had taken on a new face. Better than that, the affairs of his love life were also in a better state, since, upon entering, while placing on Georgiana's beautiful forehead a kiss that up to now could be called paternal. By the way he made a place for his lips in a swift and passionate movement, pushing back the disgraceful curls that the fashion of the period amassed almost right up to a woman's eyebrows, he seemed to act as a proprietor, moving out of the way what hampered his pleasure.

But then, if Alexis explained Georgiana's better fortune, what then explained Alexis' own better fortune in money and in his love life? To give a reason for all this change from one chapter to another, a little development is needed. Alexis had felt too threatened by losing Georgiana, and the ridiculous position of a *six vos non vobis* [58] had been found too near becoming a fact for him not to make extreme haste to consolidate his conquest in his hands. From there, renouncing his virtuous actions that hadn't succeeded for him, he had been delivered, to use the language of jurists, in block, all the good luck he had left behind, and becoming more serious than he

---

[57] From the Greek play, *Iphigenia in Tauris*, by Euripides. Orestes, having been ordered by Apollo to go to Tauris to bring back the statue of Artemis, is arrested, since the local custom is to sacrifice all foreigners. He is saved by his sister Iphigenia, who was earlier taken away by Artemis and made a priestess in Tauris. They recognize each other, escape, and Orestes became King of Argos.

[58] "For You, But Not Yours" were the words Vergil wrote on the wall when Bathyllus, another poet, plagiarized his work. Rabou footnotes it as *"Celui qui tire les marrons du feu,"* ie: the one who pulls the chestnuts out of the fire.

had been up until then, he became the successor of Mirza Babba.

If he had really wanted to get to the essence of that love, there would still have been something to say about that happiness. Having almost none of the European ideas about women, long formed to the morality of the harem, it was less to a lover than to a master that Georgiana seemed to submit. In her, instead of the charming modesty that gave in, there appeared rather a glacial resignation submitting with stoicism to the consequences of destiny. But in the absence of that chaste reserve, which is the most delicate seasoning of pleasure, Alexis found himself possessing wonderful beauty. His senses instead of his heart were filled with such gratitude, that his love, until then, passive and held in by force, underwent one of those disorderly and huge urges over which reason has no control and which can stir an existence right down to its foundations, change all its restrictions.

And that's not to say that in the middle of his victory the conqueror had the least illusion. After that situation into which Georgiana had let herself be drawn, as well as after that significant question that had surprised him as she came back into his hands, the moral level of that girl was measured. It was clear that there could never be enough love aroused in her that she would not be ready to take flight the moment an existence in which the perfumes and the other superfluities, as necessary to her as bread and air are to others, were absent. Evidently, then, that intoxicating and sensual felicity, which for Alexis had hardly begun, was at the mercy of what the publicists and economists call the financial question. To align a rational budget of expenses with a budget that didn't fall into deficit, that summed up the solution to the problem caused by Georgiana.

It was then that the traces of a wish, at first very vague and hardly perceptible, were revived in Alexis' thoughts. Let someone tell us how many men escape that fatal axiom, follow our interests, our principles! And isn't it very marvelous when between these two contradictory forces, there is established a battle that the ability of most minds can turn the question into a form where that antagonism can be reconciled?

Left to his natural inclination toward right and honesty, Alexis, at the first moment, had only seen in the condition of an employee of the *Secret Bureau* a tainted and unworthy profession. The day that the hardness of Princess F*** had condemned him to look for, at any price, a way to take care of Georgiana's future, that resource, being a desperate light presented to his mind, he had immediately discarded it, because the functions that his father wanted to invest in him continued to present themselves to him in a bad and repugnant aspect. But later, when it was a matter of having his happiness safeguarded, there is no way to imagine the prodigious number of arguments and knowledge that presented themselves to color in some other way the hereditary necessity against which he had at first rebelled.

The result of that sudden illumination, which we will dispense with giving its course in detail, was that, one fine morning, presenting himself before the worthy author of his days who, for some time, in parentheses, he had greatly neglected, Alexis said this to him:

"Father, you see before you the prodigal son. Will it please you to receive him with mercy?"

"Do you mean to say," Hulet the elder answered, "that, cured of your unreasonable prejudices, you have come around to your destiny?"

"Yes, I thought about it," Alexis answered rather hypocritically, "and dependence for dependence, I would prefer that which places me under the hand of my father to that of a foreigner."

"But I am told that you have left the house of the Ambassador from Persia," Hulet the elder remarked, no doubt to make the refractory son understand that, without it appearing too obvious, he had not stopped keeping an eye on him.

"He was a ridiculous man," Georgiana's lover answered, turning very red, because he had a horrible fear that, while learning about the rupture with Mirza Babba, his father had equally found out about the strange companion with whom he had left the Embassy. It appeared, however, that the paternal inquisition had received no detail about that subject, since the Director of the *Secret Bureau* was content to say:

"And since then, how have you lived?"

"I had a very ridiculous job," Alexis answered casually. "I gave lessons in literature and geography in an institution for young ladies."

Hulet the elder just shrugged; then he added:

"Well, then, boarding schools are not a more agreeable habitation than Embassies?"

"No, I told you, father, depending on you seems to me more honorable than going earn my bread in a hard way among strangers"

"You will not depend on me," the inquisitor of letters answered seriously, "you will depend on a function of which I suppose you have now thought about the great importance, because I warn you, it's a serious job."

"That I will do seriously, father; I beg you to believe that. But I dare hope, at my age, you will not make me have an existence as severely limited as yours. Thus, for example, so as to not t trouble your habits of retirement and solitude, as I did in the past, I would desire to be permitted not to live with you, under the same roof."

"I am annoyed that that is your desire. That great attachment to the pleasures of the world isn't a very reassuring symptom to me."

"But, father, maturity can't be improvised. You, yourself, like me have been young."

"All right, so be it! I count at least on your prudence. Now, there remains for me to explain to you the duties and engagement you are going to assume. The first, the most imperative of all, that goes without saying, relates even to the existence of the *Secret Bureau,* an absolute, inviolable discretion."

"Am I not myself one the first to be concerned?"

"Then you must wait. Many secrets that you must bury and guard as if in a tomb will come into your hands, but above all, is that at no price, for whatever reason, you must not allow yourself to serve a personal interest, or even a privileged interest any of the revelations that you might have collected. In that disinterest lies all the morality of our institution. Never act except with a thought of the public order. That is how it is lifted to the height and dignity of a magistrate."

"I understand that," Alexis answered.

"Yes, but it must be understood as one of the laws of narrow duty, the violation of which no transgression, just as no excuse, will be permitted. And, see! Here is an example of the inexorable rigor with which among us the least fault of that kind is carried out: One of our men suspected the faithfulness of his wife. A letter that he intercepted in his functions procured him the way to confront the guilty man, and in this sense he used his discovery. Well! even so excusable as a misuse of his discovery might be, before our justice, he found no forgiveness. Today, he is atoning in a State prison and he is forever banished from our ranks."

"That is perhaps a great deal of security," Alexis couldn't keep himself from remarking.

"Who would complain about it," Hulet the elder quickly answered, "when forming among ourselves a sort of family tribunal, we are the ones who judge the offense and award the punishment. There is still more. On the express demand that I made to the Emperor, when it was a question for me to accept the presidency of an association that I wanted at the same time to enlarge and moralize, invested with high and low justice, we ourselves are the executors of our arrests, apart from some extremely serious cases, we have not had to refer to the Head of State."

"I see, in fact," Alexis answered, "that in your hands, what I took at first to be a low method of espionage, has become a kind of Holy-Office, of which you are the Grand Inquisitor. And as for me, I have no more repugnance to become one of its members."

"You have said it, my son," Hulet the elder answered with a kind of pride. "It is the Inquisition, without its atrocities and its terrible torture, functioning in the interest of the State, and placed higher than the horizon of the monastic domination. Until tomorrow then—your entry into functions. The salary for the position in which I intend to place you, is twelve thousand livres a year; you will be ostensibly attached as official interpreter to Constantinople for the Ministry of Foreign Relations. You will be primarily responsible for the surveillance of diplomatic dispatches."

Now, in the boudoir of Georgiana, the comfortable and radiant Alexis, the bouquets of Madame Prevost, it seems that everything has been explained. Without being like the famous Zamet,[59] lord of seventeen hundred thousand écus of income, Georgiana's lover had at least enough for her to live on, and, in addition, a way to explain to himself his means of existence.

He would have nothing to fear, as Georgiana naively said, from the judgment of the *Qadi*.

XXV. The Woes of a Happy Lover

It was in the year 1811 that Alexis, in the disorderly state of his love affair, decided to become part of the *Secret Bureau*. That sacrifice accomplished, to say he found in the possession of Georgiana happiness without clouds, would perhaps be going too far. A hard first necessity that he had to submit to was to let his protegée occupy alone the delightful little retreat he had found for her. To share it with her was impossible; there were too many chances that scandal might reach the paternal ears and put the morality of the new employee in dangerous and regrettable suspicion.

On the other hand, in that isolated and relatively independent situation, in those circumstances, how many traps could be set for Georgiana by her radiant beauty and her inexperience! Just to see the mass of hornets that came to buzz

---

[59] Sébastien Zamet (1549-1614), a very wealthy banker.

around his good fortune, in the rare occasions when he showed himself in public with his mistress, Alexis could easily calculate how the proprietor of such a rare treasure might have some enterprising minds prejudiced against him. And in many ways, despite his youth and his personal advantages, he often felt that he played the role of Bartholo[60] having some flighty Rosine to guard.

In many ways, however, Georgiana could seem to be reassuring, because the more he lived with her, the more he saw that, lacking sensitivity and heart, she would with great difficulty be led away. But it must be admitted, also, as that strange girl made progress in European ideas and customs, she developed a prodigious instinct for flirtation. Now, without ever giving any serious cause for jealousy, a woman with that character, never ceases being an agitating and worrying possession. Attractive and provocative to all, she never was absolutely decisive. But with her airs of abandon and unsure virtue, she remained nonetheless, a guardianship that took much time. And with that eternal worry to spare himself beginning commitments and false steps, it was difficult for the patience of a lover seriously smitten not to feel himself cruelly tried.

Another matter of worry was that Herminie, the girl who had had detestable projects concerning Georgiana, hadn't given up her role and her dangerous influence as easily as one might have been believed. Alexis still got wind of some hidden intrigues against his property and his woman. At the same time, it didn't seem to him that he had all the information that he needed from the beautiful obsessed girl about those secret enterprises that caused his concern. And he didn't find that they were obliterated by the virtuous indignation and hot anger that he himself experienced.

---

[60] A character from a comic opera of Pierre-Augustin Beaumarchais, *The Barber of Seville* (1813). Rosine is an orphan and the ward of Bartholo, who plans to marry her, but she is already in love with Count Almaviva. Bartholo's clever and roguish barber, Figaro, brings about their marriage.

But independent of all these snags to his perfect happiness, the poor young man couldn't be slow to recognize that, in another way, Georgiana threatened to become a terrible embarrassment for him. Having followed that life of a recluse throughout her youth, finding before her, finally, an open field, with the ardor of someone newly freed, she tended to rush into pleasures and expensive dissipations of Parisian civilization. And, everything considered, the salary of a *Secret Bureau* employee didn't seem to be able, for an extended time, to pay for the furious passion for expenditures that the beautiful debutante showed. It was useless for him to condemn himself to the most severe economy; just in gloves, lingerie, and in perfume, Georgiana was a ruinous expense for him. And what must make the sad cashier give some thought, was that devouring creature, on one of the points where she showed herself the most incorrigible, did not have any plan formed to limit herself. Without having the least conscience, come into the world with the instincts of a courtesan, that escapee from the harem, was an abyss which, with the wave of a hand, could swallow up the best established fortune. From that, it can be judged what must be the poor twelve hundred francs Alexis poured monthly into that wind storm.

Seeing his feeble resources become more and more insufficient, nevertheless, so dearly procured, and the debts, like a rising tide, beginning to encircle his life, the desolate young man had twenty times decided to break off an attachment so menacing for his future. But he wasn't yet at that dulling of pleasure brought about by long use. Dominated by charm, he put off breaking the chain from day to day, and he clung foolishly to his dangerous happiness, as incomplete and combative as it was.

Finally, toward the month of May 1812, Alexis received from the march of political events the strength, and, to be more accurate, the Imperial duty for that affranchissement, the courage which he had never before found in himself. The famous Russian Campaign began then, and, in the middle of that mass of diverse nationalities and interests linked together by force, that he called his *Grande Armée*, the Conqueror of Europe must have foreseen as possible the chance of too many diplomatic felonies not to have surrounded himself with some precautions. An employee of the *Secret Bureau* was then attached to the head of the État-Major Général, with instructions to secretly extract information from the correspondence of a great number of people, and Hulet the elder, happily inspired, although ignorant of the irregular life of his son, obtained that important mission for him.

While often having wanted the chance for one of those ruptures which, by the force of circumstances, arrive for a gentle parting, Alexis, when the moment came for a separation, was only aware of his cruel bitterness, and leaving with heartbreak, he dared to carry with him the infatuation even to the point of believing it possible that at the distance he was going to be from his love, Georgiana would be unshakably faithful. The reasons for which he could lean on such an unlikely foreseeable future he had strongly kept from telling himself; but, after all he would hope because he had hoped and he would have been too cruel to himself not to have any hope. And Georgiana's cold disposition gave a chance for him.

To say that the beautiful child, on the subject of his doubts, gave all the promises proper to give him confidence, would certainly be useless. What woman, at the moment of a departure, refuses those sorts of words and who doesn't recall that, in similar circumstances, Ninon[61] herself didn't hesitate to give a written engagement. At least Alexis, if something unfortunate happened to him, didn't want to be blamed. Each week, while the amorous young man often delayed writing to his mother, who loved him passionately, he sent to the dis-

---

[61] Anne "Ninon" de l'Enclos (also spelled Ninon de Lenclos and Ninon de Lanclos) (1620-1705) was a French author, courtesan, freethinker, and patron of the arts, mistress of famous aristocrats, friend or benefactor of Racine, Molière and Voltaire, among others.

patch rider of the Prince de Neufchâtel a long letter to Georgiana. No less regularly, he sent a sizeable part of his salary, and, in several occasions, his good services having merited him a bonus, his dearly beloved also immediately received the generous supplement.

From the Géorgienne's side, the correspondence was less well received. Her letters, with noticeable brevity, didn't recommend themselves by their very warm feelings. But Alexis still found an excuse for that. The poor girl, as has been said before, hadn't greatly profited by the lessons he had been pleased to give her. To write, then, became a chore for her. She knew better how to be beautiful than how to express herself, and, probably, if Madame de Sévigné [62] had been more richly endowed with physical attractions, her epistolary renown wouldn't have come down to us so highly regarded and resounding.

Finally, by his great willingness to be deceived, the young man's illusions continued right down to the terrible retreat from Moscow. And if it's permitted to bring together two situations in size and importance so different, the disaster of Alexis' love life and that of the giant whose fall soon resounded throughout Europe, broke out almost at the same time.

On evening, the army already in retreat, when the disorganization was beginning to reach the ranks, Alexis was seated near a bivouac fire when a letter was brought to him which had been searching for him since the evening before. That letter was in an unknown handwriting and his astonishment can be imagined in reading the following:

---

[62] Marie de Rabutin-Chantal, Marquise de Sévigné (1626-1696) was a French aristocrat, remembered for her letter-writing. Most of her letters, celebrated for their wit and vividness, were addressed to her daughter. She is revered in France as one of the great icons of French literature.

Monsieur,

Mademoiselle Georgiana isn't ignorant of the fact that you take advantage of the boredom of absence, and she has been very carefully told about more than one friendly distraction that you haven't thought you should refuse yourself since your separation from her.

Mademoiselle Georgiana didn't need to learn by these multiple acts of inconstancy, the very mediocre attachment with which you honor her, and those constantly renewed scenes by which you make her harshly feel some small sacrifices you make for her, have made her know that she is a heavy burden to you that you wouldn't be unhappy to be free of. Your wish, Monsieur, will become fact, Mirza Babba has remembered a woman to whom he knew how, better than you, do justice. He has just given to her a sum with which my friend can in the future do without any assistance. She therefore quickly returns to you "all" your freedom.

Nevertheless, Monsieur, while doing this sensitive duty toward you, Mademoiselle Georgiana asks me to tell you that it is, in certain ways, very painful for her, because, no matter how people act, one hasn't lived for some time in a close relationship without leaving a little of her heart there. I believe that, in truth, the poor girl is still weak enough to love you. But her pride, as sometimes happens in lofty characters, has stifled her tender sentiments, and after the much forgetfulness, for which you are guilty, she has only one thing to say to you: that is, that henceforth "everything between us is over."

Please accept, Monsieur, the assurance of my most distinguished sentiments,

Your very humble and very obedient servant,

Herminie Daliron

For poor Alexis, that signature was a complete revelation. It was that of the fatal Assistant Headmistress, that he had always regarded as one of his dangers. Since he had managed to get her out of his path, during the time when that wicked woman had come to prowl around Georgiana, he thought he was certain that she was far from Paris. He had counted without her when, on his departure for the war in Russia, he had begun to calculate his good and bad chances during the absence to which he was condemned. That girl was meddling, that was sure, and he was not duped by the pretended memory of Mirza Babba. That was an honest way to explain some infamous traffic into which Georgiana must have been drawn. All that odious wealth spoken about for her, meant that girl without shame or heart was forever lost to him.

But what seemed to him to pass all limits was the shameless way and the audacity in which she wanted to make him seem guilty when he was the victim. To take as proven, what was at the most probable, to claim to have the right to throw his memory to the wind, without his having explained or defended himself, was truly Machiavellian. Now, precisely in the present case, the resemblance to reality wasn't reality. Vis-à-vis that creature that he had so foolishly loved, Alexis had been guilty of no kind of infidelity, and in the middle of the great carelessness of life in the bivouac, he had almost had to defend himself from ridicule for that rare regularity of conduct. So therefore, the imputation under which Georgiana was trying to shield herself was clearly shown to be false. And the only thing she established was an unbelievable perversity of imagination revealed by the woman who dared blame him.

What's more, that masterpiece of duplicity clearly accused its author. It showed too much stratagem and depth for Georgiana to be capable of it. It was that abominable Assistant Headmistress, who, after having destroyed all the poor young man's happiness, and had told him about his disappointment, believed she had still found a way to stifle the cry of his heart and to gag him.

However, Alexis found two benefits in the blunder of that process. By the movement of violent indignation that he felt in his heart, the stiffness of the blow he had just been dealt, was lessened and deadened. Then, almost at the same moment, caught up with the rest of the army in the horrible disaster of the retreat from Moscow, having to defend his life

173

against the fury of the elements, by not even caring, in the state of his mind, whether he lived or died, he found instincts against danger which were, perhaps, his best chances of survival.

Thus, managing to get himself out of the middle of the terrible confusion of the Imperial catastrophe, he made his way rapidly to Paris, where he flattered himself that his presence wasn't expected without a certain mental anxiety by the guilty women.

XXVI. A Woman's Revenge

The unhappy man almost always moralizes. On arriving in Paris, totally occupied as he was with his sad adventure, Alexis thought first of all about his family duties. He ran to rue Barbette embraced his excellent mother, whom we have seen he didn't always have present in his thoughts, while he kept all his memories of the unworthy passion which, unfortunately , he couldn't be said to have entirely gotten over. From the Marais, he went to the rue du Helder, to the apartment where he had left Georgiana living at his departure. He hoped to learn from the concierge the location of the place she had gone.

Everything is not rosy in the profession of the Orpheus looking for their Eurydice. And to suffer the compliments of condolences which began when he addressed the people from whom he asked information wasn't a small humiliation. But at least he obtained all the information he wanted and here's how his sad adventure was told to him.

To tell the truth, Georgiana's relationship with the Assistant Headmistress had never been suspended. Even at the time when he thought himself the most relieved of the visits of this demon temptress, they continued furtively and immediately after his departure for the army the dangerous girl had in some way taken his domicile rue du Helder, where a single day didn't pass without their seeing each other. Nevertheless, for some time, Georgiana's existence continued to appear regular.

There was no change in her habits which could incriminate her conduct. But one day, it was noticed that, brought by Mademoiselle Herminie, a tall and thin old man, who on the outside looked almost poverty-stricken, paid a visit noticeably prolonged. The next day, Mademoiselle Georgiana left with her friend, announcing that she wouldn't be back in the evening and that she was going to spend some days in the country. After that, she hadn't been seen.

But her maid had been seen, and through that girl it had been learned that, lodged in a townhouse, rue de la Chaise in the Faubourg Saint-Germain, his mistress had a carriage, servants, and magnificent furnishings. Something that rendered all these details almost unbelievable is that the author of all that fortune was the old man that could easily have been taken for a beggar. However, not content with taking care of the fate of Mademoiselle Georgiana, he had installed Mademoiselle Herminie Daliron near her as housekeeper and lady companion.

What's more, everything led to the belief that this benefactor was very unusual. Some days after his conquest, he came to the rue du Helder, accompanied by a decorator to whom he had sold all the furniture of the apartment. When everything seemed to indicate that he was royally rich, he showed himself unbelievably stingy and greedy in the bargain that he was said to have made. As for the name of that miser, the thing the only thing he could recall was that he was very well known in the financial world. That information added to Georgiana's address, was more than the amorous questioner needed to be able find the inconstant mistress and the rival from whom he intended to demand a devastating account.

Without losing a moment, Alexis went to the rue de la Chaise and the gossip there of the establishment and the beauty of the Géorgienne, didn't take him long to find the lodgings he was looking for. On entering the townhouse, immediately pointed out to him, he was struck by its grandiose proportions, but at the same time, a subject not less astonishing, dilapidation was present everywhere. After having gone across a vast courtyard, where grass grew up through the paving stones, he came to a porch which the vigorous growth of plants through the tiles had caused it to be off balance. Only the first floor seemed to be inhabited. As for the upper floor, closed off with French shutters on which thick layers of dust, joined to the action of heavy rain water had almost entirely corroded the paint, it showed abandon evidently going back some years. On the walls, where the paint was peeled off in large places, letting the dark color of the stone show through, there was the same lack of care as in the urgent reparations equally neglected on the roof, more gravely important.

An old concierge, whose rough and poverty-stricken appearance was in perfect harmony with all that appearance of ruin, responded in a tone partially polite to Alexis' demand to be admitted to see Mademoiselle Georgiana. Nevertheless, that cold reception tended rather to an instinct of that bad tempered doorkeeper than to an order given him to turn away the guests presented: "On the porch opposite!" he finally said, and at the same time he sounded a little bell connected to the apartments by which people were alerted.

After being introduced into the vestibule paved with marble, which followed the porch, the visitor was transported in some ways into another hemisphere. On the outside there was desolation, no trace of upkeep or even of simple conservation. On the inside, on the contrary, there were all the signs of the most elegant luxury. Thus, in the entry way, notwithstanding the advanced season of the year, there were flower pots filled with blossoming flowers and rare plants. Responding to the concierge's bell, there appeared a lackey wearing expensive livery. After Alexis had given his name and after the lackey left to see if *Madame was receiving,* he was taken into a drawing room where, to an experienced eye, the furnishings would not have appeared, perhaps, of a perfect and irreproachable unity, but rather as if blown from the four winds. The splendor and richness of all the furnishings that decorated that room were such that its colorfulness could as well be due to the proprietor's fantasy as to an example of his economy.

The visitor had had time to glance about at this unusual collection of riches, when, a lateral door being opened, he suddenly found himself, to his great astonishment at such rare audacity, facing Mademoiselle Daliron. Carefully dressed, she appeared with the casual air of a mistress of the house receiving an expected visit. While having noticed that at her appearance, a certain trouble, even a great manifestation of disdain and anger had appeared on Alexis' face, that girl didn't appear the least in the world worried by that menace of hostility. Noticing that served as an introduction for her. She graciously pushed an armchair toward her guest and in a tone which asked for peace:

"You seem to be very angry with me, Monsieur," she said to him.

"Angry with you?" Alexis said, continuing to stand, "that would be to say too much and not to say enough at the same time."

"Yes, let's not mince words," the young woman said, smiling, "definitely contempt.'

Alexis answered only by nodding his head sharply, meaning that his opinion had been understood.

"Well!" replied the former Assistant Headmistress, "it is against that feeling that I intend to defend myself. Will you listen to me a moment?"

"I wanted to see Mademoiselle Georgiana," Alexis answered drily.

"You know very well, Monsieur, that what I can have to say to you is not very far from the reason that brought you here."

"But, then, does your virtuous friend refuse to see me? Are you here in her name?"

"In my own, Monsieur, in order to explain to you that, very far from owing me your disdain or your hatred, you owe me, on the contrary, your gratitude."

"That at least promises to be new and original."

"Well! Please take this seat. I must go into some detail, and, to see you in this way badly situated to listen to me, I won't be completely free to tell you everything."

The remarkable serenity of the speaker and the unusual subject that she proposed to discuss, were not without exciting Alexis' curiosity. He then decided to sit down, but he was careful to keep an expression of great disbelief. This prevented at the same time that, with a studied air of impatience and boredom, he seemed to want to show a kind of moral violence which he regretfully suspended.

"Monsieur," said Mademoiselle Herminie, as soon as she was sure that he was listening to her, "to love a woman is not to understand her. It's rather the contrary that's true."

"From that you conclude?"

"That in attaching yourself to Georgiana, you dug an abyss under your feet. Believe me, Monsieur, women understand each other better between themselves. I have carefully studied that dangerous girl. I had a reason to."

"Yes," Alexis said ironically, "a noble interest."

"You don't know me, Monsieur," Herminie replied with dignity, "and you don't know my past. I have been beautiful also, not as beautiful as Georgiana, but more attractive perhaps, because I had a soul and a heart which showed in my eyes. That beauty was fatal for me. An orphan, without a future, without a protector, I saw myself, from my earliest youth, exposed to all the pitfalls of seduction. A woman of the hideous kind that you believe to be mine, managed to deliver me to the libertine appetites of a man whose immense fortune made him a most dangerous temptator. That man is the man I have brought as your successor to Georgiana. Do you now begin to understand?"

"Yes. I read somewhere that Madame de Pompadour knew how to keep herself in the good graces of Louis XV, in taking under her patronage even the Parc-aux-Cerfs."[63]

---

[63] Stag Park. Madame de Pompadour, once the mistress of King Louis XV, but later only a friend and political ally, was

Under that cruel insinuation, the Assistant Headmistress became animated. Her eyes, for the first time since she started that conversation, showed an expression of disdain and anger. Then she continued:

"It was not a question for me," she said, "of keeping the splendors of the position as a favorite. It was a matter of getting the better of an infamous process. You, yourself, Monsieur, you will be the judge. God wanted to punish me for where I had failed. One day His Hand chastised me. A disfiguring malady menaced that beauty from which I had found my ruin. Then, what did that man, made up entirely of two passions, lechery and avarice, do? Not doubting that my end was near, he had me taken to a hospice. Later, only my beauty having suffered under the attack of the evil, from a life of luxury, where he had maintained me so long as I was beautiful, he threw me to public charity. He would have had me submit to its most humiliating form if I had not kept that pride that is the salvation of the moral being, even when it has been the most profoundly diminished."

Alexis couldn't help being moved and wanted to retain his anger, that he felt himself losing it despite himself. He couldn't keep his eyes from showing a certain interest. Encouraged by the effect she saw she was producing, she continued:

"I indignantly rejected that man's insulting charity. In the middle of deadly privations, I had the courage to study and provide for myself an existence, although miserable, in a way dignified and respectable. Then, that done, I took a solemn oath to myself, that of avenging myself."

---

said to have created a house near the palace of Versailles which she stocked with beautiful young virgins, who formed a kind of harem for the King. Madame de Pompadour was said to have chosen the girls herself and to have supervised their training.

"But if, as I now believe I understand it, Mademoiselle Georgiana is your revenge, I'm the only one who has paid for it.'"

"Yes," the Assistant Headmistress said, solemnly raising her arm, "as God is God, Georgiana will be my revenge. Either by the possession of her charms, which *he* is going to foolishly wear out, must finish drying up the sources of life in him, or that the genius of prodigality that I found in her must shake the foundation of that fortune, selfishly and dishonestly acquired, and that he has never spent except on the most brutal passions, I tell you that girl will be disastrous. Your former mistress is not a woman at all; she's a beautiful envelope where I have never been able to find one heart beat. Like Helen of Troy, destined to become the destruction of all she approached, she is already beginning to have the most disastrous influence over your life. And you are so bitterly and rigorously asking me to give you an account for having taken that fascination away from you!"

"But I don't see," Alexis replied, parodying the somewhat emphatic sentence of the Assistant Headmistress, "that either the sources of my life, or that of my *fortune,* have very considerably dried up."

"Your fortune!" repeated Herminie. "Let's not talk about that!"

"Meaning?" the young man exclaimed in a menacing tone, his conscience at that moment recalling the degrading resources to which he had descended for possessing Georgiana. A thought passed through his mind as a doubt that his secret might have been surprised and penetrated.

"Yes," continued the Assistant Headmistress, "I will admit to you, should my frankness cause you anger, I didn't like to see that sudden ease which, for a moment, put you in a position to contravene my plans."

"Mademoiselle, your profound knowledge of the human heart makes you immediately think evil."

"So be it. Let's say that I am wrong. How, at least, did that windfall come about for you that I couldn't explain to myself? Did it save you from poverty? Wasn't it slowly swallowed up in that gaping black hole that you have at your side? Poor, you were rich, because you owed nothing at all. Today, the debts that you left after you at your departure, others contracted in your name during your absence, those are already the fruits of the dangerous happiness I took you away from."

"Mademoiselle," Alexis said, rising, because he was tired of always getting the worst of it in his encounters in that rough skirmish, "that's to show a great deal of concern for my affairs. I came here to speak to Mademoiselle Georgiana."

"She refuses, Monsieur, to see you, and I have gone much past my instructions which were only to relay to you that unfriendly ultimatum."

"That is to say that an audacious sequestration..."

"Do you insist on hearing from her mouth that she does not want to see you? Come, I'm going to take you to her. That's a rashness that I want to take on myself. You will see how you are welcomed!"

Alexis had given way to a bad inspiration from his ego. He believed that his presence would be a cruel embarrassment for his flighty mistress, and he savored in advance the bitter pleasure of overwhelming her with his reproaches and his contempt.

Mademoiselle Herminie went ahead of him. With her, he traversed a long series of sumptuous apartments and finally arrived at a pretty little dressing room where Georgiana, in the hands of the famous Michalon, the fashionable hairdresser, was seated in front of a mirror, in the middle of a deluge of curling papers, curling irons, cosmetics and perfumes. As soon as the door opened, Georgiana saw Alexis in the mirror. Without turning around, without even showing an emotion of impatience in her expression:

"But Mademoiselle Herminie," she said in a dejected tone, to have it believed that speaking was fatiguing for her, "I told you, I can't see anyone. If the gentleman absolutely insists, you must call my servants."

And it wasn't at all with that atrocious humiliation, buried with that immense ridicule, that Alexis was going to end. Turning around, and going toward Alexis, his curling iron in his hand:

"Go away, young man," the artist hairdresser said to him, which must have been the culmination of all his misadventure, "be calm, be reasonable, don't force *us* to resort to violence. You are not important. No one comes like this to profane mysteries. Here, believe me, is the dressing room of Venus!"

XXVII. François-Honoré Dubignon

That strange, uncultivated man who had just installed Georgiana in the kind of splendor which we have just seen, was named François-Honoré Dubignon. He was born in a little village in Limagne d'Auvergne toward the first half of the preceding century. His parents, as a lawyer, in one of the thousand and one law suits that he was involved in throughout the long duration of his financial career, said jokingly, were poor but dishonest. Having gone to Paris as an umbrella merchant, and next an itinerant salesman, during the period of the Directoire, he was far enough advanced in his businesses to find himself linked in interest with the Ouvrards, the Desprez, the Vanterberghes, and other financiers of the period.

On the way to a fortune that had already made a rapid flight, he encountered a stumbling block. Around 1805 or 1806, certain irregularities in commercial records had drawn the attention of the legal system. The Emperor, who did not like suppliers, had ordered that case to be followed closely. But thanks to a fortunate lack of proof, all the irregularities for which he had been asked to give an account fell back on a civil servant. The judgment went to the benefit of the accused and a verdict of dismissal was given. From that moment, François-Honoré Dubignon made from this modest level of innocence the rule and measure of all the rest of his life. He rapidly became rich by that elastic regime of conscience. His disposition not less than his opulence created for him a bizarre career of notoriety, which the Imperial government had not disdained to depend on occasionally. Herminie had told the truth; his passion for money and for women summed up his character almost entirely, one moderating the other, as wine and laziness in the song did in the heart of Figaro.[64]

In fact, to satisfy his avaricious carnal appetites, that man so little given to expenditure, who neither clothed himself decently nor maintained his buildings, rarely stepped back before a sacrifice. But the reader has seen how he repaid himself by a thousand base acts, sometimes sending to be cared for by charity the woman who had ceased to please him, sometimes in turning to his profit the sale of the furnishings of his new mistress' apartment, after having installed her at very little expense in one of the numerous townhouses he possessed in Paris. These were used as so many warehouses to store the products of usury and of pawnbroker establishments that he managed at the same time as his greatest business on the Stock Exchange and in industry.

We have talked about two passions, but a third one must be mentioned for François-Honoré Dubignon, that one innocent and the least offensive. He loved passionately the game of tric-trac.[65] He was too dishonest a player for an honest man not to have thrown the cone and the dice in his face. He had set up as an opponent a scapegoat for about six hundred pounds a year. Each evening, in the company of that unfortunate man, he played his favorite game for a long time. A dubious café forming the angle of the rue Gît-le-Coeur and the quai des Augustins, was the usual theater of those encounters. That was where Herminie Daliron must have gone to find him

---

[64] See Note 60.

[65] A game invented about 1500 AD played with a board not unlike that of backgammon. By the time of Louis XV, there were two variants of it: Little Tric-Trac and Big Tric-Trac, both played a board game with fifteen pieces for each of two players. Complicated rules govern the moves of the pieces around the board.

when the delicate affair of Georgiana was brought up, since another eccentricity of that person was never to actually lodge anywhere. His habit was to go sleep on a mat in some corner of one of the numerous dwellings which he owned, that he preferred to leave empty of renters rather than to undertake the least repairs.

Going to see him under the pretext of imploring his charity, the Assistant Headmistress, at first rather roughly rejected, was enormously better received when she had come to talk about an incomparable beauty, that she knew was at that time available in Paris. The bargain was not concluded immediately, Georgiana not having come around to the idea of a Croesus dressed in rags. But things explained to her better, the former harem slave had so well repaired her clumsy first encounter that never, for any other woman, had François-Honoré Dubignon been known to show so much enthusiasm and generosity. It even happened that the fascination was carried to a very extraordinary point. Notwithstanding the fact that he did not like to pay a man whose functions were becoming nothing more than a sinecure, since he now gave almost all his evenings to his new passion, he almost never appeared anymore at his game academy, where he had made an event one day by appearing in a hat three-quarters new and in clothes passably clean. No one recalled having seen that before.

Later, there was apparently a decline in his enthusiasm for Georgiana, and he returned regularly to his little café. We found him on this field of battle one evening in combat with Alexis Hulet. But, as a preamble, we must first be allowed to tell of the way in which the poor young man had governed his life since the day when he had been so pompously shown the door by the hairdresser Michalon. Following that terrible disappointment, the unfortunate young man had gone through transports of rage which summed up his need for revenge, the only thought in his life.

Something inexplicable, it wasn't toward the primary instrument of his misfortune that he directed most of his anger. Towards Herminie, that girl who had brought everything about, he still felt secret esteem. Besides the fact that she had seen through Georgiana, since he himself had never judged her a great deal differently, he admitted that a woman treated badly had a right to take revenge in whatever way she could. But to humiliate the insolent woman who had spoken of having him thrown out by her servants, to get the best of that hideous old man to whom it would have been ridiculous to have taken any notice, and who showed him the power of money under the most repulsive form, that's what had become for the rejected lover his dream every moment. The opportunity for vengeance once presenting itself to him, he had sworn to himself to carry it through at the price of the greatest sacrifices.

Misfortune never comes alone. The Malet conspiracy [66], occurring during the same time as the disaster in Moscow, had made the police extremely suspicious. There was a redoublement of activity in the control of letters. At first attached to the Ministry of Foreign Relations, Alexis Hulet now had nothing to monitor, since no European power had any longer a representative in Paris. He was recalled to the plebeian standard post bureau so as to help the employees there, his colleagues, being no longer numerous enough for the job. Aside from the distaste that the violation of private correspondence inspired in him, that necessity to do it nightly, surrounding himself with extraordinary and infinite precautions in the place where the members of that Inquisition met, caused him constant suffering. Finally there was boredom, lukewarm zeal in carrying out

---

[66] The Malet Conspiracy against Napoleon happened he was campaigning in Russia in 1812; it was led by Republican General Claude-François de Malet, a member of the *Philadelphes* secret society. He had been under house arrest in Paris from 1810 until October 1812, when he escaped. Using the name "General Lamotte" and forged documents, he claimed that Napoleon had died in Russia and that he himself had been named Commandant of a Provisional Government in Paris. The attempted coup failed and the leaders of the conspiracy were executed.

his functions, and finally a general attitude that let it be known to the clerks, his colleagues, that finding himself superior in the work that he did with them, he hadn't voluntarily become one of them. Warned several times about this attitude by his father, the young aristocrat paid little attention to his advice. It must be said that the other civil servants rather largely returned to him the same dislike and resentment, the disdain and the regrettable presumptuousness, that he clearly showed toward them.

That dismal situation continued for more than a year. So far as Georgiana was concerned, he often had the opportunity to see her brazenly displaying the luxury of her dress and her carriages in the streets. And as to his odious rival, the consolation of some possible revenge had yet to present itself. The Empire, however, was rushing toward its fall. We were now in the first days of March 1814, and to ward off financial embarrassment, which complicated the situation even more, the Minister of Finance was negotiating a loan. Pressed on this subject with some other capitalists, François-Honoré Dubignon, hadn't shown any kind of willingness. On the contrary, some time before that, some Englishmen crossing the channel into France had brought, on behalf of Louis XVIII,[67] a

---

[67] Louis XVIII (1755-1824), was a monarch of the House of Bourbon who ruled as King of France from 1814 to 1824 except for a period in 1815 known as the Hundred Days. Louis XVIII spent twenty-three years in exile, from 1791 to 1814, during the French Revolution and the First French Empire, and again in 1815, during the period of the Hundred Days, upon the return of Napoleon I from Elba. Until his accession to the throne of France, Louis held the title of Count of Provence as brother of King Louis XVI. On 21 September 1792, the National Convention abolished the monarchy and deposed King Louis XVI, who was later executed by guillotine. When the young Louis XVII, Louis XVI's son, died in prison in June 1795, Louis XVIII succeeded his nephew as titular King. During the French Revolution and Napoleonic era, Louis XVIII

Declaration. Among other promises he made to his future subjects to help rid him of Napoleon's corruption, was the very
definite way he insisted on proposed immunity to guarantee
the sale of national possessions. Georgiana's lover, the holder
of a great number of buildings having that origin, was credited
with having spoken with praise about that Declaration, and
was even accused of having spread the word about it. As a
result, very active surveillance by the police was ordered
around his person and the Director of the *Secret Bureau* was
ordered to open all his letters and to make scrupulous extractions.

One day, Alexis noticed the name of François-Honoré
Dubignon at the head of a list of suspects submitted in their
epistolary relations to the function of the *Secret Bureau.* His
life was lit up with hope, and he had no trouble obtaining from
his father that the analysis of that correspondence, the explora-
tion of which the Government seemed to very interested, be
given exclusively to his care.

From the direction of politics, where Dubignon could be
found vulnerable, nothing came to light. For some time nothing but insignificant things were revealed in his letters. But

---

lived in exile in Prussia, the United Kingdom and Russia.
When the Sixth Coalition finally defeated Napoleon in 1814,
Louis was placed in what he, and the French royalists, considered his rightful position. Napoleon escaped from his exile in
Elba, however, and restored his French Empire. Louis XVIII
fled and a Seventh Coalition declared war on the French Empire, defeated Napoleon, and restored Louis XVIII to the
French throne. Louis XVIII ruled as king for slightly less than
a decade. The Bourbon Restoration regime was a constitutional monarchy (unlike the ancien régime, which was absolutist).
As a constitutional monarch, Louis XVIII's royal prerogative
was reduced substantially by the Charter of 1814, France's
new constitution. Louis had no children; therefore, upon his
death, the crown passed to his brother, Charles, Count of Ar-
tois, who reigned as Charles X.

one fine day, Alexis bounded like a tiger that had just seen a prey, and the same evening, knowing very well the habits of that enemy that he believed he finally had at his discretion, he went to the café at the rue Gît-le-Coeur, certain that he would find him there.

The reader is certainly curious to know the content of that missive which had caused so much joy in Alexis' heart. But to tell that content now would be to make a double use of the scene which we are going to witness shortly. So please be patient and wait until the following chapter.

XXVIII. The Game of Tric-Trac

The first to arrive at the place where his interview was supposed to take place with the man he abhorred, Alexis found the establishment in some excitement. They had just learned some sad news. The poor devil to whom Dubignon gave a pension to submit to his bad humors and his insults had died some hours before, struck with an attack of apoplexy. The odious Dubignon, arriving almost at the same time, had only one thing to say about the misfortune announced to him:

"Now, I, who paid him his four-week salary yesterday! A nice evening I'm going to spend!"

Catching the ball on the bounce, Hulet's son, approaching that man so disappointed, and speaking with great modesty about his talent as a player of tric-trac, he offered himself to replace the player who had had the indelicacy to die just the day following the day when his monthly salary had been paid.

"First of all, I must warn you of one thing," the Turcaret[68] answered roughly, "I'm not at all thinking of replacing the dead man."

Alexis protested that his offer was disinterested, and that his ambition was only to show himself the least unworthy that

---

[68] *Turcaret, or The Financier* is a 1709 comedy by Alain-René Lesage (1668-1747) about a ruthless, dishonest, dissolute financier.

he could to such a clever adversary, and the game began. Having more goodwill than knowledge, Alexis hadn't completed four plays before he had revealed the most deplorable ignorance.

"Ah! come now, my dear fellow," Dubignon exclaimed, "You're a catastrophe!"

"Do you think so?" the younger Hulet ironically answered.

"What! Do I think so? You know nothing about the game."

"Actually, that's possible," Alexis replied. "But neither do you know anything about what I have to communicate to you," and he took a paper out of his pocket.

"What's the meaning of this?" the old man quickly asked, "some beggary? My friend, I am very angry; in the evening I never talk business.'"

"It's not a matter of business. It's just a letter I would like to read to you."

"Eh! What do I care about your letters!" Dubignon replied, moving with great noise the dice around in his cone in a way so as to prevent Alexis from being heard.

"Mine, yes," Alex said, raising his voice, "but those of your friend Desmarest, in Mauriac..."

"How's that? What do you mean?" Dubignon asked, changing expressions and ceasing to agitate the dice in the cone.

"Well! Don't you have a friend named Desmarest in Mauriac?"

"Demarest—the world is full of them," answered Dubignon, whose face had gone from pale to livid, and at the same time exchanging the cone and the dice for a carafe near him from which he filled a glass of water.

"What you say is true," the young Hulet answered, "but all the Desmarest don't write in this style: *My dear and excellent friend, to have spent five years in the galleys, that's something, however...*"

189

On hearing that terrible sentence, Dubignon was so troubled that, instead of carrying the glass to his mouth, he began to shake it in his hand as a moment before he had done with the cone. Next, he poured all the contents onto the tric-trac board, with the same movement that he had used to throw the dice.

"Well, what do you want?" exclaimed Dubignon. "You offered to play a game with me and, instead of playing, you come to kill me with business. Let's see; give it to me, that letter, so I can see what it's about."

"No, I prefer to read it to you."

"Oh! *Mon Dieu*! I know very well what there can be in it: it's harping about a service I was supposed to have been rendered."

"A pretended service! You're very honest! A man who pleaded guilty to a forgery that you committed , and who went in your place to Rochefort[69] and who says he has proof of all that which he threatens you with because you refused him a poor thousand francs that he needs to complete his daughter's dowry. It seems to me it's your gratitude that's claimed, and not the service."

"But, first of all," said Dubignon, who had gotten back his self-assurance, "I ask you how you can have in your hands a letter that certainly I didn't misplace, if it's true that it was written to me!"

"Well! Do you think I could be fortunate enough to possess the original that should now be in your hands? I have only a copy."

"That is to say that this droll fellow, not content to ruin me in the delivery of letters, now believes he can frighten me with copies he puts in the hands of his emissaries. Well! Tell him that I care very little about threats. Just today, I mailed an epistle which won't make him laugh. You, my fine friend, I warn you, can take back your threat."

---

[69] Rochefort prison on the Atlantic coast-, in the Charente-Maritime Department.

"However," Alexis answered, "that letter, made public, wouldn't do a great deal for your reputation."

"All right! Make it public, if that's what you want to do. My reputation is above attacks by people like you."

With that, he rose and left the café, leaving Alexis a little shocked by the self-control with which Dubignon ended after being so emotional at first.

The next morning Dubignon was with Georgiana, who was talking to him about some fantasy, we don't know exactly what, to which he didn't want to agree. He was finally made to shout:

"If I agreed to everything, I would finally be pillaged. That's like a strange man who, yesterday evening, tried to get a thousand francs from me. But you should see how I stopped him."

At that moment a servant appeared announcing that a young man was asking to be seen.

"And who is that young man?" Dubignon asked in a harsh tone.

"He says he is your tric-trac teacher."

"My tric-trac teacher? Are you crazy?"

"Yes, Monsieur, he had me repeat it twice, and he told me to say that to Monsieur."

"So, my thief from yesterday again!" Dubignon thought aloud. And following the servant, he passed into a neighboring room where he waited for Alexis.

"Do you know that the joke is beginning to bore me?" the financier said in a superior and threatening tone. "What are you still claiming today?"

"Again a letter to communicate to you as yesterday."

"But I told you I don't want to talk anymore about this strange man nor about his letters."

"Yes, but this one, not being from him and being from you…"

"What! From me?"

191

"Exactly. Didn't you tell me you had written to that man about that affair? Well, that letter, I read it, and having read it, I find, on my word! my good man, that you are very careless!"

"So then," Dubignon said, shrugging, "since I wrote that letter at my house, that I didn't make a draft of, and that I carried to the post myself, you're going to make me believe that you have read it?"

"Yes, because you didn't pay attention to those following you who were slowly collecting the letters that you believed you put in the box, when you put them aside."

"Enough of that. You would have certainly talked to me about that letter if you had it."

"But in fact I don't have it. I don't even know that I must possess it. Did I tell you that it was me who found myself able to take advantage of your blunder?"

"Ah! Then," said Dubignon, beginning to be terrified, "you are a band?"

"Oh, yes," Alexis continued, "that poor Demarest has a few friends, and to see him get justice, each one put in a little."

"Then, what did I write to him?"

"Why! Some very little encouraging things. For example, that, without his knowledge, you had managed to get back into your hands that famous proof he threatened you with; that, besides, in a few months the statute of limitations will have run out; in essence that you were mocking him."

"All right! If I had written that, and if that were true?"

"Well! my dear fellow, you would be hanged, because even your presumptuousness proves you were guilty. Putting that letter in the hands of the Imperial Prosecutor, you can see what will happen first."

"Yes, but you wouldn't do that," Dubignon replied, pretending still to speak in the conditional, to admit, at least, that it was possible. "Desmarest still has more to gain by getting something out of me than by going to get me condemned to the galleys, because what would he get out of that?"

"Agreed. But I, who am not Desmarest, and who would take great pleasure in sending you there where he spent five of the best years of his life, I tell you that the letter will be put in the hands of the Magistrate before this evening, unless you agree to do everything I tell you."

"Ah! Then there's no way to understand that. You don't come on his behalf as you told me?"

"I come for myself. I am taking care of my own interests. Providence is just. Do you know a young man named Alexis Vandel, from whom you stole with money a girl named Georgiana? That young man, Monsieur Dubignon, is me!"

"You! Then that's most unusual still, because it's completely impossible that you have gone to unearth Desmarest in the mountains of Auvergne."

"It isn't necessary for you to understand," Alexis coldly replied. "Rich people, Monsieur, are rich people; clever people are clever people. Sometimes they have their turn."

"Young man, I am truly sorry to have caused you some unpleasantness. I didn't know that you had set your heart on that woman. Someone came to throw her at me, and, as a parenthesis, she has already cost me dearly. But, then, what can I do to make amends?"

"First of all, Monsieur, you are going to send to your friend in Mauriac the thousand francs he asked you for."

"But my dear Monsieur, since you don't even know that man, what interest do you have in him?"

"The interest of right and justice. *That man,* as you call him, has done enough for you not to bargain about that service, and I find him very naive and very simple not to ask for more."

"Well! I find it's not good for me to do business with you. You're a hard man to deal with. Let's go on: a thousand francs for Demarest. And next?"

"Next, you will take me to see your mistress, and in my presence, you will make clear to her that she will immediately leave your townhouse and no longer have any kind of relationship with you."

"By my word, you couldn't ask me for anything that's easier to do. That girl is ruinous, and I've been thinking of dropping her for a long time."

"You see, that works very well. Only, that expedition completed, to break off with her properly, you will set up for her a life time annuity of two thousand écus."

"Two thousand écus! What are you thinking about! A capital of a hundred twenty thousand francs!'"

"But which will revert to you at her death."

"At her death! I am sixty-five years old and she is scarcely twenty."

"Well! Then it will be for your heirs. What's more, a hundred and twenty thousand francs in one part, and one thousand francs in another , that still will be only one hundred and twenty-one thousand francs."

"What's that? Really! It is certainly clear, young man, that your generosity is taken from other people's purse."

"Ah!" Alexis said casually, "there is still one more thing: You have with Georgiana, as a lady companion, a person who is going to find herself without a position. I have some interest in her."

"Who? Herminie Daliron, a hussy responsible for all the business of taking away your mistress, and who is the cause for my having offended a man of your value! To be concerned about a creature like that! You aren't thinking about that!"

"But be aware that you aren't without some guilt toward her. After having abused her youth, you sent her, somewhat casually, to die in a hospice, in charity. Now, since I'm settling with you, it's also necessary to take care of this. It seems to me that a lifetime annuity as a pension of three thousand livres is right."

"Then, my dear fellow, just say immediately that you want to ruin me."

"No, not at all. Let's not get upset like that. One hundred twenty-one plus sixty thousand, that just makes a little over one hundred eighty thousand francs, and, really, for a man like you, that's a trifle."[70]

"One hundred eighty thousand francs, a trifle! And then for your part, which you haven't talked to me about."

"Me, I'm not asking you for anything."

"What! Really?"

"Exactly, and don't you believe that the pleasure of seeing so many good deeds spread around you wouldn't be a nice recompense for me? Only, we certainly must agree on our facts. First of all, you're going to put Georgiana out of your house."

"That's agreed."

"Next, you will buy a postal order for a thousand francs that, in my presence, you will mail to Desmarest. What's more, you will have the two contracts for the lifetime annuities that we have just agreed on sworn to by a notary, and you will give them to me."

"And you, in exchange for all I will have done there?"

"I will give the dangerous letter back to you and promise you, on my honor, the most absolute discretion. Only, I warn you, if I learn that, near or far, you make the smallest effort to see Georgiana again, then the war begins again, and you will see if I am an enemy to underestimate. Nothing would prevent me from getting in touch with your friend in Mauriac, and helped with my good advice and my assistance, he would seem to me someone from the country to make you see."

"All right,'" Dubignon, who didn't bargain about a sacrifice where he didn't have to spend money, said pleasantly. "We can always begin by doing what you like and evicting that flighty girl who deceived you."

"No," Alexis answered, "it's the entire plan that I have had the honor to submit to you. I don't want to deal with the provisions one at a time. Tomorrow morning at the same hour, I will have the pleasure of seeing you again. You will have

---

[70] Note that here Rabou is dealing with francs, livres, écus, all in circulation throughout France at that time.

taken care of everything, and then nothing will keep us from finishing."

"Listen to me, young man," Dubignon said, seeing Alexis ready to leave, "you're acting here with a chivalrous intention. You want to force me to waste my money on a crowd of not very interesting people, and aren't thinking about yourself in all that. Let's do something better. Let's leave aside all those despicable people, and between you and me, accept fifty thousand livres that I offer you right now. Fifty thousand livres, that's a nice sum!"

"Yes," Alexis said, laughing, "that's more than a quarter of the hundred eighty thousand francs I asked. But after reflection, I hold to what I first said. So, it's understood. Until tomorrow."

"Until tomorrow, so be it," Dubignon replied, and to himself he added, "Twenty-four hours, that's still a long time, and there's time to turn things around without being seen."

XXIX. The National Debt

Some information here will give an idea of the good order and the clever direction that the administration of the *Secret Bureau* presided over at that time. While doing his best to find out how his persecutor had gotten hold of his letters, Dubignon didn't doubt that a procedure involving public safety could explain that removal. The fact is that, at that time, very few people had even suspected the existence of that governmental machinery. The sound of cannons and that of glory drowned out all the others. Besides, that's the way of all well constructed and well operated machines. They function noiselessly and without any din. Today, two side-wheels and a simple steam engine silently do all the work that the fourteen gears, the twenty-eight cranks, the hundred and thirty force pumps and suction pumps that in the past constituted the deaf-ening apparatus of the now useless Marly Machine.[71]

It was different for the regular police. As for the great reputation that Fouché had created in that section, while doing very little work, witness the Malet Conspiracy, where it had played such a ridiculous role. The Imperial Police was consid-ered by the public as a sort of magician, for whom everything was possible. It was then in that direction that, after many plans and projects made in his head, Dubignon decided to turn. He thought about a man in that administration with whom in the past he had had a relationship, on the occasion of a theft committed prejudicial to him. He knew that man to have great dexterity, had heard him complain about the little recognition they gave to his services, and about the mediocrity of his assignments. It seemed to him that there was some chance he would welcome being contacted. It was true that in that decision, there wasn't more than one weak side, and Dubignon was too careful not to have carefully weighted the pros and cons before coming to such a decision.

First of all, the employee he was going to contact might be an honest man who wouldn't worry about a lie, as poor as he was, in the exercise of his functions. But that hypothesis didn't get very far with the financier. His opinion was that every conscience has its price, that it was just sufficient to find out how much. And, besides, without compromising anything, he could feel out the employee by talking to him about the affair but keeping the anonymity of those involved. Even after the confidence thus broached, he left things as they were and in the same state as if he had never said anything. But where Dubignon saw a real danger was in the necessity that he would have to pass that dangerous letter that he wanted to get out of Alexis' hands into the hands of his affiliate. With this security, the policeman might want to show zeal at his expense and find it useful for his advancement to denounce him. It even wasn't

---

[71] Hydraulic-powered mechanism created in 1684 to pump water from the Seine to Versailles for its fountains.

impossible that, replacing his persecutor, that employee might have the thought of asking some huge sum for the restitution of the litigious paper. And extortion for extortion, it would be as well to keep the terms he had rather than merely switch enemies by increasing the number of those who held such a dangerous secret. At that point, all the question was there: to create in the one whose help you wanted more reason to be faithful than to be a traitor, and with the bait of a good round sum it seemed that result could be achieved.

In addition, one consideration seemed to carry the balance. The letter he was trying to recover didn't have a signature. Dubignon could, therefore, seem to be working for the profit of a third party, that he would pretend not to want to name. In that situation, there would be more ways to judge his man before opening himself completely to him. And then, in fact, he ended by asking himself what human affair could be conducted well if the result could be mathematically sure. To avoid paying almost two hundred thousand francs, was for a miser, a reason to risk something, and even more so as he put some ego into not letting Alexis, that he called *a type,* get the better of him. He went then to see his policeman, and, leaving his interview with him, he complimented himself very highly on the choice he had made.

The worthy civil servant had made just the resistance that was necessary to put an air of combat into his administrative modesty. The price of the service was stipulated at twenty-five thousand francs, that was for Dubignon one hundred fifty thousand francs gained. Finally, when the name of the holder of the letter was delivered to him, the employee carried his affability even to promising to get hold of it and return it *without having read it.* It was impossible to be more delicately obliging and to enter better into all the convenience of the situation. Leaving that conference, Dubignon felt himself free and in a good humor. It seemed to him that the weight of a mountain had been lifted from his chest. He fell back a little into his character, and during the time that passed until the hour that he was supposed to gain possession of the precious paper and pay the promised sum, he wondered if there couldn't be some ingenious way to obtain a lower sum. But that bad thought lasted only a moment. In remembering the manner, frank and cordial, with which he had been dealt, he was ashamed of himself. And twenty-five beautiful bank bills in his briefcase, he went to the rendezvous. On seeing him enter:

"Ah! There you are," said the civil servant, with the air of a man who has good news. "Well! If you will come with me, we are going upstairs to the Head of my division."

"How's that! The Head of your division? You gave a third person our secret?"

"It was indispensable. Without that, I wouldn't have succeeded'"

"But I don't at all want to do business with the Head of your division," Dubignon exclaimed. "Here is the sum agreed on," he added, opening his briefcase, showing the bank bills, the view of which he thought would produce a good effect. "It's ready and I'm holding you to our first agreement."

"I repeat to you, Monsieur, that the Head of my division has been told and he now expects you."

These words were said in a dry and commanding tone which appeared to the financier to be the worst omen. However, too clever not to know that in difficult positions, as much as possible, it's better not to show fear and avoid being unmasked.

"Let's go then," he said, "and meet your Chief."

A moment afterward he was taken into the office of the high functionary and left alone with him, the two seated side by side.

"Monsieur Dubignon," the Head of the division said, "some time ago the Government made certain overtures to you relative to a loan that the situation of the public treasury needed to bring about..."

"Yes, Monsieur," Dubignon replied, "but, without talking about the difficulties of the moment, I had the honor to

199

reply that my personal difficult situation did not allow me to enter into the plans of the Government.'

"The Government, Monsieur," the administrator replied, "is perfectly aware of the motives of your refusal. But today the situation has changed, and although I am not absolutely competent in financial things, I have the mission of renewing to you the entreaties in completely different circumstances from those that had opposed success."

"Ah! And how do you mean that?" Dubignon answered. "The circumstances have changed! That is to say that the state of things has become much worse. The Allies are right now at the gates of Paris..."

"From which I conclude," said the Chief, interrupting, "that the dangers to the country have been aggravated, the situation of the Treasury is more than ever difficult, and more than ever there is need for devoted and immediate assistance from all good citizens."

"Ah, put like that, it's true, and, in fact, all good citizens must be ready to make every sacrifice; but I understand that as meaning good citizens in general, the good citizens taken as a whole, since, in such great need, what can the devotion of one individual do?"

"Very much, Monsieur, as an example first of all; in the matter of a loan, contagion is very useful. Then, there are private individuals who are in a quite exceptional position, and from those, more outstanding sacrifice could reasonably be expected."

"Finally, Monsieur," Dubignon, not holding back his impatience to see his position clearly, "to leave off generalities..."

"Yes, and to get away from them in a good way, here's what it's about. The idea of a loan that was mentioned to you is more than ever present. But the Government needs someone to launch it; you understand, like the judas sheep that is put to walk at the head of the troop and make the others jump over the more difficult spots. Well! your great fortune, your high financial reputation, seems to point you out better than anyone for that role. And it's on you, I hasten to tell you, that the Government in its need, in its desire, to succeed, has believed it should cast its eyes."

"Very flattering," Dubignon answered. "But if the situation of the Treasury is worse, mine, unfortunately, hasn't gotten any better, but I am in a position to subscribe for a little something…"

"Well," the Chief of the Division replied, "some ground has been gained with you. Some time back you refused out of hand, and today you are at least disposed to help the State with something."

"Well, damn! Yes, with some amount that will not go beyond a certain figure and which I will be able better to set when I have been told the conditions."

"Here are the conditions," the Chief said, taking a paper from his desk that he presented to Dubignon.

"You are making a mistake," Dubignon replied, after having glanced over the paper. "There is no trace of figures there."

"Oh! I beg your pardon," said the civil servant. "I gave you the copy of a very unusual letter that came to us following an attempt at corruption directed toward an employee. But, even so, read it; it's curious and of a nature to interest you."

"That's not necessary," Dubignon answered, beginning to be very worried. "The conditions of the loan?"

"Well! here they are, my dear Monsieur Dubignon. By tomorrow at noon you will commit to us a sum of two million, for which you will be kind enough to write me a check on your bank. I will sign a receipt to you, and as soon as the difficulties of the Treasury are over, you will be authorized to come here to claim the capital plus the interest."

"A wonderful debtor I'll have there!" Dubignon said, carried away by the wound in money done to him, "the State that in perhaps a week will be topsy-turvy, and that is now using a forced loan."

"Monsieur Dubignon, you aren't considering the fact that foreseeing certain misfortunes of the country can sometimes be considered a crime, above all when, beyond public calamities, hopes are indulged where it wouldn't be impossible to find a smell of high treason."

"As you like, Monsieur," shouted Dubignon, ceasing to control himself. "I'm being made a victim of infamous atrocities."

"Stop right there, Monsieur!" shouted the high functionary, standing up with dignity. "You are calling an atrocity what is a very mild and paternal form of justice. The two millions that you are asked for to pay the army in Paris, until the moment that the Emperor will have come to liberate his capital, before God and before men, as the head of a jury may soon say, you owe them! That letter, that you didn't dare read as I watched, establishes that in an affair where the State got the worst of it from you, it was four times right. Do you want us to place the question before the Criminal Court? If that letter is produced, there can be no doubt. Thank us for not asking you, with the capital, as arrears, your honor, and be aware that in leading you to pay a debt, you are left the rare satisfaction and the supreme good fortune to render a service to your country."

"Considered like that, the thing can be accepted," Dubignon answered, very softened. "But at least you are going to give me that letter?"

"And a receipt in the form of a discharge of accusations," answered the Chief.

Both sides began to write and a paper was presented.

"Very good!" said the Chief, after having read the money withdrawal notice. At the same time he took from his pocket the accusing evidence and he said to Dubignon, "Here is your letter."

Dubignon, with a convulsive movement, was going to place it in his briefcase, but changing his mind, he approached a lamp and saw the post mark distinctly.

"Monsieur," he then shouted, "this is an infamy! That letter wasn't, as I was made to believe, put by accident beside the mail box; it's evident the Government has letters opened."

"You are mistaken, Monsieur," the Chief answered. "Dishonesty, committed at the office of departure, effectively made the young Alexis Vandel possessor of that document. But proof that the Government is foreign to the intervention that your temptation of corruption has made him the only one to profit is that orders have already been given that the author of the extortions practiced against you be severely punished."

"All right," said Dubignon, after having looked for his hat for some time like a man disoriented by all that had just taken place. "You win. You are the strongest!"

And he left.

XXX. Sardanapalus[72]

A quarter of an hour later, some people who met the old miser walking up and down the Palais Royal galeries, were convinced that everything about him looked like a drunk or a madman. After having made a tour of the Arcades several times, he went to sit down on a bench in the garden, where,

---

[72] Sardanapalus was, according to the Greek writer Ctesias, the last king of Assyria, although in actuality Ashuruballit II (612-605 BC) holds that distinction. In Ctesias' account, Sardanapalus lived in the 7th century BC, and is portrayed as a decadent figure who spends his life in self-indulgence and dies in an orgy of destruction. The name is probably a corruption of Ashurbanipal, the last great Assyrian emperor, but Sardanapalus as described by Diodorus bears little relationship with what is known of that king, who in fact was a militarily powerful, efficient and scholarly ruler. Ashurbanipal died of natural causes in 627 BC. Greek legend holds that Sardanapalus was the son of Anakyndaraxes, however it is known that Ashurbanipal was the son of the Assyrian king Esarhaddon. The legendary decadence of Sardanapalus later became a theme in literature and art, especially in the Romantic era, exemplified by the painting by Eugène Delacroix, itself based on the 1821 play *Sardanapalus* by Lord Byron.

despite the very cold temperature of the evening, he remained seated for almost a half hour, gesticulating, speaking to himself in a loud voice; in short, showing all the symptoms of the greatest agitation. It was also told that when he had finally gathered some people around him, he suddenly stood up, went up to Number 129 in the arcades, where he gambled, throwing on the counter napoleons [73] in tens where he lost with calmness that would not have been expected of his avarice. Only, when he had sacrificed that sum, as if he gotten the result of an experiment, he was heard to say:

"All right, that's done. It's a worn-out vein."

Leaving the gambling house, he went into several jewelry stores, where he purchased a considerable number of diamonds and gems, with which he filled his pockets. He then went into Chevet and ordered a supper that he had sent to his townhouse on the rue de la Chaise. He himself went there by carriage, which was against all his habits. It could have been eight o'clock, eight fifteen, when he arrived. He learned that Georgiana, accompanied by Mademoiselle Daliron, had just left for the Opera, which didn't seem to him unusual; he had learned about the Opera project that morning.

After that, he employed all the servants in the house to do various extraordinary errands. In that occasion, whatever could be expected from his bizarre character appeared surpassed. So, an house later, one of the people he had sent into the neighborhood, appeared, carrying with him all of the detonators, explosive fireworks, Chinese lanterns and small pieces of devices that he had been able to procure. It seemed that unusual man intended to give a party in his townhouse, although neither the outside temperature nor the political situation seemed very favorable for projects of celebration.

Two hours later, two or three vehicles filled with fodder, that he had to pay an exorbitant price for in order to get them delivered in such a short time and at such a late hour of the evening, appeared in the courtyard of his townhouse. And

---

[73] Gold coin minted in units of 5, 10, 20, 40, 50 and 100.

instead of being taken to the barns, all that hay and all that straw was, by his order, spread out in the apartments on the ground floor, even in the rooms occupied by his mistress.

While this was being done, the supper had arrived. He had the place settings laid out in one of the large salons, the only one not transformed into a feed store. He ordered that the chandeliers and candlesticks were to be filled with candles and lit. Then, as it was not yet the time that Georgiana was to return from the theater, he occupied his time by increasing the combustibility of his Chinese lanterns, pouring on them the several liters of turpentine he had sent a servant to buy for that purpose. He ordered all the windows as well as the doors of the townhouse to be lit up. Then he went to Georgiana's room to get a magnificent house coat with Persian designs, with a size not too unsuitable for his height, and thus decked out, he began to write a letter which he immediately had sent to the post. It was addressed to *Monsieur the Secretary General of the Hospices of Paris.*

That letter finished, it was sent to the post just as he heard the noise in the courtyard of the carriage returning Georgiana. Taking then a torch in each hand like a well-practiced host going to receive the visit of an august personage, he went up to the Queen of the place. One can imagine her astonishment, when, already wondering what the illumination which lit up the courtyard could mean, she saw herself greeted by Dubignon, grotesquely dressed in one of her housecoats, and showing her by the light of two torches his thin and pale face, wearing a majestic seriousness, which excluded the supposition of a joke he had thought of. What appeared even stranger to Georgiana, and most of all, what was less to her taste than all the rest of the eccentricities which she was witnessing, was seeing her apartment become something between a barn and a stable.

"Are you crazy, Monsieur?" she couldn't help asking.

"No, but I am farseeing and philanthropic. Some days from now, there will be a great battle for Paris. I want this house to be transformed into a provisional location for a hospital. For the lack of bedclothes, which I couldn't procure in sufficient quantity, I've had brought here the things to get them."

"That will be nice," said Georgiana, not entering the least in the world of philanthropy.

"Then I certainly hope right now that your beautiful hands won't disdain to tear up old linen to dress wounds. But while we're waiting, we should celebrate a little."

And he took Georgiana into the splendidly lit salon where the supper had been laid out.

"That's better," said the courtesan, who found herself in her element, "but before taking advantage of your gallantry, please allow me to go take off my frills and put on, as you have, a more comfortable negligée."

And Georgiana left, followed by Mademoiselle Daliron. As soon as they were alone, the courtesan said to Herminie as both were changing dress:

"You're going to give me a strong scolding."

"And why would I scold you?"

"That's because I've made an enormous blunder. How could I know that the old fool would surprise us this evening and would be here when we returned from the Opera, and probably will spend the night here."

"That's probably not very likely, but what does it matter? He's not always as gallant as this."

"*Mon Dieu*! What a terrible idea I had!" Georgiana continued, talking to herself.

"What's wrong?"

"Well!" Georgiana replied, speaking very fast, a rather ridiculous instinct of people who have a difficult admission to make, as if the words flowing faster would leave less trace, "tormented this evening by that young Colonel whom you know has a passion for me, I have allowed him to come into the garden with a promise to see him for a quarter of an hour, to hear the very serious and very personal thing that he said he had to say to me."

"You must have lost your mind."

"No, because I intended to take away a little of his joy, by having you find us in a tête-à-tête without it seeming arranged."

"Then why that rendezvous?"

"Ah! Because I noticed that Princess F*** never took her eyes off him all evening. I didn't want him to go back to that pedant. Besides, he leaves tomorrow to rejoin his regiment, and with his arm still in a sling, his wound hardly healed, there is every chance I will never see him again."

"And at what time is he supposed to come?"

"At midnight he must be in the big side garden. He knows the way. I drew up a plan of the house some time ago. He swore to me that he intended to have me kidnapped if I didn't show myself a little more welcoming to him."

"All right, about midnight," said Herminie, a person resolute in everything, "if we are still at the table, which is very probable, I will leave under a pretext and go tell him about the set back."

"Good dear, always my savior!" said Georgiana, embracing her confident.

And arm in arm, they returned to the banquet room. On sitting down at the table, the two women were surprised to see several gems that Dubignon had placed in their plates with very gentlemanly attention.

"Monsieur," Georgiana asked, laughing, "did business go well for you today?"

"Am I not likeable?" asked the financier. "Here, that's not all."

And he took out of his pockets a part of the jewelry he had stuffed there, so much that Georgiana and Herminie, to whom he distributed it, could hardly believe their eyes. He next told his guests, that, like at the little suppers of the Directoire and the Regency, everyone should serve himself, since, for more privacy, he had sent all the servants on errands outside the townhouse. Then they began to have supper.

Dubignon, who was usually perfectly sober, showed that, on the subject of temperance, he had equally modified his habits. He ate with sensuality, poured himself ample glass fulls, and was not less a good conversationalist than he was in doing honor to the food. He had fits of gaiety, more and more arrogant, intermingled with continual distribution of jewelry and precious stones, that gave him a distant resemblance to Aladdin in *The Thousand and One Nights.* This amusement continued for some time, right up until the clock in the salon struck midnight. The old miser, who at that moment hardly merited that epithet, with a serious expression, listened to the bell strike twelve times

."Now," he said, in a strange voice and rising from his seat, "we're going to have a laugh."

And then, with no more explanation, he left the apartment.

"What's wrong with him?" Georgiana asked immediately after he had left. "I find he has a gaiety that frightens me. Could he suspect something?"

"That's not very likely," answered Herminie, "but nevertheless the time has come to go see your handsome officer."

Saying that, leaving by a different door, she also left the salon. A few minutes had hardly gone by than Georgiana saw her come back in, her expression excited, her voice altered.

"We are lost," she shouted to her friend, "Dubignon is completely mad. He has just set fire to two or three places in the townhouse. The flames are already reaching right to here."

And as a testimony to that frightening news, they heard the noise of explosions from the devices that the lunatic had placed at several points among the straw spread out in the adjacent rooms. An odor of powder, of smoke, and the fumes of the burning turpentine spread throughout the house. Seeing their danger, the two women rushed toward a window where they tried to open the shutters which were held in place by a heavy iron transversal bar. That obstacle wasn't easy for them to move. At that moment, the madman who had set the fire reappeared. His first act was to turn the key in the door locks, as he saw his guests' preparations for evasion:

"What! my little chickies," he shouted, "you want to leave me just at the most beautiful moment?"

And passing from speech to action, with an arm to which his excitement gave an unusual strength, he interposed himself to restrain the fugitives. The women, on their side, pushed by terror, sustained the fight energetically while the explosions of the devices multiplied and thicker and thicker smoke invaded the apartment.

Suddenly, behind one of the windows that Dubignon was trying to keep Herminie and Georgiana from approaching, a noise outside sounded, indicating that someone was forcing entry through. A little astonished by that unexpected intervention, the maniac left off for a moment his resistance to his prisoners' efforts. Taking advantage of that instant's relaxation, Herminie threw herself against the bar holding back the shutters and managed to open them. Almost at the same time, Georgiana opened the lock on the window behind which there stood a young man with his arm in a sling. With his free hand he rapidly helped the two women climb across the window sill, and from there they were safe.

Thus abandoned, Dubignon didn't make any effort to pursue the prey that had escaped him. On the contrary, he closed the window again and barred it carefully. Next, with feverish activity, like a man who feels he has only some instants to finish his work, he took all the furnishings in the room and stacked them one on top of the other until the pile they formed reached a considerable height. That done, he ran into a neighboring room which the fire had not yet reached, and gathering up an armful of inflammable material, he placed it alongside that pile of rubbish, which he set on fire. Next, to speed up the activity of the combustion, he went to open a door facing a long suite of apartments leading from the salon which was already on fire.

Then the crowd that had run into the townhouse to bring help as soon as the fire broke out saw a strange sight. From a distance, across an ocean of flames, that no one would have thought of crossing without running into certain peril, they saw a man climb onto a kind of pyre, his arms crossed, seeming to wait with serenity an inevitable approaching death. That spectacle didn't last but an instant, a whirlwind of flames and fumes having come to put an end to it.

The next day, when the place that had been the theater of the conflagration could be entered, they found in the middle of the debris some calcined bones that were carried to the cemetery under the name François-Honoré Dubignon, to be buried in a rich sepulcher he had a long time before had constructed.

Many explanations relative to that tragic end were given after the fact and the care the dead man had taken to bequeath by a letter in the form of a handwritten will his immense fortune to the Paris Hospices surrounded his memory with a posthumous good will to which the conduct of his entire life didn't seem very much to have destined him.

The version prevalent in the public was that the unhappy man was overcome by a kind of amorous despair following the infidelity of his flighty mistress. And that death, let it be said in passing, was followed some days later by the glorious death on the hills of Saint-Chaumont of the brilliant Colonel who had snatched Georgiana from the flames. That was the beginning for the murderous beauty of a public craze and fashion where the terrible name of *The Bloodied Girl* was everywhere in vogue.

But Dubignon wasn't one of those men that can be pushed to the extremes that we have seen by the loss of a woman. That fine of one hundred eighty thousand francs, that Hulet the younger had inflicted on him, and the circumstances so wounding for his ego, and, at the same time, so disturbing for his future, that had surrounded that first misfortune, had naturally upset the unhappy old man.

It is understandable that a two million franc fine, as a substitute for the one he had tried to decline, didn't bring him any great consolation. Most of all, he didn't pardon himself for the lack of caution with which he had thrown himself at an incorruptible civil servant who had played him this bloody turn. In addition, like all men who have had much to thank fate for, Dubignon was superstitious. He believed in a lode of good luck, in a star, and from the day that he saw his honor threatened, at the mercy of the police, and delivered over to what he called its extortions, he judged that his good luck had abandoned him.

And after a last and visible experiment that he went to carry out at a gambling table, he took that abandonment as definitive and declared. He preferred a quick and sensational end to that slow wearing away of his happiness and fortune to which he thought he was destined. It's possible also that the perils that surrounded Paris, which saw at its gates the out-posts of the Allied Army, had greatly troubled his mind. In addition, there's one comment to make. In avarice, when it's a character's passion, there is always a certain dose of insanity. It then remains presumable that, while making the prepara-tions for his last passage with truly marvelous lucidity and presence of mind, Dubignon had succumbed to that access of cold and reflective madness that is almost always the law of voluntary death, even when it is carried out with the most ap-parent cold-bloodedness.

XXXI. Tying Things Together.

It's rather rare that Providence fully shows all the part in the action that it pleases it to take in the conduct of human things. But when it does consent, as here, to let us be present at that latent work through which it leads a destiny to the pre-cise terms it has marked out for it, the spectacle of that infer-ence is too curious to follow for us not to stop for a moment to recapitulate the march and the successive development of that very obvious fatality that hung over the Hulet family.

About '89, Hulet, the present head of the *Secret Bureau,* seemed to have been shielded by his father from the necessity of their inheritance. But, in a sad flight through so many sta-tions, priest, Dominican, Grand Inquisitor at Malta, brought back to France on the wings of the Revolution, apostate monk, member of the Convention, and finally a regicide, he has finally come back to his point of departure, and accepted, even with some eagerness, that condition of existence that a vainly foreseeing wisdom had declined to accept for him.

In his turn, the first born among the children of Hulet the Apostate, Alexis, had to pass through the same narrow path laid out for those of his race. Some years after his birth, an unexpected chance to steal him from the embrace of that destiny appeared for a moment to open up. But it was exactly the love of his mother, refusing to let him be adopted by a stranger, which had closed for him the way out. When his hour came, his father tried, if one can speak this way, to make him enter the slot marked out for him. The ardent young man rebelled and resisted, and it seemed that his instincts of honor were going to preserve him:

"You will come back," the Director of the *Secret Bureau* had calmly told him.

And, in fact, brought back by a mad love affair, the predestined man came to put on the yoke. And now, the relative honesty that at least was possible for him in that inherited position, in the middle of the tempest of his passions, could no longer be preserved. A liar in order to get revenge, he was now exposed to all the consequences of that regrettable decision. Probably the Will on High, little accustomed to giving the Hulets credit for His Justice, was not slow in demanding an account and expiation. At that point, the influence of Providence, which at first had developed slowly and patiently, seemed to have hastened its blows.

The same day that Alexis had triumphantly gone to see Georgiana's lover and dictated to him his conditions, the police had learned of the abuse of his functions by a member of the *Secret Bureau* through Dubignon's imprudent attempt to corrupt a police official. Two hours later, the imprudent young man, as well as the letter he was going to use to get Georgiana away from the miser, were in the hands of the authorities.

Here again a cruelty of destiny was manifest. In the blind calculations of human prudence, a long time before, it was Hulet the elder himself who had made it certain. It is recalled that, to set up an honest ministry, he had not wanted to have anything to do with the Police Administration. What's more, in the hope of making the *Secret Bureau* moral, as he said, he had reserved the right to hire all the employees under him. He had instituted inside that corporation, of which he was the supreme head, a kind of disciplinary tribunal set up to judge the misdeeds of its members.

Jealous of its functions, like all powers, the Police had several times made claims against that independence in which the *Secret Bureau* was placed vis-à-vis them. Some battles, with a certain amount of bitterness, were even started on that subject. Following those debates, the *status quo* had been maintained to the profit of Hulet. As little as one wishes to recall the liveliness that ordinarily the disputes of prerogatives take, one can imagine the joy of the Police in catching in a serious mistake the son of that fortunate antagonist against whom they had not been allowed to prevail until then.

As soon as Alexis Hulet was arrested, the following letter was addressed to his father:

The Minister is informed that one of the employees under your orders has been guilty of a serious breach of secrecy in his functions. A letter he intercepted, instead of being placed under the eyes of the Government, to which it could bring important information, became in his hands, the instrument of an ignoble extortion. Immediately arrested, the guilty man is at this moment at your disposition. It is believed, that in this circumstance, as in all the others, you will claim the right to submit to your interior justice, the arbitration of the punishment incurred for that forfeiture.

Please accept, Monsieur, the receipt of the present, and believe me, etc.

P. S. I notice, in rereading this letter, that I omitted to tell you that the name of the guilty man is Alexis Vandel. Might that unfortunate man be one of your relatives?

A relative of Hulet! The traitor pen that had sharpened the lines that we have just read like a dagger, knew very well that Alexis was his son. That revelation was a lightning bolt for Hulet the elder. Probably, neither for himself, nor for his family, had he counted on a happy future, but misfortune coming to visit him in this way as a stain, didn't find him prepared. What he had above all not foreseen was that, with his son, guilty, and having incurred a penalty that everything foresaw as terrible, he himself would be called on as one of the first to lend his hand to that justice. However, there was no way to misunderstand. The letter that he had received called on him to have that painful courage, and had been sent to him as a challenge.

In addition, if that intimation hadn't come to him from outside, he had to expect the same requirement even from the men who served under him. As he planted the tree, so he must gather the fruit. From a shameful institution, he had claimed to make a kind of magistrature. Beginning then as preaching his example, he had asked of his collaborators seriousness in manners and austerity in life. Then, in order to maintain that level of virtue, he had encouraged habits of vigilance and mutual censorship among his subordinates, founded on the principle of solidarity that he wanted to establish among them. From that, among those men whose occupation and common destiny should have brought them close together, doubt and defiance continually fermented, and there was a constant and almost general absence of any affectionate feeling and fraternity. Existences lowered in class by reverses in fortune, egos pushed to despair by not being able to find in society the place they were ambitious to have, or people with the disposition of Hulet himself, having a marked taste for power, and loving under that clandestine and almost infernal form which put at their mercy all the most mysterious arcana of human thought, such were the elements that made up that type of secret society, of which that former Inquisitor was the soul.

But the passions that usually ferment at the bottom of occult associations, fanaticism, pride, the disposition for mistrust, cruel instincts, are also to be found. When it's a question of keeping all those irritable, primitive natures in one bundle, because they basically do not fit well with the conscience, this result could only be achieved by inexorable firmness, tempered by the most rigid sense of justice. That *physiology* of the *Secret Bureau* once known, could it be said it was possible that Hulet could appear before those men, remembering that, in the past, he had been their judge, but this time faced with the degrading accusation that Alexis was his son? His first thought was to recuse himself, but that would be to take away that prestige for incorruptibility that was his strength. On the other hand, to associate himself with that arrest, would perhaps to hark back to Brutus,[74] because in every instance, he himself had preached pitiless severity. The accused, independent of the seriousness of the fault, must have against him the hateful austerity of his judges, which, in advance, it may be remembered, he had brought on himself by his haughty behavior and his airs of disdain.

One chance remained for the unfortunate father, that of letting the serious associates proceed according to the cruel jurisprudence that he had been the first to introduce among them, then to secretly refer the case to the Head of State, that assuredly would interpose himself before the execution of the sentence, if certain measures were overlooked. But, as we have pointed out, that was not a resource, it was only a chance, because at any moment, the Avant Guard of the Allied Army might begin its assault on the capital, and the Emperor had delayed his return from day to day. Unfortunately, the *Secret Bureau's* justice was as speedy as it was severe.

---

[74] Allusion to Shakespeare's *Julius Caesar*, Act III, Scene II, in which Brutus, alleged to be Caesar's illegitimate son, and one of his assassins, says of the Emp[eror in his funeral oration, justifying his participation in the murder: "It is not that I loved Caesar less, but that I loved Rome more." For Caesar read Alexis, and for Rome the *Secret Bureau.*

Thus it was on March 28, 1814, a date to take note of in the history of the Hulet family, that Alexis appeared before the tribunal formed of all the employees and his colleagues assembled by his father. The accused didn't try to deny the infidelity of which he was guilty, but he protested violently against the charge of trying to commit extortion from Dubignon. Either because the judges had decided in advance, or because the explanation that he gave had not convinced them, even after he had restored his true character and reasons for the act, he continued to be regarded as having been guilty of dishonesty, and all with one voice decided that he had to pay with his life because the security as well as the reputation of the Society had been compromised to such a high degree.

We are mistaken. The death sentence was not unanimous. Only one among all the members of the tribunal found that the spirit of revenge in which Alexis acted was a powerful motive for minimizing his sentence, and he refused to vote with his colleagues. But the indulgent judge was not Hulet the elder. With an appearance of inexorable firmness, he judged with the others that his son had deserved the death to which he was condemned, the first time that in the *Secret Bureau* the cruel sentence of capital punishment was delivered. There was, therefore, no precedent for that terrible formality. That fearful question that in the past, under Cromwell, had been posed to another Hulet by Lieutenant Walker was asked again here: *Who will be the executioner?*

A terrible and frightful solution to that difficulty had been given by the murderers. They had cast dice for the hatchet that struck Charles Ist of England. That wasn't the fortune of the game here, but a serious delay of fate which, as in the other cases, the judges of the Association had to designate the executor of the sentence. And here the head of the *Secret Bureau* surpassed Brutus, Peter Ist and Philippe II of Spain, *those three who drank their own blood,* as a great poet said of them. Declining the officious intervention of the one who, after having refused to pronounce a judgment of guilty, asked at least that the father of the condemned man be dispensed with wit-

216

nessing the execution, Hulet wanted his name to be placed in the urn with those of the other judges. And then, on whom do you think the providential designation fell when a Hulet dared to place himself in its path?

With that second thought of Hulet the elder to have the *veto* of the Emperor intervene, our readers will explain to themselves the prodigious tranquility he showed on receiving his bloody mission from the hands of fate. And he didn't share the astonishment which struck the harsh judges when they saw him coldly discuss with them the way in which the execution of the sentence would be carried out. The result of the deliberation was this: Absolute control was given to the executioner to dispose of the life turned over to him; he was given three days during which he could choose his time, his place, his methods. They only required of him an oath that he would not warn the victim in his hands, who must not even be told of the sentence. They acknowledged to themselves, in fact, the danger that the possible escape of the condemned man would cause the *Secret Bureau*. No longer having anything to fear from it, he could spread their secrets everywhere.

From his former opinions, Hulet had at least kept the religion of national feeling. The day following the condemnation of his son, would have then been for him full of perplexity. That day, which was March 20, he heard, with all of Paris, the famous Proclamation addressed to all the inhabitants of the capital by Joseph Bonaparte, Lieutenant General of the Empire and Commander-in-Chief of the National Guard. That Proclamation was thus conceived:

Citizens of Paris, an enemy column is advancing toward Meaux. It is moving across the road to Germany, but the Emperor is following it closely at the head of a victorious army. The Council of the Regency has provided for the safety of the Empress and that of the King of Rome. I am with you. Let's arm ourselves to defend our city, its monuments, its wealth, our women, our children, everything that is dear to us! May this vast city become an armed camp for a short while and may the enemy be shamed under these walls that he hopes to scale in triumph! The Emperor is marching to our aid. Let us second him by a short and active resistance and save French honor.

More than anyone, Hulet the elder was waiting with anxiety and impatience for the return of the Emperor so loudly announced, because it was at the same time the salvation of Paris and that of his son. But in the evening, he learned that the enemy was at the gates of the capital, and that, instead of the Emperor arriving at the head of a victorious army, Marshals Marmont and Mortier,[75] with some weak remains of the troops they commanded, had taken positions to give battle the next day.

The night of May 29 to 30, the *Secret Bureau* met as usual, but it couldn't be said to function; besides, having only a small number of letters to examine, expecting that the couriers had been cut off at a number of points, their preoccupation was too great. Some of Alexis' judges, however, had the nerve to speak about him to Hulet and wanted to find out what dispositions had been made. To that, Hulet answered drily that *he had three days* and that, when it was time, he would give an accounting. The meeting discontinued, the executioner of the sentence climbed up to the attic of the Post building near where the archives for which he had custody were located. There, in a room that somewhat resembled the famous Piombi

---

[75] Auguste Frédéric Louis Viesse de Marmont (1774-1852), French general and nobleman who rose to the rank of Marshal of France and was awarded the title Duke of Ragusa. Adolphe Édouard Casimir Joseph Mortier, 1st Duc de Trévise (1768-1835) was a French general and Marshal of France under Napoleon I. He was one of 18 people killed in 1835 during Giuseppe Marco Fieschi's assassination attempt on King Louis Philippe.

of Venice,[76] Alexis had been placed since the night before and he knew nothing about anything that had transpired on the outside.

"My son," Hulet the elder said to him on entering, "I warned you that the functions you asked to be given, after at first having declined them, were grave and serious duties. In addition, I told you that the least dereliction of duty would be punished by pitiless justice. It pleased you to use your holy ministry to satisfy your worldly passions. Punishment hasn't been slow to follow. Yesterday, you were condemned to die, and following the curse that hangs over our family, fate has designated me to carry out the sentence."

"A weapon, Monsieur," Alexis cried out quickly, "and I will spare you the terrible duty you have assumed."

"No," Hulet the elder replied, "you won't lift a desperate hand against your self, and I, your father, will not be reduced to being your executioner. The country's misfortunes leave a less sad issue at our disposition. The enemy is outside Paris. At daybreak tomorrow, the battle will begin and, on our side, at least, it will be bloody, since the Emperor, by a maneuver difficult to explain, has left only a handful of soldiers to do battle with the innumerable hordes. You are going to come with me to embrace your mother and your sister. Then, from there, in the ranks of the National Guard, we will go together to confront the enemy's bullets. At least our blood will not flow uselessly for our country."

---

[76] Piombi (The Leads in English) is a former prison in the Doge's Palace in Venice. The name of the prison refers to its position directly under the roof of the palace, which was covered with slabs of lead. In winter, these slabs let the cold pass and they acted as a catalyst in the summer heat, imposing harsh conditions for inmates. In 1756, Giacomo Casanova made a famous escape from the prison. He published the story of his escape in 1787.

"I, yes, I will go," Alexis answered quickly, "but you, father, have not at all failed in your duty and no sentence of death has condemned you."

"You are wrong. The same sentence has condemned both of us, you in your life, me in my honor. And with the horrible duty that fate has made a necessity for me, more than you, I need this refuge of a glorious death."

"But my mother! Helena!"

"We will transform their names into an honorable and respectable one, a name to which you have again increased the stain. The widow and the sister of two soldiers who died on the field of honor won't be pitied. That's a nice title to wear."

"But, without me, without my sin, you would never have thought of this sacrifice, which nothing asks of you, neither your age, nor your functions."

"Listen!" said Hulet. Hearing the sound of drums in the distance, he interrupted his son. "They're beating the call to arms. We don't have a moment to lose to join our brothers in arms. Come."

The farewells that Alexis made to his mother and sister could not be described as heartbreaking as they were. Admirable in firmness, the father and the son let nothing be seen of their own emotions, and they easily persuaded those from whom they were separating that, called up only for security services, they wouldn't leave the heart of the city and would run no great danger as a consequence.

Arrived where the Eighth Legion was assembled, when Marshall Moncey,[77] who then commanded the National Guard, addressed their battalion and told the citizens the most accustomed to the use of weapons to take firing positions outside the barriers, they were the first to leave the ranks. Going in the direction where the battle was the most intense, they were seen all morning firing from the most perilous positions,

---

[77] Bon-Adrien Jeannot de Moncey (1754-1842), 1st Duke of Conegliano, 1st Baron of Conegliano, Peer of France, Marshal of France.

notably in the attack from the woods and the village of Romainville, where the nature of the soil prevented mass engagements. Then there took place a battle so furious and so relentless that, mixed with those firing from the Boyer Division, they never ceased risking their life, taking no care to shield it. .

But death, that capricious thing that seems to refuse the encouragements of those looking for it, didn't accept their sacrifice. And while there was such a great harvest of death around them, no bullet hit them. Later, when succumbing to numbers, the defenders of Paris were forced to abandon Pré Saint-Gervais and to retreat to Belleville, instead of following the retreat, the two Hulets veered to the right and reached the Père Lachaise Cemetery. Its walls had already been crenellated for battle and a certain number of volunteers from the National Guard were still holding out against the enemy.

Remaining among the last to defend that point, it was already close to five o'clock in the evening when the suspension of fighting which had just happened, extinguished throughout the line the noise of guns and artillery. So long as the heat of combat had lasted, neither the young man nor the old man had felt their fatigue; the fever of action had sustained them. But when silence took the place of the tumult of the battle, and they had used their last bullet, a kind of prostration took hold of Hulet the elder. Before going back down to Paris, they sat down on a mound of stone and looked sadly at the immense panorama unfolded at their feet. Nature, that day, wasn't insulting, as too often happens to the sad emotion that has run its course. A gray and gloomy sky had, during the whole day, veiled the sun. Only at sunset, it pierced the clouds for a moment, and its rays drowned in the evening fog, appeared like a bloody globe floating over the great vanquished city.

"Father," then said Alexis, approaching the old man who had caught his breath, "you're resting before having finished your work, and that sentence that you must execute?"

"God apparently doesn't wish that it come about," responded Hulet the elder, "because you and I have confronted death enough. It didn't come."

"But here is its kingdom; we are alone; the place, the time, everything is favorable to settle the account that you delayed," continued the condemned man.

"We have more nobly repaid our debt; come to my arms; everything is forgiven."

"You are forgetting the kind of men you command. It will not be possible for you to maintain any discipline over them if you don't do the *thing* you have been charged with."

"And do we know that tomorrow that Association won't be dissolved? The Empire at this hour is like the sun which descends on the horizon."

"If not the Empire, another government will claim your services. Didn't you said that even the great Revolution of 1789 didn't free us?"

"That's to insist too much on a horrible idea," Hulet the elder said, standing up. "I now feel I have enough strength to start again on our way. Let's not stay here any longer."

"Take this, father," Alexis said, handing his gun to the old man. "There is still a bullet in the left chamber. I didn't send it to the enemy, reserving it for myself. I must admit to you, to make you decided to do what is your duty, that life weighs heavily on me, and in default of your hand, mine will strike."

"Then give it here," said Hulet the elder with impatience.

Taking the weapon, he stepped back several steps. But, instead of turning the gun on his son, he pointed it away into the distance and pulled the trigger. A strange thing happened. As if an invisible hand had directed the bullet, like that of Freyschütz[78] as soon as it had been fired, Alexis bent over

---

[78] From the German folk tale *The Marksman*. A contract with the Devil gives the Marksman seven bullets. The first six allow him to shoot and never miss. The Devil reserves the seventh for himself. His bullet hits the Marksman's fiancée. Carl

once, then he fell heavily, his face onto the ground, without saying a word, without giving a sigh, and he no longer moved.

"But that's impossible," cried out the unhappy father, who had thrown the murderous weapon far from him and run to the victim.

Nothing, however, was truer than the tragedy he didn't want to believe. The bullet had penetrated his son's left temple, where there was visible a little round hole. The brain had hemorrhaged and death must have been instantaneous.

"Oh! our fate!" cried Hulet the elder, striking his forehead, "but nevertheless must it be believed that it extends even to the miraculous!"

At the same time, as his eyes looked about for the bullet that must have ricoched so terribly, he noticed, some steps away from him, a white marble monument from which he had dislodged a large piece. And then he couldn't doubt the terrible Hand of Providence in what had just happened, when he saw written on the marble, in golden letters:

IN MEMORY OF
FRANÇOIS-HONORÉ DUBIGNON
Former supplier of the French Armies.

Getting up his courage to deal with the terrible blow that Fate had just dealt him, he lifted the inanimate corpse of his son onto his shoulders. He had to stop a number of times along the way, because he was bent double under the weight. He managed in this way to reach the barrier, where he put his sad burden into an ambulance.

The next day, the National Guard that, after the capitulation of Paris, remained armed and patrolled the place concurrently with the Allied Forces, and could render military honors to the young defender of the fatherland.

Maria Friedrich Ernst, Baron von Weber, made the tale into an 1821 opera. There are other versions, including one by E.T.A. Hoffmann.

His funeral services were held at the church of Sainte-Marguerite, the parish closest to the place where his mortal remains had been placed. From there, he was taken to the Père Lachaise Cemetery. The workers who formed the population of the adjacent streets spontaneously followed his convoy.

Contrary to the custom in Paris, where parents do not go to the funeral services of their children, Hulet was in charge of the mourning. He was careful to invite the *Secret Bureau* employees. Only one among them turned down his invitation; that was the man who had not wanted to vote for the death of the unfortunate young man. What's more, he did not go up to Hulet, nor come to shake his hand. Neither did he say a word of sympathy to him. He let it thus be understood that he suspected that merciless man to have profited by the sad circumstances in which the country then found itself to execute the mission which he had not hesitated to take upon himself.

PART IV. THE BELL ROCK LIGHTHOUSE

I. The Widow Cagliostro

At the time when Hulet the elder was called to direct the *Secret Bureau,* which makes our story go back to the last months of 1799, a fact of a rather extraordinary nature had been brought to his attention. Every day, for several weeks, the employees charged with unsealing letters, had seen pass under their eyes, a voluminous letter written on slick and perfumed paper that the first morning mail delivery never missed finding deposited in the central box at the Post Office Building, situated as it is today rue Jean-Jacques- Rousseau. The return address was always in the same hand: *Madame Lorenza Feliciani, Cagliostro.* After that name, there was no precise address, but always a different name, often that of one of the European capitals, and more usually that of one of the great Italian cities, as if the tireless correspondent believed his daily envoy had more chances of being delivered to the object of its vague address on the other side of the Alps.

With the advent of Bonaparte to the Consulate, the Jacobin Party had just lost its last hopes. The only chance that remained to it was that of conspiracies and underground secret meetings. The authorities then directed their serious attention to the place of the intrigues where it was reasonable to believe they were at work. In addition, that name of Cagliostro[79] was

---

[79] Alessandro Cagliostro (1743-1795). Pseudonym of the Italian adventurer, thief, magician, and freemason born Giuseppe Balsamo. He practiced medicine and occultism in Italy, France, and Spain, was a world traveler and a favorite of Louis XVI and the Versailles Court. He became a glamorous figure associated with the royal courts of Europe where he pursued

that of a man who, among the precursors of the French Revolution, had played a considerable role. It was concluded that, through that correspondence, done in some way undercover, some of the plots of which the Consular Government had a foreboding could be uncovered. As a consequence, a great number of those letters, because of the bizarre nature of their address, seemed to call for the attention of power, were opened and read. But no interesting revelations were found that seemed to merit the perseverance of that inquisition. Not carrying a signature, those incomprehensible epistles all ended with a postscript indicating that response should be directed to M. X. B. in the same city to which they were addressed. As to their content, it was comprised of an eternal reiteration of the complaint of an unhappy lover, lamenting the memory of a short felicity which had for him only the duration of a dream and to which he asked to be returned. Besides, if this subject could be reproached for not being sufficiently varied, its monotony was at least redeemed by a certain merit of style and a warmth of expression where the fervor of a passionate heart in love would be difficult to misunderstand.

However, not stopped by that apparent insignificance, the *Secret Bureau* saw only one more reason to confirm its suspicions and to redouble the activity of its surveillance. By means of that ink called *invisible* which, when applied has no color, but reappears when heated, nothing was easier than to insert between the apparently most innocent lines important conspiracy and diplomatic secrets. The amorous sighs that

---

various occult arts, including psychic healing, alchemy and scrying. He was prosecuted in the Affair of the Diamond Necklace which involved Marie Antoinette and Prince Louis de Rohan, and was held in the Bastille for nine months but finally acquitted, when no evidence could be found connecting him to the affair. Imprisoned several times in several countries, he was condemned to death in Italy but his sentence was changed to life in prison by the Pope. He had married Lorenza Seraphina Feliciani (1751-1794) in 1768.

could be thought to serve as a passport for more serious communications, were then submitted to examination by the most powerful detecting reagents and the past-master of the *Secret Bureau* in those kinds of operations used all his knowledge to bring out from the paper the mysterious information that it was suspected to contain. But that work was a sheer waste of time, and nothing inserted between the lines was revealed in the writing. There remained the possibility of a desperate sick monomaniac with a mad imagination.

No further attention was given to those letters that decidedly appeared to be only desperately erotic. Also, at the end of some time, their source, which until then had flowed so abundantly, seemed to have suddenly dried up. From that, the somewhat specious conclusion was drawn that the sad lover, wearing out his patience, had finally given up. However, he had been slandered. Four years later, at the end of November, the interrupted correspondence suddenly began once more, and the name of the Widow Cagliostro again obsessed the letter-openers of the *Secret Bureau.* After the second apparition of that epistolary phenomenon, the opinion, generally, among the employees of the mysterious little office, was that no importance should be attached to the reproduction of a fact that, notwithstanding all the cares of the most active surveillance, had ended only in revealing perfect nonsense.

The impression of Hulet the elder was, however, different. Here is his reasoning: It was about the time of the 18 Brumaire [80] that those unusual missives had begun to be noticed. Now, they began again at the time when the Imperial Throne has just been constituted. Their appearance, therefore, coincided with two serious failures by that incorrigible Republican party which always instinctively blames its disappoint-

---

[80] The coup of 18 Brumaire (9 November 1799) brought General Napoleon Bonaparte to power as First Consul of France, and ended the French Revolution. This bloodless coup d'état overthrew the Directoire, replacing it with the French Consulate.

ments on conspiracy. Thus posed, shouldn't it be admitted that, despite all contrary appearances, these irritating epistles could be attached to some underground network, whose name will be discovered later, and while waiting, shouldn't the most careful control of them be continued?

Whatever the justice of that point of view, in foreseeing plots and shady networks, the Director of the *Secret Bureau,* it must be recognized, showed a far-seeing and judicious mind, since from that time the work of those secret associations, agitated France, Italy, and Germany secretly, and weighed at the end so heavily in Napoleon's destiny. Among those secret societies that, under the Empire, had their center of action in France, two, in particular should be pointed out. The first, called the *Philadelphes,*[81] had as its historian, in the ardor of his youth, one of its members, who afterwards became a famous writer, his ardor extinguished in the bosom of that association less occult and more innocent, called the *Académie Française.* Everyone has read *Histoire des Sociétés Secrètes de l'Armée et des Conspirations Militaires* [82] and it's known that the *Philadelphes* were a moderate republican affiliation, having its most active and its most numerous ramifications in the Imperial para-military political organizations. It's known

---

[81] Masonic lodge founded in France in the 1750s and which became a centre for conspiratorial revolutionary activity. It had close ties with French revolutionary Charles Nodier who mentioned it in his book on the subject (see below) published in 1815. In the beginning it was made up mainly of French émigrés. From 1852 onwards, it had close ties with the political group *La Commune Révolutionnaire*, which it appears to have founded, as all of the prominent members of one organization were members of the other. Although some associates of Blanqui were involved, such as Jean Baptiste Rougé and Theophile Thoré, they did not play a prominent role. This was taken rather by Montagnards or Jacobins, most of them with a long track record of conspiratorial politics.

[82] Attributed to Charles Nodier. (Note from the Author)

also that its founder and its principal figure was Colonel Oudet,[83] a most distinguished officer who died at Wagram, not without some suspicion of an ambush. A fact less well known is the affiliation of General Moreau,[84] for a short while the leader of a vast military plot. Crowned by two Philadelphes' plots nipped in the bud was the famous Malet Conspiracy,[85] all this pointing out, up until 1813, the existence and the action of secret societies, without the police being, for a long time, able to catch them red-handed.

A great deal less pure in its elements, and having, besides, a rather ephemeral existence, another secret society existed under the Empire. That one was rather narrowly connected to the history of the *Secret Bureau*, so it will be necessary to give some circumstantial details about it. For several years that society was able to hide its existence and its organization completely from the vigilant eye of the police. Founded by an unusual man, whose character will be sketched in some detail shortly, it began to function almost immediately after the establishment of the Consular Government, and carried the rather significant title of *The Society of the Sleeping Lion.* To depose the great man, who, in the language of its members, was never referred to except under the name of *The Obstacle,* to reorganize the government under the naively atrocious and bloody regime of 1793, and push France back to 8 Thermidor,[86] such were the ambitions and goals of that frenetic asso-

---

[83] Colonel Jacques Joseph Oudet (1773-1809) ,wounded several times in battle, he died at the Battle of Wagram. It was rumored (by Nodier) that his death was the result of a plot.

[84] Jean Victor Marie Moreau (1763-1813), French general who helped Napoleon Bonaparte to power, but later became a rival and was banished to the United States. He returned in 1813 and joined Allied Forces against France. Wounded at the Battle of Dresden, he died a few weeks later.

[85] See Note 66.

[86] 8 Thermidor an II (26 July 1794): fall of Robespierre.

ciation. It was composed of former Septemberists,[87] ex-presidents of clubs, those remaining from the Babeuf Conspiracy,[88] and, finally, all those kinds of men that public opinion had stigmatized in mass by the generic name of *Robespierre's tail,* such were its elements.

Obscure for the most part, which explains why, after the affair of the Machine Infernale[89], they escaped the proscription

---

[87] Survivors of the September Massacres, a wave of killings that took place in Paris between 2-7 September 1792, and other cities in late summer 1792, during the French Revolution, as a reaction to a fear that foreign and royalist armies were about to attack Paris and that the inmates of the city's prisons would be freed and join them. Radicals called for preemptive action, especially Jean-Paul Marat, who called on draftees to kill the prisoners before they could be freed. The action was undertaken by mobs of National Guardsmen and some fédérés; it was tolerated by the city government, the Paris Commune, which called on other cities to follow suit. By 6 September, half the prison population of Paris had been summarily executed: some 1200 to 1400 prisoners. Of these, 233 were nonjuring Catholic priests who had refused to submit to the Civil Constitution of the Clergy. However, the great majority of those killed were common criminals.

[88] The Conspiracy of the Equals or Society of the Panthéon was a faction within the French Revolution led by François-Noël Babeuf (1760-1797), a.k.a. Gracchus Babeuf, a French political agitator and journalist. His newspaper *Le Tribun du peuple* was best known for his advocacy for the poor and calling for a popular revolt against the Directoire. He was a leading advocate for the abolition of private property. He angered the authorities and, despite the efforts of his Jacobin friends, he was executed.

[89] The plot of the rue Saint-Nicaise, also known as the *Machine infernale* plot, was an assassination attempt on the life of First Consul Napoleon, in Paris on 24 December 1800 as he was going to attend the opening of Haydn's opera, *The* Crea-

en masse which was directed against the Jacobin party. All were men of action rather than men of thought, and shortly after the foundation of their society, abandoned by the one man who had held first rank in their association, it probably wouldn't have been long before it disintegrated, if a character already seen in this story hadn't come to take his place among them in order to bring the help of his knowledge and of his energy.

That man, who in the prologue of this story, appeared to us under the name of Count Montalvi,[90] was an Italian whose true name could be found inscribed in the former Book of Gold of the Genoese nobility, under the two entries of Senator and Prince Bevillacqua. Rich, imposing by his height and his demeanor, bizarre in some of the circumstances of his life, by the ardent make-up of his mind, as well as by an uncommon depth of passion and character, he was admirably cut out to take a role of the first order in the drama of a shady conspiracy. This new affiliate had also been recognized by the *Sleeping Lion* Society as a priceless recruit. And after having rapidly stepped over the first levels of the association, he wasn't slow to exercise the supreme influence there.

---

tion. It followed the *conspiration des poignards* of 10 October 1800, and was one of many Royalist and Catholic plots. The name of the *Machine Infernale* (infernal device) was in reference to an episode during the 16th-century revolt against Spanish rule in Flanders. In 1585, during the Siege of Antwerp by the Spaniards, an Italian engineer in Spanish service had made an explosive device from a barrel bound with iron hoops, filled with gunpowder, flammable materials and bullets, and set off by a sawed-off shotgun triggered from a distance by a string. The speed of Napoleon's carriage carried it beyond the explosives, but Josephine and her daughter Hortense were in the following carriage and Hortense suffered a shrapnel wound in the arm.

[90] See Volume 1, p. 54.

Already long accustomed to the life of secret societies, he opened a new horizon to the one of which he became the leader. With a name more ambitious and more high sounding, that he had imagined for it, and, finally, by the security with which he had the talent to surround its existence and its reunions, he had managed to add to it a vitality and strength of expansion that it had not known up until his arrival. From an obscure and suffering association, to which he came to affiliate himself, the intention of the new recruit was to bring about a kind of *mother society* with the goal of absorbing in itself all the other associations of the same nature existing on the surface of the globe. He had set himself the goal of the conquest and the proclamation of the Universal Republic. Finding that to such a high aspiration there couldn't be a name too brilliant, he called his new organization *The Order of the Grand Firmament* or *Directoire des Sublimi Maëstro Perfetti.* As for the cleverness of the precautions which he had managed to set up for the security of the Association, they can't be understood except with some introductory explanations.

Everyone somewhat knowledgeable about the secret history of the Revolution of 1789, has heard tell that, even before the reunion of the National Assembly, rue Plâtrière (today the rue Jean-Jacques Rousseau), there existed a center of insurrectionist reunions from which emanated the first emotions leading to the childhood of liberty for France.

In the Committee on the rue Plâtrière, said an anonymous critic, *among a great number of facts gathered by chance, there was often precious information. It was one day a matter of setting fire to all of Paris. Phosphorous and bitumous apparatus had been placed a various points. But the organization was suddenly and unexpectedly interrupted by the National Guard. Four hundred brigands carrying arms were arrested in Paris. Not one of them was French. They had come from the other side of the Rhine, and they had been bribed for several months.*[91]

What was needed as a meeting for the authors of such horrors was an underground lair. And in fact a vast excavation remained from the former Hôtel des Flandres, that in the past had occupied all the space between the rues des Vieux Augustins, Pagevin, and Coquillière. That was the space that would shelter that odious secret conference. When the Revolution had made its furious outburst, and its public center of action had been publically transported to the Jacobin Club, the secret of its precautions became useless and the rue Plâtrière was closed and abandoned. Made aware of its existence, Prince Bevillacqua, as soon as he had taken over the direction of the *Grand Firmament,* acquired a shabby house that had an unknown entry into the cave that he proposed using. While the upper floors were occupied by members or affiliates of the society, claiming to work as various types of workmen, by the care of the *Summo Maestro* (Supreme Master), in the subterranean location a room was set up for the reunions of the society. There, at the same time, the high dignitary had brought in and organized at his expense rich material to be used in the ceremonies and the trials. He thought that imposing and theatrical decoration could speak strongly to the imagination and was of a nature to create great thoughts of prosperity for the Association.

In an unusual situation, that will be explained later, Prince Bevillacqua, with his position as *Summo Maëstro*, took over the functions as Director of the Imperial Lottery. Cleverly making that official situation serve the security of his occult work, in a boutique forming the first floor of that house where it was so important to avoid the eye of the police, he established the Sales Office for which he had been commissioned. No other position could be more favorable to the mystery

---

[91] Excerpted from *Histoire des Jacobins depuis 1789 jusqu'à ce jour; ou, État de l'Europe en Novembre 1820* by Vincent Lombard (1820). (Note from the Author)

233

which was the main interest of the *Grand Firmament* works. It is known, in fact, that a double entry existed in almost all the Lottery Offices, one open to the public and the other for players who did not want their activity known. From that it could be understood the ease of entry that, for the adherents of the secret association, resulted from that arrangement. Neither the affluence of the people who entered the house, nor their mysterious aspect, were such as to arouse the suspicions of the neighbors and the authorities. The Lottery was sufficient to cover and to explain everything

Another circumstance extremely favorable to the security of the work was the considerable number of players, or as they were then called, *auctioneers,* drawn to the Office under the administration of the nobleman from Genoa. No one as well as he knew how to make an attractive use of night lights, numbers stuck with ribbons, and illuminations in green-colored glass which were used to announce jackpots. His advertizing talents were not limited and he seemed to have unlimited resources. So, upon entering his establishment, the players first marveled to see themselves greeted by a black man wearing white silk stockings, powdered hair, his purse and his dress of magnificent livery. Then, the happy and bizarre personality of the inflexible divinity on whose altar they had come to sacrifice, in a woman placed behind a grill of green satin, and positioned so as to take in the stake and to deliver the tickets, the courtesans of chance weren't slow to find a deaf-mute.

Let us add that, already middle-aged, that woman still had the remains of uncommon beauty. Seen in the shadows with which she was careful to surround herself, and with heavy make-up, her charms created an illusion. Thus, all of Parisian society which made the fortunes of those oddities, there was no talk but of the beautiful deaf-mute on the rue Jean-Jacques Rousseau. From the most distant areas there was a rush to come buy her tickets.

Under such a surface, the operation of a conspiracy was certainly difficult to expose. For several years, Prince Bevillacqua was able to be tranquilly enthroned at the head of the *Grand Firmament.* The circumstances in which, a little later, that dangerous affiliation was dissolved, will be made known in what follows in our story. While waiting, we are going to show it at work and functioning in all the splendor of one of its ceremonies.

II. Ephraim the Jew

That black man that we have just seen in the Lottery Office who greeted the players and was transformed into a sort of bailiff of Destiny, was an African from Madagascar. His name was Britannicus, and he was very much in the confidence of Monseigneur Bevillacqua. Entered very young in the service of his master, having been with him a long time, that man had fulfilled the intimate functions of valet. But since the Prince had been elevated to the Presidency of the *Alta Vendita* in the *Grand Firmament,* affiliated by one of the lesser grades to the secret existence of the Association, Britannicus had become a sort of *Maître Jacques*[92] and didn't play a role any less important. Finally, concierge of the underground location and keeper of the material necessary for ceremonies and initiations, he was also the decorator and organizer of those sorts of solemn occasions. More than once, he had introduced fortunate details of his own invention which later found a place in the ritual.

During December of the year 1804, that clever master of ceremonies received the order from the Grand Master of the Association to arrange the room for a special occasion. That day, a double ceremony was to take place, a general chapter

---

[92] A character in Molière's 1668 comedy, *The Miser.* Harpagon, the miser, intends to marry his son and his daughter, as economically as possible, to spouses undesirable from the young people's point of view. When told to limit expenses, Maître Jacques incurs the anger of the miser and is beaten. For revenge, he furthers the interests of the miser's children to wed their own choices.

meeting and a reception of one of the high ranking members. As a consequence, in a kind of back store room intended for furniture, and which a door cleverly hidden in the wall separated from the large room for meetings, Britannicus went to get a large wall hanging of celestial blue velvet, with astronomy signs embroidered in relief. That wall hanging attached to the wall, he then set up a platform on which was place an armchair with symbolic figures, surmounted with a canopy. A quadrangular table covered with a cloth of blue velvet was set up in front of that throne. On that table the decorator placed a candelabrum with seven black candles, a crown, a scepter, an antique sword, money in coin and gems of a bizarre design hung on a serpentine chain. At the foot of the table, spread out on a cushion of blue satin, there was a white robe, a belt, sacerdotal articles and a Phrygian cap. And then what wasn't the most pleasant detail of all that theatrical decoration, a human skeleton was hung on a pedestal. And, since the springs that served to maneuver that anatomical piece didn't move it easily into the pose mandated by the ritual, the venerable relic was grabbed by the miscreant African who, after having finally arranged it as he intended, said to himself, rubbing his hands:

"Now the Maestri can come. Their lodge is well prepared."

The first to the rendezvous was the *Summo Maestro,* Prince Bevillacqua. Wearing all the insignia of the Grand Master, the high dignitary took advantage of the solitude in which for a short time he was left by the brothers and friends to try out a certain number of majestic poses from the throne and to glance at a paper, undoubtedly the manuscript of a discourse that he was going to pronounce.

As the room began to fill up with Associates, wearing blue robes sprinkled with stars, which made them resemble astrologers from a comedy, the Grand Master went to meet them, greeting them politely, but at the same time with cold dignity. It was clear that he made it a principle to keep them at a distance and to clearly mark the height of the distance that separated him from them. Besides, a sentence that he repeated to almost every one entering would have been enough to justify somewhat the melancholy gravity in his demeanor.

"Messieurs," he said several times, "we have sad news to report today."

But he didn't explain anything more, reserving for the entire assemblage the more complete tenor of his communication. As soon as the *Alta Vendita* was complete, the Prince went to take his place on the throne. After some preliminary acts meant to be sure no stranger could see the mysteries, he rose and, his head uncovered, he seized with his left hand a flaming sword, the pommel of which he applied to his heart. With his left hand he took a mallet and struck the wood on his chair three times and declared the meeting open to receive a candidate at the rank of *Epopte*, or enlightened priest. The reading of the minutes of the preceding séance complete, the noise of a kind of altercation was heard at the door of the room. Asked to go find out the cause of that disorder, the brother who was on watch, said, as he returned:

"Grand Master! It's a blind man who is looking for a star."

The order to bring in the profane was immediately given. He walked in with bare feet, his hands bound in irons, and a blindfold on his eyes. After having conducted him to the middle of the room, the brother who had brought him in approached the Grand Master and gave him a document. It was the will of recipient, who had, according to the statutes of the order, just drawn it up in the antechamber in the Masonic language, *the small thing*. After having examined that document for a moment, the Grand Master motioned that the blindfold of the profane be removed. Then with an air of disdain, he asked:

"Who brings us this slave?"

"He came of himself," replied the brother who had brought him in. "He smelled the air of liberty from afar."

"So, what does he want?"

"That someone remove his chains."

"Why does he not ask those who enslaved him?"

"Those refused to break his bonds. They had too great an interest in the continuation of his slavery."

"Those merciless masters, who are they?"

"Society, government, the sciences and false religion."

"Is this man, like us, resolved to have done with all those evil things?"

"What he is commanded, he says his heart and hand will do."

"Let that enemy of tyranny be set free, but before conferring on him the title to which he aspires, we need additional guarantees."

Then the profane was freed of his chains and brought to the table on which were spread out the objects already enumerated.

"Look!" the Grand Master said to him, "fix your eyes on the shine of this scepter. Now if those jewels, that crown, that gold, hold attractions for you, they can be yours, and we will know how, outside of this enclosure, to make you rich and powerful. Would you prefer to learn wisdom? You will see all the insignias of it on that cushion. Don't be afraid to say which you want. Each man has his vocation, marked by his character. Decide. Choose. "

If the recipient had fallen into the trap and had chosen the symbols of power, he would have immediately been greeted by this curse:

"Monster, leave and cease to contaminate this sanctuary. Go, flee, while there is still time."

And from that moment, he would have been put on the index for the society's vengeance. But it didn't seem the candidate had made such a misguided choice. He chose the sacerdotal signs and the white robe. Then the Grand Master said to him:

"Greeting to the great and noble soul! However, he isn't yet permitted to wear that robe. First learn what we are and the goal to which we hold."

The profane man was then seated in the middle of the room on a chair without a back. The Grand Master then gave a long discourse, the sense of which was that with civilization despotism was installed and had ended the reign of Nature, that had been the only period of equality and liberty. The goal of the secret society was to return man to that happy state where each individual was sovereign and the only King over himself. To obtain that result, the method was to abolish all royalty, all magistrature, all religion, all science, the source of inequality and error, all property.

That said, the recipient was invested with a white robe and took the oath of absolute and blind obedience to the mandates of the Grand Master of the order and to *Unknown Superiors*. He was then anointed with the oil of palm, a tuft of his hair was cut off and burned in the flame of the candelabra with seven candles. Then they placed a Phrygian cap on his head, telling him never to take it off, understanding that it was more valuable than the crown of kings.

The ceremony thus terminated, the newly-initiated was again led outside the room. The rank he had just attained did not give him access into the chapter of strict observance, where the general business of the society was going to be discussed.[93]

A dramatic incident led to the sad revelations expected, to recall the words pronounced by the Grand Master at the beginning of the séance. The door of the room opened loudly and a man, his clothes in shreds, his hair in disorder and spread with ashes, in whom those present had some trouble recognizing one of the members of the Association who, some months before, had been sent to Ireland, England, and Scotland to propagate the work of the *Grand Firmament* and to visit the correspondents, or *provincials*, that the society had placed in the United Kingdom.

---

[93] The strange details of that ceremony bear great similarities with those of ceremonies conducted by the famous sect of the *Illuminati* in Germany. That coincidence will be explained later. (Note from the Author)

239

"Vengeance, brothers," cried the new arrival. "Vengeance! Our *provincial* is dead! He is dead, Ephraim, the zealous Levite. Vengeance, Vengeance, against his murderer!"

The emotion caused by the announcement of that death was immense. It seemed the Association had just learned of the loss of one of their most venerated members. The usage was when the *Grand Firmament* saw the eclipse of one of its *stars,* one of the surviving members delivered his funeral elegy before the assembled chapter. That time, it was the Grand Master who took the floor. Told of the disastrous news in advance, he had been able to prepare a discourse, the manuscript of which was only a short time ago seen in his hands. The orator stood up. A solemn silence awaited his speech. Then, in the words that follow, he began to throw flowers on the tomb that he had been charged with honoring:

"Yes, brothers and friends, that light and that great intelligence from which the first thought of our Association sprang, is extinguished. Yes, Ephraim is dead, that man of such powerful genius and such strong will. That man who can be summed up in one phrase, in calling him: *the great unknown philosopher.* A long friendship united me with him. His life has been for me without secrets and without a veil. I can tell you about it in its entirety. Ephraim was born in Denmark in the Israelite religion. It is enough to say that, in his youth, he was unhappy and persecuted. The tortures to his ego inflicted by prejudice and intolerance brought to birth in him a profound hatred of social institutions, and an instinctive ardor to return the world to the state of nature to which its regeneration must one day begin.

"To persuade men, even for their happiness, that great intellectual effort was needed. Ephraim spared himself nothing. At thirty, he had gone through the circle of sciences, although he felt contempt for them, and all the languages of the Orient were familiar to him. It was then that he left for Egypt to find at their source the mysteries of Memphis, the birthplace of all the initiations. His discoveries, in the secular sands of the Pyramids, hastened the last irresolution of his powerful mind. He was sure that, in the secret societies, there lay a force to lift the world. That was the lever that he took.

"In Malta, where his apostolate opened, he began by opening a lodge according to the teachings of *Misraim,* but his sojourn in that isle was, above all, marked by the perpetration of a courageous sacrifice, that he dared envision without terror and that, in the same conditions, no man, one can say, had accomplished before him. Aspiring to raise himself to the supreme heights of intelligence, and having noticed that, during that ascension, the weight that the cortege of senses caused him, he resolved to abolish them in himself, at least in the proportion where that separation was consistent with life continuing. What Origen [94] did by fanaticism, he did to himself for the cult of reason. In the archives of the Inquisition of Malta, which by a lawsuit directed against him forced him to flee, there is a recipe for a mixture by the means of which he managed to extinguish the sensual man in him, to leave nothing alive but the thinker and the regenerator of humanity. From Malta, Ephraim went toward Germany, and it is in that country that the trace of his most elevated title we can imagine can be found. He founded the sect of the *Illuminati,* the most marvelous instrument for conspiration that perhaps has ever been

---

[94] Origen (184/185-253/254), one of the most influential figures in early Christian asceticism who was born and spent the first half of his career in Alexandria. He was a prolific writer in multiple branches of theology, including textual criticism, biblical exegesis and hermeneutics, philosophical theology, preaching, and spirituality written in Greek. He was anathematized at the Second Council of Constantinople. Unlike many church fathers, he was never canonized as a saint because some of his teachings directly contradicted the teachings attributed to the apostles, notably the Apostles Paul and John. His teachings on the pre-existence of souls, the final reconciliation of all creatures, including perhaps even the devil (the *apokatastasis*), and the subordination of God the Son to God the Father, were rejected by Christian orthodoxy.

241

established. But, so strong by the mind and the will, that great man carried into action a kind of meditative timidity which made him decide to entrust this marvelous creation to one of his disciples. Adam Weishaupt,[95] who, until then, had obscurely lived at Ingolstadt, and was then was enthroned as the founder of the Order of the *Illuminati.* But, in reality, at the depth of one of those unknown retreats, Ephraim was the continual inspiration for his actions and for his thoughts.[96]

"For several years, immersed in a kind of revolutionary Platonism, our illustrious friend waited until the germ of social

---

[95] Johann Adam Weishaupt (1748-1830), German philosopher and founder of the Order of the Illuminati,

[96] In his *Memoirs Illustrating the History of Jacobinism*, Abbé Baruel, who gave detailed information about the *Illuminati* sect, said that Adam Weishaupt, before bringing about his detestable creation, had an initiator and a master. (Note from the Author) *Mémoires pour servir à l'histoire du Jacobinisme* is a book by Abbé Augustin Barruel, a French Jesuit priest. It was written and published in French in 1797-98, and translated into English in 1799. In it, Barruel claims that the French Revolution was the result of a deliberate conspiracy hatched by a coalition of philosophers and freemasons. The conspirators created a system that was inherited by the Jacobins who operated it to its greatest potential. The *Memoirs* purports to expose the Revolution as the culmination of a long history of subversion. Barruel was not the first to make these charges, but he was the first to present them in a fully developed historical context and his evidence was on a quite unprecedented scale. Barruel wrote each of the first three volumes of the book as separate discussions of those who contributed to the conspiracy. The fourth volume is an attempt to unite them all in a description of the Jacobins in the French Revolution. *Memoirs* is representative of the criticism of the Enlightenment that spread throughout Europe during the Revolutionary period and is considered one of the founding documents of the right-wing interpretation of the French Revolution.

dissolution placed in the *Code of the Illuminati* had begun to bear fruit. But when the time had come, and during the revolt of the Low Countries against the House of Austria,[97] Ephraim could hear the first rumblings of the European storm of 1789, he left his contemplative role. A letter from the Minister of Foreign Affairs to Louis Capet [98] shows him being involved in the most active way to advance the work of the humanitarian regeneration.

> *Master Ephraim, whom I told you about in one of the last letters,* wrote Montmorin,[99] *appears to have been sent to Paris by the Minister of His Prussian Majesty, Bischoffwerder,*[100] *to intrigue and even in the most criminal way. He frequents secret societies and tries to agitate journalists. I am almost certain that he spreads money around and I know that he can obtain considerable sums from bankers without its being known where they come from. You will recall that Master Ephraim was sent into Brabant to help the revolution, and that he has come to Paris when Brussels no longer offers material for his zeal.*[101]

---

[97] The people of the Austrian Netherlands rebelled against Austria in 1788 as a result of Joseph II's centralizing policies. The different provinces established the United States of Belgium (January 1790). However, waylaying Joseph's intended concessions to the Belgians to restore the height of their autonomy and privileges, Austrian imperial power was restored by Joseph's brother and successor, Leopold II by the end of 1790.

[98] The King of France.

[99] Armand Marc, Count of Montmorin de Saint Herem (1745-1792), French Minister of Foreign Affairs and the Navy under Louis XVI.

[100] Johann Hans Rudolf von Bischoffwerder (1741-1803), a favorite and adviser to King Frederick William II of Prussia.

[101] Excerpted from *Histoire des Jacobins*, page 60. (Note from the Author) See Note 91.

"Immense, in fact, my brothers, was that zeal! Other foreigners, Fournier,[102] dubbed the 'American,' the Prussian Anacharsis Cloots,[103], Thomas Paine,[104] the Pole Lazouski,[105] can be considered as the most ardent workers of the work, but while working in the shadows, the arm of Ephraim delivered blows more sure and more efficacious.

"There was often seen in the halls of the Convention a tall man with a pale complexion, bright, animated eyes and an unspeakable expression of calm irony who it was impossible to forget when he had once been encountered. Seeming to lend his hand to nothing, that man was nevertheless seen everywhere there was a marked expansion of the Revolutionary

---

[102] Claude Fournier L'Héritier (1745-1825), nicknamed "The American" because he'd gone to Haiti to seek fortune. Returning to France, he joined the Revolution and distinguished himself by organizing a popular armed force which became involved in all major insurrections of the capital. He spent much of his life in prison, all governments regarding him as an agitator and accusing him of inciting to insurrection..
[103] Jean-Baptiste du Val-de-Grâce, baron de Cloots (1755-1794), a.k.a. Anacharsis Cloots. Prussian nobleman who was a significant figure in the French Revolution, nicknamed "a personal enemy of God," he was elected to the Convention, but was expelled from the Jacobin Club, accused of being a foreign agent by Robespierre and was guillotined.
[104] Thomas Paine (1737-1809). English-American political activist and philosopher, one of the Founding Fathers of the United States, he authored the two influential pamphlets at the start of the American Revolution, and inspired the rebels in 1776 to declare independence from Britain.
[105] Polish citizen who had moved to France and been promoted Inspector of Manufactures but joined the Jacobin Party and became Captain of the National Guard and lead the march against the Tuileries on 10 august 1792. He was arrested on 13 March 1793 and died on 23 April 1793.

fluid. October 6,[106] June 20,[107] August 10,[108] at the massacre of the Champ-de-Mars,[109] at the September verification of the credentials, he was there! On January 21,[110] a man was seen, a smile on his lips, busy dipping a handkerchief in the blood that had just flowed from the Place de la Revolution. That unknown man, that was our friend. If it can be believed, he was venomous and fatal for the health of Kings. On March 2 1792, when in three days Leopold of Austria died from dysentery, Ephraim was in Vienna; two weeks later, on March 16, when in Stockholm, in the middle of a masked ball, Gustav III of Sweden was struck by Anckarstrom, our zealous propagandist was in Stockholm. He stayed there six weeks more when every morning, without the police ever being able to account for that audacious bravado, the cadaver of the royal murderer exposed, according to the Swedish custom on a scaffold of infamy, wore a laurel wreath on its head. A note was in its right hand on which was written: '*Blessed be the courageous hand that saved the fatherland.*' "

The Prince de Bevillacqua was at that pointing his funeral oration when there seemed to a certain movement in the audience. He stopped speaking as if to ask the meaning of that interruption. An explanation was immediately given to him that, probably, he didn't expect to be so clear and so precise. A man stood up. It was one of the former butchers of October and September to which the annalists of the Revolution had given a sort of celebrity under the name of *the man with the long beard.* Compared to that knife wielder, Ephraim couldn't be given great consideration. Being bored by the long panegyric, with a brutal and audacious frankness that he had retained from his bloody profession, he said:

---

[106] October 6, 1789. Women's march on Versailles.
[107] June 20, 1791. The Royal Family flees Paris.
[108] August 10, 1792. Storming of the Tiuileries.
[109] July 17, 1791.
[110] January 21, 1793. Execution of King Louis XVI.

"Grand Master, you are laying out for us some beautiful phrases and reciting what we already know. It's known that the Jew Ephraim was a good bloke, but as for me, I have never thought much of all Jews. But the way this brave man died, that's what it would be good to know. Do us the kindness to tell us that, and afterward, if you want to, you can speak for three weeks."

Thus called to task, the Prince bit his lips. To a dark scarlet the pallor of anger rapidly showed on his face. However, he controlled himself and despite the unanimous murmurs that had greeted the brutal outburst, he folded his manuscript, placed it in his pocket and limited himself to saying in a disdainful voice:

"Monsieur is right. When the life of a man is written, it is logical and interesting to start with his death. That procedure cuts short a great deal."

Nevertheless, docile to the lesson, the orator passed on to a rapid improvisation where all the flowers of rhetoric were omitted. He explained that after the 9th of Thermidor,[111] feeling that the future of the Revolution was already compromised, Ephraim had taken refuge in Italy, where he had founded a society which, for a moment, under the name of the *Awakened*, had enjoyed a certain credit. Later reappearing in France, Ephraim was the secret inspiration for the Babeuf Conspiracy,[112] and following that, by the foundation of the society of *The Sleeping Lion,* he gave a new form to his tireless need for revolutionary agitation. After the 18 Brumaire,[113] as he saw nothing immediately realizable against the First Consul, he went to England. There, insinuating himself into

---

[111] Thermidorian Reaction, in the French Revolution, the parliamentary revolt initiated on 9 Thermidor, year II (27 July 1794), which resulted in the fall of Robespierre and the collapse of revolutionary fervor and the Reign of Terror in France. See Note 86.

[112] See Note 88.

[113] See Note 80.

the councils of the emigration, he took an active part in all the attempts against the life of Bonaparte. But his alliance with the aristocracy was only momentary, and soon, leaving the foyer of the counter- revolutionaries, he transported his center of action to Scotland.

From time immemorial, there existed in that land a Masonic Order of *strict observance*, which was considered to be a continuation of the Order of the Knights Templar.[114] Rising quickly to the highest levels of that Association, Ephraim wasn't long in communicating to it the political aspect that, until then, it had lacked. But it didn't seem to him that the time had come to attack the British Monarchy, which he thought there would be of great help to overthrow Napoleon. He went to meditate in solitude and, through the patronage of his fellow Masons, he was named guardian of a lighthouse in the middle of the sea some miles off the coast of Scotland.

No place was ever better suited to become the lair of a conspirator. There was constantly a great stream of travelers who wanted to visit that lighthouse, whose history as well as position were curious. From there, without exciting the least

---

[114] In 1128, Hugues de Payens met King David I in Scotland. The Templars then established a seat at Balantrodoch, now Temple. In 1189, Alan FitzWalter, the 2nd Lord High Steward of Scotland, was a benefactor of the Order. About 1187, William the Lion granted part of the Culter lands on the south bank of the River Dee, to the Templars, and between 1221 and 1236, Walter Bisset of Aboyne founded a Preceptory for the Templars. In 1287, they built a Chapel dedicated to Mary the Mother of Christ, and, in November 1309, the name of a William Middleton of the "Tempill House of Culter" was recorded. It has been claimed that in 1309, during the trial of the Templars in Scotland, Bishop Lamberton of St Andrews, gave the Templars his protection, although there is no evidence to support this. It should also be recorded that John of Fordun's Chronicle of the Scottish Nation, a major Scottish mediaeval source makes no mention at all of the Templars.

suspicion, Ephraim was able to receive from every country in the world the affiliates of the revolutionary propaganda who came to receive enlightenment from the councils of his experience and to communicate with him. For several years, with the title of Provincial of the *Grand Firmament,* Ephraim lived in that retreat.

"Two months earlier," said the Grand Master, "he was left full of health and hope by the brother voyager who now has brought us the news of his baneful end. Following a tour of England, Ireland, and Scotland, this brother voyager wanted, before returning to France, to make a last visit to his venerated brother. But on arriving in the little village of Arbroath,[115] which is the place of embarkation to the lighthouse, he was greeted by a thunderbolt of news: Ephraim had just perished, assassinated.

"In addition, the circumstances surrounding that crime," the Grand Master added "were such as to merit the highest degree of attention from the *Sublimi Maestri Perfetti.* During a stormy night, it was noticed that the lighthouse beam had not been illuminated, a fatal neglect causing several vessels, bodies and goods, to be lost. The next morning, the locals went to reconnoiter the cause of that disastrous eclipse of the star designed to guide sailors. Then, in that tower isolated in the middle of the ocean, the blackest mystery was revealed. First of all, the disappearance of a man named Matiphous, who, concurrently with Ephraim, the English Admiralty had made guardian of the lighthouse; then that of a female traveler, who, the evening before, accompanied by her husband, had gone to visit the lighthouse. That was nothing yet; in going into the travelers' room, the unfortunate Ephraim was found stretched out on the floor, struck in the heart with a knife that the murderer had left in the wound.

---

[115] Arbroath, or Aberbrothock, is a former royal burgh and the largest town in the council area of Angus in Scotland. It lies on the North Sea coast, around 16 miles ENE of Dundee and 45 miles SSW of Aberdeen.

"No one in Arbroath doubted whose hand must have struck the blow. No one had, for a moment, thought that the husband of the woman who had disappeared, and who himself had remained at the lighthouse could be the murderer. On the contrary, Matiphous, that man who hasn't been found, who was from Malta, a kind of adventurer with a most deplorable background, was the one who attracted all the suspicions.

"Without mentioning the other mysteries in his life, in London he had become the valet of the executioner; then had been outlawed, and it had yet to be explained by what protection he had managed to occupy the confidential post that he shared with Ephraim. Therefore, Matiphous must have committed the crime—but for what purpose?

"That purpose," said Monsieur de Bevillacqua, terminating his rapid exposé, "the Arbroath magistrates were not in a position to explain. But for us, brothers and friends, one word is enough to explain it. In Ephraim's hands were deposited a mass of papers, both his personal papers and those concerning the future and the security of all the Associations with which he corresponded. He usually kept those papers locked in a secret red portfolio. Now, there was no trace found of that portfolio. Therefore it was in view of appropriating that precious set of documents that Ephraim was put to death. Therefore, the murderer must be the agent of some government wanting, at any price, to steal those papers. Now, brothers and friends, faced with such grave occurrences, can you see what you must do?"

Thus opened, the discussion was long, confused, complicated; in a word, it had all the character that must decide us to not reproduce it here. Only one positive result was deduced, knowing that Matiphous was a terrible scoundrel and at all costs the *Grand Firmament* must pursue him with its vengeance.

III. The Lighthouse of Bell Rock

Very serious accusations have just been lodged against Matiphous, our former acquaintance. Let's see what foundation they have.

On the northern coast of Scotland, between the Gulfs of Forth and Tay, there is an immense rock in the sea that, on a clear day, can easily be seen from the little village of Arbroath. At ebb tide, that rock clearly shows its bare sides covered with a luxuriant vegetation of seaweed, algae, and innumerable varieties of shellfish. But when the tide comes in, it is covered by the surface of the sea and in the event that the sea becomes strong and stormy it becomes a reef just below the water, impossible to detect. For a long time it was the terror of navigators in the area of the North Sea between Edinburg and the Orcades.

It's recounted that about the 13th century, a philanthropic thought pointed out that dangerous area to seamen. If an old tradition can be believed, a Superior in the Arbroath Abbey thought of attaching a buoy to the rock and placing a bell to that buoy. When the sea was calm and the rock was visible, the bell was silent. But when the waves became higher, hiding the reef, their agitation set off the bell and it vibrated louder as the storm became stronger, warning the sailors to keep their distance. This dangerous place was then given the name of Bell Rock. However, that means of safety was found insufficient and was soon given up. Finally, the frequency of shipwrecks brought about a general clamor and the Admiralty decided to build a lighthouse at the summit of the rock.

The difficulty of the enterprise was immense. The violence of the sea made it difficult to conceive of trying to work there. Even the base seemed to lack a foundation for the edifice that must be set up on the unequal rock surface, constantly menaced by waves and criss-crossed with crevices and deep cracks. That construction took forty-five thousand pounds sterling and six consecutive years of battle with the ocean, which seemed to set its anger against the audacious talent of

250

the engineer, Stevenson. Successfully completed by the perseverance of the English genius, it remains today one of the
most astonishing works of this kind that has ever been constructed. The tower, rises one hundred and sixteen feet, of
which seventy are a massive wall, thus its entrance is more
than half way up its height. Eight and one half feet from the
level of the sea, its walls at the summit are no more than a foot
and a half near the ledge. Mounted on the dome of the edifice,
there is, at night fall, a rotating light alternating white and red,
which can be seen from fourteen miles in the distance. During
stormy weather, very frequent in that region, a mechanism
puts a carillon of bells in motion which supplement the
dimmed light. [116]

Toward the end of 1799, one of the employees guarding
this lighthouse was, in fact, the man from Malta, Gregorio
Matiphous. The misfortunes for which he was reproached in
the preceding chapter are recalled here. Confined in Newgate
Prison, following the botched hanging of the boxer Broughton,
delivered through the intercession of Sir Sidney Smith; compromised by that inexplicable personage who called himself
sometimes Colqhoum and sometimes the Marquis de

---

[116] Most of this is historically accurate. The Bell Rock Lighthouse, off the coast of Angus, Scotland, is the world's oldest
surviving sea-washed lighthouse. It was built between 1807
and 1810 by Robert Stevenson (1772-1850) on the Bell Rock
(also known as Inchcape) in the North Sea, 11 miles east of
the Firth of Tay. Standing 35 meters (115 ft) tall, its light is
visible from 35 statute miles (56 km) inland. The masonry
work on which the lighthouse rests was constructed to such a
high standard that it has not been replaced or adapted in 200
years. The lamps and reflectors were replaced in 1843 and
used in the lighthouse at Cape Bonavista, Newfoundland,
where they are currently on display. The working of the lighthouse has been automated since 1988. The challenges faced in
the building of the lighthouse have led to it being described as
one of the Seven Wonders of the Industrial World.

Samaniego, by whose order he had to undergo Colqhoum's atrocious revenge. Suffering the terrible pain of that treatment, near then to giving into a thought of suicide, nevertheless he was stopped at the edge of that desperate resolution. His charitable decision made him the adopted father of a young girl, terribly abandoned by the death of her mother. That's where Kitty Ketch's sad and unhappy suitor was at the end of the earlier part of this story.

To live any longer in London had become impossible for him. His adventure with the hangman's daughter and the terrible stain the Marquis de Samaniego had inflicted on him, had had too many repercussions. On the other hand, it wasn't with the some hundred guineas that made up his fortune at that moment that he could undertake moving and providing honorably for his existence and that of the young girl that he had promised to protect and support.

The day Sir Sidney Smith had remembered him and had officially intervened to get him out of the hands of the Sheriffs, Matiphous hadn't been able to take it on himself to go offer his thanks to that liberator before whom he would have had too much to be ashamed of. Now the pressing duties of paternity that he had assumed soon made him put aside that ego. Soon after Madame de Limeuil's funeral, no longer hesitating to go see his protector, he had asked him to procure for him some employment in one of the numerous colonies that England had under its domination. Sir Sidney Smith had gladly answered that wish and, some days later, having asked the man from Malta to come see him, he announced that, instead of sending him far away to expiate all the follies of which he was guilty, he had a position, passably remunerated, whose functions were perfectly easy to fill. Taking him away for a while from that world where he had great need to be forgotten, would not, however, force him to leave the territory of the United Kingdom.

To live on the Bell Rock Lighthouse, at the distance it was from the coast, to often remain for weeks deprived of all communication with the land, to live there like some vestal charged with the eternal upkeep of that beam of light, and as a price of that reclusion, nourished and clothed by the State, to receive fifty pounds sterling as a salary, such was the fate offered by Sir Sidney Smith to his protegé. Certainly, at any other time in his life, Matiphous would have found that a cruelly monastic life that he was proposed. But considering the harsh necessity in which he had placed himself, to conceal himself from the attention and the memory of all those he had known, no proposition could be made to him that would better fit his needs. He gave himself only the time necessary for his preparations and less than a week afterward he had rendered the last duties to Madame de Limeuil, accompanied by the young orphan, the new functionary departed for Bell Rock.

He found more numerous company in that place than he at first supposed, and in his somber mood at the time, the presence of two colleagues with whom he had to share the habitation and the guardianship of the lighthouse seemed to him more a burden than a lessening of his exile. However, he soon recognized that his great taste for solitude would not be as completely opposed as he had at first imagined. In terms of the rules that organized the service of the lighthouse, each guardian was authorized every three weeks to spend one ashore. Matiphous' intention being to reduce his time to an absolute reclusion and never to take advantage of his turn to leave, one of his colleagues hurried to appropriate for himself that part of his liberty which he didn't want to use. As for Ephraim, except for some short escapes that he liked to make to go to Arbroath to preside over the Masonic lodge to which he belonged, he was no less a stay-at-home than his new colleague. Vast correspondence, numerous visits he received and a great many very deep meditations about his plan for a radical regeneration of humanity by means of a universal upheaval, absorbed his time so completely that he almost never thought of leaving. Matiphous equally then benefitted from the conspirator's habits of retreat. To tell the truth, the third guardian was a true sinecuriste who only at distant intervals, and then to salve his conscience, came to spend three or four days at the lighthouse.

In that continual close working relationship that Matiphous lived with Ephraim, it seems there should have resulted a warm intimacy. But between the two men, to tell the truth, there was no sympathy. Matiphous was open, a man with drive, athletic, and, on the contrary, with his very pronounced conspirator temperament, Ephraim was somber, suspicious, little communicative, and strongly introspective. On seeing Matiphous arrive, his propaganda instincts had immediately tried to make a convert of him. But it must be remembered that Matiphous had served as a military surgeon during the first Italian military campaign. As far as his former General Bonaparte was concerned, he practiced a kind of cult to which the ideas of a Jacobin were at opposite ends of the pole. Since then, in the short but disastrous rapport he found himself to have with the somber *Sleepers' Club*,[117] the former substitute for Jack Ketch hadn't taken a very marked inclination for secret societies.

When Ephraim began to touch on something relative to certain projects of affiliation to him, he expressed himself in a way so as to make it known that he would be neither an easy nor reliable recruit. A great coldness wasn't long in developing between the two colleagues of that profound divergence of instincts and, while living under the same roof, they were as much as to say total strangers to one another. Exchanging only at very distant times some insignificant words, they did not even sit at the same table at mealtimes. Ephraim, who wanted to leave little place for bodily needs, always ate standing up and just what was needed to conserve the breath of that feverish existence that he had entirely committed to the cult of evil and anarchy.

It must be said also that in addition to those three guardians, the lighthouse counted still a fourth inhabitant, but without an approaching encounter where we will see him play a

---

[117] See Volume 1.

rather considerable role, it will hardly be necessary for us to go into great detail about him.

He was a poor idiot child whose history was as touching as it was unusual. Born some years before at Bell Rock, his parents, at the establishment of the lighthouse, had been its first guardians. Never having left the place of his birth, after the death of his parents, he had conceived for the lighthouse such an attachment that all the energy of his miserable intelligence seemed to be concentrated there. At about eight years old, he had seen his parents, who had given him the sad gift of life, die several months apart. At their funeral, there was not a tear in his eyes. But after their removal, when there had been a question of his leaving the lighthouse to be taken to Edinburg to an orphanage, he went, with lamentable cries, to take refuge on the platform of the tower. He clung to the balustrade and gave the strongest resistance to the efforts made to pull him away from it. Touched by that attachment to the place that had become for him like a country, the successors of his parents, the predecessors themselves of the guardians we find in place, asked that the poor child be left with them, promising to take care of him. Since that time, in some sense immobilized at the lighthouse, the idiot, each morning climbed to the dome and there, crouched under the apparatus of the beam, he spent long hours contemplating the sea and rocking himself in a monotonous and plaintive voice. He seemed to find a kind of voluptuousness in being battered by the wind.

As a result of that almost constant isolation where Matiphous found himself between the conspirator, who represented in some fashion the abuse of intelligence, and the idiot who represented the last degree of its negation, he rapidly developed the sentiment of paternal affection. From the first moment Mademoiselle Limeuil had inspired him, and on her side, she repaid him with such strong gratitude that on both sides it seemed to be tenderness inspired by ties of blood. In addition, in the fervor of his devotion for the one whose future he had so solemnly guaranteed to her mother, the man from Malta poured into the thought of an enterprise that only the heart could dream of, but that the strength of will nevertheless conducted to a good end. Resolved to make himself the teacher of the orphan, and not feeling himself necessarily prepared in the past very near the work he was undertaking, he had the courage to begin by acquiring knowledge in order to be able in some measure to communicate it. The result was truly miraculous. That man, whose faults of every kind, and even a murder, had been so strangely predisposed to the role that he had dared to dream of, came to make of his pupil, a chef-d'oeuvre of innocence, and she became at the same time a model of solid instruction and ravishing beauty.

In the middle of these pious cares, the years flowed by more rapidly than would have been thought. Despite the rigors of the sequestration to which Matiphous was condemned, he was more than once heard to regret the time of his sojourn at Bell Rock, as having been the best of his life. Brought up, as will be remembered, under the roof of a poor fisherman on the little island of Gozzo, he had kept as the first impression of his childhood, a passion for the sea. It could be said that the habitation of the Lighthouse where he now spent his life replaced it in some way. In case, however, that his young companion might seem to tire of that severe reclusion, he voluntarily released her from her vow of Saint Simeon Stylites.[118] He sometimes insisted on taking her to Arbroath, so that she might enjoy some distractions. It was not truly conceivable that, beginning to come to the age of reason when she left society, that child didn't want to know the pleasures that she had already seen. But the more Diane de Limeuil's intelligence de-

---

[118]Saint Simeon Stylites or Symeon the Stylite (c.388-459). Syriac ascetic saint who achieved fame for living 47 years on a small platform on top of a pillar near Aleppo. Several other stylites later followed his model (the Greek word *style* means pillar). He is known formally as Saint Simeon Stylites the Elder to distinguish him from Simeon Stylites the Younger, Simeon Stylites III and Saint Symeon Stylites of Lesbos. Miracles were attributed to him during and after his lifetime.

veloped with the years, the less she seemed to wish to see anything modified in the tranquil uniformity of her life.

What's more, it must be said that rarely did several
weeks go by without curiosity bringing to Bell Rock some
strangers who were not all, fortunately, agents of demagogu-
ery coming there to plot conspirations with Ephraim. Often,
also, with a sudden change in the atmosphere, those visitors
were kept as prisoners at the Lighthouse. For that occurrence,
a room for travelers, containing a library, maps of geography,
newspapers, instruments of optics and mathematics, and, finally, an album, where it was customary that visitors write their
name with some comment, served as an asylum for those cap-
tives of the Ocean. As the mistress of a well appointed house,
Diane de Limeuil did the honors of their prison with charming
grace, and the animation that those guests' presence momen-
tarily added to her existence was enough to temper its constant
monotony. But when the visitors became rare, in her studies,
in some housekeeping cares, in the elegant women's hand-
work in which she excelled, in her play with the idiot to whom
to a certain point she had made herself loved by her gentleness
and goodness, but most of all in the contemplation of the
grand scenes of nature, the young scholar found sufficient
diversions in her isolation.

For her, from the dome of the lighthouse which embraced an immense horizon, a series of sublime spectacles
unfolded that the harmonies of heaven and earth made incessantly to pass before her eyes. As soon as she arose, she went
to greet the morning splendors of the East reflected in the
shining waves of light. Sometimes she contemplated the almost setting sun in the vapor of the evening, inundating with
gold, purple and emerald the two immensities she had over her
head and under her feet. Dreaming under the star of the night,
when with its pale light it turned the top of the waves to silver,
melancholy with the fogs and the mist balancing on the liquid
plain, filling her imagination with the feeling of the infinite,
one day, in the sight of the sea sleeping and united as an im-

mense cloth, she found again with happiness the image of her life so calm that a care never troubled it.

The next day the scene was different. In the distance, at the edge of the horizon, she saw an enormous sleeping wave awakened by some ripples that rapidly criss-crossed its surface. Then as the wind turned cool, those ripples multiplied and changed into regular furrows like that of land which a plow has passed over. The wind, catching its breath, to that sight there followed waves, further apart and higher, rolling heavily on themselves and turning to white foam. Then there was a curious phenomenon that made seamen say that the sea was turning into sheep, because, in fact, it looked like a huge troop becoming detached with its white fleece from the dark green of prairies. Still tormented by the wind, that more and more pressed on it, the passed on to present the spectacle of deeper and deeper cavities until they came to break themselves in curls of foam against the obstacle that the rock and the lighthouse that surmounted it presented. Then after the rough weather, gales came and pushed before them those roaring mountains which seemed at the first shock that they must carry away the slender column of Bell Rock.

During the terrible heavy seas, the fearless girl found a strange pleasure in feeling under her feet the trembling of that airy tower, which, moving from its base to its summit, seemed to vacillate in space and vibrate like a sounding board under the effect of the denotation of waves coming to hurl themselves against its walls, reproducing the sound of lightning and of canons.

After a while, the two solitaries were so very familiar with those magnificent horrors, that during the long winter nights, the bellowing of the storms and the furious sea, instead of keeping them awake, seemed rather to put them to sleep. Rocked by the oscillations of their granite vessel, always anchored, they never slept more soundly than when the unleashed elements brought the strongest movement and the most desperate shakes.

More than four years had gone by in that way without any event troubling the course of that existence of uniform tranquility. It still seemed possible to hide for a long time from all the agitations of the world, where, from time to time, there came a vague echo. Nevertheless, in appearance the simplest in the world, an incident suddenly came to modify Matiphous' projects of indefinite retreat and throw him back into that tumultuous current of adventures that seemed to be the law of his life.

IV. Big, Fat and Widowed

In December 1804, as everyone knows, the coronation of Napoleon, who became Emperor of the French, took place. Curious, in general, about those sorts of occurrences, the English newspapers, despite their hatred for the fortunate soldier, published his coronation ceremony in great detail. Matiphous, in one of the gazettes with which he often passed his free time in his voluntary captivity, could read in a very detailed and very complete story all that had taken place in the Notre-Dame Cathedral in Paris. In the middle of a long list of the dignitaries of the new Court who figured in the Imperial pomp, there was a good number of names belonging to the old aristocracy. On that subject it was even recounted that a candid emigrant, reading, at Hartwell, the list of those outstanding deflections, exclaimed that it was false reporting on the part of the *Moniteur* and that all the officers of the usurper's crown listed must be *bad subjects* dressed up in the names of the former nobility, who hadn't forgotten themselves to that point.

Matiphous, who didn't at all have such a high idea of the infallibility of those St. Peters of legitimacy, remained, on the contrary, struck by the name of Lady Octave de Limeuil, listed among the number of ladies in the Empress' palace. Without speaking to his adoptive daughter about that discovery, he managed soon to get access to a genealogy of the Limeuils that he recalled having noticed among the family papers left by Diane's mother. After having read those titles, he believed

259

he could with authority think that person so well connected in the Imperial Court was a near relative of the young girl for whom he was caring.

He was in the process of finishing his research in the visitors' reception room, where he was consulting those old papers, when his colleague, Ephraim, entered. If the man from Malta had looked at the maniac closely, he would without a doubt have noticed that his eyes were shining and haggard and his face greatly distorted. But, occupied as he was with those documents, Matiphous wasn't struck by that look on his face. On the contrary, finding an opportunity to begin a subject with the unexpected arrival on which he often took pleasure to vex him:

"Well!" he said to him, pushing toward him the newspaper in which the Coronation Ceremony was printed, "the French have an Emperor, and the Pope himself crowned him."

"Pope, Emperor, two things which must disappear," replied Ephraim angrily, "and the Republicans allowed it to happen!"

"Well, yes," Matiphous replied, "and everything took place marvelously. Your friends, the Democrats, were well behaved, and to make up the cortege of the Great Man, many of the great names of the former nobility were mingled among them."

"Evil days! Evil days !" shouted Ephraim, lifting his arms toward Heaven, "that's discouraging for the future."

The man from Malta was going to answer him that, on the contrary, with the reign that was beginning, the future seemed to him rich in hope. But his colleague had already left, since it was almost always in that way, with some short exchange of words, that their encounters ended. Laughing to himself about the way in which he had put to flight that maniac, for whom hatred of Bonaparte was a kind of religion, Matiphous picked up the papers he had just consulted and went to replace them in his pupil's bedroom where they were usually kept.

In the interval, a cutter, a small boat that remained constantly in the Arbroath port that had charge of replenishing supplies to all the lighthouses along the coast, reached Bell Rock and disembarked two strangers who wanted to visit the lighthouse. While one of those visitors, a lively and alert lady, quickly climbed the bronze stairway which led to the rock's platform and to the door of the tower, her companion, a person with an excess of corpulence, needed the help of two sailors to hoist himself the length of the steps which usually the vapors of the sea and even sometimes waves made humid, slippery, and dangerous to access. Arrived, however, without any problem, that kind of Falstaff didn't seem to have done his share of the perilous ascent to which he had just been constrained. On entering the travelers' room, where he had been preceded some instants before by his agile companion:

"The Devil!" he shouted, "women and their curiosity! They have to see things, even if you must break your neck following them...'"

And in the middle of his imprecation, becoming aware of the graceful figure of Mademoiselle de Limeuil who, seeing him out of breath, had immediately come forward to off him some refreshment, he continued:

"At least, I'm not talking about you, charming miss. You appear to me to be a fortunate exception, God be thanked, in your sex. I will accept a pot of ale, port, or beer. I drink them all indifferently."

"And thanks to the welcoming nature of your stomach," the female traveler said disdainfully, "God knows the zephyr that you've become. Twenty steps to climb, and there you are all in sweat."

Immediately leaving to go look for something to use on that two-footed sponge, Diane didn't hear the rest of the dialogue which, by the tone of sweet pardon which he inserted, seemed to take place between two spouses. However, at the young girl's return, a happy modification seemed to have been made in the respective attitude of the strangers. Having taken off her traveling cloak and straw hat, shaded by a veil, a ravishing face appeared. The young lady, a batiste handkerchief in her hand, was busy drying the sweat that had run three quarters down his bald forehead to the face of her massive companion. A good and tender mother couldn't have taken more affectionate and more concerned care with a cherished child.

However, Matiphous, who wasn't present at the arrival of the travelers, had come forward to greet them, and his behavior toward them wasn't long in astonishing Diane de Limeuil. Usually hospitable and in a good humor when he saw some guests disembark, the man from Malta, that day, had taken on a disdainful and dark expression that his adopted daughter didn't remember ever having seen on him. Noticing that he was pale and that on his very altered features there showed something like indignation caused by the basically rather ridiculous spectacle of the beautiful stranger bestowing passionate cares on her monstrous companion.

"My good friend, what's wrong with you?" asked Mademoiselle de Limeuil. "You seem to be ill."

"Me! no," the man from Malta answered, with a grimaced smile.

"However, something extraordinary is happening to you."

"Once more, there's nothing wrong with me," Matiphous continued impatiently, "or to put it better," he continued, "I have something to reproach you for. I don't find it proper that you play the role here of a tavern servant."

"But, my friend, never before have you forbidden me to be welcoming and helpful to our visitors."

"That's because there are visits and visits," the man from Malta quickly answered.

Then, seeing that Diane was looking at him with a kind of astonishment, he brusquely took from her hands the little pitcher of ale and the glass she had arrived carrying. After having placed them roughly in front of the stranger:

"Yes," he continued, "it is perfectly useless for you to go to any trouble for people of this kind. So, go to your bedroom; I will take care of doing the honors for them, and please, I ask you, don't come out until I tell you to, and when we are delivered of this nice company."

Accustomed to defer to her adopted father, and understanding by the tone of harshness so unusual in their relationship, that Matiphous must have been struck by some unusual circumstance, Diane did her duty and left the room, very intrigued, if not worried, and shut herself in her room.

While the words that have just been reported were being exchanged in a low voice between the man from Malta and the pretty hostess of Bell Rock, the stranger had done well by the ample measure at his disposal of that well beloved liquid, but not content with that tacit approval, he said to Matiphous:

"Monsieur, that's a good brand of ale which must help you pass the time in this place of humidity and solitude."

"Yes, generally our ale is found passable," the man from Malta answered, "but probably that's the least thing of interest which has drawn you here. You have probably come to visit the lighthouse?"

"To tell the truth, without offending you, all the lighthouses in the universe couldn't be situated so as to make me take a step. But my lady, here present, persuaded me that your marine nest must be very curious to explore, and, me, in everything her humble servant, I had to consent to come with her."

"You will permit me to agree with the lady," Matiphous replied. "But to satisfy her desire, I advise her not to put off satisfying her curiosity. The cutter which brought you won't be long in coming back, and I doubt very much that he will be able to await your good pleasure, because all atmospheric conditions point to a wind storm."

"Let's go, My Lord," the female voyager said quickly. "Let's get moving; you heard him; we have just enough time."

Thus commanded, the stranger emptied his glass of what remained of the ale, and, after having slowly savored one for the road, with his large hands on the table before him he made a flying buttress and managed to get to his feet. And with a somewhat disinterested air, followed his petulant companion to whom Matiphous was showing the way. When they had glanced at the lower floors, opening the door to a stairway that led to the dome, the man from Malta said:

"What there is really curious here, that's the beam and the magnificent horizon which it shows from where it is placed. But, Milady," he added, "I suggest you adjust your hat and your shawl. Up there, the wind is a little strong, and it's not convenient to wear something that can be carried away by the wind."

"What!" asked the stranger quickly. "Is it dangerous up there?"

"Oh! no!" Matiphous answered, "especially in the company of My Lord, your husband, who is a man for balance and resistance."

"It's true," the fat man said, entering willingly into the joke, "that to lift a man of my importance it would take a very strong wind."

As if to calm her feminine fright, as soon as she had taken the precaution that her guide had suggested, the female traveler had begun to climb the stairs quickly. There was no need to show her the way; a passage opened up in front of her, only wide enough for one person. The man from Malta was walking behind the young lady, and, at some distance, forming the rear guard, the bulky stranger was trailing painfully behind. At about halfway up the height of the tower, at a spot where there was almost total obscurity in the length of which he was hoisting himself, the heavy person began to shout:

"Eh! You others, impossible to go any further..."

"Come on, have courage," answered the female voyager, "we will soon be at the top."

"But it's not a matter of courage," the mass of flesh replied, "the architect didn't take my measurements, and neither forward nor sideways, I can't get through."

"In fact," Matiphous said, laughing, "the stairway follows the pyramidal form of the tower and always gets smaller as it progresses; therefore at a given spot that unusual structure prevents an obstacle to corpulence beyond the ordinary."

Very annoyed by that ridiculous occurrence, the female stranger started to go back down.

"Not at all," Matiphous said, blocking that movement backward, "we have almost arrived. It's simpler to ask this poor gentleman to go back down. We will give only a glance up there, but the view, I assure you, is worth the trouble, and why deprive yourself of that spectacle that you won't have available any other time in your life."

"Well said! Go wait for us down below!" the female traveler shouted to her husband.

And while the unfortunate blocked man turned around backward, she arrived at the summit of the monument, followed by Matiphous.

"My God! What a wind there is up here, but what a magnificent expanse!" exclaimed the female traveler in the presence of that immense panorama which unfolded under her eyes.

Matiphous let her gaze around that vast space for some time; then a moment afterward as she asked him if that point she saw on the horizon wasn't the village of Arbroath, Matiphous answered:

"You are far-sighted, My Lady. How is it that with such eyes you don't recognize people better?"

The young lady looked at him, but in a face covered by a long beard that he no longer shaved since he had become an anchorite, and in traits it was impossible for her to recognize since she hadn't seen them in at least four years, when it was about that time Matiphous hadn't set foot outside the lighthouse, she couldn't make out anything that revealed a memory.

When she admitted that absolute lack of memory, Matiphous continued:

"Me, I'm less forgetful, and I recognized you marvelously; you are Kitty Ketch, the daughter of the London hangman."

"But I don't know who you are," replied the woman, without accepting an identity very little flattering to her ego, but also without expressly denying it.

"Oh! Well, me, I remembered you at first sight, you and the boxer Broughton accompanying you. Only, I found him a little out of shape."

"If that is so," the traveler said drily, "to whom do I have the advantage of speaking?"

"To a man, Milady, you cruelly played with. To Gregorio Matiphous, your fiancé and the former aide to your father."

"You! Monsieur Matiphous! Here?'"

"Where, charming Miss, I'm paying for the happiness I had to love you and to believe your word."

"My God!" the young woman answered, "I know very well that I committed great wrongs against you, but my aunt must have told you, I was then under a charm, and for many years I had thought about Monsieur Broughton."

"And then," said the man from Malta, whose face took on a sinister expression, "it was very natural that I served as a stepping stone to that very ancient and very respectable love?"

"I don't say that, but, then, after some years, you don't hold a grudge against people."

"Grudge!" Matiphous repeated. "Oh! I have something better than that for you."

That word was said with an accent so menacing that Kitty immediately felt herself in danger, and, with an instinctive movement, she moved toward the entry to the stairway, saying that the violence of the wind didn't allow her to stay very long in that place.

"Not at all, not at all!" Matiphous said, barring her from the passageway. "It's here, alone, between Heaven and Earth that you have to listen to me. You probably took great pleasure in the game you played with me..."

"Oh, no, Monsieur," Kitty answered softly. "I've already told you: I gave way to a bad inclination from my heart. On the contrary, I regretted very much those actions which circumstances made a necessity."

"And you think that, wounded in my feelings, my honor stained, condemned for more than four years to seclusion and exile, everything will be forgotten because you have consented to tell me about your regret'"

"But, Monsieur, what better can I say to you? Isn't the past with God?"

"Men have, at least, the present," Matiphous answered, raising his voice. "And tell me, do you remember a statement that you once made to me?"

"I don't know. During the time that I was honored with your acquaintance, many things were said between us."

"Yes, but among all those things, one sentence I still remember: *People from Malta,* you said to me one day, *are possessed by demons of vengeance.*"

"I must have said that in a moment of bad humor."

"Well, you didn't lie. A man from Malta can wait ten years, twenty years, his whole life, but, when the day arrives, he reaps his justice."

"Monsieur," Kitty exclaimed, frightened at the tone with which those words had been pronounced, "you wouldn't give way to some violence?"

"Say your prayers," Matiphous said in a tone of cold resolution, "because as God is God, you won't go down in the way that you came up."

"Have pity! Have pity! Monsieur Matiphous," said the poor woman, throwing herself at the knees of the furious man.

"Pity, and you! Did you have any for me?"

And seeing the man menacing her with some terrible death, Kitty left her begging posture and, in a desperate effort, she tried to push aside Matiphous who was barring the access to the stairway. But that violent action only hastened the catastrophe. Receiving, without being moved, the blow that the weak creature had intended to give him, Matiphous took advantage of the moment and, seizing her with his strong arms, lifting the victim, he already held her horizontal, suspended over the abyss, when behind him, a long burst of laughter broke out, as if some demon had found himself there to applaud that tragedy.

Surprised at the last moment by an intervention that nothing in that place and at that moment should have made him expect, the man from Malta turned around and saw the idiot crouched under the beam apparatus. He should have remembered that the poor imbecile spent three quarters of his life in that spot. Either brought back to reflect by that hideous laugh, his action appeared to Matiphous in all its horror, or that sudden interruption was sufficient to calm the violent movement to which he had been on the point of ceding; or finally, because he had never had the intention of terrifying his deceitful mistress, he said to her:

"You see, My Lady, that I could take revenge," and at the same time putting her back upright, "go," he added, "go join your lovable Broughton, that man of weight and importance for whom special stairs have to be constructed."

But Matiphous' cruel act had had more regrettable results than he at first thought. Just as Kitty's feet touched the floor, he saw her legs give way under her and, looking at her face then, he recognized that, under the effect of the terror, she had entirely lost consciousness. That posed a great problem for the irascible man from Malta. In the place where the scene took place, he had no way at hand to take care of that fainting. On the other hand, given the layout of that narrow spiral staircase, carrying down that inanimate body would have presented the greatest difficulties.

Without taking much time to think about it, Matiphous thought of another way. He left for a moment and came back soon afterward provided with a stimulant. On entering the place from which he had been absent for only a few minutes, he was at first surprised to no longer find the unconscious woman where he had left her. But his astonishment took on another aspect when, after having looked around the narrow space that took only a glance, he determined that decidedly Jack Ketch's daughter had disappeared.

That she had escaped by means of the staircase was impossible. The armoire in which the anti-spasmodiques which he had brought back were kept, was located at the bottom of the stairway to the tower, some feet from the door through which the fugitive would have had to pass. Should he think that having naturally regained use of her senses, she, herself, in an excess of fright and of despair had inflicted on herself the treatment with which she had only been threatened? Or, finally. should that mysterious disappearance be attributed to some supernatural intervention?

While those ideas went rapidly through his mind, Matiphous noticed that the idiot had a knot of blue ribbons in his hands that he recalled having seen a minutes before attached to Kitty's blonde hair.

A horrible suspicion suddenly occurring to him, he threw himself on the idiot and shook him violently by his arm.

"Williams," he asked him, "where is the lady?"

The imbecile looked at him without answering and again began rolling the ribbons in his fingers, continuing his eternal murmuring.

"Will you speak!" the man from Malta then shouted, angrily gripping his arm. "I'm asking you where the lady is!"

And he seized the ribbons. That time the idiot seemed to have understood. A dazed look spread over his face. At the same time, he quickly got up and ran to the balustrade that ran completely around the platform of the monument. There his pantomime became terribly expressive. He made the movement of picking up something from the floor, and then, with both his arms held out in front of him, he reproduced the violent act by which a heavy object is thrown far away.

So, there was no longer any doubt. That imitative and malicious instinct in the man with as much intelligence as a monkey, had just caused a terrible misfortune. Witness of the wicked action that Matiphous had not completed, the miserable idiot had taken it on himself, and by the hand of that brute, in whom the detestable appetite for destruction had been raised, always more developed in human nature to the degree that it is less directed by reason, the unfortunate Kitty had been sent to a horrible death.

By a natural comparison, led to recall the daughter of the Gozzo fisherman who had the first affections of his heart and whose very sad end he had later learned, *It is then written,* the man from Malta thought, *that after having outrageously deceived me, all my loves would have the sea as a tomb?*

And he shed a tear for those two victims of their own duplicity. But the troubles of the present were too vivid in his mind for him to take the leisure to be sorry about the past. How to make the stranger accept as a fact the catastrophe of which Kitty was the victim? To claim that, seized with vertigo, she had herself fallen, that explanation was very unlikely. To mention the deadly intervention of the idiot was hardly any more believable. There was no way to deceive himself.

Assuming that Broughton immediately showed himself easy to persuade, the return to Arbroath or even on the cutter, during the trip, he would learn the name of the guardian he had left alone with his wife. That name alone would be a total revelation, and, from there, blaming Kitty's disappearance on an atrocious impulse for revenge, he wouldn't be long in referring it to the law, where it would find all the elements for an accusation of murder.

From that rapid review of the situation, Matiphous appeared to deduct a very regrettable necessity. If he didn't want to let himself be hanged in Scotland, as before that he almost had been in Malta, he must leave the lighthouse immediately. Risking the loss of all the cost of that sacrifice, he had to find a way to prevent Broughton from being on the voyage.

Thus, with a violent or clever procedure, to keep the ex-boxer at Bell Rock, and to do so as to prevent him from embarking on the little boat that was coming to pick him up, that was the problem. We will tell the solution that Matiphous found and it can be read in the following chapter.

V. The Flying Fish

The first concern of the man from Malta was to go find his adopted daughter and instruct her to make, as quickly as possible, a package of some of her clothes and toilette articles. He advised her most of all to put into that little baggage the documents and family papers which we saw him researching at the arrival of Kitty and Broughton. As for the motives of that sudden departure, he reserved an explanation of them to his pupil for later. It was expected that the cutter could come back at any time. They didn't have a moment to lose if they wanted to get on board.

The man from Malta made the same preparations for himself, and he didn't leave out of his provisions for the journey a little chest containing a nice round sum, a result of the savings he had been able to make during his sojourn at Bell Rock. Those dispositions taken, there remained the difficult question of sequestering the boxer, and while taking care of the arrangements for departure, Matiphous hadn't stopped thinking of that problem. Here's the way he finally decided to take care of it. Going to find his man in the travelers' room, he was going to tell him that Kitty took such an unusual pleasure in contemplating the view of the panorama from the dome that he wasn't able to persuade her to come down. He then deemed that he would be unnecessary company for her, and while waiting for that ardent nature admirer to rejoin them, he suggested to Broughton that he empty another pot of that ale that had had the honor of his approval. It was believed that, mixed with that beer, a strong dose of alcohol would transform the boxer's reason in a rather perfidious manner so that he wouldn't put up a long resistance. Then the worthy man would be put under lock and key, and before he had drunk the vat of poison, Matiphous counted very much on having reached the coast and being in safety in Arbroath.

This beautiful plan set up, the man from Malta, hurried to prepare the traitorous mixture; then, after glancing at the preparations he had told his adopted daughter to make, and

271

that he found a good way toward completion, he went back to Broughton, almost sure that ingestion of that insidious liquid by that intrepid drinker wouldn't be a great problem. But, as he entered the travelers' room, he saw that his star had made useless his expense of imagination. Because of his excessive corpulence, habitually of a sleepy disposition, the boxer, at his return from his abortive ascent, had thrown himself into an armchair, whose comfortable position alone would have been enough to induce sleep. As Matiphous appeared, a harmonious and sonorous snoring was for him, if one can speak this way, the trumpet of good fortune that in the middle of his ingenious arrangements, he hadn't the least idea of counting on.

Nevertheless, he didn't want his preparations to be proved wrong, and since he also had an old account to settle with the boxer, he placed on a table near him the pot of adulterated ale. When he awoke, taking the presence of that unusual refreshment for a delicate attention, it was a good bet that the boxer would be led to drown his reason there by himself. That innocent revenge thus arranged, Matiphous had only to board the cutter as soon as it touched Bell Rock. Here, more than ever, in the fortunate slumber of Broughton, an unusual favor of fate was revealed, because, just as the man from Malta opened the lighthouse door to have news of the little boat, whose arrival he was watching for, he heard the captain's voice hailing the passengers for them to get aboard without delay. So, as Matiphous had foreseen, the sea, from one moment to the next, was becoming worse.

The appearance of the man from Malta and his pupil was a kind of event on board the cutter. During the almost five years that they had resided at Bell Rock, they were moving to ground for the first time. Matiphous was greatly congratulated on the sacrifice that he had decided to make of his anachorite beard, and the absence of the two travelers remaining at Bell Rock seemed completely natural, when he had explained that fear of stormy weather had held them back. Despite a sea that had become threatening, the crossing, happy and rapid, was not marked by any incident.

As soon as he had disembarked, the man from Malta, informed himself about departing ships. Having the luck to find a three mast which that same evening was setting sail for Hamburg from the English docks, he immediately booked passage there, so that he would already be a great distance from the coast of Scotland before anything of his unfortunate adventure had reached the village of Arbroath.

Once in safety, Matiphous became more communicative, and consented to give his adopted daughter the explanations relative to their sudden departure that until then he had left her hoping for. About eleven years-old, at the time she came under the care of the man from Malta, Diane de Limeuil, in 1804, was in her sixteenth year. In physique as well as in morality, she appeared notably developed. That would explain then the nuance of feminine second thoughts very easy to catch in the conversation which will follow. That conversation took place between the tutor and his pupil the day after they had taken passage aboard the three mast.

Pressed to tell the reason for his rapid departure:

"Yesterday morning, Matiphous began, '"reading in the newspaper the account of the coronation ceremony, I noticed the name of a Lady Octave de Limeuil serving as a Lady of the Empress' Palace."

"So?" Diane asked.

"Then I went through your family papers, and being sure that Monsieur Octave de Limeuil, that I saw there a number of times, was your father's brother, I concluded that the Lady in the Palace called by the same name, must be his wife, and consequently your aunt."

"That couldn't be more logical; but what does that have to do with us?"

"You should understand it. I was happy to discover that you have a relative with a position in the Imperial Court."

"I don't think it was to put us in contact with her that you carried me away like a holy relic."

"Not absolutely. But, nevertheless, for a long time something has worried me. Until the age where you are now, I have been able, alone, without help from anyone, to fulfill the promise made to your poor mother on her death bed."

"And now," Diane asked, with some bitterness, "carrying out that promise has ceased being possible for you?"

"Probably, because the time has come for you to think of an establishment. Without fortune, with no standing at all in the world, no person less than I is in a position to provide you with that."

"But, *Mon Dieu*! Who then is talking about getting me an establishment?" the young girl asked, shrugging.

"Me, whose duty it is, and who, right up until the day when I have led you to that port, will be responsible to see to your future before the saintly and worthy woman who, from up above, is probably watching us."

"That responsibility must weigh very heavily on you," Diane de Limeuil then replied, putting in her voice more bitterness than the tender evenness and the habitual sweetness of her character would have expected.

"Far from being a burden to me," Matiphous replied, "the care I have given you up until now has been my greatest consolation, as it will perhaps be the honor of an existence where the fatality of evil has had up until now more place. But now, not being in a position to crown my work, I thought about asking for help from your relatives. The ties of blood and her high position could give you a very useful protector."

"Certainly," Diane said, ironically, "I should count a great deal on my relatives. In London, they were so kind to my mother!"

"You are talking about your relatives, the ones who emigrated, who were prejudiced against the birth of the Marquise, your mother. But your aunt, accepting a responsibility at the court of the Usurper, as he is called, must have very different ideas."

"So," Mademoiselle de Limeuil asked, still in the same quarrelsome tone, "'it was to run to the probable contempt of that aunt that we left our poor Bell Rock so suddenly?"

"To tell the truth," Matiphous answered, "I hadn't fore-seen leaving in that way, on such short notice. But an adventuress and a knight of industry, encountered in the past, and to whom there was nothing less agreeable than to renew their acquaintance coming to trouble our solitude, to take you away from that low contact, I only hastened a trip by several weeks that I had first thought about. What's more, I intended to tell you about it the same day we started."

"It is still rather unusual," Mademoiselle de Limeuil, obviously hostile to Matiphous' project, observed maliciously, absolutely wanting to quarrel with him, "that as much in a hurry as you are to approach my aunt, you have thought about reaching France."

Matiphous had more than one good reason to take that detour. First of all, fear of being followed by Broughton, he had boarded the first ship he had found available; then, it must be added, before trying his luck on the soil of a country where his former participation in Sir Sidney Smith's escape had somewhat badly repaid hospitality, he wasn't sorry, as it's said, to see the lay of the land, and in this way, the detour through Germany was going to do that. But independent of his two prudent motives, which he had no intention of telling his pupil, the fierce war at that time between France and England, was an absolute obstacle to an English ship landing in one of the ports of the English Channel.

That was how he victoriously challenged the girl's reasoning, and he pointed out to her in addition that the strait was infested with pirates and that he wasn't in any hurry to meet them in his path. As far as wolves on the sea and wolves on land, the proverb is all the same, because at the moment the man from Malta was talking to his pupil about the danger of finding on their route some *letter of marque*[119] the man placed at the top on the crow's nest signaled there was a sail in sight.

---

[119] In the days of fighting sail, a letter of marque and reprisal was a government license authorizing a person (known as a privateer) to attack and capture enemy vessels and bring them

The Captain immediately took his spyglass and after having considered, to speak his language, *what it was all about,* shaking his head, he said:

"Hum! Too close."

And he began to look with doubled attention, at the ship that from its equipment didn't seem to have anything marvelously good for them to foresee.

"Captain," said the Helmsman, taking it on himself to interrupt that long observation, "doesn't that look a lot like a privateer?"[120]

"Take this. See for yourself, if that doesn't look like it," the Captain responded.

The sailor respectfully took the spyglass and after having followed with his eye the unknown ship that the wind was pushing with full sails in the wake of the three masts.

"It's small," he said. "It's light and it could be a kind of three masts along coastal waters carrying a twenty-five to thirty member crew with a few pairs of little bronze trumpets to start a conversation."

"And if that young adolescent," the Captain asked, "did us the favor, as it seems to want to do, to capture the *Flying Fish,* Captain Lantonne, what would Monsieur the Helmsman think of that?"

"Damn! I think I would prefer something else in our path. But the gazettes that I read yesterday at Arbroath indicated that it had been seen very recently off the waters of Gibraltar."

"Aren't there always some eels somewhere that slip through your fingers when you think you have grasped them! That wild pirate never does anything else but grow like bad

---

before admiralty courts for condemnation and sale. Cruising for prizes with a letter of marque was considered an honorable calling combining patriotism and profit, in contrast to unlicensed piracy, which was universally reviled.

[120] A privateer was a private person or ship that engaged in maritime warfare under a commission of war.

sea weed where it's the least expected. Let's go, let's go," said the Captain. "We have to be ready for anything; prepare for combat!"

At that order, all the crew ran to their stations. The sailors raised the cannon portholes and a dozen cannons[121] were put immediately in batteries to show the audacious *mosquito*[122] that, since he acted as if he intended to give chase, he would find out what he was dealing with.

During those preparations the pirate had approached in reach of the cannon and came alongside the three masts. It had deployed its tricolored flag. A strong and resounding voice then shouted:

"Strike your colors for France!"

On his side, the Captain of the English ship had ordered the national flag to be raised to the top of the mast, and as the only response to the insolent intimidation of the pirate, he had sent him a barrage from his cannons. But as he expected, he was faced with the most fearless and resolute adversary. The sailors manning the cannons hadn't had time to recharge when the little ship came along side, and the adversary, using grappling hooks to come aboard, he saw itself invaded with cries of "Long live the Emperor," by about twenty some odd devils incarnate and soon the French fury had conquered the English vessel that was then immediately occupied, taken over and conducted to Dunkirk.

There, with all the crew of the captured vessel, Matiphous and his pupil were at first treated as prisoners of war. But by means of the documents and papers of the family that the man from Malta had in his possession, it was not difficult for him to establish French nationality for Mademoiselle

---

[121] Rabou here uses the word *caronades*, a light-weight cannon used at the time, less accurate than later cannons.

[122] In contempt for the usually small boats that the French corsairs sailed, the English called them *moucherons*, tiny flies or mosquitoes. But they often bit the British lion in a cruel way. (Note from the Author)

de Limeuil. As for himself, under the catch-all name of "Deschamps," he passed himself off as an emigrant who had embarked with the intention of coming to be repatriated and the position he occupied with the young girl whose nationality had just been confirmed caused his own to be accepted without being contested, and in some sense was part of the bargain.

There was something better than that. The name de Limeuil was known by the Assistant Prefect of Dunkirk as being that of a woman very well placed in Court and who occupied a high position near the Empress. The gallant administrator then thought it would be an act of clever courtisanship to put at the disposal of the young emigrant all the good services that he was able to render her, including that of money, just in case in she was experiences some difficulty in that manner. Put back in possession of all his belongings and those of Diane, which had not been declared, Matiphous, in all that unexpected goodwill accepted only a good legal passport, that, under his new name of Deschamps, consolidated in his hand the full enjoyment and entire title and quality of Frenchman. In that fashion, and thanks to the good fortune of his short captivity, he was reintegrated into France much more easily than he would have hoped. A little less than a week after his departure from Bell Rock, and in company of his pupil, he arrived in Paris.

VI. The Paris Lottery

Matiphous didn't find it as easy to see Madame de Limeuil as he had supposed. It was only after having gone to her townhouse several time to no avail that he decided to let her know the object of his visit if he wanted to be received. And also, what was he thinking about to assume that name of Deschamps, and what do you expect a mistress of a house to answer someone who comes to announce that Monsieur Deschamps solicits the honor of an interview? There are so many people of that name that, to tell the truth, it belongs to no one. Without considering the fact that it absolutely lacked elegance, for the mind it was only an abstraction. One could be ready to see an unknown but only if its personality offers something for the imagination. Deschamps! Just as well say it's a good third of humanity who is asking you for an audience. Matiphous then decided to write. But it took time for any letter to arrive and then to be answered. Let's add that, kept busy with her service to the Empress, Madame de Limeuil couldn't make use of her time as she wished. In brief, all that detour caused at least a delay of a week. However, Diane was triumphant and held to her presentiment of a detestable reception that was already going to be realized.

On the contrary, the man from Malta forced himself to find that delay explainable, claiming that he didn't prejudge anything. Besides, he took advantage of it to take his adoptive daughter to see the beauties of the great city, And although Mademoiselle de Limeuil showed herself rather cold to all those marvels, claiming that the view from the top of Bell Rock, the spectacle of a sunset, left very far behind it the splendors of Paris civilization, her tutor insisted on taking her everywhere and the least entries from *The Stranger's Guide* book were oracles for him.

A dead institution today,[123] replaced by repeated acts of charity, the lottery at that time flourished under the official patronage of the government which claimed, perhaps with some justification, that, of all taxes, that one which was paid spontaneously is the best invented and the most sustainable. By this reckoning, the drawing of chances by fate had been surrounded by the power of a certain solemnity. It was on the rue Neuve-des-Petits-Champs, in the former palace of Cardinal Mazarin, later the building of the Companies des Indes, that the administration of the lottery was installed. There a vast room, decorated picturesquely in the form of an ancient temple, offered to the view of the public a colossal statue of Destiny, the patron divinity of that temple. The statue held its fatal book on its knees. Presided over by the Minister of the

---

[123] The present Loterie Nationale was resurrected in 1933.

279

Police when winning numbers from a wheel of fortune came to be proclaimed by an orphan from the National Orphanage, by means of an ingenious mechanism, they appeared to be written as if by magic on the page where the book of destiny was open. The effect produced by this coup de theater on the idle Parisian looking on can't be described. So it was that on the days of the drawings, the crowd which filled the room where the scene took place was exclusively composed of professional players or those with tickets. For some, the appeal of the spectacle was limited to the eruption of numbers as soon as they fell from the hand of fate. For others, they never tired of coming to look at the poor orphan, dressed in red, like the children in a choir, his eyes blindfolded and his hands covered with a kind of military glove to avoid any idea of fraud.

In all, a lively emotional atmosphere, an apparatus cleverly calculated to impress, the dramatic aspect of the disappointment and the joy in the expression of the most the most stressed and the liveliest was well beyond what was needed to justify a big crowd. There was nothing more natural, therefore, than to see Matiphous, some days after his arrival, having taken his pupil there as a spectacle worth her attention. The drawing had just finished. Giving his arm to Mademoiselle de Limeuil, the man from Malta had left the room in the middle of a compact crowd. But they had already gone far enough that, each one pushed from his side, the great crowd in the middle of which they had walked for some time, began to thin out. Matiphous was then rather disagreeably affected when, turning around by chance, he believed he saw an unknown person purposely measuring his pace to his own, and making an effort not to pass him. That notice struck him so much more strongly in that, in the location of the lottery, he had already noticed that the radiant beauty of Mademoiselle de Limeuil seemed to have been a continued attraction for that unknown man.

The man appraised, he was in every country of the world, what would have been called a shining cavalier: dark complexion, black hair falling in thick curls from under his

hat, a tall and well-formed physique, irreproachably fashionable, a distinguished air, and even a little presumptuous, that's
what the man from Malta inventoried at a glance and which
seemed to him to very well mean the unknown person was an
audacious amorous adventurer. He was patient for some
minutes more, then very sure that the unknown man hadn't
stopped following them, he stopped short, and when the observer was beside him, he asked him heatedly what he meant
and why he was walking in cadence with him. Thus called to
task, the unknown man didn't seem to be discouraged and, on
the contrary, an affable smile spread over his face. At the same
time, from one of the pockets of his coat, he took out several
brochures with different colored covers, and with a rather pronounced Italian accent, he said graciously to the questioner:

"Monsieur, I am the author of some little works about the
lottery, and I wish I may be permitted to present you with
one."

"Eh! Monsieur," replied the man from Malta, who
wasn't at all satisfied with that response, "to give people your
production, to walk as you are doing, in their shoes, doesn't
seem necessary to me."

"If you would like," the unknown man continued, without letting himself be turned from his intention, "I can offer
you the *Livre d'or,* the *Trésors of Mameluck* and *The Quintes
Égyptienne,* the *Vrai et gros Cagliostro,* the *Tables d'argent,*
and the *Traité de la sympathie universelle,* that most of all I
recommend to your attention."

"Just a minute," the man from Malta replied, pushing
away the brochures, "your manner of following on my heels
displeases me extremely. If your path is in the way you are
heading, I have nothing to say, but I'm going to take the opposite direction, where it is not presumable that suddenly you are
also going that way. Now, I tell you, I will take as a terrible
insult your persistence in walking behind me."

That said, and without waiting for an answer, he started
on his way again, and while the importunate man remained in
place, seemingly very occupied with returning all his library

into his pocket, the tutor and his pupil walked away from him, going back in a way from where they started, defying him in that way to continue his maneuver to that point.

While the young girl argued with her adopted father about his idea of exposing himself to some regrettable dispute, Matiphous, from time to time, turned around to see the effect of his demand. He had the satisfaction of verifying that his reprimand seemed to have rid them of the annoyance. However, as they approached the rented house where, since his arrival in Paris, he had lived, the idea came to him that, without his knowing it, he had perhaps been followed at a distance. He judged it prudent by some clever backtracking to ward off, if need be, a furtive maneuver of the enemy. That inspiration was well taken. And he quickly retraced his steps. As he turned into a street, he discovered his man hidden under a carriage entrance. So the tenacious person had not left the trail and had only put a little more cleverness and discretion into his insistence on persecution. The man from Malta immediately made his decision. Seeing a haberdasher shop, he pushed, rather than escorted, his pupil into the shop, telling her to choose some knitting wool and tapestry work which they had earlier talked about. Then, running to this pursuer, who in the meantime had remained firm, waiting for him, he said:

"Monsieur, you obviously want things to go badly between us."

The unknown man again put his hand in his pocket, and Matiphous thought that it was once more going to be a matter of the ridiculous brochures, but not at all. Searched for in an elegant card holder for a moment, it was a calling card, golden on the edges, and courteously presented to him, asking him to look at it.

"Monsieur," the man from Malta observed to him on receiving what he took to be a challenge to a duel, "I can't return the same to you; I don't have on me either a card or card holder, but if you will take a piece of paper out of yours and your pen…"

"Not necessary," interrupted the unknown man. "You have misunderstood my intention. Just take the trouble to read the card."

Matiphous didn't think he should refuse that invitation and on the card was written, because the luxury of the engraved card was no longer in fashion: *Prince de Bevillacqua, Director of the Imperial Lottery.*

"Monsieur," then said the clerk prince, otherwise known to us as the *Summo Maestro* of the *Grand Firmament,* "I gave you that card so that you would know first of all who you are dealing with, and that I am not an adventurer."

"An adventurer, no, but a disagreeably obstinate man who seems to take for what is not his own, me and the young person that I had the honor to accompany."

"Well, Monsieur," the Prince replied, "that is precisely where you are wrong. A while ago, in the lottery room where my presence by the nature of my functions will, I think, sufficiently explain my presence, I followed with my attention a very graceful young girl whose arm you had taken."

"To that point," Matiphous interrupted with a feeling that somewhat resembled paternal pride, "there is nothing much to be said. That young girl is charming, and to a certain point I don't pretend to prevent people from looking at her."

"I looked at her," the Prince continued.

"And followed her," the man from Malta said in a meaningful tone.

"And followed her," repeated the Prince with good grace, "but with a completely different sentiment than that of admiration or covetousness.'"

"Then, Monsieur, why this insistence?"

"Because a young and beautiful woman is always interesting when it's known she's threatened with very great danger."

"Danger!" Matiphous quickly said. "What do you mean by that?"

"An immense, a terrifying peril," continued the Prince with a great appearance of truth, "and it was to tell you about

283

it, away from the presence of the one that I know is threatened, that I have maneuvered around you for an hour, exposing my well-meaning action to the most ridiculous interpretations."

"But that danger, what's its nature?" asked Matiphous, that the serious and convincing tone of the Prince wasn't without disturbing him somewhat.

"To tell you where the lightning will come from, I am not permitted to say, but I can tell you the way to get it, assuming, however, that a deplorable distrust doesn't paralyze the value of that information in your hands."

"Excuse me, Monsieur. It seems there is some misunderstanding here. The young person in whom you wish to trouble yourself to take an interest is a foreigner, arrived in Paris just a few days ago, not having, except for me, any kind of relationship. How could she be the object of some ill-will?"

"That's right," Bevillacqua continued, "a foreigner, and probably from some country in the Orient, from which you yourself seem to have originated."

"Well, that's what confirms your mistake. My young pupil has passed the better part of her youth in a country to the north, and that's the country she has come from."

"So be it! But you will not confirm that she has never been in the Orient, because I think you do not know either her parents or the place of her birth."

"The place of her birth, I don't know exactly, but what I can guarantee you is that I knew her mother very well."

"Who was an Italian?"

"Eh! No, Monsieur, a French woman. As you see her, there is no one any more French. There is between us some mistake."

"It is possible," the Prince continued after having appeared to reflect for a moment, "that from a certain direction my information hasn't had all the accuracy desired, and that explains the position of a man who accidentally discovered a secret, nothing of which was conveyed to him. But as a whole, I'm unfortunately sure that I haven't made a mistake. Now, you've been warned, you'll make a reasonable use of it. Only please take it for certain that taken in a vacuum and with ill-defined information, all the precautions you can take will be absolutely without a result."

Having said that, Bevillacqua gave the man from Malta a friendly wave; then he acted as if leaving him without insisting any further. Matiphous at first let him go, but the perfectly cold and indifferent tone with which his questioner was leaving him could with difficulty not leave an impression. He then retraced his steps, and, like a man who had changed his mind, approaching the man giving advice, he said:

"Monsieur, our situation is something so unusual that you will certainly excuse me for having to think twice before making a decision. But a moment ago, if I'm not mistaken, you kindly told me that the danger against which you wanted to forewarn me, you knew a way to get to it?"

"It's true, I said that. But just because of the extreme simplicity of that means, how easy it is to use, and I will go so far as to say, how agreeable it is, leaves me greatly in doubt that you will decide to use it."

"Why?" Matiphous insisted.

"Because you take me for someone making a bad joke."

"What does that matter, if I'm a man who will listen to a joke?"

"You say that, but faced with something you can't understand, the ego intervenes and you aren't at all what you had promised."

"Oh, no!" the man from Malta said quickly, "I promise to take your information seriously and to be nothing but perfectly grateful."

"You finally want it?"

"Absolutely! Speak, I insist."

"Well, this evening," the Prince said, weighing his words, "you and that young lady, between eight and nine o'clock, be at the Opera, but sitting where you can be easily seen."

"And who will see us?"

"Me and a woman I will accompany."

"And then?"

"Nothing. I will not speak to you or approach you; I won't seem to recognize you, but my wife, because it's good that you know I'm married, my wife will have seen you, and at that the peril disappears."

"I have to admit that your way of safety appears a little farcical," Matiphous then said. "I will also admit, however, that it can have its serious side, and the mysterious stranger of that encounter?"

"The important thing is that she exists," the Prince interrupted with some dryness. "I would add, however, to encourage you, I will not make any obstacle to the procession of some friends and even to the intervention of the police, if that suits you, and will see nothing inconvenient. That well explained, I leave you, and I am your servant."

Matiphous' perplexity could be understood. The man who had just spoken to him had a great appearance of good faith, joined to all the appearance of a good social standing, and had been, in any case, a conspirator of good company. In the procedure he presented as efficacious in clarifying an unknown danger, he could probably find more than one inconvenience. And to look at it from the bright side, it had at least put off an unusual perfume of oddness. But on the other hand, did the peril in question really exist? There are so many strange encounters in life! And if one had to reproach himself for incredulity or for a refinement of caution, which had left an opening for a disaster that could have been brought to light, what a regret and what a responsibility to incur! Such was the interior monologue that occupied Matiphous during the time he took to conduct Mademoiselle de Limeuil to their domicile. The same remained in his thoughts the entire day. Finally, toward the dinner hour, after several times walking up and down, he had, it seems, made a decision, because, returning to his pupil, he said:

"Diane! You must make yourself beautiful and put on the new dress brought to you yesterday. You haven't yet seen the

Opera. I've just bought tickets; we are going there this evening."

VII. The Limeuil Household

Matiphous certainly had in his past more than one memory that must have made him hesitate a great deal when confronted with such a suspicious and so unusual a situation as that to which he was summoned. But a character's disposition creates the events of the life right to a certain point. Before everything else, the man is the man he is, and it's indirectly and in the long run that in each individual the moral temperament is modified by experience. Adventures are accepted by the adventurous, and in accepting, in the end, the strange rendezvous from the Prince, Matiphous was obeying his inclination and a kind of gravitation. Let us say, nevertheless, that in letting himself, perhaps, be drawn into a trap, he had surrounded his actions with all the precaution that prudence had suggested. Having taken his officious savior at his word, he hadn't spared expense for a method that he himself had set up. And the proof was that, on his entry to the theater, a man who looked like a policeman had made him a sign of recognition. The same man had then followed him at a distance and had not left him until he had seen where he was going to sit with his pupil. There was another testimony that the vigilance of the man from Malta had surrounded Mademoiselle de Limeuil with adequate protection. If the contents of his pockets had been inventoried, there would have been found in the form of two small pistols called *fight-starters,* with which, in the present case, he had decided to be well armed.

But despite all those preparations and notwithstanding the great dramatic airs of the business started that morning, it must be said that its denouement unfolded in a very ordinary way. Almost across from Matiphous and his pupil, Monsieur de Bevillacqua and the lady he spoke of, came to take seats in a box they occupied by themselves. The Prince's companion was a woman that much make-up and the mirage created by the lights made appear more beautiful than she really was. A great look of lack of interest, boredom, and even suffering showed in her expression, and the man from Malta could see that during the duration of the drama, not a word was exchanged between her and Bevillacqua. As for the attention that lady was supposed to give to Diane's presence, that attention was, if not undetectable, at least infinitely less marked than he had been led to expect. For a few seconds, Madame de Bevillacqua, if that name could actually be given to her, held her lorgnette pointed at Mademoiselle de Limeuil. And it would have been impossible to confirm that following that hasty examination the eyes that had looked at Diane were wet with a tear, but in that symptom of nonconfirmed emotion, the quick, lustrous shine of her lorgnette as well as a movement of sensitivity could have had their part.

Sure of having been seen, the man from Malta had fulfilled the role required of him, and at the end of a certain time, he thought he could leave. That evening the spectacle was only mildly interesting. Mademoiselle de Limeuil seemed to take only very cold interest in it. Matiphous, preoccupied as he was with some attempt at a possible kidnapping at the exit, because that was the direction of his apprehensions, still less than his pupil he was not disposed to be amused with what was taking place on the stage. As a consequence, he suggested to Diane that they leave, a proposition immediately eagerly accepted. At the intermission they left the theater and got into a rented cab without any trouble. By means of the promise of a good tip, they were returned to their lodgings post haste. It must be thought that during the trip nothing disquieting happened, because while Mademoiselle de Limeuil had already gone through the door, leaving Matiphous busy settling with the coachman, that same man with the equivocal appearance who, under the peristyle of the theater, had appeared with information for him, passed by rapidly and said in his ear: *Nothing new!* A sacrosanct comment in police language revealing that on the surveillance horizon everything is dead calm.

Worried, nevertheless, by what could follow, Matiphous took the precaution of moving from the house where he had been staying, taking care not to leave a forwarding address for the new domicile he had chosen. For several days he took all the precautions that prudence could suggest. But his apprehensions being far from justified, two weeks later, Bevillacqua having encountered him in one of the *galeries de bois* of the Palais-Royal,[124] that unusual man pretended not to recognize him, since he maneuvered in a way so as not to be approached and was obviously in a hurry to be lost in the crowd. Notwithstanding his very natural desire to know the answer to the mysterious plot in which he had been mingled, Matiphous, as a result, didn't feel very relieved and satisfied in receiving that apparent notice of a definite conclusion.

As far as we are concerned, that exemplary discretion of the noble man from Genoa, can only be convenient for us, because it will take us to a less nebulous matter: to know the success of Matiphous' letters to the grand lady to whom he had written. Madame de Limeuil, born a Limeuil herself, and for the present we don't give her the title of Countess, because the titles of nobility were only restored in 1807 in the Imperial Court. Madame de Limeuil, as we say, had married the Count Octave de Limeuil, the younger brother of the Marquis who had died in the emigration, the one whose widow we have seen die in such a sad way in London. Madame de Limeuil was, then, the aunt by marriage of the young girl it was a matter of placing under her protection. And, besides, bearing the same name, she was still related to Diane, although in a more distant degree. Even so, by the marriage she had contracted with the uncle of the young person, the natural ties of that relationship couldn't be closer. Considering this, Madame Octave de Limeuil would have had very bad grace not to have given great consideration to Matiphous' request.

---

[124] Taking inspiration from the souks of Arabia and the forums of ancient Rome, the Galeries de Bois were the artistic, social and political centre of the French capital.

Also, as soon as the duties of her position with the Empress gave her free time, she hurriedly authorized Matiphous to visit her, bringing all the documents which he said he possessed. It couldn't yet be a question of receiving Mademoiselle de Limeuil. As a first step, it was indispensable that her relationship be authenticated.

There was not the least difficulty for that proof. Matiphous' clear and precise explanations, the family documents, and the genealogy that he placed under the eyes of the Lady of the Palace, soon convinced her. What's more, the personality of Diane, when she was allowed to appear before her noble relative, would have culminated, if it was needed, in the demonstration of her ancestry. The living portrait of her father the Marquis, she had, with the Count Octave who resembled his brother a great deal, such a uniformity of traits so perfect that everything about her showed such a great family resemblance that just the view of her gracious face in the absence of all the other proofs, she could claim to have her parentage accepted. It was astonishing, nevertheless, in recalling the very wicked actions that, in England, had marked the rapport of the Marquise with her relatives who emigrated, that now, in Paris, his daughter was welcomed properly.

But Matiphous had guessed right. In the Limeuil family the events of 1789 had changed a great many things. Although begun as a misalliance, following the democratic movement of the époque, the Marquis de Limeuil had emigrated and died following a wound received in the ranks of Condé's army.[125] Remaining, on the contrary, on French soil, his brother, the Count Octave had joined the services of the national armies

---

[125] Louis-Joseph de Bourbon, Prince de Condé (1736-1818). Cousin of Louis XVI of France, headed an army of émigrés comprised of so many of the French royal family that it was sometimes called "The Princes' Army." It also included young members of the French aristocracy. The army fought in conjunction with Austria but was paid by Spain, Portugal, Naples, Britain and Russia. It was disbanded in 1807.

and in 1792 he was Aide-de-Camp to General Beauharnais, Commander-in-Chief of the Army on the Rhine.[126] The man who had taken that position in the Revolutionary battle, couldn't be too strongly dominated by the prejudices of caste. Also, he was the only one in the Limeuil family who had seemed to give his approval to the conduct of his brother, the Marquis, when he had given his name to a girl without rank of birth, but worthy in all other ways of his choice. Nothing, therefore, could prevent Count Octave from accepting with enthusiasm a niece born of that marriage. Only, as will be seen, drawn to appeal to the wife rather than to the husband, without knowing the lay of the land, Matiphous had made a very fortunate choice.

Count Octave didn't take part in anything that concerned his household. Just to suspect his existence, it was necessary to be on a certain personal footing. Come into the world with admirable talents, high intelligence, a great taste for art, a physique at the same time pleasant and imposing, that very distinguished man had, for a number of years fallen into an incomprehensible effacement of himself. To confirm the period and the cause of that moral decadence was difficult. From the moment a Revolutionary decree had nullified the *former nobles* in military employment, after having given his resignation from the rank, he occupied in the Armies of the Republic, Count Octave had left France and had never ceased traveling to various countries. But at his return, which took place during the year 1799, everyone was struck by his black humor, certain lapses of mind, and in a word, extraordinary distractions that, without going to the point of suggesting a mental disorder, constituted at least the best characteristics of an attack of hypochondria. After some time, nevertheless, his state of mind improving, advantage was taken of that to have him marry a

---

[126] Alexandre François Marie, Viscount of Beauharnais (1760-1794). General during the French Revolution, he was the first husband of Joséphine Tascher de la Pagerie, who later married Napoleon. He was arrested in March 1794 and guillotined.

cousin, a girl without a fortune for whom that marriage was fate. It remains to be understood why, far from being declined, in addition to Count Octave's being completely passive, the girl of whom it was the object had agreed.

To say that union was unhappy wouldn't have been exactly true. After all, the young person who was resigned to it, had gotten almost the complete sum total of matrimonial benefits that many women, no longer girls, look for exclusively in marriage: a fine name, a beautiful fortune, on the outside great freedom, on the inside, the most absolute power to direct and administer everything. Those were the results of her bargain for Madame de Limeuil. Only, among all that conjugal felicity, what seemed the least understandable was on the side of the husband. He, who had promised to give himself, had in some way entirely kept himself back, and had only indirectly given himself. Traveling often, always alone, and with just a trusted servant, on his return to France he made long visits to his chateaux. When Count Octave came to reside in Paris, he was hardly a more real and more tender presence for his sad companion. When, by chance he found himself with his wife , he was put to flight by the least visit. With a number of pretexts, and often without even explaining that caprice, he had dispensed with appearing at the same table. In a vast townhouse, he had chosen to lodge in a pavilion lost in the depth of the garden. Negligent in his dress, taciturn, and not letting the secret of any predilection for work that occupied his long days of solitude, that man for everyone around him was a sad and inexplicable problem.

No one would be able to tell how Madame de Limeuil had become accustomed to that strange regime. She was one of those women which a strong sense of their dignity keeps them from confiding their bitterness, and never, despite the provocations and the insistence of her friends, had she consented to admit the secrets of her household to anyone. Nothing showed that she was happy, but also nothing showed that she had a wounded heart. Never complaining, even careful not to let it be perceived that she had some reason to complain, all her concern was to save appearances the best way possible and to avoid the bizarre behavior, which she was at the same time victim and witness, becoming too great a scandal.

"Yes, Monsieur de Limeuil has a few eccentricities," was the most complete admission, or almost the greatest blame, that on the subject of her husband, anyone had managed get from her. At the end of several years, society had accepted that situation at face value and no one commented any longer on it. Passed on to become a chronic state, her married widowhood had ceased to occupy public curiosity and remained just friendly interest. To that interest and to the friendship of Hortense de Beauharnais, with whom she had been reared in the pension of Madame Campan,[127] she owed the position of Lady of the Palace of the Empress. And by giving her duties outside her household, that work had brought a very fortunate simplification to the falsity of her existence.

In addition, the sadness of her abandonment was consoled by a brother, a young man with a great future, whom the Emperor had attached to his State Council. In society, he gave his arm to his sister, was her tablemate, and even with the approval of the owl, her husband, who seemed charmed to have abdicated a notable portion of his conjugal duties, he moved into the de Limeuil townhouse, as little as that arrangement had pleased him. In addition, without living under the same roof as his sister, Anatole de Limeuil didn't let a day go by without visiting her. It was he who, when Matiphous came to present the documents and family connections, took charge of examining them and determined that Mademoiselle de Limeuil was definitively accepted.

However, Diane didn't immediately take the place in her aunt's house that her age and that recognition of relationship

---

[127] Jeanne Louise Henriette Campan (née Genet) (1752-1822). Educator, writer and lady-in-waiting in the service of Marie Antoinette before and during the French Revolution, she was afterwards headmistress of the first *Maison d'éducation de la Légion d'honneur*, as appointed by Napoleon in 1807.

would have suggested. The duty as Lady of the Palace, often caused Madame de Limeuil to be absent from her home, so propriety did not allow her niece to move into her townhouse. In addition, while including in his plan of instruction an introduction to the important chapter on religious education, Matiphous hadn't been able to make his adopted daughter a perfect Christian. She was sixteen years-old and had not yet received the Sacrament of the Eucharist. For this reason, and in view of taking care of this pious interest, a stay of some months in a convent was judged to be an arrangement perfectly fitting for Diane. It was with difficulty that the person principally concerned could be persuaded to that point of view. A kind of daughter of nature and in a long tête-à-tête with the man from Malta, never having had to adjust her will to anyone but him, Mademoiselle de Limeuil was naturally horrified at the idea of seeing herself shut up between four walls, without a horizon, to all the severities of monastic pedagogy, and that decision taken for her, was a great bitterness in her life.

"You see where your beautiful inspiration has brought us," she said to her adopted father, who recognizing the necessity for a separation, had accepted the idea only with displeasure. "You are no longer anything to me. Under the name of parentage they have taken your place and have taken over your daughter."

A little contrite, Matiphous tried to make the future pensionnaire listen to reason. He promised to visit her often in the parlor. Then he pointed out to her that it was only for a short while and that soon, returned to her freedom, a marriage in the future for her was foreseen. But already before rather badly received, that great passion that her tutor showed to see her married, didn't find Diane any more sympathetic. At that comment, on the contrary, she broke off the interview brusquely, ending it in a very bitter way, saying:

"Finally," she said, " in a few days you will be completely rid of me!"

And at that point, showing on the outside the most total resignation, without resistance, without a complaint, the poor sea swallow let herself be put in a cage.

With a feeling perfectly suited to propriety and his dignity, Matiphous, when the Limeuil's came to talk to him about paying for with money the care he had given to their young relative, answered with a noble refusal and wouldn't hear of any settlement of that sort. He had decided on his own plan of existence, and, counting on taking advantage of his former title of military doctor, he proposed, after having up-dated his studies, to live as a surgeon. All he consented to take was the recommendation of a family well placed in society and which without another concern but that of a little declared goodwill could help him form a clientele. As a beginning, Madame de Limeuil gave him her servants to treat. Setting a broken leg with a great deal of skill for a footman almost immediately put him in high regard in the opinion of that domestic staff. The lady of the palace, in addition, showed him some marks of politeness. Returning home one day, he found a magnificent case that in a note very nicely stated she asked him to accept. Two or three times also, he was invited to a small dinner and was free to go see Diane in her convent, on condition, however, of not multiplying his visits too much, since too frequent visits were contrary to the rules of the holy house.

But there suddenly appeared a great modification to those very friendly relations. Once very coldly received by Madame de Limeuil, some days later, Matiphous was no longer received and soon he was certain that in that sense a general order not to admit him had been given. At the convent, there was the same treatment. Mademoiselle de Limeuil had become invisible to him and despite his insistence to see her in the parlor, he was up against an evident bias to refuse him all communication with her.

To that sudden change, to that rapid falling out of favor that he had first had with his adopted daughter's family, there must be some mystery. Soon that sad exile was only too clearly explained. One morning, he was brought to the police station. There, he learned that the secret of his pseudonym of *Deschamps* had been exposed and that he was known as a man named Matiphous, who, under the Directoire, had undertaken to bring about the escape of Sir Sidney Smith. All his adventures in England were also known, including his quick departure from Bell Rock and the accusation of the murder of his colleague Ephraim, that he was suspected of committing.

On this last accusation, which inflated the record of his past, already fairly muddled, Matiphous, as can be imagined, defended himself, but without his denials finding much belief. As for the rest, that was not the important point of the communication. Following a demand for extradition by the Admiralty, the police knew the unfortunate outcome that the desertion of Matiphous without lighting the beam had for the English Admiralty. The night of his departure, two schooners and a frigate of the Royal Marine were lost and as the author of that catastrophe, the former liberator of Sir Sidney Smith, had been condemned to death. The question now was to know if he would be turned over to the English Government, which despite the state of war that existed with France, reclaimed the condemned man in the name of civil rights.

In the Council of State, to which that question had been submitted, it was almost unanimous that the question should be asked of the Admiralty. The act for which punishment was asked was a truly international crime, and notwithstanding the objection of a member who pointed out that the unfortunate man that was going to be hanged had won, without striking a blow, a real naval battle against England, our sworn enemy. In the name of principles and for the respect the French owed to themselves, the request for extradition had been approved. However, at the urging of a great lady, who had revealed a very honorable fact about the condemned man, the Emperor had decided not to hand him over, but he had been told that, until told otherwise, he would remain under the surveillance of the State Police. And that was the first kindness of that regime that at the time Matiphous had been invited to enjoy.

From that, the reaction of the Diane's family was perfectly explained. In the Council of State, in which Monsieur
Anatole de Limeuil sat as an auxiliary member, he had known
a portion of his deplorable past, and after having gotten him
out of a harsh arrest, Madame de Limeuil must have believed
she was quits with him. His life saved, she considered him a
man no longer to be accepted as a guest, and according to all
appearances, she thought she had used great forbearance in
dismissing him without saying a word and without wanting to
give him any kind of explanation.

VIII. The Sleepwalker

It seemed that Matiphous hadn't undergone all the dis-
paragement among the servants of the Limeuil Townhouse
that he had fallen into with the mistress of the house. Some
days after his discomfiture, he saw Count Octave's valet come
to him. That was the old servant who was the only one with a
little of his master's confidence and who accompanied him on
his trips, as has already been said. That man began a conversation with Matiphous in a rather solemn voice, telling him that
he came to let him in on an important secret, for which he demanded, most of all, the most inviolable discretion. Following
the ordinary formula of people of his profession, Matiphous
answered that doctors were a kind of confessors, and that he
could speak openly to him in all security. Those preliminaries
established, the old servant, who was one of those eloquent
and ingenious valets after the manner of Figaro, and whose
type since 1789 is almost lost, continued in the following:
"To a certain point in his household, my master is a liar
as a husband. I am the only one who knows that, and I am
telling you here. The very night of his marriage, at the time
that nothing should come between married people until the
morning, it was a matter of correspondence. My master rang
for me and I was surprised to find him shut up in his apartment
sealing a letter. I was ordered to carry the letter immediately to
Madame la Contesse and then to come back and pack the

297

bags. The next morning at five o'clock the post horses were in the courtyard and without waiting for a honeymoon that had begun in such an extraordinary manner to reach its first quarter, we left for Venice, then we passed on into the Tyrol and Dalmatia, where for several months we shuffled about in every direction without a goal known to me or admitted. Evidently, during his trips, as in Paris during his short appearances, my master remained under the domination of a single thought, the trace of which must necessarily be found in the voluminous writings with which he was furtively occupied until daylight when he kept up the appearance of being completely lazy. Unfortunately he never left out anything he had written. As soon as he had put down his pen a secret strong box was an inviolable asylum for all his paperasseries.

"As for how Monsieur and Madame la Comtesse lived, it was unusual in this way: as a cast off wife, in every meaning of that phrase, Madame appeared not to have either hate or anger against her husband. In the intervals, which were, besides, very short, which brought them together, there never stopped being a friendly rapport between them. Attached from time immemorial to the service of Monsieur, like everyone one, I finally became blasé about his eccentricities, but for some time, the mysterious nature of his life has become complicated in an extraordinary way. I have to say, first of all, that when he returned from his last trip, Monsieur stayed for several days at the Charterhouse of Parma;[128] then, when he arrived in Paris, there seemed to be established a very unusual new level of good understanding between Madame and him. He ate his meals everyday with her. Like a man who is trying to please, he took some care with his dress. The two spouses have already been seen out in public together several times, and they have often had a friendly tête-à-tête together right up to a very late hour at night. In short, in all of Madame's personality there was something radiant, and an unusual well-

---

[128] A famous Carthusian monastery located in the city of Parma, Italy.

being. The difference has made me think that a radical change and a revolution must have come about in his life.

"Well, Doctor, it is exactly since that very fortunate transformation in his life that Monsieur, to today's baggage, his old originalities out of fashion, has judged it useful to substitute a new bizarre behavior which very far surpasses the rest of what I have told you. Despite his return to conjugal tenderness, it must be said, my master continues to live at the bottom of the townhouse garden, in a pavilion that he likes. The garden has, on that side, an exit onto a little used street, greatly convenient for those leaving during the day as well at night. Now, for some time, every night, the Count leaves by that door. He remains five quarters of an hour outside. Then, following that, he comes to get back in bed, where, until very late in the morning, he sleeps deeply and peacefully."

"That's what's very surprising," said Matiphous, interrupting.

"The first time," the old servant continued, "that I heard the Count get up in the middle of the night, I thought he might be ill, and I hurried to his bedroom, in case he needed me. Entering his bedroom, I found him in the dark, seated at a table where, nevertheless, he seemed to be writing. When I spoke to him to ask him if my services were necessary, he didn't look at me or answer, and his pen continued to race across the paper. Soon afterward he took a briquet, lit a candle, and sealed his letter. But then I saw that despite his wide-opened eyes, his look was dull and fixed and that he was looking in front of him without stopping on anything. Then he stood up and began to walk around the apartment. Having always heard it said that it was dangerous to awaken sleepwalkers suddenly, I stood to one side, to let him pass. I followed him into the garden where I saw him reach the door to the street. My first movement was to follow him, less to know where he was going than to lend him assistance in case he encountered some danger in his path. Then I hesitated, recalling that he was very secretive by nature, and a man who wouldn't pardon me for what he would call my curiosity if, by chance, he happened to wake up with me present.

"However, the thought of the dangers he might run into was more important than all other considerations. I began to follow him resolutely, being careful to leave enough distance between us to be sure not to be seen if his sleepwalking suddenly ended. From the townhouse that you know is on the rue de l'Université, he reached the quay, picked up his path by way of the Pont-Royal, the Place du Carrousel, that of the Palais-Royal, the rue de Grenelle-Saint-Honoré, and he finally stopped at the rue Jean-Jacques Rousseau, near the big mailbox. He threw in the one I had seen him writing in the darkness that he still held in his hand. Next, without waking up, he went back to the townhouse. It will soon be three weeks that the same little scene takes place each night.

"I haven't opened my mouth to anyone, always hoping that nocturnal habit would stop of itself and fearing, besides, that the phenomena of his sleep might hide some important secret. But other than my having finally decided to speak to you, dear Doctor, to know if your medicine couldn't do something about it, my confidence has today become a necessity, because a task that unfortunate man has given me must keep me away from Paris for several days. I can't let him wander around the streets at night where so many bad things could happen to him. I would dare then to ask you to trouble yourself to take my place in my approaching night surveillance. At the same time, you would have an opportunity readymade to study that medical case, and to recognize the symptoms on which you could then base his treatment."

"But are you sure that he is asleep?" Matiphous asked.

"His walk, his facial expression, doesn't leave any doubt."

"And you have no idea what kind of mental preoccupation could give birth to that habit?"

"I told you that," the old servant replied. "My master is the most impenetrable of men."

"Then I will have to see this for myself," Matiphous said with importance. "Is there an hour when he leaves?"

"Every night when three o'clock strikes, he get up."

"All right! The coming night, about that time, I will be in the vicinity of the hidden door, but I must know how to recognize it, because I don't know exactly where it is situated."

"I can take you there right now, if you will allow me, since in two hours I must have left Paris."

And they left together. The following night, Matiphous was on time at the hour stated. The somnambulist wasn't less so himself and following the itinerary the old domestic had indicated, he conducted his new surveillance right to the rue Jean-Jacques Rousseau. It hasn't been forgotten that in the same street and not far from the Post Administration building was situated the famous Lottery Bureau administered by Prince de Bevillacqua. At that hour of the night, it goes without saying, that establishment of the Temple of Fortune, was closed. But in passing, Matiphous had noticed two men stopped at the doorway. These men seem to have been overcome by wine and were speaking with excessive animation. One of them was Britannicus, the black factotum already seen at the *Grand Firmament*, the other was one his compatriots with whom he had spent the evening drinking. And following that, they had not been able to agree mutually on what to do, and now, not being able to leave each other, they had begun to quarrel. At first, their debate had been only comic, and during more than a quarter of an hour, they had been glad to exchange with all levels of tones and with a variety of inflections which supplemented that of words, the eternal and well-known refrain of *me good neg'o, you bad neg'o!,* an affirmation with which, in the colonies, it isn't unusual to see an ardent debate continue for several hours.

Either the noise of that quarrel or some other circumstance that remains unknown, just as the sleepwalker was about to throw his daily letter into the mailbox, his sleepwalking suddenly ended. Matiphous, who was at that time following him rather closely, heard him say to himself, hitting himself on the forehead, "Still that damnable habit!" and at the same time, he angrily tore up that letter that represented the importunate persistence from which he wanted to be released.

Back in control of himself, the sleepwalker didn't need Matiphous to take him back. The man from Malta was less in a hurry to continue his role as guardian angel, since at hand at the same moment he encountered an employment for his zeal much more needed. The noise of the debate he had heard had become very animated. From words, they had come to blows, and when Matiphous came to go back by the two friends, Britannicus was lying on his back on the pavement. Held by the throat and near suffocating under the pressure of a furious hand, his blood was flowing abundantly from a wound to the skull that he had gotten in falling.

To run to the combatants, to take the side of the most mistreated and the weakest, by that intervention putting the winner to flight, such was the result of that act of generosity that Matiphous willingly incurred when he encountered on his way an opportunity to redress a wrong or to calm suffering. Not content with having snatched Britannicus from the most imminent peril and seeing him losing a great deal of blood, he thought, if it can be said that way, to transfer to him his zeal as a conductor which he hadn't been able to use with Monsieur de Limeuil. He asked the wounded man where he lived so that he could accompany him to his dwelling and dress the wound. Britannicus was at the door of his domicile. For the safety of his cash register, Monsieur de Bevillacqua had him sleep in a loft above the back boutique of the Lottery Office. And, as a parenthesis, it must be admitted, that night the African was rather negligent in his position as a guard.

Matiphous then had only to take the key to the boutique from the wounded man's pocket. A light once illuminated, he could be sure that the wound to which he put on a preliminary dressing, was not serious. He promised Britannicus that he would come see him the next day.

The following day, he did, in fact, see his patient He had the satisfaction of finding him on his feet. His wound had already developed a scab and he didn't have to suspend his functions as doorman for the Lottery Office. While talking with the Malagasy,[129] and while receiving assurance of eternal gratitude, that can in fact be expected of men of that race when they have been rendered some important service, Matiphous glanced at the green velvet grill which hid the deaf and dumb card dealer, to whom the reader has already been introduced.

Now, Matiphous' astonishment can be understood when he recognized in that woman the one that Bevillacqua had said was his wife and who at the Opera by a single one of her looks was supposed to have kept Mademoiselle de Limeuil from such an imminent danger. On her side, the card dealer, as soon as Matiphous had turned his face toward her in order to re-member her better, that time, instead of the unusual lack of expression that at their first encounter was so apparent, every-thing in her seemed to show strong emotion. There was some-thing better than that. Not being seen by Britannicus who, at the moment, had his shoulder turned toward her, she rapidly showed the man from Malta a lottery ticket with some words written on the back and indicated that she wanted to give it to him. But by a finger placed over her lips, she indicated discre-tion and caution to him, and showed him she shouldn't be ap-proached except with great skill and great circumspection. In such a place, the means to communicate secretly wasn't diffi-cult to find, and Matiphous soon found a way by saying casu-ally to Britannicus:

"Well, since I'm here, I must place three numbers that I've had on my mind for some time."

And he approached the grill with green velvet curtains, taking out the money for his bid. A complication arose. Britannicus decided to intervene in the preparation of the tick-et.

"She doesn't hear or speak," he told Matiphous, explain-ing the infirmity he had encountered, and offering to serve as an intermediary between Matiphous and the ticket clerk who

---

[129] Native of Madagascar.

usually did marvelously well without his officious intervention. But there, too, the man from Malta showed cleverness
and presence of mind. Seeing that the tiresome watcher still
had his eye on the woman in the office while she was writing,

"Come now!" he protested, "don't look while she's writing my ticket. You'll bring me bad luck. In your devil's country, all of you have the *evil eye.*"

The variety of superstitions of gamblers is infinite and
the one that at that minute Matiphous pretended to have was
not unusual, so that it had the intended effect. The woman
behind the grill had just finished writing at her ease the secret
communication that she intended, when, seeming to come
from the ceiling, a voice shouted.

"Britannicus! You animal! See how you watch! Will you
please tell that gentleman to give back that ticket on which
something other than numbers has just been written right under my nose!"

Caught in the act by a method which, at first, would have
seemed to have something supernatural about it, Matiphous
raised his head and saw in the ceiling an open judas hole, a
treacherous invention that never justified its name more than
in that circumstance. A maneuver, up until then well carried
out, was suddenly aborted. To give back the paper that the
man from Malta already had almost in his pocket, was something easy to say. But Britannicus, as could be seen by the
adventure in which he had his head cut, wasn't a very rough
player. Immediately deciding on strong resistance, Matiphous
thought it first prudent to reach the street to have the intervention of passers-by if it was needed. But just as he lifted the
door handle, it suddenly opened bringing reinforcement to
help the African. That reserve body was none other than
Prince Bevillacqua.

"Monsieur," he said to Matiphous, clearly showing that
his was the voice heard from above, "your way of coming to
surreptitiously get the secrets of my household is the ultimate
disloyalty. Fortunately for you, you don't know anything yet,

because you would pay dearly for that. Please return that paper to me."

Matiphous tried to put the question on an administrative footing. He claimed that the ticket really was a lottery ticket, that he had paid money for it, and as a result no one had the right to take it out of his hands.

"No equivocation, Monsieur," said the Prince. "I know what I know. It isn't a question here of the Imperial Lottery, but of my personal business. Here's a weapon," he added, drawing a pistol from his pocket, "that, wind charged and not powder charged, has the advantage of blowing people's head off without causing a scene and without noise. That paper then! Or you're a dead man."

"Go ahead and give the paper back to my master," said Britannicus in a more conciliatory tone, which didn't match his desperate efforts, useless until then, to take the litigious paper out of the hands of the man from Malta.

There is no way to know where that battle would have ended if it was prolonged much longer, but another unexpected event occurred to solve it, because everything that happened around Matiphous that day inclined a little toward the miraculous.

"Monsieur," the deaf-mute woman, suddenly recovering the power of speech, said to him, "please, I beg you, don't resist any longer. The answer that you might have been able to give me, would scarcely tell me more than what happens here. That would be to expose your life uselessly. The secret that you are being kept from knowing regards no one but me, and so far as you are concerned, I can swear to you that you have no reason to know anything more about it."

"Well spoken! for a person who doesn't do that very often," Bevillacqua said in a tone mingled with bitter irony. "You hear her, Monsieur. A friendly person also exhorts you to give in. All right, now, one last time, will you have done with it?"

Solicited in that way by both sides, Matiphous believed he should resign himself. But he couldn't return exactly what was asked of him in such a commanding way. He threw the ticket on the ground, and wanting to pass his anger on to someone, he said to Britannicus:

"You, I will remember the way in which you show your gratitude!"

However, the Prince, instead of bending down to pick up the paper, just put his foot on it and the said to the Malagasy:

"Open the door for the gentleman!"

Britannicus hurried to obey and as Matiphous looked at him with contempt when he passed by:

"Me good neg'o," the black man said to him, "but me not betray my master, when my master is right!'"

IX. Diplomacy and Secrets of the Heart

If Matiphous had only followed what his disappointment and anger told him to, at that same step he would have denounced the shady plot by which he had just found himself compromised. But after a little thought, he told himself that Bevillacqua definitely seemed to be a dangerous adversary with whom, in all the encounters, he himself had gotten the worst of it. In addition, the vanquished man also asked himself, was it prudent, when he knew himself to be under surveillance by the State Police, to go point out his suspicious vigilance, as being mixed up, in whatever way, in mysterious complications whose nature and character were completely unknown to him.

Everything considered, since their first encounter Bevillacqua had faithfully kept his word not to try to carry it any further. In the last engagement, it was he, Matiphous, who had been the aggressor, while his adversary had simply defended himself. What seemed to him to be established by the words of the deaf mute, which he had not initiated, since she had been surprised trying to get in touch with him, was that the intercepted confidence didn't concern him in any way. Then why, in a situation where he was a stranger, go assume new hatreds for himself, and why attack in a war where the result of curiosity satisfied seemed to be the only prize of the victory, even if achieved with great effort. These different considerations well thought out, Matiphous took the position of remaining quiet. He only promised himself to be on his guard and to keep a cautious and armed observation.

Once set on the path to wisdom, he included in his plan of discreet reserve the other not less nebulous confidence about Monsieur de Limeuil. He resolved not to get mixed up any further in an affair where there could be foreseen, if not other ambushes, at least new problems. Excellent results seemed to crown that behavior full of sense and restraint. Having escaped that cloudy atmosphere that seemed to have threatened to surround his life, Matiphous soon concentrated entirely on his medical studies and caring for the small clientele he was not slow in forming. One care, however, continued to preoccupy him, to know about the cruel embargo put on his relationship with his adopted daughter. His truly paternal tenderness didn't easily accept his part in that very strict seclusion.

About six months passed without another cloud when a very serious complication arrived that he took very much to heart. One morning, Madame de Limeuil sent Monsieur Deschamps (the pseudonym of Matiphous) her hurried compliments and asked him come by her establishment. A young person in whom he took a strong interest would be subject of their interview. Having no doubt that it was a question of Diane, Matiphous quickly accepted that invitation, and some hours later, he was at the home of the Lady of the Palace. This time, in the antechamber, he was welcomed as a man they were expecting.

Madame de Limeuil's opening was that of a person whose former disobliging behavior seemed not to embarrass her the least in the world. And the proof of that was that she didn't think she owed her guest either an excuse or an explanation.

"Monsieur," she said, getting immediately to the matter, "if I remember correctly, at our first interview you gave me the honor of telling me that what most decided you to put into my hands the care of Mademoiselle de Limeuil's future was the feeling that you couldn't give her a proper establishment."

"It is, in fact, Madame," the man from Malta answered, "in that interest that I intended to call on your patronage. I only dare to allow myself to find that what you call my abdication, may have resulted in consequences perhaps somewhat absolute. "

"Let's go over it," said Madame de Limeuil. "The justification that I might undertake on that delicate subject will have nothing precisely pleasant. Besides, the direction that I intended to give to relations with my niece is becoming a completely idle question, since it's a matter a short time from now of making her the mistress to chose them herself, or at least to transfer the control to an authority which will have ceased to be mine."

"That would then be, Madame, if I understand you correctly, a marriage that you have in view for Mademoiselle de Limeuil?"

"Precisely, a marriage, and that affair presents itself surrounded with such circumstances that, after having hoped for your approval, I would dare go even to soliciting your help, if you would allow it."

"Truly very honored," said Matiphous, "and, in that what seems to me more precious, is that it is most unhoped for."

"What you don't know, Monsieur," continued the Lady of the Palace without taking into account Matiphous' new allusion to the very little helpful treatment that he had been able to receive from her, "is that my niece, right now, finds that she has become a rich heiress."

"Through your benefaction, no doubt?"

"No, but by the munificence of the Head of State. He has at his disposal all the national wealth which remains unrecovered, and has just, in this case restored to Diane the fortune of her father."

"But at least it was to your kind intervention that this result must be attributed?"

"Not at all. The merit belongs entirely to my brother Anatole, and it's exactly for the marriage I told you about that presents a difficulty."

"How is that?" asked the man from Malta.

"I like to think," the Lady of the Palace continued, "that in telling you the name of my brother Anatole as the person Monsieur de Limeuil and I intend to make Diane's husband, we would encounter no serious opposition from you. Anatole, if the eyes of a sister do not deceive her, is perfectly fine on the exterior and in manners. Still very young, he has, by his talents, been able to attract the attention of the Emperor. He is, in respect to Mademoiselle de Limeuil's age, perfectly acceptable, and what's more, her relative. Having rather often accompanied me in the visits I have been able to make to the convent, he has developed a very strong feeling for Diane. With the serious character I know him to have, I believe I can say that the duration of that attachment would be at least comparable to its warmth."

"You have deigned to speak to me of my approval," Matiphous answered. "I've had the honor to meet Monsieur your brother several times, and I can only agree heartily with your assessment of him."

"Since that is so, Monsieur, we dare to call on the very natural influence you have with a girl you have brought up, because our overtures have been, as far as Diane is concerned, met with an almost final refusal."

"Couldn't it be that she would like to know her husband better before agreeing, and that it would be nice to see her own heart sharing a sentiment that Monsieur de Limeuil would have already developed more rapidly?"

"I don't know," the Lady from the Palace answered, "but I'm very afraid that an explanation that appears to me, as to you, very natural and sufficient, is not acceptable here. A very witty answer, but which had a certain perfume of offensiveness, seems to me to offer a better key to Diane's refusal. And I admit that without Anatole's insistence, so far as I'm concerned, at that simple reply, every kind of negotiation would have been immediately broken off."

"But, *Mon Dieu!*" Matiphous asked, "what is that terrible word?"

"In order for you to understand, Monsieur, I must first tell you that my brother has no fortune, so that, from the money point of view, when she has taken possession of her patrimony, Mademoiselle de Limeuil may be considered for him what is usually called a very good match."

"Oh!" the man from Malta said, interrupting, "I believe I know Mademoiselle de Limeuil well enough to confirm that the possible insinuation that you saw, couldn't have any serious foundation."

"Let me continue," the Lady from the Palace said, "the situation we are talking about here is very unusual. Anatole, as I told you, is not rich, but it happened that the restitution of Diane's paternal fortune was because of him. My brother had begun the process. The situation came to the Emperor's attention, who, with a political thought, interferes rather willingly in family affairs. He noticed that the young girl, in whose favor he had been asked to intercede, was going to find herself becoming a very eligible match. At the same time, Anatole, who, because of very pronounced near-sightedness, was unfortunately unfit for a military career, still had an entire career to make in the civil functions to which he had to resign himself. From that, the restitution that he, in his great position, decided in favor of my niece, was so narrowly tied to the idea of a marriage between the young people that, sending back to me the decree in favor of Mademoiselle de Limeuil, returning all the unsold property remaining from the Marquis, her father, he told me in his own words:

" 'It is most of all in consideration for your brother that I am making the decision for which you thanked me. And I hope that, a few weeks from now, you will present your niece, who will have become your sister-in-law, at court. With that title, she will have every reason to be welcomed there.' "

"Well!" said Matiphous, flattered by the thought that his adopted daughter would be married by the Emperor, "what could Mademoiselle de Limeuil answer to that?"

"Just one thing, but something that strikes a blow. She said, the first time I talked to her about that project of marriage: 'Then it's Monsieur Anatole who is bringing me my father's fortune as a dowry.' "

"What does that matter!" Matiphous answered, becoming rather comically passionate about the success of an affair in which his idol was concerned. "It is Monsieur Anatole who obtained the result; what is simpler than to see him profit by it, when, besides, in every other way he justifies the choice that has been made for him?"

"Considered from that point of view, the situation doesn't seem to present any difficulty, but you can understand that close to the refusal that shortly afterward followed it, my niece's comment implies the most insulting idea. In all this affair, wouldn't it seem that we have been above all preoccupied with the thought of appropriating her fortune? After that insinuation, any insistence on our part is repugnant to us, whatever our conscience tells us and even though her true interests have been our only concern."

"Just a moment," Matiphous replied. "I believe Mademoiselle de Limeuil incapable of a bad feeling. What is frightening her, I am sure, is rushing into a marriage when she hasn't been left enough time to think about it. But very certainly, by reasoning with her a little, her hesitation will be easily overcome."

"That's exactly why we thought that your influence could be used in a useful way, if you don't see any inconvenience in taking charge of that reasoning."

"How's that? But you will find me, on the contrary, very eager to do that confidential mission in that way, if I could hope to be received…"

"You will be, Monsieur, because, I admit to you , I had counted in advance on your helpful intervention, and as of yesterday, Diane is as approachable for you as she has been in the past. Only one thing to point out to her, that is, to put away from us, as far as possible, all sordid interest, we have decided that her marriage contract would expressively carry the clause *separation as to property*. She would remain, therefore, mistress of her fortune and would have full and entire use of all her revenues."

"Madame," said Matiphous, rising, "I will go from here to the pension immediately and I hope in an hour or two to bring back to you the consent desired."

"No, the rule of the Order does not permit you to see Diane before four o'clock and I am due at the Empress' service in a short while. It is only after tomorrow, in the morning, that we can resume our conversation, but that delay is not important and will allow you not to be too hurried in your intervention and to take, if necessary, more than one meeting to bring about our result."

Thereupon, the two negotiators separated in good agreement, as is seen. But just as Matiphous returned home, a letter was given to him. From the address as well as from the handwriting he recognized the handwriting of Mademoiselle de Limeuil. She wrote what follows to him:

Monsieur and dear Tutor,

This letter will come to you by the way of a friend that I made here and who just today is leaving the pension. That opportunity to deceive the close surveillance to which I am submitted doesn't promise to be often renewed. It will not appear astonishing to you that, all at once and without mincing words, I try to make you part of the development of my most secret thoughts.

A marriage has been proposed for me, but I see there a very great objection; that is that it can't make me happy. The person spoken to me about, has, they say, a great deal of love for me. But I don't have any for him and I can't see how that feeling could come to me.

In addition, I don't have any taste for society. To live at Bell Rock as I had lived until the moment you had the unfortu-

nate idea to leave that happy stay, that is my dream. And the Court, where it is now a question of presenting me, has nothing that can make me forget it. But you are going to say again, because for you that is a fixed idea, 'a girl must marry.' As for me, I don't see the necessity at all. And I am here in a house which proves that many persons of my sex can escape that imperious law. But after all, if it is not in my destiny to avoid it, what could a woman desire in the companion of her life? A proven friend, a man whose devotion it appears, she can appreciate, and who, some years older than she, can guide her by his advice and surround her with his protection.

Isn't it at Bell Rock that this portrait could be immediately found? Among that crowd of strangers who came there constantly, and several of whom showed themselves very attentive toward me, couldn't there, in the long run, be encountered someone who would consent to share with me that dear solitude in which the happiest years of my life were spent.

If you would not agree with me, Monsieur and dear tutor, that I could dispense with going very far to look for a husband, and if your feelings are very far from mine, then I will resign myself to going through with this marriage, which will, as you said at another time, free you of your responsibility. Whatever may happen in the future, I will not remain less grateful of the care you surrounded my youth, and despite many of the suspicions they have tried to give me about you, I will continue until the last breathe to call myself your very affectionate, devoted,

Diane de Limeuil

A postscript followed in which Matiphous was given an address that he could safely send the response that letter seemed to require.

X. The Hotel d'Angleterre

The wicked place where we are going to take the reader was an establishment which no longer has anything like it in

313

Paris today. The licentious morals that the Directoire had willed to the Consulate and to the Empire, it must be said, those two époques when the life of the camps became, to a certain point, that of the nation, were perhaps a little too complaisant in accepting that inheritance that since then the progress of public morality has made us more honestly repudiate. Situated on the rue Saint-Honoré, at the angle of the Place du Palais Royal, l'Hôtel d'Angleterre[130] adjoined an establishment no less famous, but with a more honest celebrity and less noisy, the scholarly and peaceful café, the *Régence,* where from time immemorial checker players gathered. To get an idea only approximating the disorderly and almost pandemoniacal appearance of the strange local which it's a question of at this moment, one has to call to mind an immense room that, closed neither day nor night, held at the same time a restaurant, a public dance hall, and a bar. Just opening the door of that cave will let escape suffocating gusts of a horrible atmosphere formed of the combined exhalations of the pipe, alcohol, wine, foamy beer, charcuterie, frying and some foul human smells.

If anyone had the courage to go inside, it is not only the heart which would be disgusted, but a sort of terror would seize oneself in finding himself transported into the middle of a tumultuous group of vagabonds, former jail birds, and prostitutes, so many there, that the select and relatively honest society in the middle of that impure assemblage was comprised of wanderers who had a little money, cab drivers, former club barkers, and undercover police agents.

In the evening, while the center of the room was very imperfectly lighted by a few smoky oil lamps, a space was reserved for rowdy dancing, circled by two rows of tables, at which a crowd of drinkers can to take a seat. One detail can give some idea of the high esteem the owner of the establishment held for that clientele. At each table, a strong little iron

---

[130] Not to be confused with the historic Hôtel d'Angleterre on the rue de l'Université in the 7th arrondissement of Paris.

chain riveted an iron chandelier and knives and forks of the same metal. That precaution had two purposes; on the one hand to maintain the ownership of the one who put them there; on the other hand, to keep them from becoming, in the daily combats that took place there, instruments of murder, or at least arms of combat.

Around those tables, and in a few small rooms called *society offices*, where debauchery and crime had a place to go shelter their secrets, where every night plots or shady affairs were numerous, that precisely explains why that den was so long tolerated. In addition to the fact that the police had its agents permanently stationed there to gather first hand much valuable information, often, just by a simple verification of the hours that either the absence or the presence of certain individuals on its list of suspects, they obtained for their investigations illuminating points of departure. Even today, in the traditions of public surveillance, the Hôtel d'Angleterre remains as a regrettable auxiliary, that it can't be consoled for having lost.

To find Matiphous in such a place could appear extraordinary, especially at the moment in which we have just seen him honored with a communication of a nature to give him some pride and to raise himself in his own eyes. He had read Mademoiselle de Limeuil's letter several times before understanding its meaning and its significance. His affection for his pupil was so perfectly paternal that the most faraway thought of another sentiment had never complicated it. It was therefore with extreme surprise that he saw the secret movements of that heart which, notwithstanding a studied reserve in the form, opened itself to him in such a naïve way. He immediately understood that, faced with that unexpected situation, the management of his diplomatic intervention must, of necessity, be modified. Not that he thought of taking advantage of the gracious suggestion made to him. That feeling that he had just received in confidence, if he had shared it, he would have recoiled before the simplest act that could contribute to encouraging it. Aware of his own unworthiness, the fear of seeing Mademoiselle de Limeuil's fortune compromised, everything made it a duty to cut short that emotion of which he suddenly saw himself the object. Now, in that frame of mind, could he go confront the knowledge of an admission that, renewed, would be only more embarrassing to decline straight out, and wasn't caution a law for him? Before going further, should he go see Madame Octave de Limeuil to confer with her about the unexpected occurrence which he had just encountered?

These honest and wise reflections took the place of going to the pension as he had at first intended. In the dreamy solicitude in which his pupil's letter had thrown him, Matiphous went to take a walk in the Tuileries. In the Tuileries, in the person of a young assistant in the administration that he had in the past intimately known in the Italian Army, he made an encounter, with all the appearance of the most complete insignificance, that must have the most marked influence on the rest of his life. Moreover, in that way that at any moment in existence the most serious complications come to birth and develop, once in the hands of that former friend, it was impossible for Matiphous to think of getting rid of him. Giving in to his strong insistence, he even had to accept dining with him. After that meal, where we wouldn't want to swear that they were of exemplary sobriety, under the promise that he would see the most magnificent bacchanal that could be imagined, the imprudent man let himself be drawn into the Hôtel d'Angleterre, where it was agreed that they would stay only a moment.

At some distance from the table where Matiphous took a seat with his friend, two men were seated and seemed to be conversing rather mysteriously. One of them, when the man from Malta appeared, began to look at him with unusual attention. That attention soon was also that of the other diner, who, several times, turned to look in that furtive, curious way, at an object pointed out to him, tried to conciliate with discretion. Very little patience by nature, Matiphous wouldn't have endured for very long the continuation of that behavior. But at the end of several minutes, the one of the two men who had taken the initiative, got up from where he was sitting and approached the table occupied by the former army companions.

"Is it really to Monsieur Matiphous that I have the honor of speaking?"

So simple in appearance as that question was, it wasn't without embarrassment for the one to whom it was addressed. To deny his identity in the presence of his friend to whom he had not told about his change of name, would have given an opening to some troublesome comments. To accept the person he had ceased to be could have some inconveniences in the future. Getting himself out of difficulty by averting the question, that, besides, in the place where he had been asked, had nothing that wasn't explainable.

"What does my name matter to you?" he answered, and it must be added, that in that answer he affected a less than welcoming accent.

"It's because not very long ago," the unknown man answered, "it seems to me I had the pleasure of meeting you in Scotland, at the Bell Rock Lighthouse."

"And when would that be?" asked Matiphous, persisting in avoiding the question.

"In that case, I would have been delighted to renew your acquaintance, and then I would have asked you for news of your colleague Ephraim, that worthy man for whom you showed such great attachment."

"Monsieur, in a public place, I neither make nor renew acquaintances. I am with Monsieur," he continued, pointing to his friend, "and his society is enough for me."

"On my word, my dear Monsieur, allow me to tell you that you are almost as polite as a hangman's valet."

At that comment, which in the circumstance had a very special meaning, Matiphous turned purple and got up with a threatening air, notwithstanding the intervention of his friend who advised moderation and caution to him.

"Will you do me the pleasure," he asked his questioner, "to leave me in peace. I repeat that I do not know you and do not wish to know you. So, not another word."

"Really, one more word," continued the unknown man, "how's the certain bobo that we have on the shoulder?"

That obvious and terrible allusion to the vengeance the Marquis de Samaniego had taken on him didn't leave Matiphous in control of himself. Faster than thought, his hand sought the face of the insolent man and a resounding slap across the face, with the same blow made the hat he had on his head roll to the ground. At the sound of that violence, the friend of the man slapped hurried to his aide. But the man he had come to aide told him not to get mixed up in the debate, and while busy, with marvelous self-control, restoring the luster to his hat that he had picked up all covered with dust, he said:

"Monsieur, I think that in this case we must exchange our addresses, because I am sure we will see each other again."

Since the day when, in his encounter with Prince de Bevillacqua, Matiphous had seen himself in the impossibility of responding immediately to the politeness of that card that he had at first taken as a challenge, he had begun carrying business cards on him. He could therefore immediately defer to the just claim that he had put himself in the position of not being able to refuse. On his side, his adversary gave him a printed card, that could be called an address, in all the meaning of the word. Following the name of François de Meilleret, was written:

Wholesale Fabric Warehouse and Linens of Every Kind:
Batistes, Cretonne, Alençon, Lille, Cortrai, Scotch
and Irish Linen, Sheets, Towels and Packaging Material
In General All Kinds of Textiles
Rue des Bourdonnais, nº51, Paris

From that, Matiphous drew the conclusion that he was dealing with what could be called an *established man,* and not with a tavern brawler, as he had at first supposed. However,

the linen merchant had read aloud the card Matiphous presented him; the name inscribed there was:

Deschamps
Public Health Officer.

"It seems," he said, "that I have made a mistake, but I
have nevertheless the right to reparation. Monsieur," he said,
pointing to his companion, "will be my witness. I choose the
pistol, because that's the right of the person insulted. Now,
when shall we meet?"

"Whenever you please," Matiphous replied.

"All right! Tomorrow morning at nine o'clock, at the
Bois de Boulogne. Rendezvous at the Porte d'Auteuil."

"Perfect," replied Matiphous.

And seeing that he had become the object of general attention, he took his friend's arm and left that cavern where the
chance of a courtesy duel was still one of the less bad adventures that could be encountered. Before asking his friend to be
his second, Matiphous needed to give his friend some explanation, since the name change, revealed by the reading of his
card, and his violent outburst at just a simple question, which
didn't have a very clear meaning, could, for a man he had lost
sight of for years, present him in a very nebulous light. He
then recounted the part he had taken in the evasion of Sir Sidney Smith, and attached to that imprudent act of his life numerous persecutions directed toward him by the police, as
much in France as abroad. After having been forced to hide
under an assumed name, the harshness in the scene just
passed, would have made the appearance of an active resur-
gence, and that would explain his quick temper.

His friend from the wars easily accepted these explanations, and the two friends soon separated, setting up a rendezvous pour the next day at seven thirty o'clock at Matiphous'
house. Back at his house, he didn't reproach himself too much
for the error he had made in letting himself be led into the
wicked place where he had encountered that misadventure.

After all, that cloth merchant didn't seem to him a very formidable man and nothing seemed to indicate that any repercussions of a duel with him was much to fear. But couldn't some mysterious complication be associated with the circumstances that had preceded or accompanied that conflict? Such wasn't Matiphous' impression. He thought that, according to all appearances, having come from Scotland for affairs associated with his linen business, his adversary had visited the lighthouse where he must have met him, and he had tried to renew acquaintance in very good faith. Some people are like that. It's enough for them if, during a quarter of an hour, they had seen your face at the other end of the world, to claim that you should remember them at all costs when you meet them again.

"But," Matiphous continued to say to himself, "not being ready for the intrusion, and the bad encounters of my life having had in the United Kingdom only too much impact, it remains presumable that, in his annoyance at seeing his advances badly received, my adversary tried to avenge himself by some cutting allusions to my sad past he had heard about, and nothing, probably, should be suspected beyond that."

Whatever the merit of that explanation, in presence of his chances the next day, Matiphous' thoughts must necessarily return to Mademoiselle de Limeuil. First of all, as the only affection he had in the world, he had to tell her goodbye. Then he found himself bound by honor to give as much weight as he could to the question of that marriage he knew she was predisposed to be against. As a consequence, he prepared a letter for her in which he asked her in the most pressing manner to give her hand in the marriage her aunt desired. In that letter, he joined a will in which he made her heir to the small amount he could leave.

These two writings, placed together in an envelope, were to be given to his witness at the time of the duel, to be sent to their address in case of misfortune. Everything thus organized, Matiphous went to bed. Going back over the prodigious number of adventures that fate seemed to take pleasure putting together in his life, he was finally visited by that courageous sleep that since Alexandre and the Battle of Arbelles[131] biographers always attributed to their hero the evening before battle.

XI. The Alarm at the Secret Bureau

The next day, at the agreed upon hour, Matiphous left with his friend from the Italian wars and, he was not seen back at his domicile during the entire day. But something that should seem surprising is that, several times in the same day, his friend came to ask his concierge about him and seemed to be intrigued to learn that he hadn't reappeared since that morning.

Still absent the following day, when coming to inquire of news of him, and always given no information, that time his friend from the Italian wars became to be terribly worried. Finally, the third day, things being in the same state, the friend of the absent man decided to go to the Police Station of the neighborhood where Matiphous lived and made a declaration. The substance was like this:

After a quarrel in a public place with an unknown man which ended in an assault, M. Deschamps a.k.a. Matiphous made a rendezvous for a duel with the man. As is usually done in similar circumstances, the two adversaries exchanged their addresses. The next day, accompanied by the person making this declaration, M. Matiphous went to the Bois de Boulogne, at the Porte d'Auteuil, which was the place assigned for the encounter. M. Matiphous' adversary was waited for a long time. All the delays exhausted, the two friends got ready to leave that place. But just at the time they thought they should leave, a man, with all the appearance of great emotion came

---

[131] Battle of Arbelles (Battle of Issus) 33 BC. Defeat of Darius III of Persia by Alexandre of Macedonia- source of artistic inspiration, notably paintings by Jan Brueghel, the elder (1602) and a 17th century Aubusson tapestry.

out of the bushes, and, speaking to them, asked them if they could point out the nearest doctor to help an unfortunate man who had just been struck by a sword in a duel. The wound, he added, was so serious that the witnesses hadn't dared to move the wounded man before he had been examined; they were so afraid of seeing him die in their arms.

Being himself a surgeon, M. Matiphous generously offered his services. Nevertheless, in case, very little probable, that his adversary arrived in the interval, he agreed that the person making this declaration should remain at the rendezvous to await the return of his friend. He then left with the man who had greeted his devotion with every testimony of the greatest appreciation.

M. Matiphous had not reappeared at his domicile. Now, in going back over the circumstances of the conduct of an adversary who, after he himself demanded satisfaction, didn't come to keep it, couldn't the officious surgeon be believed the victim of some trap?

The Magistrate received that declaration with a very natural objection. Since the addresses had been exchanged, the address of the man with whom the encounter was to take place and now suspected of an ambush, was known. Hadn't some information about him been obtained? Hadn't any inquiry been made about him?

The friend from the Italian wars answered that he hadn't neglected such an act that came so easily to mind. He had therefore gone to the address given at the time the rendezvous had been made. But what seemed to unusually deepen the suspicion of some shady revenge was that Matiphous' adversary was found to be nothing but a fraud. He had appropriated the name of another person. But between him and that other person, there was no likeness. The linen merchant that the person making the declaration went to see on the rue des Bourdonnais did exist. However, he was an honest businessman of a herculean height. He bragged that he had never in his life accepted a duel. Given the fact that his personality was too calm to ever be an aggressor, he felt he had a strong enough fist to kill on the spot, without any other formality, any man who allowed himself to seriously insult him.

All information gathered elsewhere indicated that merchant was a man who enjoyed the highest reputation. The Tribunal of Commence, answering for how he had directed his life, he escaped the suspicion of possibly conniving with the one who had stolen his name. Besides, in his favor, he was led to think that a salesman, holding by that title a certain number of his cards, had been able to work against him. Some time ago, following several serious abuses of confidences, he had dismissed that employee whom he had never heard anything about since he had dismissed him from his house.

Following that declaration, an inquiry was begun by the police to discover what had become of Matiphous, an incident even more serious since the letters of the Widow Cagliostro had suddenly stirred up concern about the mysterious Administration of which Hulet, the member of the Convention, was the Chief. Justifying in every way its name, the *Secret Bureau* was installed at the Poste Building, in a vast vaulted room at least twenty steps down below the level of the rue Jean-Jacques Rousseau, adjacent to it, and had no outside daylight. The employees, as in a mine, never worked without a lamp and in a silence where no outside noise could trouble its solemnity. The astonishment of those somber workers can be imagined when, one morning, when they were assembled in the usual place of their séances, they began to think they heard some dull blows striking the wall, as if some strong hand were used to demolish it or pierce it. Listening carefully, the noise more and more distinct, soon left no doubt as to the intention of the worker, who coming closer and closer from moment to moment, must soon manage to make a hole in the wall he was trying to undermine. Thus, indiscreet, and very probably those with malicious intent, were going to penetrate the mysterious sanctuary and find the letter -opening industry in full activity.

That was a frightening prospect for everyone there, but Hulet, the Member of the Convention, who in his father's manuscript had learned the terrible end of the *Apostles of Nuremberg,* wondered if the *Secret Bureau* was not threatened by some similar treatment. His first care was to go out to be sure that freedom of communication with the outside was not disturbed. At his return from that reconnaissance, which fortunately didn't show him anything he had to fear, the work had made more progress. Limited to a more and more narrow radius, the blows struck with extreme violence were concentrated on a single point. It became perfectly possible to determine the place where, with a very close delay, the breach would be made.

Now, in this instance, this unusually remarkable detail: according to some old employees, the point which seemed to give access soon to a mysterious invasion must have been chosen with premeditation and with perfect knowledge of the surroundings. To support this estimate, here are the proofs that two or three of the old employees were able to give. In 1757, they said, the King bought the Hôtel d'Armenonville, situated on the rue Plâtrière, to establish the Administration of the Postes which has always remained there. In doing the work of reconstruction, it was recognized that between the edifice being built and a house situated on the same street, some distance away, there extended a long subterranean conduit, probably the remains of the former Hôtel des Flandres, on the basis of which the Hôtel d'Armenonville and almost all the adjacent area had been built. The idea then was to put that distribution to advantage. In the house on the rue Plâtrière that tied that subterranean passage to the new Poste building, there was established a liquor boutique which was given to a police agent to manage. Given the proximity to the Halles, that shop could stay open all night without causing any suspicion.

The liquor store communicated with the entrance to the subterranean conduit, that itself ended at the place where the *Secret Bureau* had been established. In that way, its employees had a way as simple as easy to get in. Seemingly entering to get a drink at the liquorist, they furtively slipped into the back of the boutique, without having to use the door of the building, where in the long run they would have been noticed by the concierge or the official employees. They arrived at the usual place of their reunions in the most perfect incognito. That state of things continued without any inconvenience right up to the reign of Louis XIV. But at that epoch an indiscretion by a policeman that had been made a sort of concierge of the *Secret Bureau,* having put in peril the secret which he held, the entry hidden by the rue Plâtrière had to be abandoned. Another secret entrance to the Postes Building had been made on the side of the rue Verdelet.

It was on the part of the room bordering that unused subterranean passage and right at the place, formerly an entrance, that the work in question at the moment was done. It wasn't therefore illogical that those who remembered the former layout saw in what was happening the result of a plot that threatened the security of all their future. Whatever the value of all these commentaries, in his inability to prevent the piercing of the wall, Hulet father rapidly picked up all the material used in the operation of opening letters. Then he ordered that lights be extinguished and he retired with all his staff to a kind vestibule that preceded the meeting room, He waited behind a half-opened door the results of what happened after his actions.

Hardly had the associates left the room than a sound of gravel rolling between the walls and the woodwork around it announced that the enemy had nothing more in front of him but the obstacle of some boards, and those were soon loudly broken. There followed a long silence in which there could be heard a sound like that a chimney sweep makes when he hoists himself along the inside of a chimney. Almost at the same moment there came the sound of a heavy body falling on the floor. After that nothing moved any more. At the end of a minute, followed by some of his most resolute collaborators, Hulet ventured reentering the sanctuary. When they reached, on tiptoes , right to the edge of the window made in the wall, revealed to them by a current of cold air hitting them in the face, those reconnoitering, were not a little astonished when they ran into a human form stretched out on the floor in a state of complete immobility.

A light was immediately brought. In that inert object they recognized a young man whose torn and disorderly clothes showed the trace of the furious efforts to which he must have gone to get into the place where they had found him. Some feet from him, fallen from his weak hand they noticed a half-broken antique sword with which he must have done all his work. What's more, from the livid pallor of his face and his state of complete unconsciousness it remain doubtful whether life had not left that strange guest just at the moment when the success of his audacious intrusion was finished. However, following some care he was given, he seemed to regain consciousness and his fainting spell was not long in being explained. Since his extreme weakness seemed to keep him from using speech, by a gesture of carrying, with agony, his hand to his mouth and his stomach, he made it understood that he was suffering all the horrors of starvation. Good fortune willed that one of the assistants, recently recovered from a malady, had some pieces of a chocolate stimulant in a cabinet, that in view of hastening his convalescence, his doctor had ordered frequent usage. No nourishment could have been more helpful in a case of exhaustion caused by lack of nourishment carried to the point of putting live in peril. In fact, accompanied by some glasses of water that remedy brought the sick man so much to life that soon he appeared able to respond to the curiosity about all he had undergone. However, when he was questioned about the end and the circumstances in which he had acted,

"Oh!" he answered, "that would be too long to tell. I feel I'm falling asleep; it has been so long since I have slept."

"But at least," they asked him, "are you alone, and no one is coming after you?"

The traveler answered nothing distinct; irresistible sleep had already lowered his head on his chest and suspended a sentence that had begun mid-way.

"At least say if you have accomplices," Hulet shouted to him in a resounding voice, shaking him vigorously by the arm.

But as he did not respond and seemed more and more under the influence of sleep, one of the assistants had the idea of a more energetic way of eliciting a response.

He went to pick up one of the iron rods that served to melt the sealing wax. He heated it a moment on the lamp and suddenly approaching the sleeper, he applied it to his neck, at the beginning of the spinal cord. The effect that could be expected from this cruel method was immediately produced. The man jumped with a cry of pain, and after he was again pressed with questions, some disconnected explanations were then obtained. It was learned that the law should immediately be called to investigate the house on the rue Jean-Jacques Rousseau, where the Lottery Office was installed. Master of this information, vague as it was, Hulet didn't lose a minute in going to the Ministry of Police. While waiting for his return, his collaborators were busy barricading the breach through which, from one moment to the next, they could fear being invaded. As to the author of all that emotion, as soon as the first feeling of pain wore off, he had fallen again into his deep sleep that no one tried any longer to trouble.

XII. Lorenza Feliciani

Some hours after the events just reported, Prince Bevillacqua, several of the affiliates of the *Grand Firmament,* Britannicus, the Black and the so-called deaf-mute woman, all the inhabitants of the house where Hulet the elder had gone to fill out a request for a police search, were arrested. At the same time, it was learned that the man whose information had made that capture possible was no one else but Gregorio Matiphous, whose disappearance the police had for several days searched for an explanation.

Following that unfortunate sleep that at first had made him so laconic, he gave the most detailed information. From his deposition, from the examination of the archives of the association, from the interrogations of all the people that he had contributed to place in the hands of the authorities, and finally from the minute investigations the police had conducted, were deducted the curious ensemble of facts that we are now going to summarize:

That woman that Prince Bevillacqua had placed under the surveillance of Britannicus to manage his Lottery Office was a woman from Genoa named Lorenza Feliciani. In the course of his long wanderings, the famous adventurer, Cagliostro, when passing through Genoa, had fallen in love with her. Speculating on her rare beauty, and to make her a part of his prodigious industry, he had irrevocably linked her to his destiny by marrying her in a legitimate marriage, making her a part of all the secrets of his life. Until then, Cagliostro had only been considered by his biographers as an audacious and clever charlatan. But if the history of secret societies is studied, a very different aspect of that man is discovered. With the famous Count de Saint-Germain[132], he appears to have been, acting as a travel agent, one of the instruments of that deep and mysterious framework that the sect of the *Illuminati* had contrived for the subversion of European States.

Toward 1789, forced to leave France following the famous Necklace Affair[133], Cagliostro had the unfortunate idea

---

[132] Count de Saint-Germain. An 18th century mystery man. His death in 1784 is documented, but his birth place and year of birth is not. He was said to be a talented composer, musician, artist, and had remarkable abilities to disintegrate and reform diamonds, turn cheap metals into gold, etc. In addition, he was supposed to have been seen in almost all parts of Europe and Asia.

[133] The Necklace Affair. Complicated history of a necklace Louis XV commissioned from two Paris jewelers, Boehmer and Bassenge, for Madame du Barry, his mistress. Before the necklace was completed, Louis XV died and Madame du Barry was banished from the Court. The finished necklace was presented by the jewelers to Louis XVI for Marie Antoinette,

to appear in Rome. The Inquisition, that knew about his relationship with the *Illuminati,* had him arrested and put on trial. Following the confessions obtained by that fearful tribunal, he was condemned to death, a judgment that Pope Pius VI commuted to life in prison. Jailed in the fortress of San Leo, Cagliostro died there about 1795.

Condemned with the same sentence, his wife Lorenza Feliciani, was destined to finish her days in the Sainte-Apolline Convent, but, in 1793, two years before the death of her husband, she managed to break out of her seclusion. Returned to Genoa, her native country, under the name of Signora Melissa, one of the numerous names that the adventurer, her husband, had successively used, she opened a fortune telling business and began to make herself known as a divineress and card dealer with a reputation equal to that which the famous Demoiselle Lenormand[134] had toward the same epoch in Paris.

---

but, she, supposedly, suggested using the money for national defense. An adventuress, Jeanne de la Motte, a descendant of an illegitimate son of Henry II, in a complicated series of forged letters, impersonated Marie Antoinette, colluded with the Cardinal de Rohan, who was in love with the Queen, and stole the necklace in 1785. The scam was discovered. Jeanne de la Motte and Cardinal de Rohan were arrested and tried. Jeanne de la Motte was sentenced to life in prison; Cardinal de Rohan, despite his obvious guilt, was set free. Madame de la Motte died miserably in London at age 34, jumping from a second story window to escape the bailiffs who were about to arrest her for unpaid debts. Her husband, the Comte de la Motte lived on into the reign of Charles X, became a beggar and died from misery. ardinal de Rohan emigrated and died in exile. The jewelers became bankrupt and their firm sank into oblivion.

[134] Marie-Anne-Adelaide Lenormand (1772-1843). Active for more than forty years as a fortune teller. She claimed to have given readings to leaders of the French Revolution as well as to Empress Josephine. Imprisoned several times, she was al-

Some years later, in the same city in Genoa, there was nothing talked about but a very unusual program that Prince Bevillacqua, one of the great names of the Genoese aristocracy had made part of his life. The lottery of Genoa, under the name of *Seminario,* had always been one of the most famous in Europe. What set it apart from the other establishments of the same type, was that the chances, instead of being made up of numbers, were in that establishment determined by proper names. In the mechanism of the former Genoa Constitution, a certain number of public functions were conferred by chance. As a consequence, all the names of those who could claimed the right to public office were kept in a box carefully sealed. And when the legal drawing took place, the names taken from the box were also used to establish the makeup of the *Seminario.*

Now, one unusual thing was noticed. Since 1620, the time of the foundation of the lottery in Genoa, until 1797, that is, for nearly two centuries, the name of the family of Benedetto Gentile had not once been drawn. Now, since it was precisely a Benedetto Gentile who founded the lottery in Genoa, people said that it was to punish him for his damnable creation that, after his death, the Devil, after having carried away his soul, had also taken away his name. Without accepting such a naïve belief, Prince Bevillacqua, had also been struck by the bizarre caprice of fate. At the time he noticed that, youthful dissipations had greatly compromised his fortune. He persuaded himself that, because of the length of time it had not been drawn, it must be taken to mean that it soon would be, and by betting on that name, he would win a great fortune.

Therefore, he began to bet relentlessly on that fatal name. Then, because of his long series of losses, stubbornly fixed on a ruinous series of bets following the law of probability, toward 1797, he had come to the point of having nothing in his possession but the sum necessary to buy a last ticket, a su-

---

ways shortly thereafter released. She was also the author of numerous books on occultism.

preme test of his star. What's more, his action taken as a resolution decided on, if in that final engagement, chance continued to be against him, he had, it was said, the intention of asking by suicide a refuge from poverty. Announced in advance
to the public, that determination gave his bet the interest of a
duel to the death. And before his bet, all eyes were fixed on
that terrible all or nothing which was being prepared.

In that frantic player's state of mind, the perplexity of
thinking about the likely alternative, it is understandable that
he decided to go consult Signora Melissa, whose fame had
reached him. To predict to him that the name of Benedetto
Gentile wouldn't come out of the urn, wasn't a great effort of
knowledge for the Sybil. The past almost certainly warned
him about the future. But to take on herself the announcement
that at subsequent drawing, the result vainly awaited since
1620, would precisely be produced was assuredly great audacity on the part of the prophetess. It must be added that a caprice of chance, however, wanted to justify it.

Having bet, according to the directions of Signora Melissa, Bevillacqua made an enormous profit and re-established
his fortune. What's more, the recompense paid to the advice of
the pythoness was as unexpected as magnificent. Three weeks
after the fortunate success of his audacious prophetess, Signora Melissa was transformed into the Princess de Bevillacqua.
So that, in the place of a denouement of a tragedy, the ending
was that of a comedy.[135]

That misalliance was so much more astonishing in that
Lorenza Feliciani, just after her return to her country, had giv-
en birth to a charming little girl that the well established impossibility of cohabitation with the prisoner of the Inquisition,

---

[135] Application of the Aristotelian definition of comedy and
tragedy. (A very short definition of a complicated theory): A
tragedy involves important and virtuous characters and arous-
es pity and terror in the viewers. A comedy deals with the
problems of less virtuous and important people and shows
their weakness and vulnerability, but in general all ends well.

placed into the most interesting way into the category of bastard and adulterous children.

However, there could be more than one explanation for the extreme form which the gratitude of the noble man from Genoa had taken. First of all, at the time that marriage took place, Signora Melissa was still remarkably beautiful. During the long life of intrigue that she had led following the charlatan, her first husband, she had always practiced, somewhat, the work of a siren, and she knew how to use all the resources of seduction that her charms could command. It could also be thought that, paid as he had been by believing in the divinatory science, from her long habitation with her first husband, Lorenza Feliciani had knowledge of a mass of precious secrets. From that, with the turn of adventurous spirit that could be assumed from the unusual battle in which Prince Bevillacqua had previously engaged, a matrimonial speculation having as an object inheriting all the secrets that had created European fame for Cagliostro can easily be understood. Finally, a third explanation, not less plausible, at the time when Bevillacqua took a wife from such a low position in society, the principles of the French Revolution had penetrated into Italy. By that invasion of the Constitution, the existence of all the aristocracy of the Republic of Genoa was seriously threatened. Bevillacqua had come close to ruin. Therefore, he was a democrat and he foresaw with great sympathy the approaching overthrow of the government of his country.

Now, since ambitious aspirations were always hidden under that democratic spirit of failure and bankruptcy, the man whose ease the aristocratic Constitution of Genoa made tremble, counted very much on being called on to play a considerable role in an approaching revolution. His game, then, wasn't it to flatter that passion for equality always sure to trick the crowd. In his marriage with the card dealer, hadn't he seized an opportunity naturally made to popularize him even more?

As is reasonable, from those great and marvelous secrets he had hoped to acquire in following Cagliostro, the man from Genoa must have found a great number of disappointments.

Instead of a supernatural power which he had perhaps expected to be put in his possession, a few recipes of doubtful efficacy, combined with many sleight of hand tricks, such were, finally, the result of the shameful matrimonial bargain that he had made. But in compensation for his intended power, it seemed to him that his wife had opened to him a very different horizon when she told him that it was due to the patronage and the complicity of the Freemasons and secret societies that had most of all led to the notoriety with which Cagliostro had surrounded his name. Immediately curious to reach that path, through the intermediary of Lorenza Feliciani, who, while in Italy, had met a former acquaintance of Cagliostro, Ephraim the Jew, Bevillacqua didn't lose any time in being put in touch with that notable revolutionary. Soon, under his patronage he became a member of the *Awakened*. A detached branch and a direct heir of the *Illuminati,* the goal of that society was to combine all of the Italian peninsula into a great federal republic.

In the archives of the *Grand Firmament,* that he himself had received from the Society of the *Awakened,* is found an account of the initiation of *Brother* Bevillacqua as a member of the second of those affiliations. The immense curiosity of that document, which the author of *The History of the Secret Societies of the Army* [136] knew as we do, explains why we decided to reproduce it here literally:

It began, that account says, *by having Brother Bevillacqua undergo an extremely simple initiation which often was accorded to entire villages, and which was proportionate to the most ordinary ability. Two months went by without his having heard anything from the Society or of its projects. He presumed that it was nothing else but what it had appeared to him at the first meeting; that is to say, an insignificant Masonic association that had usurped the great fame on the faith of which he had desired to see himself affiliated.*

---

[136] See Notes 81 and 82.

Brother Bevillacqua began then to regard it as a pure game of the imagination, when a letter conceived in the terms he distinctly remembered from his reception, called him into a forest of rather bad reputation where he was to find a great number of his brothers assembled. He went to that rendezvous without any precautions, since the terms of his first initiation and the character of the persons who had served him as godfathers, seemed to offer a very sufficient guarantee against every type of ambush. He recognized the most obvious signs of the place designated to him, having before and afterward, walked through the whole area, still waiting and not seeing anyone appear. A few days afterward, the same notice was again given in the same terms and the rendezvous made to the same place. He obeyed with the same punctuality and was not any more fortunate in his search. That particular test practiced on his patience was renewed four times with the same denouement in the space of three weeks. Following a fifth call to which he submitted with a certain annoyance, he was coming back somewhat embittered by that constantly repeated deception, when he heard, a hundred feet from him, what seemed to be the call of a man in distress, which kept him in the forest where, that time, he had gone further than he had up until then. The day was at its decline, the season very bad (It was toward the end of November) and continuing to go forward into the woods he didn't recognize, Brother Bevillacqua ran the risk of getting lost. But no consideration could stop him in an occasion where humanity made such a commanding appeal to his courage.

Armed only with a dagger, he rushed into the thicket, cutting down the brambles in front of him which were an obstacle, always directed toward the voice asking for assistance and to which he was drawing closer and closer, he finally came to a more open space. There he saw three men of bad appearance take flight at his call, firing their carbines at him. Remained alone, he saw stretched out at his feet a man covered with blood illuminated by the last lights of twilight. With that doubtful light he could, however, discern clothes in tatters

and soiled with blood, and see that the victim had been violently strangled.

Brother Bevillacqua had hardly the time to look at that
sad spectacle and see some signs of life near being extinguished in the unfortunate man whose agony he was contemplating. Looking around him with an uneasy eye he measured
the depth of the brambles, where in twenty places death could
traitorously reach him. Just then a detachment of armed force,
drawn by the cries which he himself had made from a point
opposite the one by which the criminals had retreated, rapidly
surrounded the place where the victim was stretched out. He
died, but his last words were to point out as one of the murderers the one who had run to his aid. What's more, the hour,
the place, the weapon found on Brother Bevillacqua and the
emotion as a result of the surprise, everything seemed to accuse him.

Despite his protests, he was bound, thrown into a cart
that was requisitioned from the nearest farm and taken to a
farm house of sinister aspect which was used as a prison in
the village where he had to spend the night. There, contrary to
his expectations, he had come to the end of his journey. For
the next two days he remained in that place of detention in the
most absolute seclusion, hardly receiving any nourishment,
and prey to that inexpressible agony that the innocent undergo
when under the accusation of a major crime. Providence
seemed to have dispossessed at its pleasure any way to justify
himself.

He was finally brought before a magistrate, interrogated,
heard the witnesses who were deposed against him, and confronted with the men who declared him their accomplice.
Brought forward with unbelievable rapidity, the procedure
was the same day far enough advanced for the affair to be
brought before a judge. His defense heard, on the indictment
of the public prosecutor, he was judged and condemned. That
ignominious death was to serve as reparation for his crime
that the overwhelming accusations of the evidence seemed to
support in the greatest degree. Broken by the fatigue of that

judicial battle, by hunger, by despair, the condemned man learned with a kind of joy that the time of his death was hastened by an unusual circumstance. The following day was consecrated to a celebration of great religious importance, and to avoid delaying the execution to the day following the next day, it would take place the same evening under torch light during the most silent and most sinister hour of the night. Conducted by the hideous hangmen, with a rope around his neck, under the gloomy light of torches, Brother Bevillacqua heard a nearby church ring the funereal knell from a bell that added to his agony.

After a rather long walk, he came into an immense courtyard in the middle of which the scaffold had been erected. A circle of horsemen, whose uniform was unknown to him, kept at a distance the crowd of spectators over whom the light of the torches spread light the color of blood. The condemned man mounted the scaffold. His sentence was read to him, and he was going to be given over to the executioners, when the running hoofs of a horse and soon the voice of an officer who jumped from his horse that was covered with foam, led to the thought of a reprieve.

Taken to one side, Brother Bevillacqua was told that an order of the government had pardoned every man condemned for whatever crime, if he could give the words of initiation and of recognition of a secret society whose name he was told. That was the society of the Awakened precisely the one of which he had become a member and whose command he was executing just at the moment when he became entangled by the fatal accusation which was going to make him lose his life. However attractive the temptation might be, Brother Bevillacqua did not give in. The object of the strongest and most well meaning entreaties, he remained unshakeable and demanded that they finish with the hanging.

Not being able to be pushed any further, the test, because it was one, was declared terminated. Brother Bevillacqua was given the fraternal kiss, and as homage rendered to his invin-

cible constancy, he was conferred the highest degree of the
initiation, and they dispensed with the swearing in ceremony.

There was no one around him who was not a member of
the association and in the bloody drama of which he had been
the principal author, all the associates had played a role di-
rected to the same end, which was a study of the firmness of
his soul before pronouncing his acceptance.

XIII. The Deaf-Mute

However powerful the organization of a society might
appear, in the ceremonials of its receptions, in luxury deployed
similar to the one that has just been described, the society of
the *Awakened,* to speak like Job, *lived a short time and was
full of many miseries.* Divisions among its chiefs, the infideli-
ties or indiscretions of several of its members led rapidly to its
dissolution, proof that for the solidity of those kinds of aggre-
gations, the solemnity of the test is of mediocre importance.
Even to a certain point, it could be said that the grand apparatus was a cause of their ruin, in the sense that the splendor of
the methods finally at last hid the goal from view.

Free from his engagements with the *Awakened,*
Bevillacqua, who in the interval had seen a revolution in Genoa in which none of his ambitious hopes were realized, judged
it prudent to leave Italy and pass into France. There, he at first
he was occupied more with business than with politics. Involved in supplies, and investing successfully in public funds,
although a foreigner, he took an active part in a legislative act
of the period, for which it couldn't be denied he was eminent-
ly qualified. W

When the Directoire thought about proposing the re-
establishment of the National Lottery, abolished by a decree of
the Convention, a commission was named to discuss the basis
of the system for the projected law. Bevillacqua, who, in his
long battle with the name of Benedetto Gentile, had looked
into the matter with very profound studies and calculations,
was consulted as a man of experience, and as recompense for

the light he had brought to the commission, he was, at his request, given the situation as director of an office that we have seen furnish such precious commodities to the *Grand Firmament* reunions. But before becoming the Supreme Head of the association of the *Sublimi Maestro Perfetti,* Bevillacqua had to spend some time in the order of the *Philadelphes.* And if, politically speaking, his rapport with that society had no considerable outcome, it is going to be seen that, on the contrary, in his private life, it exercised an influence that modified all the administration of his household.

At the time when Bevillacqua became a member of the *Philadelphes*, between his wife and him, for a long time, there had been marked coldness. Both sides regretted the tie which united them, because both sides had overrated their expectations. Lorenza Feliciani had seriously counted on becoming Princess Bevillacqua and on taking advantages of all the considerations of that title. Now what that hope had led to was to become the companion of an obscure conspirator who could claim, by his fortune and by his great intelligence and his character, every social distinction. For herself, she had to swallow being reduced to the level, in the middle of the interference of obscure secret societies, of being nothing more than the unhappy worker in their nameless work. As for Bevillacqua, it has already been said that he had to lower his sights considerably as to the presumed benefits of his association with the Widow Cagliostro. At that point, all the bad sides of that marriage had become for him an immense burden. In particular that compromising maternity which, at first, he had not asked for an accounting, had become one of the worries of his life. Soon a pronounced diversion of political opinions came to crown such a well established misunderstanding. Having the opportunity to approach Josephine Bonaparte, and even having, it is claimed, predicted to her the high fortune to which she was destined, Madame de Bevillacqua was deeply sympathetic to all the grandeurs of Napoleon. In his positions as a *Philadelphe,* Bevillacqua was, on the contrary, violently hostile to the First Consul, and from there the cause of frequent violent storms in the household.

It seems that in the middle of one of those conjugal quarrels, the affiliate of the *Philadelphes* was led to make a threatening allusion to an attempt that the society was thinking of making against Bonaparte. That incomplete warning that she had thus received, Madame de Bevillacqua believed that she should immediately transmit it to Madame Bonaparte, who, herself, passed it on to Fouché.[137] Put thus on the way, the clever Minister of Police wasn't long in discovering that it was a matter of waylaying the vanquisher of Marengo in the middle of the mountains when he was crossing them returning from Italy. Thanks to the clever organization of the *Philadelphes* plot, the authors remained unknown and couldn't be captured, but their design fell apart. Having themselves informants in the Police, the conspirators managed to learn the origin of the denunciation which caused their failure. It can be imagined in what a false position that revelation immediately placed Bevillacqua in the bosom of the association.

Strongly called to task about his wife's indiscretion, the man from Genoa energetically defended himself from the suspicions that she had let be traced back to him. Then, when he saw that despite his denials, he continued to remain under the shadow of an injurious doubt, thinking about the attractions of Brutus[138], to put himself in a better posture, he offered to sacrifice the guilty one.

"We don't kill women," he was disdainfully answered. "You must be careful of all intemperance in speech, if you don't want to be taken any more seriously than they are. No

---

[137] Joseph Fouché (1759-1820). Minister of Police under Napoleon I.
[138] Second allusion to Brutus' speech to the Romans after he helped assassinate Julius Caesar, saying "not that I loved Caesar less, but that I loved Rome more." Replace Caesar with the Widow Cagliostro and Rome with the *Philadelphes* Society.

man can be part of any business who doesn't know how to keep a secret."

After those hard words, Bevillacqua ostracized himself. But at the same time, animated with a violent desire for vengeance against the one who had caused him that humiliation, he had her leave with him precipitously for Livorno, where he claimed he was called by an important business affair. He didn't forget to tell her that the young girl that he reproached himself so strongly for having assumed the parentage was also part of that trip. Several days after the arrival of the two spouses in Livorno, the unfortunate child had disappeared.

Suffering from every anxiety and every doubt, Madame de Bevillacqua nevertheless had no suspicion of the angry hand that had stuck that blow to her maternal heart, but one morning her husband said to her:

"Lorenza, there's a debt between us. Would you like to settle it?"

"A debt?" the unhappy woman asked with dread, because there was a menacing tone in what Bevillacqua had asked her.

"Yes, a debt," and at that, the terrible man from Genoa, who until then hadn't said a word to Madame de Bevillacqua about his complaint against her, began a long expose of the consequences of the report of which she was guilty. Then, he continued, "My first thought was to make you pay for that betrayal with your life."

"Well! What kept you from doing that?" resolutely answered Lorenza, who immediately saw implacable resentment in her husband.

"No, you will live," continued the man from Genoa, "but you used your tongue in a not very loyal and reflective way. I will take care that in the future your tongue will be sealed."

At the first moment Madame de Bevillacqua had the idea that it would be one of those horrible mutilations such as are practiced in the Orient. But immediately understanding what she thought, the terrible man of justice said:

"Come now! Am I an executioner? You will stay healthy and keep the instrument of your fault. But, for an example, I forbid you use it to express your thoughts with anyone other than myself. In that way you will be spared a great many foolish words."

"Eh! Monsieur, if I intended to obey you, will it depend on me not to transgress your orders?"

"You will obey me, I'm sure, and with the most scrupulous attention, because after all, do you love your daughter?"

"My daughter!" cried out Madame de Bevillacqua distractedly. "Why are you talking to me about my daughter! Ah! You are the one who kidnapped her!"

"You're right," the man from Genoa answered calmly. "I put her in a safe place so that she can be a hostage for your obedience. Now do you want to hear the details of what must remain an agreement between us?"

"Monsieur, kill me instead," cried out the unhappy mother.

"I won't kill you. On the contrary, I will continue to treat you as a cherished and honored spouse. Only, beginning tomorrow, news will be spread around that due to the emotion and the shock that the disappearance of your daughter caused you, you have been struck with paralysis. Now, you can choose: that infirmity can be whichever you like, either intermittent or continuous. If, for your daughter, who is lost to you for a long time, but that I myself will have always at hand, you desire all the happiness that a mother could wish, you will obey me in every way. If you want her life to be a little less happy, from time to time, you are free to begin speaking again, it being understood that your child will experience the opposite at your least word. Finally, if it should be convenient for you never to see her again, let's say that I didn't at all condemn you to silence and keep the liberty of your tongue, as from my side I will keep the freedom of my deliberations."

"But to what age will I be deprived of my daughter? What length of time do you assign to this odious torture?"

341

"I don't know. Obedience will determine the duration of the expiation."

And, despite the supplications of the victim, asking for herself a more cruel chastisement, on condition that an innocent creature was not punished, the infernal Genoese persisted in his refinement of vengeance. He understood very well that to strike the heart of a mother, there was nothing more sure than to deliver the blow to one of her children.

Madame de Bevillacqua found in her love for her daughter the courage to endure the terrible redemption to which she had been condemned. Greater still was her sacrifice, because on the promise that that willingness would be the price of her seeing her daughter, she consented to work at the Lottery Office on the rue Jean-Jacques Rousseau, giving there, as it has been seen, the spectacle of her pretended infirmity. But since, following that cruel punishment, Bevillacqua put off from day to day bringing her the consolation which with false promises he had deceived her, the poor woman was finally so discouraged that she thought of suicide. For more than one reason, the threat of that outcome worried her persecutor. First of all, he calculated that if Lorenza Feliciani decided to turn her desperate hand to take her life, that would be because she no longer had any hope that her daughter was still alive. After that, no longer having anything to worry about before dying, she might perhaps find a way to have come before the law certain revelations that caution demanded not to be confronted. But this danger, if not considered, for a man who had taken such an odious pleasure in distilling his vengeance, wouldn't it be a gross miscalculation to see it so suddenly concluded. Could he not with delight continue the suffering so ingeniously cruel he had devised, and wasn't it for his heinous nature a great pleasure that he didn't want to lose?

He then looked for a way such that he then could keep his promise. We must hastily add that he himself had long since placed that realization outside the sphere of his own will. Little by little his aversion for that illegitimate fruit, which put a stain on his marriage, had taken on such a character that already, even before the indiscretion that Madame de Bevillacqua had committed, he had thought of getting an object he couldn't endure out of his sight. When, then, he had taken the innocent creature from the love of her mother, he hadn't kept her at hand as he had claimed. A crime had been the cost of his hatred. There too was marked the refined genius of evil that definitely seemed to be one of the salient traits of his character. He knew that at Livorno, where there was immense commerce with the Orient, there were purveyors of harems coming to search for European products for which they were sure to find advantageous placements in Muslim countries. Now, Lorenza Feliciani's daughter promised to be remarkably beautiful. Bevillacqua had only to get in touch with one of those infamous traffickers and just as surely as a tomb the walls of a seraglio must have swallowed up his worry.

In taking care of the future of that unfortunate child with one fell swoop, her executioner probably had not hidden from himself that an unforeseen necessity coming to force him to produce her, that sudden denouement could, at another time create more than one problem for him. But before anything else, he had ceded to this consideration: the younger the victim was when taken from her country, the less she would have the chance to react against the destiny that he had set up for her. Now, when he had completely lost trace of her, Lorenza Feliciani's despair had just given him formal notice, a situation that remained outside his calculations. Nothing therefore seemed more difficult to refuse to accept than the imperious demands of maternal love, when, suddenly fate, one of the great masters of the world, took charge of bringing him that solution which for several days he had been cruelly prevented from finding. How it was that Diane de Limeuil was found to have great resemblance to the young girl he was going to place under the eyes of her weeping mother, that is what, later, will be very naturally explained.

It has previously been shown how Matiphous's pupil found herself, one day, in the path of the Prince, and the advantage he knew how to take from that encounter. Diane de Limeuil, it is useful to know, was some years older than the unfortunate infant, of whom she was, without knowing it, supposed to play the role. But seen at a distance, in an audience, when, besides, Bevillacqua had taken care to flatter the maternal pride of Lorenza Feliciani by mentioning development of rare precocity in the girl he was going to present to her, the illusion produced the expected result to the suppliant.

Having thus calmed for a time the anxieties of the unhappy mother, he had her again obedient and resigned. Later, however, having had time to reflect, Madame de Bevillacqua had, if not disbelief, at least doubt about the young girl, already so completely grown up, that had been placed before her eyes. Every calculation meant that her daughter must not have been more than twelve-years-old. The express condition that her husband had made was that she should not give way to any demonstration of maternal emotion. At the same time, the absolute impassiveness that she had noticed in the one showed to her as the child of her womb, and who had not left her at an age when she would not have kept a memory of her mother, everything made her think of some trickery. From that, she determined to have an explanation from Matiphous when, one day, in the Lottery Office she had recognized him for the man who had accompanied the suspicious apparition in which she no longer believed. In that encounter, to get to the bottom of the truth, Lorenza Feliciani had decided to no longer count on any consideration from her husband. At that point, her husband had absolutely sequestered her, and while letting her see the most sinister projects against her, he had taken minute precautions to prevent her from taking her life. He reserved for himself, if the unhappy woman was to end in a violent way, at least to be her executioner.

In using Matiphous and his pupil for his infamous comedy, Bevillacqua didn't know that he had under his hand that man from Malta that the *Grand Firmament* accused of murdering one of its members. The scene at the Opera played out, he had no more interest in the marionettes that he had set in operation. He thought nothing would come of his adventure. But, one day, at the Hôtel d'Angleterre, the former Bell Rock guardian had been met by the traveling salesman, one of the conspirators, who had brought to Paris the news of the homicide of Ephraim. Immediately recognized by that man who had seen him at the lighthouse in the exercise of his functions, Matiphous believed himself to be the object of a duel, when he was going to be the object of an ambush. That rendezvous of honor that had led him to the Bois de Boulogne, that pretended wounded man for whom he had let himself be drawn into a remote alley of the woods to give him medical attention, was so much cleverness.

There, several armed men had forced him to climb into a carriage that had rapidly conducted him to a country house in the area. Until the evening that house had been used as prison for him. Then his hands tied, a gag in his mouth and his eyes blindfolded, he had been placed in another vehicle, and during a part of the night, as much as he could tell, he had traveled on the road toward Germany. The men who accompanied him pretended to name all of the relay stations on that route and where they stopped to change horses. Coulommiers, a little village situated fourteen leagues from Paris, was the place that the prisoner thought he had ended his trip. Taken into an underground location, he found himself facing a kind of tribunal where three men wearing a mask on their face had demanded that he give an account of Ephraim's murder. However, they offered him clemency if he agreed to restore the red briefcase which he was accused of having taken after the crime was committed, or, even if he limited himself to indicating the hands into which that precious depository had passed, supposing that he no longer had it.

Innocent of all the acts he had been charged with, Matiphous knew only vaguely the sad end of Ephraim which he had learned after his appearance in the Police Bureau. It was then impossible for him to give him any of the information demanded.

But, without giving any credence to his denials, they warned him that he was going to be taken into the *room of reflections*. He would stay there until he decided to talk. In a way, his fate was decided on the arbitration of his stomach, since he wouldn't be given any nourishment until he decided to talk. That amounted to saying that, condemned to the question of hunger, the terrible fate of Count Ugolino [139]was reserved for him.

During the three long days and the three long nights that Matiphous spend in the dark prison where he was confined, at regular intervals a voice came to call to him through the door, asking him in a tone of kindly interest if he had *reflected*. Then, as the unfortunate man was profuse in oaths and in protests trying to persuade his executioners that he knew nothing about any of the charges, he was told:

"As you please. If the diet is to your taste, you can consult with yourself some more. We have a lot of time."

And after they had thrown him that statement, everything around him returned to deadly silence until another voice (because a number of men seemed to work in a relay for that torture) came to begin the same irony again. Toward the beginning of the fourth night, the prisoner, who had had only short periods of intermittent sleep agitated by painful dreams, began to be dizzy. He had periods of fainting that made him believe life was leaving him. Although plunged in thick shadows, he saw as if there were tongues of fire and shining clouds dancing in front of his eyes. At the same time, dull sound struck his

---

[139] Count Ugolino della Gherardesca of Donoratico (c.1220-1289). Italian nobleman, politician and naval commander. He was frequently accused of treason and features prominently in Dante's *Divine Comedy*. He was walled up with his sons in their prison which would also be their tomb. He watched his sons die of starvation one after the other, then driven by hunger, ate their flesh before he died himself. His punishment is described in Dante's *Inferno*. Auguste Rodin also used it as the inspiration for a statue.

ears. A waking sleep peopled with frightening and bizarre hallucinations little by little took hold of him. In that situation he no longer thought of trying to make his persecutors reconsider. He ceased to respond to the voices that came periodically to speak to him. But his senses, as he became weaker acquired an unusual subtlety. He heard a kind of conversation in taking place in a low voice, not far from the door of his cell.

"It's clear. He won't talk," said one of the speakers of that conference, "and he'll carry his secret with him."

"Well! At least our Ephraim has been avenged."

"Let's put fire to his feet," was the opinion of the third, who had perhaps been a party to the bands of criminals who had merited their name from the usage of that terrible method of torture.

"What's the use?" he was answered. "Isn't dying of hunger the most terrible of tortures? He's a determined man. We will get nothing from him."

"Perhaps, Messieurs," said a voice that Matiphous vaguely remembered having heard somewhere before.

"Tell Britannicus, who should be up above in the Lottery Office, to come down. I believe I have an idea."

Britannicus! The Lottery Office! Those words were a complete revelation to the man from Malta. In the voice that had named the African, he believed he had recognized that of Bevillacqua. From that moment, he could guess the place where he had been taken and the hands into which he had fallen. Some time went by. There was a certain movement in front of his cell. Then suddenly the door was opened. The miserable man, who was dying of starvation, was surprised by seeing a table filled with food. At the same time, one of the masked men who, before, had interrogated him, was standing on the threshold of his prison.

"Monsieur's food is ready!"

Immediately brought alive again by the sight and by the odor of the food, Matiphous rushed toward the meal offered him. Despite the obstacle of several masked men standing on either side of the table with a naked sword, he was able to reach with his hand one of the dishes and seize some food that he carried to his mouth with a totally animal avidity. But held back by the men who surrounded him, he was told to confess the truth before taking a place at the festive table. Not knowing anything about what was demanded of him, the unfortunate man couldn't give in to the temptation that torture creates in an innocent man to admit guilt. And with an accent of truth that would have convinced hearts less inaccessible to pity, he continued to protest his inability to make any revelation.

"That's all right!" said one of the masked men, whose height and accent Matiphous recognized, and no longer doubted, as Bevillacqua. "What he took could prolonger his torture for some hours. Put him back in his cell!"

The order was carried out the same moment and without a great deal of violence. Exhausted by hunger, the prisoner wasn't in any condition to pose any great resistance. Nevertheless, his return to the place that was supposed to be his tomb, was not done without a little fight and disorder. And, taking advantage of that movement, one of those in the most hurry to carry out Bevillacqua's order slid into his hand a paper that his fingers grasped with a convulsive passion. He instinctively felt immediately that some method of escape was indicated to him on that paper. But once the door was closed again, seeing himself plunged into the inextricable shadows, the unfortunate man believed it was a new refinement of torture imagined by the executioners to increase his agony. It was horrible torture, in fact, to feel that under his eyes his salvation could be written and not to be able to decipher it.

About an hour passed in that agony which, however, didn't remain purely passive. Persuading himself that in some corner around him he might find some method to procure light, Matiphous started to feel in all directions the different decorative objects that were used for the initiations of the *Grand Firmament,* since he had been given as a prison that kind of cellar adjoining the great room for meetings. But at the moment when he had finished moving about all those second hand clothes, the prisoner despaired of seeing his research crowned with success, some soft knocks at the door drew his attention. At the same moment he recognized that the kindly thought of the one whose instruction remained useless in his hand, had found a way to let him profit by it. Placed exactly right, from the keyhole of the lock, a light projected a ray of clarity on the paper that he hurriedly placed near it, permitting him to read these few words that he saw written there:

Me good neg'o! You save Britannicus that other time. Now I save you. Me not able to take key from my master, but you can make a hole in the wall where wall sounds hollow, with piece of iron I searched hard to find for you. You not make noise and chew up paper from Britannicus so no one know what I wrote.

After having read the note, Matiphous was astonished at not having himself the idea of such an evasion. That was explained, however, by the belief he had always retained that the men whose prisoner he was wouldn't want to carry things to the last extremities. But after the judgment that had made the African help him, knowing that kind action made him apprehensive for his own safety, the condemned man could no longer doubt that his death was seriously resolved. In the middle of the mass of objects he had explored before, he began to look, without stopping, for some instrument for a prolonged search, and he wasn't long in discovering that Roman sword that it will be recalled was part of the reception ceremony.

Sounding then the wall in every direction, he recognized a rather large space where it sounded empty and without being well aware of the exit he might find in that direction, he immediately undertook to make a breach. The hope of escape and the small quantity of nourishment that he had the good luck to steal from his executioners had to that point overexcited his strength and his courage. His work was carried out rapidly, and soon, after having pierced the wall and crossed over the encumbrances, he found himself in the underground passage that had formerly served as communication between the

Lottery Office and the Administration Building of the Poste. That long tunnel where an inspection hole had been cut in the top, letting in a little air and light, he passed through without an obstacle. Soon he found himself in front of the door that had been boarded up which, in the past, had opened into the *Secret Bureau.* There, encouraged by the sound of voices that he thought he heard through the wall, and, despite his exhaustion and his weakness, finding in the instinctive conservation of energy the supreme effort, he succeeded in joining the personnel of the *Secret Bureau.* But, as was seen earlier, that unusual stimulation didn't sustain him beyond the moment when he had crossed the last obstacles and his feet had at the same time touched the floor of the room he had invaded. He fell, deprived of feeling and giving no signs of life.

XIV. The Perfect Lover

The Imperial Government had a good principle; that was to make public the least possible information about the plots that had come to its attention. On the information given by Matiphous, the *Grand Firmament* had been taken in the act. When visiting his prisoner, that he believed he would find dead or in final agony, Bevillacqua had just become aware of his escape. Accompanied by several of his affiliates, he started to enter the underground passage in pursuit of the fugitive, when a squad of police agents invaded and surrounded the location and the society. The registries and the papers, as well as all the material for initiations, were immediately seized. All the people, without exception, that a thorough investigation had discovered in that suspected house were put into several carriages. After that seals had been placed on the door. Then whatever curiosity the neighborhood had showed, nothing happened and the excitement had hardly extended to the limits of the neighborhood. No free newspaper existed then which could have commented on that expedition or found out about it. The dispersion of the society and a penalty applied, its members, some hours later were tracked throughout all points of Paris with the same secrecy and the same rapidity of execution.

Following some confrontations with Bevillacqua and other principal persons of that shady affair, the Prince was sent to Vincennes, some others of his association sent to other State prisons. Several were taken to the frontier of the Empire with the threat of being turned over to military commissions if they dared to reappear in France, and the rest placed under the surveillance of the State Police or thrown into beggars' prison. As for Madame de Bevillacqua, after having with great ingenuity recounted all the travels of her adventurous life, she herself had asked to seek asylum in a religious community. From the depth of that holy asylum, aided by Minister Fouché, who, in return for the frankness of her confessions, had made her hope for his help, she had done all that was necessary to find her unfortunate child of whom Britannicus had finally revealed to her the deplorable fate. If, as it was only too much to be feared, her searches must finally be without result, she had decided to end her days in that pious house.

As for Matiphous, while he had not exactly stumbled on the *Secret Bureau's* existence by accident, it was feared that, his imagination, processing what he had seen, he might commit some harmful indiscretions. The best thing, then, was to confront him with that fact and let him choose between perpetual life in a State Prison or to let himself take a place in the secret Administration that had been revealed to him. His choice was not in doubt. Naturally he opted for the second choice.

For the courageous devotion that he had shown to Matiphous, Britannicus the Black had demonstrated a very exceptional attitude in the middle of the kind of den where he had been found. Besides that, the magnificent roundup the police had made was due to him. He was therefore left free. To replace the condition that he lost by the sequestration of Prince de Bevillacqua, another soon appeared. By means of the salary attached to his employment in the *Secret Bureau,* Matiphous became a man of comfortable means. He offered to take his savior into his service. Britannicus, having eagerly and with gratitude accepted, it could be said that in the long episode of the *Grand Firmament,* everything was definitely liquidated, if the account of Count Octave de Limeuil didn't remain to be explained. For some time, the reader has been curious about his incomprehensible passion for the Widow Cagliostro. He can now see into that so persevering and so unhappy love.

Soon after the close of the legalities which had just shed light into that complicated situation, at first inextricable, where, despite all Bevillacqua's concealments, the combined explanations of Lorenza Feliciani, of Matiphous, and of Britannicus, left nothing obscure or not understood, the Minister of Police asked Monsieur de Limeuil to come to his office.

"Monsieur," the high functionary said to his visitor, who was greatly intrigued by that invitation, "if my information is correct, for several years an Italian woman named Lorenza Feliciani, the widow of the famous charlatan Cagliostro, has been the object of your most active research, has she not?"

"Where did Your Excellency learn that?" Monsieur de Limeuil asked in a tone showing that a deeply sensitive cord in him had just been touched.

"How do I know that? My job is to know everything. And it's also somewhat my claim. So, I can also tell you, as little as that proof of my good information may please you, the profoundly secret interest you have in finding that woman and even how you knew her."

"I am here," Monsieur de Limeuil replied, "to listen to everything Your Excellency may judge useful to tell me."

That was cleverly phrased, because without admitting anything and without denying anything, Count Octave put the man questioning him in the position of continuing and telling just to what point he had information.

"All right, then!" the Minister continued, "since you seem to challenge me, I will begin by reminding you of the period when the Revolutionary Government dismissed from the military those called nobility in the past. You resigned your commission at the rank of Adjutant-General, that you had very valiantly earned on the field of battle. Almost immediately your friends, with regret, saw you go abroad."

"My Lord," Monsieur de Limeuil quickly interrupted, "I left my country to avoid the scaffold, which took Custine[140] and Beauharnais, my companions in arms. But I did not, as did the émigrés, did take service against France. It is to be hoped that the conscience of those who forced me into exile have nothing more to hold against me."

"But," replied the Minister, without showing any emotion to the rather transparent allusion made to his Revolutionary past, "I don't mean to say that your conduct abroad had anything about it that was reprehensible. You had a taste for

---

[140] Adam Philippe, Comte de Custine (1740-1793). As a young officer in the Bourbon Royal army, Custine served in the Seven Years' War. In the American Revolutionary War he joined Rochambeau's Special Expedition. Following the successful Virginia campaign and the Battle of Yorktown, he returned to France and rejoined his unit in the Royal Army. When the French Revolution began, he was elected and served in the National Constituent Assembly. At the dissolution of the Assembly in 1791, he rejoined the army and, the following year, replaced Nicolas Luckner as commander-in-chief of the Army of the Vosges. In 1792, he successfully led campaigns in the middle and upper Rhine regions. Following Dumouriez's apparent treason, the Committee of Public Safety investigated Custine, but a vigorous defense mounted by Robespierre resulted in his acquittal. Upon return to active command, he found the army had lost most of its officer corps and experienced troops. In 1793, following a series of reversals, the French lost control of much of the territory they had acquired the year before. The following year, Custine was recalled to Paris. He was prosecuted in a lengthy trial before the Committee on Public Safety's Revolutionary Tribunal, found guilty of treason on 27 August and guillotined the following day.

art. Italy offered you an attractive asylum. For several months, occupied with archeological excavations, living with the boarders of the School of Rome and the artists who assembled there, from all points in Europe, it could be said that you led in the capital of the Christian world an existence as completely honorable as it is possible to desire."

"Is it then to say that after that time my conduct had no merited the approval of Your Excellency?"

"I don't claim that at all, but only that in a certain convent of Sainte-Apolline, a woman that the Inquisition had judged proper to enclose there and that you yourself judged proper to have her leave, all that, it must be noted, modified your way of life a little."

"It probably isn't a trick that I was supposed to have played on the Inquisition in Rome that is at this moment the object of your saintly zeal, is it?" Monsieur de Limeuil asked in a sharp tone.

"No, Monsieur, so much more so in that the Inquisition wasn't slow in being avenged. In your imprudent passionate ardor, you gave refuge to a serpent."

"A serpent?" Monsieur Limeuil said, smiling disdainfully.

"There's no doubt, because what other name do you call a woman who, after having done everything to make you intoxicated with a mad love, some days scarcely elapsed, furtively left your hospitable roof, writing you as a goodbye: *I don't at all like to be loved with that lack of reason: love instead of a convent for a prison. Having the honor to be the widow of the great Cagliostro, in view of paying a debt of gratitude, I can very well 'lend' myself for a day, but give myself, never. Consider that you have seen me in a dream, and forget me, as I will forget you.*"

Struck by the emotion that memory had caused him, Monsieur de Limeuil was drawn to depart from the system of denials where until then he had been retrenched, and he exclaimed:

"That note, who could have told you its content? I told that to no one, and I am sure it has never left my hands."

"I know many other equally hidden things," the Minister continued. "For example, all the secret change that abandonment produced in you, which, what's more, I must tell you, was brought about mostly by the fear of falling back into the hands of the Inquisition. It was not even that sublime feminine caprice of ingratitude and fear that affected your behavior."

"I have lived long enough, Minister, to believe a woman capable of every kind of duplicity."

"It hardly seems that way, because the cup you have begun to drink from, taken away from your lips, she was like a terrible thirst that has not ceased dominating your life. You soon left Rome, and on some vague information, persuaded that the fugitive must retrace her steps to Dalmatia, you rushed after her traces, that you next relentlessly followed her over all of Europe with a passion that became greater in proportion to the futility of the search, and finally came to make you doubt your sanity."

Suddenly throwing off his mask completely, Monsieur de Limeuil exclaimed:

"Then, Your Excellency, you who know so many things, must be able to tell me if *that woman* still exists and where it would be possible to find her."

"There is no doubt, and it's precisely to keep you from writing to her haphazardly in all the capitals of Europe, and to conduct you, myself to the place where you will be at leisure to see her and talk to her, that I have taken the liberty to ask you to come here."

"Oh! Let's go, Monsieur!" exclaimed Count de Limeuil, no longer trying to hide anything of what he was experiencing.

"I am at your service," the Minister answered, and an instant afterward his carriage carried them rapidly toward the asylum where Lorenza Feliciani had decided to spend the rest of her life.

On the way, Monsieur de Limeuil learned the edifying biography of the Widow Cagliostro from the time he was separated from her. Only, he was not told of that girl, the so un-fortunate fruit of their short liaison, because it must be said, what was being prepared at that moment was a radical cure for that love that had thrown into the Count's life so prolonged and very obvious trouble. The revelation of that paternity would have furnished him one more tie to that woman, from whom it was a matter of detaching him and could only have the opposite of the desired effect.

Monsieur Fouché, who was certainly an eminent and in-contestable politician, one of the most remarkable Ministers of Police who has ever existed, had never imagined that he could, with equal superiority, interfere in a question of the heart! In any case, all the plan being executed was due to his genius and to his wisdom. Once he had learned everything about this case of pathological love, he believed he could carry great news to Madame de Limeuil, in making her understand that the enig-ma of her husband's coldness was finally solved.

"I knew," Madame de Limeuil then replied, "that I had, in fact, a rival. On the day of my wedding, my husband told me of that misfortune, because of which I was condemned to a long widowhood. But finally, after a retreat Monsieur de Limeuil made some time ago to the Grande-Chartreuse, he told one of the fathers of that house about his fatal passion and received through his exhortations enough courage to break with that fatal preoccupation that made him more to be pitied than blamed. Since that time, he has changed greatly toward me and seems to have come back to me."

"But what you don't know,' the Minister then answered, speaking like La Bruyère [141]or Monsieur de La Rochefoucauld[142] of *Les Maximes,* "is that rival you believe

---

[141] Jean de La Bruyère (1645-1696). French philosopher and moralist.. Rabou may have been thinking of a quotation by LaBruyère: "Women are extremes; they are better or worse than men."

[142] François VI, Duc de La Rochefoucauld, Prince de Marcillac (1613-1680). Author of maxims and memoirs. It

you have triumphed over, remains so much more to be feared, because all her seductions, to tell the truth, exist only in your husband's imagination. Having possessed her for hardly a moment, and having spent years regretting her and searching for her, he thinks she still has all the attractions she had. But time has taken its toll. And such is the domination of these memories, that, put aside from his thoughts during his waking hours, they have taken refuge in his sleep that each night pays a deplorable tribute to the phenomena of somnambulism. To-day, that woman, author of all that evil, is positively in our hands. The course of the years, while taking away her beauty, has struck her, through the events of her life, with moral degradation which alone is enough to take away all her seduction. In my opinion, then, the way to have done with her, is to throw her, such as age has made her, in the path of our maniac. We will kill the dream with reality and make the phantom vanish by walking straight at it."

Seen in that way, where certainly its specious side is seen, he had persuaded Madame de Limeuil and with her formal authorization, the officious moralist took it on himself to arrange that encounter where he was expecting such happy success. Exactly twelve years had passed from 1793 until 1805 since Count Octave de Limeuil had undergone the fatal fascination which they hoped this dramatic encounter, called in the language of the theater, the *recognition scene*, would finally end.

Assuredly, in the history of the heart, isn't it something very exceptional that, during those years, having created a life unto itself, and which, nevertheless, in its intimate memories didn't at least find again a faraway equivalent? Who knows but if, for love, an obstacle isn't the first condition for its duration? Who hasn't in the same way, at a distance and in the void, more or less possessed in thought a woman who, finally

---

was said that his world-view was clear-eyed and urbane, and that he neither condemned human conduct nor sentimentally celebrated it.

come near, ends by losing all her prestige, because the perfections instead of existing in her, were all in the generous imagination of her would-be lover?

What differentiates that case from the case of Monsieur de Limeuil is only the intensity and the duration of the infatuation which, little by little, came to be clothed in the sick character of a single idea. But sensual possession, rapid as a dream, that sentiment preceded in him, wasn't that also totally unusual and could explain the deep furrow that Lorenza Feliciani had created in his memory? However that may be, that woman whom Monsieur de Limeuil had so loved, he was seeing her again. He had gone into the saintly house, the Widow Cagliostro was called to the parlor. Certainly, a dozen years more on her head, the cruel tortures to which her husband had submitted her, and most of all the certainty of the terrible destiny of her daughter, that was much more than was needed to have brought about such cruel changes in her charms. Perhaps, then, Monsieur Fouché was right. If Count Octave had had time to gaze on that ruin, probably his love, suddenly, like a balloon stuck with a pin, would have been deflated. But another denouement, more glorious for the human heart, was reserved for that test of the solidity of the strongest aspirations.

Monsieur de Limeuil didn't even have the leisure to verify the terrible changes that the years had made in the woman of his memories. As soon as he saw her, he felt something like a cloud pass before his eyes. He was seen to turn pale, tremble, and fall over. Then, when he was raised up, he was dead. He was dead with joy like Argus, Ulysses' dog at the return of his master. Or, if a more noble comparison is needed, dead like the old Saint Simeon, crying out in his cantical of the actions[143] of grace: "*Now, Lord, you can recall your servant to yourself, because my eyes have seen the Savior: Nunc dimittis servum tuum,Domine, quia viderunt oculi mei saluture tuum.*"

[143] Rabou gives the words of Saint Simeon in both French and Latin.

XV. To Descend in Order to Rise

Recovered from the emotion that his disagreeable adventure had caused him and the new face so quickly given to his life, Matiphous had also in mind the events that he had been constrained to neglect. He went then to see Diane's aunt to confer with her about the difficult matrimonial negotiations that so many incidents had suspended and to be available to the noble lady in everything she judged useful for its success. Arrived at the Limeuil townhouse, learning about the death of the Count, Matiphous believed he shouldn't ask to be seen by the widow. He just wrote to her to let her know that he would be available as soon as the *"preoccupation with her understandable sorrow allowed her to receive him."*

Either the *understandable sorrow* of Madame de Limeuil had left her with a great deal of self-possession, which, what's more, was understandable when she had lost a husband of such an unusual kind, or she took strangely to heart the marriage of her brother Anatole, because almost immediately Matiphous received authorization to come see her, an unhoped-for eagerness for which on his side he hurried to take advantage of. His embarrassment was great when it was a question for him of explaining the unexpected discoveries in Diane's heart. For the moment that presented the greatest obstacle to the desired result. But he was helped very much in that difficult exposé by Madame de Limeuil's insight

"Yes," that great lady said with an imperceptible nuance of disdain, 'what must happen, happened. For years you lived tête-à-tête with that child. As soon as her heart was old enough to speak, you were there under her eyes. She took gratitude for the attraction and character of another sentiment. But in my opinion, that's nothing serious, so long as that inclination is not shared. It could appear to you pleasant and *useful* to follow up on that admission you've been told."

That word, *useful,* had been pronounced with marked affectation and its effect was decisive. Calling attention to

Matiphous's care kept him from being too strongly struck by the light and cavalier tone with which she treated the revelation of that love of which he was the object. If the man's integrity was not thus called in question, perhaps his ego would otherwise have noticed what there was disobliging in that manner of considering it as impossible that he could ever inspire a somewhat serious passion.

But faced with the clever suspicion addressed to his selflessness, he didn't have a choice of attitudes. To accept blindly all the actions that the prudence and wisdom of Madame de Limeuil could claim from him, such seemed to him his role; therefore he made no objection to her when she added:

"The end justifies the means. This marriage I have suggested seems proper to you. Without bargaining we should cut short the intention that has just been thrown across it. My advice is now no longer that you have an interview with Diane. It's just necessary to write to her. And in your place, I would do it with a tone of authority, and perhaps with a little dryness, that would leave no opening to bring up again that impossibility which you consider no differently than I do."

"I will gladly write," Matiphous answered, "but the terms of that letter put me in a difficult position."

"Why?" asked the Lady of the Palace, "when it's agreed that in the interest of Diane herself, breaking off with her by telling her unpleasant things is what is best?"

"But in being firm, and even severe, I wouldn't want to go so far as harshness."

"Oh! then," Madame de Limeuil said quickly, "if we want just to untie instead of breaking, we may just as well resign all influence."

"Well, then, you Madame who appear to know so well what must be said, couldn't you inspire me? In that way, in case of failure, my responsibility, at least would be covered."

"That has no importance," said Madame de Limeuil and going to her secretary, at the end of several minutes she placed in front of Matiphous a note thus conceived:

My dear Diane,

You are a child. Your aunt knows better than you do what is proper for you, and I can, for my part, only give her ideas my full and entire approval. It is enough to tell you that I do not take seriously that totally new and unexpected form that you seem to want to give to your gratitude. The best way to show me your gratitude is to show yourself docile to the thoughts of those who have the right and the duty to direct you. In that way, also, you will prove that the education to which I gave all my care has made of you a wise and reasonable girl of whom I will continue to be proud as in the past.

Although a little less sharpness could be wished in that rough draft, it went straight to the goal proposed. Matiphous reread it twice. Either because he wanted to shield the temptation to modify something, or because he found it proper to agree with the absolute frankness of its tone, he asked permission to have a copy that Madame de Limeuil would have sent to his address.

That arrangement agreed on, he left Madame de Limeuil on receiving from her the promise that he would ultimately be kept abreast of the solution and even the somewhat remarkable phases that the affair going forward could present. His heart, however, was saddened, because there was no way to hide from himself that he had just signed the death notice of his relations with the girl that, until then, he had called his child. But in addition to the fact that the feeling of a great duty accomplished was a consolation to him, it must be admitted that in the unforeseen and even the strangeness of the horizon that his affiliation with the *Secret Bureau* had just opened in his life, there were great distractions. In any case, that new situation that it wouldn't have depended on him to decline, had constituted between Diane and him a barrier that couldn't be crossed, supposing that other obstacles had not already preexisted. Their separation then was, in all the strength of the word, an accomplished fact. Before an irremediable necessity, the resignation, without being less bitter and perhaps sooner, patience put it at the level of a sadness where the extent could be measured with less pain.

As for Madame de Limeuil, personally persuaded that the feeling expressed by her niece couldn't be in the least well founded, she didn't judge it necessary to confide it to her brother, a situation that created new and useless complications.

"Anatole," she told herself, "wouldn't take the thing as it should be taken. He would brood infinitely on his delicacy wounded by such a rival, about the moral violence it would make to his future, and about the danger to a union to which a heart wasn't committed. In the middle of this deluge of scruples, all the work already done could finally fall apart. It's useless then to provoke them."

The question thus settled on the side of Anatole, on the side of Mademoiselle de Limeuil, it didn't even seem that she should suffer that small amount of deliberation. Matiphous' letter was immediately sent to her, and the next day, her aunt arrived at the convent to take in the expected effect. Believing in very good faith that the marriage projected would bring happiness for her niece, Madame de Limeuil hadn't paid attention to a situation that, however, stared her in the face. Evidently, in the sudden change that took place in the poor young girl, in a sort of feverish hurry, without any transition, she began to show, for a very near conclusion, all the symptoms of a decision taken violently and desperately, and not that of happy, or even a considered decision. But halted at the letter and not at the spirit of the consent that her niece let fall from her mouth, Madame de Limeuil rushed to take her at her word, and after the strict delay necessary for the formalities of the law, the sacrifice was consummated.

However, Monsieur de Limeuil had certainly made some objections that naturally came to mind about that quick execution. For example, was it proper that, close to the still recent mourning in their house, a marriage should be celebrated in their house? In the same way, he had not been without a certain instinct about some violent pressure put on the will of his future wife. When, from one day to the next, he had seen her giving up all resistance, he had asked himself if that rapid resignation was very natural and very spontaneous.

But Mademoiselle de Limeuil was a courageous girl who felt her ego engaged not to appear to save herself for Matiphous, since he had greeted the offer she had made of her hand with a refusal so harshly formulated. Monsieur de Limeuil was at the moment less a husband for her than a sort of living reply to an insult that she believed herself obliged to answer to a procedure that had deeply humiliated her. Because of that, she had the courage of her determination, the unusual strength to do everything to bring it about. In view of that result, with hypocritical resignation, when she saw the doubt and hesitation of Monsieur de Limeuil, she pushed impatience even to comedy, talked of her ardent desire to be finally snatched from the insupportable sojourn in the pension, and, finally, if she didn't exactly act out a feeling that she didn't experience to any degree, at least she let there be seen in herself a seductive hope by which all of Monsieur de Limeuil's scruples couldn't keep from being conjured away.

There was something strange in the wedding ceremony, but inevitable, however. Matiphous wasn't invited. For having too much wanted to bring him close to her, the imprudent girl had dug an abyss between them. The next day after the wedding, the precise date of which he didn't know, a note from Madame de Limeuil told the *exile* that all had been consummated. By a very transparent insinuation, Diane's aunt intimated that as a duty of honor he resolve not to make any effort to have even the shortest access to the new household. The poor young man had, for himself, understood that conventional propriety and he supposed that after a few years, at the most, he could be relieved of those instructions.

While waiting, and as cruel as that ostracism was for his heart, he never stopped thanking Providence for the, according to him, rather fortunate turn of events with the people of the *Grand Firmament* that had finally been given to his life. After so many obstacles and so many storms, couldn't he consider himself as having come into port? He now perceived a logic to his existence, until then so chaotic. The functions of the *Secret Bureau,* that others had considered only as stigmatizing, were particularly suitable for him, and he valued all the price as the crowning of a too regrettable past. In the general lack of integrity of the work to which he was going to contribute, in some fashion they settled for him, absorbed and lost for him all the bad memories of his life.

A benefit still be considered was that he was out of reach of the police of different countries, vis-à-vis with which he had been successively compromised. A member of the Holy Inquisition of Letters, he had nothing more to fear either from the law in Malta, or from the English Admiralty, or from the Imperial Police that could not refuse him his full pardon for the story, which was, besides, very ancient, of the escape of Sir Sidney Smith. Now he was no longer under but one jurisdiction, that of the *Secret Bureau.* Probably, after the particular care with which Hulet the elder had explained to him the incorruptible honesty that was expected of him and the inexorable strictness of the punishments to which the least infringement exposed him, he would be careful to give no reason to incur the severities of the domestic tribunal whose existence had been revealed to him.

As for the arrangement of his life, with the help of Britannicus, who was an alert and experienced domestic servant, he was put on a very comfortable footing. The twelve thousand francs that he earned as an employee of the *Secret Bureau,* and the approximately three thousand francs that a good year/bad year, could bring into his practice as a surgeon, amounted to fifteen thousand pounds of income. In addition, his medical profession served him as a way to explain his morning outings that his functions required of him. He was supposed to be attached to the hospital clinics where health services always required him at any time at a very early hour. Thus the forced unusualness of his habits escaped all embarrassing commentary.

To complete giving to his establishment the ease and consistency that, until then, had been lacking in his life, his instinct had been to proceed to the great denouement of marriage. But a reason of delicacy put an obstacle in the way of that honest vague desire. Unless he became the husband of some tarnished woman, like the one from whom he knew he was descended, no more by his past than by his present did he feel himself a suitable party. His resources then made him return to the friendly sinners that we had already seen him frequent under the Directoire, when he had to banish from his thoughts the daughter of the fisherman from Gozzo, that flighty fiancée, his first love. But to place himself once more on that dangerous slope, he was careful not to let himself be carried away by those prodigal follies that had led to such regrettable decisions. Far from that, exploiting to the profit of his medical clientele, the use of all the virtuous ways which he desired in short love affairs, he made his way closer and closer so well into the world of kept girls and women of the theater that he became for them the fashionable doctor and got from their nerves, from their fainting spells, and from their migraines much beyond what their good graces paid him.

As sweet as the calmness of that epicurean existence was, it didn't, however, leave him without remembering his adopted daughter and without worrying about how her marriage had turned out. From some gossip that came to him that all the happiness that he had hoped for her had not been realized, he took it on himself one day to write to Madame de Limeuil in order to have some first-hand news of that household which she hadn't permitted him to see with his eyes. The answer that she deigned to give him was triumphant. Diane was presented as no longer having her first opinions and described as enjoying with her husband a cloudless happiness and on the point of becoming a mother. She was going to place the last crown on her prosperous married life. But after that letter was received, two months had not gone by when, asked by Madame de Limeuil to come to see her, Matiphous saw wiped out by very different information that seductive family tableau that had been presented to him. The first and saddest misinformation was that Diane had given birth to a child that hadn't lived, and that in coming into the world, had put his mother's life in danger. Then, to that misfortune, that didn't definitely have anything that wasn't reparable, had followed the saddest complications.

Up until that point, without showing a very strong passion for her husband, Diane had behaved completely properly toward him, and nothing seemed to contradict Monsieur de Limeuil's hope that his wife's heart would come to beat in unison with his. However, after the misfortune she had gone through, as if that maternity Providence had taken away had been the only reason for Mademoiselle de Limeuil to endure her husband, she had begun to have a more marked coldness toward him. She had seemed to accept with impatience the solicitude with which he surrounded her still uncertain health. And, finally, she continued to remain darkly melancholy, which seemed to be a constant regret of the union to which she had consented.

But the trouble didn't stop there. Soon the last limit of the most frightening unexpected in that sad path was reached. By a kind of supernatural revelation that no logic had been able to persuade Monsieur de Limeuil not to take the impact seriously, he had come to consider his conjugal honor as highly compromised. Several times while his wife was asleep he had heard a name on her lips and that name was often accompanied by passionate exclamations. These appeared to him to be an accusing echo of the secret emotions that agitated Diane's heart when she was awake. The name addressed in the nocturnal aspirations of Madame de Limeuil can be guessed. Now, here is what happened.

The jealous husband wanted to find where to vent his anger, and although Madame de Limeuil had tried to place on herself all the problems by admitting that she knew Diane's sentiments and it was by her instigation that they was put aside. Monsieur de Limeuil tried to find a way to find Matiphous guilty. He accused him of having created an unworthy obsession in the mind of his pupil. But, finally, when at the end of all arguments, he was forced to recognize the injustice of his suspicions directed to the integrity of his rival, he summed up to himself:

"Still, there is one too many of us upon the Earth!"

From that could be deduced the approaching prospect of a duel for Matiphous, a deplorable last resort that without being a remedy for anything, was going to compromise two existences not having, in reality, any debt to settle. In addition Diane's reputation would be open to one of those nasty attacks from which the life of a woman can never recover.

We know that Matiphous was brave and the sword or pistol of Monsieur de Limeuil didn't worry him very much, but what moved him in that confidence was the happiness of Mademoiselle de Limeuil that showed him was so seriously at risk. They talked a long time. Several methods to remedy the situation were discussed, one after the other. Finally, since nothing that had been proposed or debated had seemed to bring the result looked for, the man from Malta said:

"I believe I know what should be done, seeming to have an inspiration. T"

hen, without explaining himself any further, he left Madame de Limeuil, asking her only to set up an interview with her brother for the next day. He hoped with that encounter to make everything return to peace.

The next day, in fact, he found Monsieur de Limeuil had come to the rendezvous at his sister's house that he had asked for. And with no other opening, going to the heart of the matter, he said to Anatole:

"Monsieur, Heaven has permitted that, looking into the handling of the sad situation that brings us together, it was given to me to establish by the most convincing proof, the absolute uprightness of my conduct. This letter," he added, in presenting a paper to Monsieur de Limeuil, "was written to me by Mademoiselle de Limeuil at the time a question of your marriage began. Having been sent to me by the mail, it bears a postmark, which assigns it a specific date and removes any suspicion that it was written afterwards for the need of the moment. That letter will demonstrate to you, I hope, that, far from obtaining from Mademoiselle de Limeuil anything other than that of daughterly affection, I was very surprised at a confession that nothing had made me foresee. And that confession, by its difficulty in being made, shows sufficiently to what point it was spontaneous."

As Monsieur de Limeuil seemed to wait for Matiphous to continue:

"Please read the letter. After you do that, I will continue."

"Well!" said Monsieur de Limeuil, "that proves that you should keep for yourself that love offered to you and not at all push it in my direction."

"As for the propriety of a marriage between me and Mademoiselle de Limeuil, I believe that no one so well as I could be the judge. No, Monsieur, I should not have become the husband of Mademoiselle de Limeuil, because a father doesn't marry his daughter. I didn't feel anything for her beyond a totally paternal sentiment. Nevertheless, my pupil was gifted with qualities amiable enough without the inducement of a great passion for her, and I would gladly have consecrated my life to her, if I had thought myself worthy of that happiness, but I wasn't."

"And nevertheless she was in love with you," the husband said, "and even today…"

"Yes," the man from Malta said, interrupting, "that's a misfortune that I deplore and which I will do something about, if God wills."

"But how?" Madame de Limeuil quickly asked.

"From the character of the young woman I know, I can be sure. I have followed all her moral development. Love cannot live in her heart from the moment it is separated from esteem."

"I don't know about that," replied Monsieur de Limeuil, "but I, who have some claim to that last sentiment, I can testify that in the woman you are talking about, esteem can live very well separated from love."

"Until now," Matiphous continued, "the girl who was my child has known me only as a man passionately occupied with her happiness. I found grace in her eyes because, rehabilitated in some way, purged by charity and contact with her innocence, my life, in her eyes has been irreproachable. But considered in another way, my existence is cruelly burdened, and if someone decided to place a mirror under her eyes…"

"But who would do that?" Monsieur de Limeuil quickly interrupted.

"I," answered Matiphous, "who would prefer to sacrifice even my honor that my daughter could be happy; I, who wish at any price to restore peace to that troubled soul; I, that she will feel contempt for and hate perhaps, but that her mother, up in Heaven, will bless, I hope, on seeing how well I know how to keep my promises."

"That's good what you're doing there!" Madame de Limeuil said with enthusiasm.

"Yes," the jealous husband answered, "that's really noble devotion, and I regret very much not being able to decline it. But it is, alas! so deplorably necessary that instead of trying to place an obstacle to it, I would dare worry under what form it seems to you to be able to accomplish it."

"Nothing simpler," Matiphous replied. "I will write to the poor soul in pain that from everywhere in Paris information comes to me about the great happiness of her household. From that I will go on to point out to her the blessing that's found by following the advice of prudence rather than that of passion. 'If you hadn't given in,' I will add, 'to the far-seeing suggestions of your aunt, consider whose wife you would have been!' There then will follow the story of my life that I will throw in there in a rather indifferent tone, having less the appearance of caution for the future than of liquidating the past. Then I will end by letting her see my intention to leave France forever, and make of myself a kind of living-dead man who, at the last moment, wants to put his conscience in order and make restitution for the good will that he had usurped."

That said, he handed Monsieur de Limeuil an unsealed letter. Then he continued:

"It may not be necessary, Monsieur," he said, "that the sad revelations intended to modify the sentiments of Mademoiselle de Limeuil, come in their entirety to you. However, if you still have some doubts about the sincerity of my intentions, and if it becomes useful for your peace of mind to be able to measure exactly the extent of my devotion, you can read and reassure yourself if, that letter written, I must remain a rival to be feared. "

"I don't want to know you," replied Anatole, "except as a generous man who, having had along with some faults I don't know, the genius of an admirable sacrifice."

At the same time, he rang for a servant, asked for a lighted candle, and after having sealed with his signet ring, the letter presented to him open, he said:

"Take charge, Monsieur, of making it happen, and may Heaven recompense you for your virtuous action."

Then the two enemies separated with feelings very different from those that would have been predicted the evening before.

"Your hand, Monsieur," said Madame de Limeuil, conducting him with a kind of respect to the door of the apartment. "I will never forget what you have done for our family! In confiding the future of her child to you, the Marquise, my sister-in-law understood you well."

XVI. A Letter Sealed with Black Wax

Matiphous didn't do things half-way. Like people who have resolved to commit suicide, who put their pistol in their throat, fearing to miss, in the exposé of the bad side of his life, he had even gone beyond the truth. So, he told not only about the murder of a chevalier that he had committed in Malta, but he presented himself as guilty of the suicide of the fisherman's daughter, his fiancée, a misfortune to which he was a stranger and which he had found out about a long time after it happened. He had equally presented under the less venial aspect the insignificant betrayal he had committed against his country when he gave the Directoire some vague information which didn't even help the audacious rapidity which led to the occupation of Malta. His prison break with Sir Sidney Smith, his foolish love with the daughter of Jack Ketch, his cruel adventure with the Marquis de Samaniego and the material stain which had followed, all that in the interest of the cure he was undertaking, he had made venomous with extreme art. Assuredly, never had a man put the quarter of the care and the ardor that this unusual criminal had employed to defame himself when preparing his apology. Going even further, even to wickedness that he had not committed and which he was not even very sure he had ever had the thought of doing, he had carefully put down to his account. Thus, without any restriction, he accused himself of having committed atrocious vengeance against Kitty Ketch when, at the most, he had become the indirect instrument of the misfortune that had happened.

However, we are going to see what human caution is and how our most cherished enterprises often find a pitfall even in the excess of precautions with which we flatter ourselves to have prepared their success. In order to second the effect that could be expected from Matiphous' confessions and also to create a diversion from the sad feelings that they were likely to cause to Diane's heart, almost immediately after Matiphous' letter was sent, Monsieur de Limeuil had suggested a trip to Italy to his wife. Having for a long time the habit of completely passive resignation to the will of her husband, Diane agreed without resistance to his project of a trip. And although a doubling of sadness in her was easy to see, since the moment when the disenchantment prepared for her should have reached her, the departure of the spouses took place without being marked by any extraordinary circumstance.

But three months later, Matiphous received a letter from Rome sealed with black wax that Monsieur de Limeuil had written to him:

What have we done, Monsieur, or, rather, what deadly behavior has been mine? Become the cause of a terrible misfortune by giving way to my jealousy, will I have the courage to tell you the terrible truth? It is necessary, however, that the sad news reach you. In all the brilliance of her youth, Madame de Limeuil has seen the tomb open for her. Now she is near her mother who had willed her to you, and whom you had so piously accepted the inheritance. The sad consolation that I find in tracing the details of that so premature end for you, you yourself, I am sure, you will experience in hearing them. Besides, there is now a debt between us. You should at least, having known the fault, also learn the expiation.

There didn't appear any violent change in Madame de Limeuil following the letter that I had caused you the necessity to send her. There was only a more profound melancholy in her behavior. By the advice of my sister, who, in advance, had taken care to arrange with the Emperor for an opportunity to travel, about two weeks after the interview that I had the honor to have with you, we left for Italy. In my position as a younger member of the Council of State, I was charged with delivering dispatches to the Holy See. The sojourn in Rome seemed at first to please my afflicted angel, not by the worldly aspect, which didn't appeal to her at all, but because of that strong and ardent religious atmosphere that was everywhere present in that great Capital of Catholicism. Saint-Peter's Basilica, and that world of monuments where art, over and over again, recounts the glory of God, awoke in our unhappy love a feeling of pious admiration which could serve to blot out her sad preoccupations. On seeing her, for me, if not more tender, at least more easily affectionate, I began to congratulate myself on the inspiration that my sister had in advising me to take this trip.

But Heaven willed that, hardly begun, that commence-
ment of moral convalescence was troubled by an unexpected
rendezvous, which was more probable in Rome than in any
other place in the world, given the extraordinary number of
foreigners who, from all time and from all countries seem to
rendezvous there. One day, when visiting the Church of Saint
Peter in Montorio [144], *we were stopped in front of the famous*
Madonna de la lettera[145] *when a young woman passed by us*
who, by the cut of her somewhat strange outfit, as well as by
her blonde hair and the shining freshness of her complexion, it
was impossible not to know she was English. A man accompa-
nied her, and his appearance showed that he was of the same
nationality and he could easily pass for being her father.

Following just a glance at that woman, I saw Madame de
Limeuil tremble and change color. From her side, the woman
who by her appearance had just produced such a strange
emotion, had turned toward Diane as if her face had recalled
a vague recollection. Claiming a sudden indisposition, my
wife asked to be taken back to her room and that same evening
she had a violent fever. Immediately called, one of the most
renowned doctors in Rome observed the sick woman for a
long time, and with a frightening accuracy of diagnosis, he
told me, on leaving her, the case could become serious. Given
the sudden appearance of a fever, that he couldn't yet give an
exact name to, it seemed to be the last part of a harrowing
moral malady, which, after having smoldered inside, had just
suddenly exploded.

In fact, during the following days, there was no im-
provement, and what became more than anything depressing

---

[144] Saint Peter in Montorio was built on the site of a 9th century church dedicated to Saint Peter and tradition lists it as the site of his crucifixion. The interior is decorated with art by 16th and 17th masters.

[145] *Madonna de la lettera.* Painting of the Virgin and Child, one of many with the same motif. The one here mentioned is venerated as being the source of many graces and miracles.

was that nothing let me find a way to have some access to the confidence of the sick woman. In vain, using the most extreme measures, I alluded to the encounter from which all the trouble had started. She dismissed my idea, seeming to find it ridiculous, and with that she only confirmed me in the suspicion of some strange mystery. However, I made inquiries; some research was done in Rome. But all I was able to find out was that the woman, whose encounter was so disastrous, was named Lady Stuart, that she was married to the old man that I had seen accompanying her, and that I was told was a Scottish Laird. What's more, there was no more precise information on these foreigners who had already left Rome, after having lived there for some time in a very secluded way.

For more than three weeks, the sickness hadn't stopped making progress, and a letter that I knew had been given to Diane in secret, had appeared to determine new deterioration. Finally, in agreement with the doctor, who promised to give more helpful care if he could know the exact nature of the malady, confronting the question head on, I said to Diane:

"There is no use trying to pull the wool over my eyes. Obviously, your encounter with Lady Stuart is the point at which the cruel indisposition we can't conquer started."

And at the same time, I begged her to have more confidence in me, if only in the interest of her getting well.

"Lady Stuart," Diane then said to me with supreme disdain, 'that woman is named Lady Stuart! Well" she added, "that adventurous woman can take on all sorts of shapes."

"Then you know that woman?"

"Yes, I know her, and I know very well now that she is not dead, since I've seen her alive with my own eyes, unless she's an apparition."

I thought that the fever was making the sick woman delirious, and I asked her to explain herself more clearly, telling her I didn't understand her. She then asked me to bring to her bed, which she no longer left, a little box where she usually put her secrets. Then, taking out a paper that I recognized *immediately, she showed me your letter, asking me if I recognized it.*

Without exactly betraying the truth, I could confirm that I didn't know its contents.

"Ah! You don't know it," Madame de Limeuil answered, with a touch of bitter irony. "Well, I tell you it is only a long tissue of lies and the proof is that the one who is supposed *to have written it, told me about his intention to leave France, and information that has recently come to me, demonstrates that on the contrary, he has not stopped living in Paris. The additional proof is that he accuses himself of having cruelly put to death a creature that I saw the other day was still alive, and who recognized me as I recognized her."*

"But the handwriting," I then asked her, "is it so little familiar to you that you can doubt it?"

"The handwriting," Diane answered me in a tone of contained indignation, "isn't it known that in Paris, for money, people can be found who will do to everything?"

And what the unfortunate woman thought, then, Monsieur, appeared to me in all its horror. Her detestable suspicion was attributed to me. I had, however, presence of mind enough not to jump to my justification. Thanks to our daily visits, I held the character of the doctor in great esteem. In the circumstance, not to take his advice could pose infinite dangers. I then decided to reveal to him, without reserve, the sad secrets of what I had done. His opinion wasn't slow in being given:

"Your wife," he said, "could suffer in secret from a love that is not returned. But you yourself said that, since your stay in Rome, she seemed to have come back to you and overcome her foolish passion. Now it's evident that what she's dying from is having her existence tied to that of a man that she believes capable of forging a letter, with a view of suppressing a rival. For her salvation as well as for your happiness, an explanation couldn't come too soon. Hurry and prove to her that you are not the vile and base soul that she thinks."

That necessity to tell everything was also what I instinctually felt. I went then to find Diane, and after having told her about your generous sacrifice, I believed I could explain all that that unusual desire that you put into blackening yourself, even beyond the truth. It was by a very natural wish to give to a bitter remedy all its efficacy.

She believed me, Monsieur, because what I had revealed to her, fit well into what she knew of the affectionate confidence she had always had in you. Her belief in my explanations surpassed even the purpose we had wanted. At the moment I finished, I saw tears come to her eyes. She clasped her hands emotionally, and said, looking toward Heaven:

"Oh, my mother, that I will soon rejoin, you were not deceived about him."

All that scene, as could be expected, had deeply moved our dear sick one. But contrary to what the doctor had predicted, the situation had only gotten worse. In the evening, her thoughts began wandering. In her incoherent speech, the name of Bell Rock often returned. It seemed she believed she was still in the presence of those sublime spectacles which had made there the joy of her young years.

How can I tell you, Monsieur, my mental state that was so grateful the victim never stopped showing the strong attachment to the thought that had been the dream of her life? Anyone else, perhaps, would have felt himself cruelly offended in his ego, but I already saw the denouement of our drama moving forward. It cast aside human thoughts and under the pale lights spread by its funeral torches, I judged myself! Yes, I told myself, I am the one who caused all the wickedness! Should I have come then to throw my love in the way of that heart who knew so well what she wanted? Should I, above all, have made necessary the use of that fatal resource that has now turned out to be so cruel? Oh! Monsieur, I addressed to Heaven such fervent prayers! I begged it to keep on earth that very exemplary soul bound to the only thought of love that had ever flowered in her. And if my prayers had been answered, divorce that day would have seemed to me a good and saintly thing. I thought I would be able to see in her again the happiness I had taken from her.

But such were not the decrees from on High. The night following our explanation she was horribly agitated, and the doctor, when he saw her the next day at his usual hour, promised me scarcely a day of reprieve. Toward the middle of the next day, as if the sickness, sure of having done its work, thought it should leave off useless rigors, the sick one became somewhat calm. Her thoughts became clearer, and soon, of herself, she thought of receiving the help of religion.

After having been confessed and having received the Holy Eucharist, she had the courage to try to think about me. And it was to ask my forgiveness for what had made her die that her last moments were used.

"Monsieur," she said, "I didn't make you happy, and I see that again, by death, I am going to increase the amount of your suffering. Do not hold it against me. In loving the man who had brought up my youth, I thought I was carrying out my mother's will. And then, for such a long time, he was the world for me! I should have resisted your hurry better, knowing that I had only given you a heart full of another, who, probably, was worth less than you. But me, I loved him as he was. He had always shown himself very good and devoted toward me. And you, yourself, Monsieur, didn't you applaud the sacrifice he made of his honor so that I could give you what I owed you? If God had let me live, I would have recompensed you for all your patience and generosity. My mother would have obtained the happiness for me to give back my heart to you in its entirety and to turn my other foolish passion into a calm friendship. Death is now going to restore order into all this trouble that, a poor creature like me should not have made around her. Try, Monsieur, not to keep a too bitter memory of her, of the one who, very involuntarily, has done you much harm. Give, I ask you, your protection and your advice to help, through the pitfalls of life, that nature so very weak against them."

The thought of you, Monsieur, was the last one of the dying woman. After that sort of legacy, giving you to me, she spoke no more. Death hugged its prey closely, and still holding my hand in hers, your adopted daughter was carried into a tranquil death. I lost so much by that death, and it weighed so heavily on my conscience, that after that misfortune, I felt, so to speak, as if there was no more breathable air around me. I searched vainly in my life; no horizon appeared there. There was one, however, and in that one, God be thanked, I found at the same time expiation for the past, consolation for the present, and the hope of eternity.

Some days after my solitude had begun, I encountered in the streets of Rome some poor Lazarite missionaries, who, coming to receive the benediction of the Holy Father, were getting ready to go to Africa to spread the Word of God there. Suddenly, I had a great desire to accompany them in their perilous journey, and if it had depended only on me, I would now be with them, in the middle of the savage peoples to whom they are going to carry the light of the Gospel. But the Reverend Father to whom I then went to ask him to make me a part of the holy mission, told me that, to be allowed to have the happiness I asked for, it was not enough to be a man of good will. It was still necessary to be one having the necessary instruction, and that even showing a sufficiently tested vocation, one must, by some particular merits be made worthy to rush toward martyrdom. All he could do was to admit me as a novitiate into the House of Rome, and it is from this holy place that I write you.

I cannot then carry through the desire of our well-beloved Diane and help you in the hard pilgrimage through this world, where I am leaving you. But at least believe, Monsieur, that all the fervent prayers that can be addressed to Heaven will be for you. For your part, ask God that He sustain me in the pious dispositions from which I am writing you, and believe that if ever the hazards of life again place us the path of one another, you will find in me a devotion without

limits and all the feelings of a fervent charitable love, with which I dare to call myself
  Your affectionate,

Anatole de Limeuil.
From the Monastery of the Lazarite Brothers,
Rome, July 28, 1807.

XVII. Benefits of the Secret Bureau

The news that Matiphous had received affected him so much more strongly since a month earlier Madame de Limeuil had taken the care to send him an extract from a letter that that she had received from her brother Anatole. In it he spoke with happiness of a notable improvement in the moral state as well as in the health of his wife. Faced with that harshness so little expected of Providence, dark discouragement took hold of the man from Malta. He told himself:

"Goodness doesn't succeed any better for me than wickedness."

And in fact it has to be recognized, none of the faults with which he had burdened his life had been crowned with outcomes as disastrous as the generous devotion that he had showed in regard to his adopted daughter. The regrettable slope on which the cry of his despair placed him can be understood. The one who can say to virtue, *You are nothing but a name* is very near failure. On reading Monsieur de Limeuil's letter, Matiphous had been at first only struck by the terrible news, the death of his cherished child. But when he began to go over all the details of that frightful event, another circumstance necessarily drew his attention. That woman that he had accused himself of killing, but that in reality the idiot had thrown from the lighthouse, Madame de Limeuil had seen her alive: Kitty Ketch, in that case, was still in this world, and what extraordinary event had been able to preserve her? It could be, however, that Diane was deceived by a resemblance, because at Bell Rock, she had not looked at the daughter of Jack Ketch long enough to be sure of recognizing her on sight.

But, on the other hand, so many unexpected and romanesque changes had, until then, marked Matiphous' rapport with that deceptive creature that, for him, the miracle of her resurrection was not absolutely impossible to imagine.

In any case, if Kitty had survived, the irascible man from Malta, indignant to see her eternally his stumbling block, promised himself to take care of that unusual favor that fate seemed incessantly to place before him. The number of his accounts against that fatal girl was thus increased by the fatal influence that she had on the destiny of Mademoiselle de Limeuil. It was her bad luck if she ever again found herself in his path. He felt himself very decided, this time, on an pitiless vengeance.

Not much time had passed before that encounter could be seen with great probability. In fact, it was in Rome that Kitty had been seen some time before, and shortly afterward Matiphous received the order to go to Florence to exercise his functions. Toward the end of 1807, by a rapid movement of his all-powerful will, Napoleon had decided to break the crown of Etruria [146] that, some years earlier, he had placed on the head of Marie-Louise, the Spanish Infante. The government of Tuscany thereafter divided into department and reunited to France, had been given by him to the Duchess of Lucques and Piombino to her sister Elisa Bacchiochi. But

---

[146] The Kingdom of Etruria was a kingdom between 1801 and 1807 which made up a large part of modern Tuscany. It took its name from Etruria, the old Roman name for the land of the Etruscans. The kingdom was created by the Treaty of Aranjuez, signed at Aranjuez, Spain on 21 March 1801. In the context of a larger agreement between Napoleonic France and Spain, the Bourbons of Parma were compensated for the loss of their territory in northern Italy (which had been occupied by French troops since 1796). Ferdinand, Duke of Parma ceded his duchy to France, and in return his son Louis I was granted the Kingdom of Etruria (which was created from the Grand Duchy of Tuscany).

since the Emperor didn't have absolute confidence in the infallibility of that female government, he had at the same time decided to send from France a certain number of civil servants who were supposed to guarantee the good administration of the duchy. Those sent were supposed to include an employee for the surveillance of correspondence. Speaking, French, English, and Italian, Matiphous owed that polyglot aptitude for being chosen to exercise those occult functions. The title of the Grand Duchess' veterinarian was to serve to hide his real function.

The man from Malta had been installed in his new residence for some weeks when, one evening at the *Pergola* Theater he encountered one of his former acquaintances, that Fauntleroy, who, it will probably be remembered, was one of his companions in captivity at Newgate.[147] That man, to tell the truth, had the greatest obligations toward him. Without the courageous denunciation of the Marquis de Samaniego that Matiphous had carried to the Customs Agents, free to live in England, that terrible enemy would not have , in his letter of farewell to the people of London proclaimed *in extremis,* the innocence of the victim that his devilish cleverness had led within two steps of the gallows.

Matiphous' sad disappointment can be understood when, on seeing a man who owed him his life, pretend at first that he didn't know him, and finally retrench into the coldest and most formal greetings. It has to be assumed that, prior to their encounter in the criminal prison, that ingrate had heard about the regrettable things his savior had done in London, and in particular, the punishment that Colqhoum's henchmen had inflicted on him. Now, as the forgetful gentleman had appeared in Florence on a grand footing, it must not have been very pleasant to have to renew acquaintance with a man whose past was so burdened with such unfortunate memories. But that was an explanation and not at all an excuse. So, Matiphous first impulse was to react strongly to a treatment

---

[147] See Volume 1.

for which nothing had prepared him. He even went so far as to ask himself if he should, carefully, invoke the help of the police to make a man disappear who, knowing all the sore spots of his life, could, from the way he acted toward him, be considered capable of the most grave indiscretions. Nevertheless, in the matter of vengeance, the man from Malta liked to take care of his business himself. Feeling himself sufficiently protected against Fauntleroy's loose tongue by the reprisals that he was in a position to make, he added his resentment to Fauntleroy's account and left it to time to inspire his conduct, in the future of a relationship that, considered in any manner, seemed to him to merit being carefully studied.

In fact, everything about his former companion at Newgate excited his curiosity to the highest point. He had left London completely ruined and escaped a major indictment only with great trouble. And now, he finds him in Tuscany, making his way among the most elegant society and having the appearance of opulence. Now, how could such an unusual reversal be accounted for? And what were the mysteries of that existence where expenditures were apparent everywhere and revenue not apparent at all? Having thought about it, Matiphous persuaded himself that diplomatic espionage must be at the bottom of that espionage, because nothing was more common than to see that obscure methods of existence serve as an explanation for astonishing fortunes of suspicious origin among certain foreigners in the great capitols. As a consequence, using a power, almost discretionary, left to him to draw up a list of letters to be watched, he placed Fauntleroy's name there, attributing to him the status of secret agent for the British Cabinet. A week had not gone by when a letter addressed to that name placed on the index arrived postmarked from England. As soon as it was unsealed and read, that letter was for the employee of the *Secret Bureau* a gift from Providence, because coming suddenly to illuminate his past, it summed up for him facts that, of a nature to pique his curiosity to the highest degree, had remained, until then, unknown or not understood.

A single word will tell the prodigious interest of that document. It came from Broughton, the ex-boxer we left asleep at Bell Rock in the travelers' lounge when Matiphous took ship to embark for the continent. That man, as it had been thus easy to record, when we saw his rapport with Matiphous, disputing with him the hangman's noose, gave the lie to the proverb: *Stupid as an ex-boxer.* He was naturally intelligent, and probably, since he had left the ring, by means of society, travel, and perhaps a little reading, he had developed an intelligence that for a long time he was content to have at the end of his arm. In addition, it is known that before every other passion, he had that for money. And whoever is said to be a miser, almost always is said to have an alert and sly mind, and certainly Broughton's correspondence had just supported that analysis, when, using the name *MacLeod*, he wrote:

London, 21 December 1807
Dear Fauntleroy,

I have much to reproach you for. Your last shipment is deplorable; either the plate is used, and if so, another one will have to be engraved, or the print out was done with negligence that could, from one moment to the next, put everything in danger. My advice is not to make any use of those miserable parodies of Bank Notes that you have just sent to us. This is so much more necessary since the Bank of London has begun to be worried because of the tainted products we have managed to put in circulation. You didn't want to believe me; you thought you should limit yourself to one printing and that it could be done without any inconvenience using the least defective of this printing. Events have not been slow in justifying my opposition. A few days ago, a poor devil was arrested just as he tried to cash one of those clumsy counterfeits. Who knows what would have happened if that man, losing his head, had not done us the service, before being interrogated by the magistrates, to kill himself in prison.

It wasn't with that casualness and with that carelessness that the famous Colqhoum had acted. And continuing his "af-

fairs," would we try to walk in his mistakes?. For him, a bill was never put in circulation that wasn't a masterpiece of counterfeiting, and he, however, didn't have the resource of that admirable artist that you have discovered in Florence, and who would be capable of imitating the bills of the Eternal Father, supposing that the Eternal Father had a bank, and judged it convenient to put bills in circulation.

Would you, dear friend, wish me to tell you all my thoughts? You are sleeping in luxury and in my opinion you have received too much of the good parts of the benefits of the association. Is that what would have been expected of you when we met in Venice some years ago? We were immediately drawn toward each other by our mutual confidences, led to recognize a romanesque likeness in our destinies. We saw each other every day at that time, and between us how many project of fortune and vengeance! "Ah!" you said with an enthusiasm I can still remember, "you want to make me a counterfeiter. All right! So be it! A counterfeiter I will be, and by inundating it with my bank notes, I will hasten the bankruptcy, of the miserable trafficker shop, known under the name of Pitt, Georges III and company.".

That pledge, it depends on you to keep it. Thanks to that incomparable man that fate sent to you in Florence, and which you had, to tell the truth, only to supervise his work, there you are, sheltered from any danger, on the point of having a princely fortune, while me, in England taking care of the delicate chore of distribution, I, every day, actually put my life in danger. With this division of roles, don't I have the right to expect from you a more active and a more devoted participation? And can I tolerate the negligence, the consequences of which will be so terrible for me?

I can hear what you will say from here. My job, you're going to answer me, is less difficult than I want to say. I found that magnificent organization that the Marquis de Samaniego, on leaving England, had left, already set up and ready to function again and with the precious elements that just had to be put to work. It seems there was nothing to do but cross your arms and watch it work. Certainly, I don't want to deny that in the participation of those great men who had so advantageously served the man called Colqhoum, I didn't find a great simplification of my task. But, do you know, Monsieur, what the complicity of those useful auxiliaries cost me? You have never been aware of the price at which I bought it. And I never thought about being reimbursed. But since we are calculating, clerk to master, then learn my sacrifices and the cruel extremities which the interests of our association have finally accumulated for me.

To go back to things a little faraway, you remember Kitty Ketch, my young and pretty liberator who, following my false hanging I took to England to make a debut at the Fenice Theater [148] where she collected so many admirers.

You, yourself, my Fauntleroy were excited in the wings, and though you had tried to make me think differently, I know very well that the real principle of our liaison was the tender feeling that you had let yourself take for that charming girl, and the charitable hope for a moment that you thought you could take her away from me. In fact, that enterprise didn't seem to me absolutely difficult. Didn't I have every appearance of being the husband of the virtuoso? And in the manner that I encouraged your solicitous attempts, instead of being an obstacle for them, didn't you take me for one of the complaisant husbands who coldly accept, sometimes even exploit with premeditation the conjugal fortune without consequences. The misfortune in all that, my poor friend, is that you didn't know the end of things.

Instead of being that patient and predestined husband that you imagined, I was a man who was the cold possessor of that beauty that so many admirers sighed for. He would actually have found it very charming if some clever thief had come to take her away from him. But that attachment that Kitty

---

[148] The Fenice Theater was founded in Venice in 1792. World premiers of famous operas have been given there, or under their auspices. Here, the location for Kitty Ketch is London.

Ketch honored me with, had something so romanesque that after having put me to the necessity of going off with her, she refused to regularize our situation with marriage, saying that denouement was the tomb of love and that she didn't want to place an epitaph on our liaison that had hardly begun.

Soon, I have to say, exasperated by the tumultuous expressions of that disorderly passion, I despaired of finding myself so loveable. Twenty times I would have broken my chain of flowers if I hadn't had great obligations toward the poor child, and in case of a rupture, the fits of passion of her despair would have been more fearful for me than the fatiguing felicity of her possession. However, neither you, dear friend, nor others have had the ability to uproot me from her heart. And even though my ever increasing corpulence continues to make me a less and less adorable suitor, that love, with a frenzy and a tenacity without parallels, began to wear out my patience when, everything ready for the execution of projects meditated for a long time, one fine day following our distribution of roles, you summonsed me to get on the road to London, the general quarter of our operations.

To confide our "banquicide" to my young companion, was truly something impossible. I don't think I am ridiculously superstitious in admitting that just the simple closeness of her name was enough to bring misfortune to the best organized enterprise. Arriving alone in England, thanks to my Scotch pseudonym of MacLeod, and to the notable bulk that had almost quadrupled my person, I could be almost certain not to be recognized. On the contrary, being accompanied by my ardent mistress, made my incognito run the most serious perils. I had notably every chance of being called to the attention of her amiable family. I was then forced, that time, to finish with poor Kitty. What's more, there was nothing more beautiful than the stoicism with which I had armed myself for the accomplishment of my resolution, once I had made it. I broke off so neatly and so sharply that the abandoned woman didn't have any suspicion of my departure and nothing could make her guess the country where. In leaving her, I was going to *direct my steps. But those who would have congratulated me with having thus accomplished the work of my emancipation, would have been short-sighted people.*

Scarcely had I disembarked in London than my troubles began. To return there with Kitty Ketch would have been to cause my downfall. To return there without her put me in the necessity of giving the most rigorous explanation. You yourself probably remember that Kitty was the niece of Mistress Aston, hostess of the former Tavern of the Bottle and the Magpie. Now, in the past, the least honorable characters that the Marquis de Samaniego had made such useful auxiliaries for the distribution of his counterfeit bills came together at that honorable lady's place of business. When it was a matter of putting their group back together, dispersed at that time, to whom should I then turn? To Mistress Aston, who had been so much in the confidence and in the secrets of the Marquis. And if, in going to see her, I didn't bring with me that adored niece, that she had in a way thrown into my arms, wouldn't her first word be that of God to Cain: "What have you done with my niece?"

To answer her: "You didn't give her to me to keep," would have been, first of all, perfectly contrary to the truth, and then it isn't with Mistress Aston, a woman of a resolute and not very easy character, that it could be a question of using that casual and cavalier tone. The dear woman knew in depth all the miracle of my resurrection. What's more, she was in possession of a will by which, the evening before my promenade to Old Bailey, I had made in her favor all my wealth, to avoid the inconvenience of my pretended death which, without that precaution, opened my succession to the profit of my heirs. I was then forced to deal uprightly with that worthy lady and furnish her an explanation that would satisfy her.

At that point, Broughton had been interrupted. In a hurry to send to their address the reproaches that constituted the principal object of his letter, in order not to miss the hour of mail pick-up, he had put it on the way unfinished, promising

Fauntleroy, what's more, to send him the continuation with a brief delay.

XVIII. To finish with Bell Rock

Fauntleroy didn't want to stay under the jolt of the reprimand addressed to him. Without waiting for the completion of the epistle announced by Broughton, he immediately put his answer in the mail. It is useless to add that, before it was dispatched on its way, that response was unsealed and read by Matiphous. Once the name of a suspect was put on the list for surveillance, not only the letters addressed to him, but also those it was thought to have come from him fell under the control of the *Secret Bureau.*

However, with London as its destination, the name of MacLeod, henceforth the pseudonym known to be that of Broughton, a letter could hardly be attributed to anyone but Fauntleroy. That gentleman wrote:

Florence, 20 January 1808.
Dear MacLeod

You are talking about this at your convenience, and apparently believe that artists are people easy to handle. I would very much like you to see that damned Hans Kraft, who won't do the least work, even if you cover him with gold. With his prodigious talent, that man, if he wanted to work at his profession, would have made his fortune a long time ago. But he has two passions, one in daytime and the other at night, which will make him die in the hospital, because they occupy most of his time. And to tell the truth, when he works, it's only during his spare time. The "owl," or "The owl hunt," a very popular sport in Florence, and the game of dominos, a deplorable importation from France, take up all the life of that maniac. It is literally only when there is no bread in the house that he begins to start a plate and to use cutting tools. Add to that, communication with that man is most difficult. He has a daughter, for whose dowry he has, it's said, decided to accept the dirty chore we have given him. That daughter is a prude, pretending to have beautiful sentiments and great character. And that imbecile father thinks he would be lost if she happened to find out that he helps us with "the great work." So I am absolutely forbidden to appear at that maniac's house, and it's only on the fly, so to speak, that I can manage to meet him.

That's why, for my last shipment, I was reduced to using a plate that was, in fact, three-quarters used, and that it was impossible to have him retouch. So, while you think me wallowing in pleasure, I am seething with impatience and annoyance, notwithstanding all the threats to break it off in case I descend on his domicile. It means nothing to him that I don't descend on his house to violently express all our discontent. The best thing to do, however, is to calm down, because that isn't a man who can be replaced, and with a little diplomacy and perseverance, we will finally get from his hands the plate that he is working on and which he has promised us for a long time.

I am rather curious to know, I admit, my dear Reprimander, what is the great effort of devotion that you have been able to bring about for the interests of our enterprise. As for Kitty Ketch, from the moment her love was settled on you, all I can see in the fact of your separation, is a reduction and not a sacrifice. What's more, I'm not like you, and since you have put me at ease about it, I admit that charming girl really made a great impression on my heart. I met her in Rome some time ago, married and in a very brilliant situation. And picking up again a tone of flirtation, I had the satisfaction of seeing her completely detached from your memory and a lot better disposed to accept my courtship and my care.

I believe that, Monsieur Hans Kraft having finally finished, I will be able soon to spend several weeks in the Eternal City. And since you have really wanted me for your successor in relation to the beautiful lady, I will put all my study into making you realize that pleasant wish. Haven't I also met again that Matiphous, the almost-husband of that charming Miss, whom you so pleasantly spirited away. Under the pretext of the service that he had indirectly rendered me by forcing the false Colqhoum to leave England, that gentleman, if I had let him do it, would have taken on a tone of familiarity which wouldn't have suited me, and which forced me to put him in his place. The miserable man has found, I don't know how, the means to have himself attached to the household of the Grand Duchess, who probably isn't aware that she has in her service a wanted man. Everything about that ingrate shows comfort and elegance. And hasn't he given himself the affectation to have, like a Mogul, a Negro as a valet. But with such adventurers should fortune and impudence be astonishing?

One more time, be patient. I am not losing a moment to put the society in a way to usefully and surely continue its operations. While you are waiting, please believe in all the friendly sentiments of your devoted collaborator and friend,

F.

It's easy to understand that with that letter and, most of all, with the cruel play on words that he allowed himself, Fauntleroy managed to become mortally at odds with Matiphous, who, in addition to Broughton and Kitty, was definitely placed in his book for vengeance. But before doing anything about him, the man from Malta wanted to know the end of that correspondence from the boxer. He didn't have to wait for that following correspondence and we are going to see if it was such as to modifier the feelings of a hurt soul.

Broughton, without answering the letter of his associate which had crossed his in the mail, continued:

,,,,that obliged me to parley with Mistress Aston and to answer first of all what she asked me concerning her niece, I was expecting a very rude reception. However, a half-truth was sufficient to save me the delicacy of that encounter. I told her, which was true, that Kitty had never wanted to consent to be my wife, but I added, a detail a great deal less exact, but on Kitty's side, lack of faithfulness had made her lend an ear to the demands of a Russian prince, who, having all that was

390

needed to take her away from a husband, had tyrannically required Kitty to send me away.

The idea of seeing her niece become a princess, kept her from seeing clearly into the lie I had told her. Instead of the anger I was dreading, my pretended desertion gave me all her sympathy. The social arrangements that I came to set up were therefore so much simpler, and soon, thanks to the help of that clever lady as an accomplice, all the former personnel of the Colqhoum corporation were re-united and put at my disposition, allowing me to announce to you that we were able to function.

Up until then everything was marvelous and I thought it was clear sailing when, in the middle of my beatitudes a suspicion slipped in. Arrived well into the age of forty-five, Mistress Aston hadn't yet thought of lighting the torches of marriage. Like our glorious Queen Elisabeth, she had never wanted to place her proud disposition under the conjugal yoke. And for her, the title of mistress was only a respectable exit which she had cautiously provided for herself when she was daily in contact with her turbulent clientele from Newgate.

Me, I was free again, and, in addition, by the fact of the will I had been obliged to make in favor of that inflammable person, a kind of community of goods had been established between us. There existed something definitely attractive between my personality and the members of that damned Ketch family. At first seen with terror, soon the tender dispositions of Mistress Aston no longer permitted me to have a doubt. The unhappy woman! I had to admit to myself that she aspired to my hand in marriage. And God knows to what extremities the heart of an old maid is capable of when, seeing herself slighted, she has only to say the word to send the object of her affections to Old Bailey. There is no easy way to get out of such a situation, and in fact, I only escaped at the price of another embarrassment. Kitty, as you may believe, had not taken her abandonment lightly. There she was, one fine morning, come to meet me in England. And continuing the fatality which follows me in all that affair, she encountered me in a London street almost at the moment of her arrival. The dangers that apparition made me run were incalculable. On the one hand, to be denounced to messieurs the sheriffs; on the other hand to see myself exposed to the jealousy of Mistress Aston, or to her just fury when she learned that I had deceived her, such were the pleasant perspectives open to me and which I had to decline at any price.

As terrible as the danger appeared, no less heroic was the remedy. Before anything else, I had to give an account to Kitty for having left her. Taking a tearful and emotional tone, I asked her to believe that her resistance to becoming my wife had led to the desperate resolution to separate from her. Duped by that comedy, she declared that henceforth her will would be subject to mine and that my matrimonial eagerness would encounter no obstacle. Apparently delighted with that resignation, without giving her time to show herself to any of her relatives, as if it were a question of eloping with a rich heiress, I threw her into a carriage and there we were, rolling toward the frontier of Scotland, where the Gretna Green marrier was to cement our union.[149]

---

[149] Gretna Green is one of the world's most popular wedding destinations, due to its romantic wedding traditions dating back over centuries, which originated from cross-border elopements stemming from differences between Scottish marriage laws and those in neighboring countries. It has usually been assumed that Gretna's famous "runaway marriages" began in 1754 when Lord Hardwicke's Marriage Act came into force in England. Under the Act, if a parent of a minor wishing to marry (i.e., a person under the age of 21) objected, they could legally veto the union. The Act tightened the requirements for marrying in England and Wales but did not apply in Scotland, where it was possible for boys to marry at 14 and girls at 12 with or without parental consent (see Marriage in Scotland). It was, however, only in the 1770s, with the construction of a toll road passing through the hitherto obscure village of Graitney, that Gretna Green became the first easily

When we arrived at the nuptial boutique, I would very much have liked not to carry things to the end. Therefore, I feigned having some scruples about the moral violence done to my future, and I told her that, satisfied by her resignation, I had decided to live in an open marriage. In the future, I added, after the proof of her submission, that I had just obtained, I thought that union would be more indestructible than if the formalities of marriage had actually taken place. But either through the spirit of contradiction natural to women, or the fear of some new attempts at departure, Kitty answered me that, having coming to finish it, she didn't intend to take advantage of my generosity. Then, as I insisted, nevertheless, digging in her heels, more and more for the denouement she had set her mind on, she showed some doubts relative to the sincerity of my procedure. I then had to take the big step, whatever I wanted. After having received the sacraments from the marriage smith, I let him write in his register the act that took away my liberty forever.

Now, my dear Fauntleroy, will you admit that vis-à-vis our association, I have shown proof of rather great devotion? Having escaped the aunt only to fall into the hand of the niece and introduce eternity into a relationship that was hard to bear in the provisionary status, isn't that a sacrifice that already gives me the right to be a little concerned in the debate about our interests?

Well! that sacrifice, today it's lost! Everything has to be started over; the danger that I thought I had conjured away is standing at my side more threatening than ever. To avoid becoming the prey of Mistress Aston, only one way is offered to me. But before submitting it to you and asking you for your precious cooperation to put it into effect, let me first tell you the manner that door of salvation was opened for me. If the

reachable village over the Scottish border. The Old Blacksmith's Shop, built around 1712, and Gretna Hall Blacksmith's Shop (1710) became, in popular folklore at least, the focal tourist points for the marriage trade.

story is a little long, it's unusual, and while it's being told, one's troubles are asleep.

The matrimonial denouement that I had to go through with the charming Kitty, wasn't really something to worry me a great deal. In a marriage like those that are rushed through at Gretna Green, annulments are never very hard to get. And, besides, to save my incognito, obliged to sign the contract with the assumed name of MacLeod, didn't I have a hidden door through which, when I really wanted to, it would be possible for me to get back my freedom? I would even add that to become the husband of Miss Ketch was, at the moment, rather convenient for me. Summing up, I had arranged for myself against the aspirations of Mistress Aston a kind of balustrade, and to reap the benefits of the situation, as soon as our union was celebrated, I was careful, without contradicting the version of the Russian prince, to have my wife tell her aunt what had just taken place between us. I was counting on the fact that, respecting rights of the most ancient date, the worthy lady would impose silence on a love that was, in some way, only left over from that of Kitty. However, since nothing guaranteed me the way the lovable tavern keeper would take her disappointment, I didn't find it prudent to reappear in London. And, at any rate, to let die down, the first fire of an anger which was not unlikely, I suggested to Kitty that we take a tour of Scotland. What place could be better chosen to spend a honeymoon than in the dreamy country of Ossian![150]

Our excursion didn't go beyond the little town of Arbroath. Kitty wanted to visit a lighthouse there which someone had told her was a curiosity to explore. But, as you are going to see, evil came to that poor child because of that fantasy!

---

[150] A series of poems supposedly found in a Scotch manuscript from the early dark ages translated and published by James Macpherson (1760). In the poems, Ossian a blind poet described the battles of Fingal, King of Selma.

Here Broughton recounted his visit to Bell Rock, his abominably ridiculous adventure and the deceptive sleep that followed. Then, having given the details that the reader already knows, he continued:

The moment I woke up in the travelers' lounge, it was almost daybreak, and nothing made me suspect some wicked plot. Far from that, during my sleep, a delicate attention, a pot of ale, that some hours earlier I had found delicious, had been placed near me. It seemed someone had wanted to invite me to toast my awakening. But what I took for a friendly attention, was only the most abominable treachery. That drink had been adulterated. In fact, hardly had I drunk some glasses, than I felt my head become confused, and from the armchair where I was seated, I would have sworn that around my voluminous body the room and all the objects in it were rotating rapidly. In that state of feverish ecstasy, imagine, dear Fauntleroy, what must have been my emotion when suddenly the door, just opened, I saw something like a ghost enter and come over to me. Tall, fabulously thin and dressed in a kind of simarre[151], the phantom carried under his arm a big red portfolio, and a torch in his left hand; and in his right he carried a dagger and walked with all the solemnity of an apparition. Suddenly, noticing me in my armchair, the ghost stopped, quickly placed the torch and the portfolio on the floor. Then, rushing toward me, he shouted: "Ah! Bonaparte, vile despot, you had yourself crowned!" And at the same time he lifted his dagger to strike me.

If I had been calm, I would have just avoided the blow, but in that vast room, with hardly any light, troubled by the long whistling wind, my head exalted by the disturbing visions with which that infernal drink had filled it, and having only too well remembered my former profession, with a blow of my fist directed to the middle of his forehead, I sent the aggressor rolling ten feet away. And once downed by that strong attack,

---

[151] Ample robe used in the 15th and 16th centuries.

he no longer made any movement. That violent act must have brought out animal spirits, because, hardly had I seen the result of my reaction than I was again at myself, and then I regretted having so strongly answered my adversary. All his bearing showed he was a demented man rather than a dangerous assailant.

Immediately busy with counteracting the effects of my brutal action, I made every effort to recall the poor devil to life. But seeing that all my efforts were a pure waste of time, I thought of getting some help from outside and I went out to call on the aid of Kitty or that of the employees of the place. As no one answered my call, I began searching from room to room. But there was no trace of a living being. The lighthouse keeper, a young girl who had received me on my arrival, and finally Kitty, my tender and faithful spouse, everyone had disappeared.

At the close of night, a horrible tempest beginning to shake the foundations of the tower, obviously Kitty and the guardian who had served as her guide could not still be occupied contemplating the horizon from atop the light. Finally, going into a bedroom, I was struck by the disorder that always marked the readiness for a departure. Almost at the same instant, in the middle of wrapping papers, I saw a letter on the floor. The broken seal invited me to look into it. Who knows but that I wouldn't find some information there? Just by the address, there was illumination. The letter was addressed to Gregorio Matiphous, Keeper of the Bell Rock Lighthouse. It was from another guardian, his colleague, who, following the indisposition of his mother for some days, couldn't resume his services.

"Gregorio Matiphous," I shouted, striking my forehead. "That's who was under that long beard, I had an idea that was a face that was not unknown to me. Gregorio Matiphous! He was the man who cut my throat to save me from the gallows, and I stole Kitty from him when he intended to marry her! No doubt, having recognized his former fiancée, he stole her away in his turn. And, evidently, to put me out of a condition to oppose his design, he prepared that perfidious drink that made me a murderer."

That last word reminded me of a pressing concern. I returned to the unfortunate man who lay stretched out on the floor and again began to do my best for hm. But, soon, forced to recognize all the symptoms of confirmed death, I found myself a prisoner in the lighthouse, where that cadaver I had just made remained as my only companion. It was necessary at least to know who was my victim. And the portfolio I had first noticed under the dead man's arm gave me some hope to be edified on that subject. After a little work, I managed to break the lock. I found myself looking at the most unusual archives that certainly no antiquarian had put together. There, jumbled pell-mell, were the diplomas of twenty secret societies, plans for conspiracies, and political upheavals embracing all the countries of the world, lists of conspirators by cities, correspondence in all languages and in all kinds of codes with their keys, designs for incendiary devices, procedures for laundering account books, for unsealing letters, for the fabrication of paper money, instructions for changing inheritances, quick poisons and those time controlled, and finally under the title of prodigies of chemistry, the formula for the famous "aquatophana"[152] and that of the terrible "water of wisdom" used to sterilize the marriage of Charles II, King of Spain and open the succession to the advantage of the grandson of Louis XIV.

Picture to yourself, dear Fauntleroy, your friend having under his feet and in his head the howling of the ocean's tempest; at his side the spectacle of death, and under his eyes that immense revolutionary repertory which, during an entire night left him stupefied and lost. So that night was for me a

---

[152]Some studies into the composition of poisons claim that "*aquatophana*" was taken from the slobber of a rabid swine, by the blow of a baton that struck him while he was hanging by his feet, upside down. In the highest levels of the *Illuminati,* one was told: "Respect and honor the *aquatophana.*"

long waking dream, and only with the first morning lights was a little calm re-established in my thoughts. However, that calm couldn't be given to me except escorted by a worry. What bothered me wasn't my captivity. With a large amount of provisions, my prison didn't give me any solicitude relative to satisfying the needs of life. Besides, my seclusion couldn't be for very long. The light not having been illuminated the preceding night, someone was perhaps already on the way to find out the cause of that eclipse. But when my deliverance arrived, found alone with my dead man, wouldn't I naturally be thought to be the author of the murder? My first thought was to give the defunct a furtive grave. But all around me were walls and floor of granite; after a lot of work, I had scarcely managed to work out the details. Another method was to throw the cadaver into the sea, but it would still be necessary to wait for the hour of the high tide. The receding tide had left a vast dry space around the tower that I would have to walk over with that sad burden under my arms. I was sure that at Arbroath, with a telescope, I would be seen doing that hideous chore. Following a rather long examination of the situation that really wasn't convenient, an idea came to mind. Matiphous, the true author of the misfortune, wouldn't it be easy to turn against him the wicked trick which he had done me? His reputation as an adventurer had been well established for a long time. During my sleep, he had furtively left the lighthouse, kidnapping my wife I had brought there the evening before in sight of and known by all of Arbroath. That flight and that kidnapping wouldn't he very naturally be suspected of the murder? And helping appearances along, would it be very difficult to place them definitely on the fugitive?

I was thinking about this when some hours later a police magistrate came to find out why the light had not been illuminated the preceding night. To cover up the way he dead man had been struck, after having carried him outside the travelers' lounge, I had carefully planted his own dagger into the region of the heart. So when the cadaver was discovered, I spoke about a loud cry and a fight I claimed to have heard in a confused way as in a dream. From that I came to the conclusion that the unfortunate man must have perished trying to keep my wife from the intentions of her abductor.

I don't doubt I will encounter a rather outstanding difficulty to my version. It will be objected that the evening before Matiphous and the young girl who lived on the lighthouse with him, had embarked on the cutter that had brought me and Kitty was not with them. But then, in attributing the murder to that damned man from Malta, the only thing I didn't have was the name of the victim. He must have thrown her from the top of the tower, because he had gone up alone with her as my pot-bellied shape will demonstrate. What's more, I will claim that the adulterated ale which in any case establishes premeditation of wicked intentions. As for the death of the man I had sent on his way, I will attribute that to the probable knowledge he had of the crime involving Kitty and the need the murderer felt to protect himself against his talking.

With anyone other than Matiphous my accusation would have to be discussed a great deal, but because of his past that man offered such a beautiful place for all the suspicions. Two things were acquired by the inquest: he had deserted the lighthouse suddenly and my wife couldn't be found. Therefore he must have done something to her, since there was no apparent reason to accuse me, given the way I lived with my other half truly like a turtledove. As for the other crime, the body of the dead man under their eyes, there were a thousand reasons that could be attributed to the man I was accusing.

First of all, at one time he was the assistant of a hangman, which supposes him to have a ferocious nature; then, he is from Malta, and it's known that men from that country are accustomed to knife play in the most pointless quarrels. And it was known that there existed between that man and the other guardian, his victim, a constant quarrel. With all of these motives, my insinuations were crowned with total success, and Monsieur Matiphous having become the scapegoat, I was free to go back peacefully to Arbroath, where I took care to show a little more despair than I really felt about my wife's disappearance.

After some days of futile searches, it was necessary, however, to go back to London, where the concern for our interests called me. There I again found Mistress Aston, who was at first content just to mingle her tears with mine and to do credit to my conjugal sadness with her eager zeal. But after a year of my widowhood had passed, the dear lady had again become tiring. She wanted to console me at all costs. It was useless to object to her that my not having any positive proof of Kitty's death, I couldn't, without running the chance of an accusation of bigamy, be wed in a second marriage. She claimed that an honest minister who was one of her friends, would marry us without paying too much attention to that. And she would guarantee thanks to some sleight of hand, by another of her intimate friends, that the Gretna Green register kept no trace of my preceding union.

To expose myself again to being hanged or acquiring a goddess changed from the former owner of the "Bottle and the Magpie," that idea, you will agree, dear Fauntleroy, was not supportable. But, what's more, that shrew is insistent, and already some rather sharp comments have given me a glimpse of seeing her decided to use her advantages excessively. The moment has therefore come, dear friend, to submit to you a plan that I was reserving for events further away, but which the cruel anxiety of my situation forces me to advance.

It would be useless to hide it from ourselves, whatever cleverness we bring to the conduct of our delicate industry, its exploitation is not of a nature to be prolonged indefinitely. At a certain time, prudence, if there is not some catastrophe, will put us in the obligation of shutting it down. I promised myself that at that point I would set into operation the resource that I now propose to you to set up immediately. God be thanked! It isn't one of those dangerous games that can't be played, so to speak, with a noose around your neck. No danger, setting it up easy and simple, and instead of seeing ourselves on the wanted list of governments, an almost sure way of putting us in the

most friendly relations with them, and I dare to say the most
gilded. Such is, my dear associate, a summary of the opera-
tion.

At that point, Broughton, brought up the greatest political considerations, not putting in doubt that all the revolutionary movement brought about since 1789 right up the time he
was writing, must be attributed to the influence of secret societies. That was the point of view developed some years earlier
by the Abbé Barruel,[153] the famous book entitled *Memoirs
Illustrating the History of Jacobinism*, that the ex-boxer seems
to have read. Since the discovery of the portfolio left by
Ephraim, which seemed to him to be priceless, and whether
they wanted to deliver the information found in it as a whole
to one of the European police agencies, or if they preferred to
let them flow out in detail by mutual agreement with each
government, it seemed to him that possession of those archives of demagogy must be seen both as a fortune and as a
point of departure for those of the State police, whose horizon
could be felt rather than calculated. For these reasons Broughton had not let the existence of those precious documents be
known to anyone. Not being able on leaving the lighthouse to
carry the famous red portfolio with him without having to account for its contents, before the arrival of any uninitiated, he
had stashed it in a secure place. And now, to get to that hiding
place, to take out part of it, such was the question. Here the
cooperation of a resolute and intelligent associate became necessary. They would go together to the lighthouse, and while
one of the visitors found some way to distract the guardians,
the other would lay his hands on the treasure and slip away
with it.
A remark needs to be made. Telling only two thirds of
his secret, so to speak, Broughton, in his letter, avoided giving
even the place where the portfolio had been hidden, information without which it would appear difficult to mount a

---

[153] See Note 96.

401

fruitful search. This was a touching and delicate attention testifying as to the rare esteem in which the two entrepreneurs of suspicious industries held their mutual counterparts, and served to measure the confidence with which they found prudent to honor each other!

Epilogue

We knew Frantz Hoffmann, the young medical student that we talked about in the Prologue to this book, very well. He was a naïve and candid German. After finishing the reading, with blonde Clara, his fellow countryman, the manuscript that had come to him by the *pale and thin man,* he came to talk to us. We must say that, in the manner he recounted his encounter in the bar of the rue de la Harpe, with the presumed author of the work he wanted us to publish, we were not in very much of a hurry to acquire that manuscript. We dismissed the young man with all the politeness that the great literary name he had inherited deserved. Sometime later, he left Paris and his negotiations remained without results. It had almost slipped out of our memory when, some years later, we were dining with one of our friends, in company with one of the Paris doctors most renowned for the treatment of mental sickness. Led to talk about his field, after having led us through a certain number of cases of alienation, some grotesque, others dramatic, that he had the opportunity to observe, the doctor finally said:

"One of the strangest cases of madness that I have encountered was that of a man named Carbonneau, who died at Charenton, not too long ago. Born with imagination, that man had tried a literary career but having found he couldn't earn a living by it, he had finally been reduced to taking a position as a clerk in a ministry, a position in which, moreover, he had never done very well. At the beginning of the Restoration, at the time of the Patriots of 1816 [154] conspiracy, a master himself of writing named like him, Carbonneau, was found compromised; brought into to law court, that poor devil was declared guilty, condemned to death, and pitilessly executed.

"Although there existed no blood relationship between the two Carbonneaus, the tragic death of his homonym unusually affected the man whose job it was to ship merchandise. Just the fact of someone holding the name having been guillotined, left in his mind, naturally disturbed, a more profound trace so that his colleagues at the office, having noticed that weakness, frequently made stupid and boring jokes on that subject. After that, as if his name constituted a fatal predestination for the role of a conspirator, that unfortunate man let himself be affiliated with I don't know what secret society. From that point, some harassment from the police took immense proportions in his eyes. To believe him, he was watched day and night by a cloud of agents, all his letters were opened by the *Secret Bureau*, a little known problematic institution, about which he claimed he was in a position to give the most precise information. All that imaginary trouble led him to see himself very seriously implicated in the Berton Conspiracy,[155] then, since during the course of fact-finding, he had given unequivocal signs of madness, instead of being tried in the criminal court, he was administratively confined at Charenton.

"The intelligent cares with which he was the object in that house considerably improved his condition. Surviving the

---

[154] A supposed plot by twenty-eight men against King Louis XVIII. They were all tried, found guilty, and executed.

[155] General Auguste Berton (1774-1822) led an army insurrection to take the city of Saumur, continuing an insurrection begun in Thouars. Calling themselves the "National Army of the West," they proclaimed that the King's government had been overthrown and that a provisional government had been established. The Conspiracy was crushed and Berton was executed.

Revolution of July some former *carbonari* [156] friends remembered him. Without being cured, his mental state no longer required that he be institutionalized. He was released and a pension was allocated to him as a former political prisoner. He was permitted to devote himself exclusively to literary occupations, for which he had always felt an inclination.

"Unfortunately, when cholera first appeared in Paris,[157] he underwent a very violent attack, and under the influence of that last shock, the vague and continued disposition of his mind toward aberration, was transformed into a fixed idea which, right up to his last hour, never stopped tormenting his life. Following his sickness, having looked at himself in the mirror, he was very shocked at the ravages cholera had made in his physique. He saw himself so gaunt, so thin, so haggard, that he thought he was seeing a specter escaped from the grave. Come then, by the most bizarre imagination, to be obsessed with himself, he persuaded himself that the specter, unceasingly attached to his steps, inflicted a thousand tortures on him, and especially that of forcing him to write every night, under his dictation, an interminable history of the *Secret Bureau.*"

"But, Doctor, in writing about the visit of that unfortunate man, some manuscripts must have been left of the account of the young Frantz Hoffmann?"

---

[156] The Carbonari (Italian for "charcoal makers") were groups of secret revolutionary societies active in Italy during the first three decades of the 19th century. The Italian Carbonari may have further influenced other revolutionary groups in France, Spain, Portugal, and Russia. Although their goals often had a patriotic and liberal focus, they lacked a clear immediate political agenda. Theories suggest that they may have spread to France with Napoleon's army, or that it was part of the work of the Freemasons.

[157] 1831; in Paris, 20,000 died (of a population of 650,000), and total deaths in France amounted to 100,000.

"He left one," the Doctor replied, "which he multiplied to infinity, and I must have one in my library, which, from the point of view of science it seemed interesting to me to conserve. In fact, in his actions and in his speech, that man showed such a complete absence of reason that he had managed to seriously relate to you that, for several months, he had been part of the anatomical display at the School of Medicine, taking the place of a figure showing the muscles of the body, which had stolen his skin. However, this madman, when he took his pen in hand became perfectly lucid. I have read the manuscript that remains in my possession. It's a novel of an excessively complicated intrigue, and which he has held together all the events with rare sureness of hand."

"This manuscript, Doctor, would you be so kind as to make it available to me?"

"Absolutely. I will look for it, and you will perhaps not have too much trouble publishing it."

The next day we were at the home of the famous psychologist. Unfortunately, his library, as the head of his Administration, was in great disorder. With great trouble he put his hands on the first three parts of the wild imaginings he had talked to us about. The remainder had gone astray. However, the Doctor committed himself to find what followed after a little research, which he didn't have time for at the moment. And with that assurance, we have decided to begin publication.

The Doctor died in the meantime. His library was sold and dispersed. In spite of all our diligence, it was impossible to put our hands on the two last parts of the unfortunate manuscript. However, we are not without some hope of completing it somewhat later. We have learned that in Germany, at Leipzig and at Vienne, two histories of the *Secret Bureau*, more or less complete, have been published.[158] Those two translations are supposed to have been made from the manuscript copy

---

[158] *Das Schwarse Kabinet*, Leipzig. Kollmann, 6 volumes 1849. (Note from the Author)

405

that Frantz Hoffmann must have taken with him when he returned to his country. Next autumn we intend to take a trip to the other side of the Rhine and we will be very unfortunate if, managing to contact the young Hoffman, we aren't able to get from him a continued conversation among us at the point where we had left it some years ago.

The reader can then be reassured that to arrive at that very desired result, we will spare no cares, no initiatives, and also no expense.

**TO BE CONTINUED IN
THE BLOODIED GIRL**